Russ,
Thanks for

# James A. Hunter

# MUDMAN

*James A. Hunter*

J. A. Hunter

# Dedication

For my brother, Aron. Where you're coming from doesn't have to determine where you're going. I've always believed in you and I always will. Love you, bro.

J. A. Hunter

## *ONE:*

## **Awakening**

*June, 1943*

He blinked his eyes open for the first time: a newborn stealing his first look at the world, which, in a way, is exactly what he was. Except no squealing, rosy-cheeked infant had ever been so big, so ugly, or so filled with blood-boiling rage. Never had a child been so appalling. He squinted at first, letting in only the merest trickle of light because even the wan illumination from the moon, which loitered over the world like a fat thumbnail, was harsh to his virgin eyes.

Smells came next: the scent of musky earth, the harsh tang of powdery slaked lime—used to mask the reek of decay—and buried beneath that, the sour stink of rotten flesh and burnt hair.

The sky spit down a misty drizzle, fine droplets of cool water that turned his gray skin slick. After a few moments more his eyes adjusted fully, allowing him, at last, to survey his surroundings. Mud and muck, deep brown and goopy, lined everything. It squished beneath his shoulder blades, clung to his arms and legs, and liberally coated the corpses crudely piled to his right.

Despite the mud, the bodies appeared almost white, like angry specters waiting for him, welcoming him to this new hell with silent screams and vacant eyes.

How he knew *anything* was beyond him, since this was the first day of his life, the day—or rather night—of his unnatural birth. Surely, no baby pushed and fought its way into the world with dark and grisly thoughts of murder and death lingering in its mind, with knowledge of mass graves, heinous experimentation, and hasty executions. But he *knew* such things. Fragments of memories floated and swirled inside his skull, dancing a slow funeral dirge, parading incoherent snatches of imagery through his head.

*The Wehrmacht march through the streets in their black spit-shined boots and high-collared, gray wool uniforms. Smart and dashing, those uniforms, dressing up the face of murder in civility and pageantry ...*

*The Luftwaffe soars overhead. The buzz of the single-prop Focke-Wulf and the thunderous roar of the colossal Messerschmitt transport planes fill the air with their racket ...*

*He clutches a small boy to his chest, his body trembling as he hides, holding his breath for fear of being heard. Terror and panic wriggle in his guts as the black-garbed Schutzstaffel—the SS—make their way from door to door, fists rapping on wood, rifle buttstocks smashing out windows, booted feet kicking their way inside ...*

*Then, train cars, loaded to capacity, roll through his thoughts. Bodies press up against one another so tightly he can't breathe—except he isn't a he, but a she. And she is searching for her sister. They'd been separated in all the chaos ...*

So many images, circling around, each screaming more loudly than the last, each demanding he lend them an ear or an eye or a hand. He clutched at either side of his head. Broad, fleshy palms pressed in as though he could simply pulverize the images and send them back to whatever nightmare they'd come from. But they kept coming, and as they came—faster and faster, like a hail of automatic machine gunfire—his chest began to itch and burn. It felt like someone had taken a cherry-red fire iron and jabbed it into the meat covering his breastbone.

A huge hand flew to the pain, his fingers finding crude markings etched directly into the skin, cut deep into the muscle below. As he touched the mark, the jagged wound, the voices and visions coalesced into a single demand. A demand for retribution. The anger came next, flowing from the brand like gasoline pumping through his veins, scorching his insides and propelling him to action. He lumbered to his feet, the muck squishing around his thick toes, and made for the muddy wall of his earthen womb. In reality, an open grave. He dug his digits in and used his flabby, though powerfully built, arms to pull himself upward and free.

He lay on the edge of the pit for a long beat, charting the lay of the land, eyes scanning the dark, which covered everything like a velvety blanket. In the distance, not so far off, he saw a squat building. Some sort of bunker, outlined by the faint glow of light bulbs. He wasn't sure *what* he was. *Where* he was. Or *how* he'd gotten there. But, as the brand burned in his chest, he was certain of one thing: someone—or, perhaps, lots of someones—had quite the butcher's bill to account for, and he was ready to collect.

## TWO:

### The Deep Downs

*Present Day*

L evi crouched low on his haunches, fat fingers pressed against the dusty rock beneath his bare, oversized feet. The vibration of fleeing Kobocks trickled up through the stone, each distant footfall like an electric blip on his internal radar. So many feet, so many Kobocks, all scampering in different directions: some searching for him, desperate to end his murderous assault, others just as frantic to escape. To escape his crushing fists. To escape his bone-breaking kicks. To escape the fate he'd already dealt out to ten or more of their filthy ilk.

He smiled, a thin twitch of the lips more closely resembling a grimace. For Levi, that *was* a smile. A rare thing, reserved for his hunting expeditions.

He peered into the darkness of the subterranean cave, even as his fingers quested over the ground, tracing lines in the gritty sand coating the surface, absently sketching out a crude map. The rough tunnel stretched out in either direction for a hundred feet before disappearing into murk, while a stream of black, brackish water trickled by on his right. Levi's gaze drifted to the stream for the hundredth time, lingering only for a moment. He subconsciously scooted away, edging closer to the wall on his left.

Then he resumed his scan, eyes roving ceaselessly, plump digits once more picking their way across the dirt. The rocky passageway was dark, though sporadic patches of bioluminescent fungi—so common beneath the Hub—ran along the coarse walls and clung to the ceiling, casting pale-green foxfire into the air. The light was marginally useful, but Levi didn't really need it, not with so much stone around him. The bedrock of this world was foreign to him, different from the rich earth of Inworld, but the golden ichor flowing in his veins resonated all the same.

Stone called to stone. Stone guided him onward.

There: a trio of the bolting creatures—these running only with escape in mind—approached from a southerly tunnel, drawing unwittingly nearer, even as they tried to leave Levi in the dust. Travelling at a fair clip. Moving together as a pack, thinking their numbers would make them safe. The smile broadened a touch. A pack of ten or fifteen of the glimmering, blue-skinned creatures *might* dissuade the Mudman. But three? He shook his meaty head, mostly devoid of a neck, at the ridiculous notion.

Levi stood, back hunched, hands flexing in anticipation of the kill to come, and continued his trek further into the heart of the Deep Downs—the cavernous subterranean network running beneath the Hub. A warren of earthen caves and passageways, home to the Kobock Nation and a thousand other horrors. He was surrounded on all sides by darkness and death, and he couldn't have been happier. This was what he was made for. This was his purpose.

He moved forward with a gimpy stride, his right leg dragging along, working only at half strength. A tremendous puncture wound, the size of a two-by-four, shot clean through his thigh. A gaping hole wide enough for a man to reach through, though the Mudman could already sense the network of thread-thin strands of golden tissue knitting his leg back together, restoring Levi with every passing second. His ichor at work.

A stupid mistake, that injury. The Deep Downs were dangerous, even for Levi. The haphazard passages were rigged with countless traps to snare the unwary. False floors filled with columns of rocky spikes. Bottomless chasms, eager to swallow the careless interloper. Rudimentary pressure plates which might trigger a gout of magma-hot molten rock or a javelin of poison-coated granite. And *water*. Levi once more glanced at the underground creek carving its way through the deep rock, flowing alongside him.

Water was the worst of the lot.

Yes, the Deep Downs were a regular death house for nonnatives. Of course, Levi could *read* the earth. Here, he was as sure-footed as even the most well-travelled Kobo. But he'd been careless—his blood lust had gotten the better of him. He could see it in his mind:

A pair of Kobocks scampered away, loping along on all fours, distorted and disproportionate limbs carrying them into a crude alcove. A dead end with no possible means of escape. The duo turned, twisted lips pulled back in scowls, revealing gnarled, rot-black teeth. Their milky eyes grew wide in fear at his lumbering approach. They hissed—a pair of dirty tomcats backed into a dead-end alley—and held up filthy hands with spidery-fingers, each tipped with blackened, dirt-caked claws.

He'd been so hungry for the kill, so eager to pulverize their frail forms, to feel the hot, putrid blood brush up against his clay-flesh, that he'd lumbered in without even half a mind for the traps so common in this place. Stupid.

A pressure plate.

One wrong step.

A javelin of razor-sharp stone—coated in gobs of slick green Kobo poison—burst from the wall, slicing through gray skin and lumpy muscle, pinning him in place. Careless. The Kobos howled in victory and scampered away while he was left to smash his way free from the stone spear.

To a mortal, the wound would've been a death sentence. For Levi, it was a mild inconvenience. Painful, true, but far from life threatening. Had he been up on the surface, back in Inworld with the great expanse of Earth stretching beneath his feet, he would've healed the injury long since. Hunting in this dark and unnatural place, so far away from the muddy womb which had birthed him, was always a dangerous game. But then dangerous games were also the most exhilarating. The most satisfying.

Onward Levi trudged, slow but steady, listening for the sounds of the approaching trio he'd sensed. After a handful of seconds, the faint scuffle of bare feet on stone and the labored pulls of deep breathing drifted to Levi's ears. Good, good, good.

Levi reached over and ran a hand across the craggy wall. Close now. The Mudman could crush all three, but an ambush was best. He ran a finger around the lip of the gaping wound in his thigh. *Better to play it safe*. Not to mention, he needed them closer. These three were fleeing, not hunting. If they saw him too soon, they might turn and dash away, escaping their well-deserved punishment. Levi was many things, but fast was not one of them. If they ran, he'd be hard pressed to stop them, especially with his leg.

Plus, the right side of his body was going numb around the edges. The digits on his right hand were fuzzy and indistinct, and his right leg—complete with puncture hole—was little more than dead weight. Had to be the gooey poison from the javelin, worming its way through his system. That and the substantial blood loss—*ichor* loss, in his case—he'd suffered from the blow. Still, no poison could kill Levi, just as no poison could kill a mountain. It'd take time, but his body would heal, would cleanse itself. Only God knew how long, though.

This new development, however, only reinforced the necessity of an ambush. He wouldn't let one tiny mistake ruin his night out, but he would be more cautious. It was only prudent.

A short distance up ahead was the perfect spot for his attack. A narrow section of tunnel formed a tight bottleneck: On the right side, the stream swelled inward, forming an eddy of swirling black water. On the left, a minor cave-in had created a sprawling pile of rubble—a mound of rough stone and glimmering crystal—which left a path, only five feet wide, running straight between the rock heap and the stream.

A good spot.

Levi inched forward, inspecting the layout with an experienced eye. On the backside of the rock pile was a niche he could squeeze his bulk into, though barely. The space wouldn't conceal him, not completely, but his intention wasn't to hide. He only needed to draw the Kobos in close enough to strike his blow.

The footfalls grew louder by the second, followed by the hiss of inhuman voices and the panting of tired lungs. As quickly as he could muster with his damaged leg, the Mudman shimmied into the tight space, bald head peeking out just enough to offer him a view of the tunnel.

Even in the dark of this place, a colony of fungi adorning the walls offered sufficient light for Levi to catch a glimpse of his prey: humanoid in shape, but a crude parody of homo sapiens. Upright, the Kobocks might've stood at five or six feet, but they skittered about on all fours, their movements almost simian—disproportionately squat legs and scrawny arms dangling all the way to the ground.

A pronounced hunch adorned each form. Bluish, opalescent skin covered lanky limbs and potbellies, while flabby tits wobbled on all the creatures—women and men alike. One had lank, greasy hair, while the other two were bald as eggs. Each wore a dirt-caked loincloth wrapped around their nether bits, and each carried a pitted weapon made of rough stone or crystal—the kind of rudimentary tools some prehistoric Neanderthal might fashion.

Levi stood in stark contrast to the Kobos.

An enormous creature, he was seven feet of towering fat, gristle, clay, and muscle. Built like an old brick shithouse: arms the size of small tree trunks, hands like dinner plates, fingers thick as bratwursts, a great barrel gut, and an irregular, bald dome. Levi wasn't a looker, not by anybody's definition. His beady black eyes sat recessed in his uneven face, and he had a sloping *Cro-Magnon* brow and the square jaw of a silverback gorilla. He sported a pair of flimsy black shorts—worn only for modesty's sake—leaving the rest of his chalky gray flesh exposed to the world.

In this form, his true form, he'd never win a beauty pageant. In the Deep Downs below the Hub, however, there was no one to impress anyway. Just monsters, horrors, and ancient godlings biding their time.

Here, Levi fit right in.

The three Kobos continued their mad dash toward the narrow gap, unaware their death waited only moments away. They couldn't see the Mudman yet, not enfolded in the rocky wall, and that was good. Levi smiled again. He could take three, even badly wounded and poisoned. One of his enormous, ashen-gray hands distended and distorted, fingers intertwining and melding together, forming a colossal shovel where meaty fingers had been a moment before. He scooped up a load of rock chips and broken stone with a *scrape.*

The Kobos hesitated at the sound, but didn't stop.

Too bad for them.

Closer they drew, thirty feet, twenty, ten—near enough for Levi to taste the fear radiating off them in pulses and see rivulets of sweat cutting tracks into the dirt covering their bodies.

He swung out from behind the rubble pile, the motion awkward with his numb right leg. His massive arm whipped forward—the limb like a rubbery slingshot—unleashing the hail of deadly projectiles at the oncoming creatures. The rocky shrapnel bashed into lopsided bodies without mercy, bludgeoning flesh in places and tearing great chunks of meat away in others. One boulder, large as a volleyball, collided into the leader's skull, caving in the side of its head and splashing the ground with purple blood.

The Kobo dropped like a sack of potatoes, its body hitting the deck with a wet *smack,* then slipping into the dark stream.

The other two let out shrieks of surprise. One tumbled to the side, clutching at a badly broken arm, the bone protruding through its feeble bicep. The other likewise took a fall, one of its legs mangled below the knee. Broke-knee cried out, a strangely human squeal, and tried to drag itself to safety; claw-tipped fingers dug down, scrambling for purchase as it pulled its body back the way it'd come.

A twinge of guilt surged up inside Levi's chest as he watched the pair battle to live, crying out in pain and fear.

Pastor Steve's words lingered in the back of his mind. *"We all wrestle with sin, we each have our crosses to bear. You have to die to those darker parts of your nature, turn your back on those baser instincts. It's not easy, sometimes, but you have to choose the better way."* It's not good to kill: so says Pastor Steve and so says the Good Book. And that was true. Tonight's expedition was a relapse, a mistake. But it felt *good*. That was Levi's darker nature. He wanted to control it, but he *needed* to kill—to shed blood, rend flesh, break bone. He'd been created for it and his nature compelled him, drove him onward.

His blood pumped and his soul sang as he watched the Kobos perish. Life and fierce joy welled up in him, unmatched by the boring routines of the everyday—AA meetings, church services, client commissions, grocery trips. But he also felt sick. Self-loathing writhed around in his guts like a brood of snakes.

*Better these monsters than some hapless mortal up top*, he reminded himself.

And these creatures *were* monsters. Living down in the stony depths, worshiping dusty, forgotten, evil Principalities and Powers of old. Though most of their kind shunned the surface, that didn't prevent their raiding parties from stealing into the human world: abducting children for their dark rituals or snatching women—breeders to propagate their twisted race. He saw death in the two remaining Kobocks, saw the murderous deeds swirling around them like a dark cloud.

*Guilty.*

That was part of his gift, too. He could read murder on people. See it in their aura as clear as the stars on a cloudless night in the backcountry. Murder, the greatest of desecrations, left a mark no one could hide, not from Levi's beady eyes.

Still, this *was* a relapse. He'd have to pay penance when this was all over and done with. His hands itched at the thought of the flames lapping at his skin, searing his nerve endings though leaving the skin unmarred—his own unique form of self-castigation.

He shivered, then rudely shoved the thoughts of guilt away, his bloodlust winning out for the time being. *It's not good to kill*: so says Pastor Steve and so says the Good Book. Except sometimes it *is*.

He scooped up another load of rubble and sent it flying, *plop, thwack, crack.* The creature with the mangled leg took a jagged chunk of rock to the throat—its windpipe crumpled inward like an empty soda can. The creature clawed at its ruined neck, its feet drumming on the ground as it fruitlessly attempted to fill its lungs. A lost cause, that. The beast was dead, even if its body didn't know yet, and good riddance. Levi watched its struggles, waiting for the usual rush of bright-hot satisfaction that came with a kill. The dying beastie writhed on the ground for another few seconds before its eyes grew dull and lifeless and it gave up the ghost.

Levi watched on, waiting. No surge came. No satisfaction at all. Just an empty spot in his center.

That was good, maybe. He'd never felt empty before, not when it came to killing. Maybe the AA and church services were working after all?

A *splash* floated to his ears and drew his attention away from the body splayed out before him.

It took only a second to locate the ripple spreading out in the slow moving stream. The third Kobo, the creature with the fractured arm, was gone. Disappeared into the murky water. The smile gracing Levi's blunt face vanished in an instant, stolen by the tricky fiend. He ground his teeth in frustration, a low growl burbling out from his chest. The beast Needed. To. Pay. Levi couldn't let it escape, not with retribution so close. The Kobo was badly wounded, and trying to swim through the water with its brutalized arm would be near-impossible. Plus, it would need to come up for air eventually.

Levi just needed to bide his time.

Wait and be patient. Patience was hard, though, especially with a victim near at hand. Still, he restrained himself. He wanted that Kobock's head on a spike, but he wanted nothing to do with that water. Castigation by flame was awful—excruciatingly painful—but the thought of dipping into the water was too revolting a notion to consider. So he waited. And waited more. As he waited, he turned the situation over and over in his mind, his need to dispense justice balanced against his fear of drowning.

This was taking too long.

After a moment, vengeance, and his bloodlust, won out. After all, how could he let a little moisture prevent him from executing his duties?

Cautiously, Levi left the makeshift sanctuary of rubble behind and trudged forward, his movements ungainly with the poison flowing through his system. His left hand reverted to its normal form, shovel giving way to fingers, as he crept toward the water's edge, moving to the place he'd seen the ripple in the stream.

Then, another *splash*, not far off, followed by a greedy gulp of air. He wheeled about, eyes running over the surface of the murky creek, finding nothing but uninterrupted swirls of black. He took a deep breath, suppressing the anxiety swelling inside him, and hobbled a few steps closer to the bank. He crouched down, laying his left palm flat against the rocky shore, mere inches from the stream. He didn't sweat—couldn't sweat, in fact—but had he been human, great beads of the stuff would've rolled down his lumpy noggin.

Levi redirected the ichor inside him, sending a surge of molten gold toward his palm, calling out to the earth below, probing at the water. After a moment, Levi grunted and shook his head. Useless. The creek was a dead spot in his mind. He could feel the presence of the water, or rather the void it created, but the Kobock in the drink was invisible.

Nothing he could do about it, then. Chances were, the Kobo's wound would do it in anyway. Might be, the creature would do the world a favor and drown—a fitting end. Or maybe the arm would go septic. Gangrene was a worry even for Kobos.

Levi turned with a sigh, resigned to carrying on. There was still plenty of game afoot, after all—

A geyser erupted on his left, the Kobo with the gimp arm propelling itself through the air, its stone blade, scalpel-sharp, outstretched. Levi moved, but too slowly. The blade plunged into the Mudman's side, the pain like a lance of flame burying itself in his innards. The Kobo retracted the knife in a flash and danced back, water flying from its body as it evaded. The Mudman hadn't been expecting such a bold play, and the gash in his side was the price.

Levi advanced, his steps ponderous, the right side of his body useless now, the puncture in his ribs a spike of agony. As with the wound in his leg, the blow to the gut wouldn't kill him, but neither was it pleasant. Levi wasn't sure what exactly it would take to kill him, but he'd survived worse than this.

The Kobo shot in again, lightning quick, his stone blade thrusting upward, seeking out Levi's heart like a homing missile. Levi threw up a beef-slab arm, the block narrowly arriving in time to intercept the thrust. The blade stabbed into Levi's forearm, gouging a deep trench in his skin. The knife tore free, and the creature danced away again before Levi could respond. Despite the Kobock's injury, it was still fast, faster than the Mudman, and smart, too. Always lingering outside Levi's strike radius.

The Mudman moved forward, circling right and pushing in toward the tunnel wall, hoping to back the creature into a corner where he could pummel the beast into a pile of vile, tainted blue meat. He shifted his left hand, letting the ichor beneath the skin melt and bulge, his fist transforming into a spiked mace the size of a bowling ball. The Kobo dove left as Levi lunged forward with a snarl, lashing out with his spiky bludgeon. Levi's strike was awkward and clumsy, his deadened right leg working against him, but still the mace collided into the creature's flabby gut with a *crack*—shattered ribs—swatting the Kobo to the ground like a line drive.

In a flash, the creature scrambled gracelessly to his feet, one arm dangling, the other outstretched, its blade clutched in a white-knuckle grip. Levi charged forward again, raising his club-hand for a killing blow—

The creature darted in low, first feinting left, then hooking right, ducking as it shot inside Levi's guard and buried the blade up to its rocky hilt in Levi's good leg. The Mudman faltered at the sudden pain and pressure. He reeled backward, his upraised mace throwing off his already shaky balance. He staggered onto his worthless right leg—a terrible mistake. His weight came down on the numb limb, only to find the leg refused to support his considerable bulk. The knee buckled and he tumbled, his good arm pinwheeling as he crashed toward the ground.

Except it wasn't ground that met his back. It was water.

Liquid—frigid and merciless—surged around him, rushing over his face and dragging him toward the bottom. Levi couldn't swim—his body was too heavy and dense to ever be buoyant, and all his flapping, flailing, and kicking did little to slow his descent. And, despite his resilience to pain and damage, he *did* need to breathe. He didn't have the full range of human organs—no proper stomach, no kidneys or liver, no intestine zigzagging through his center—but both heart and lungs were present, though they functioned only to redirect and channel his ichor.

The Mudman, a millstone thrown into the sea, drifted down four or five feet before his shoulder blades thudded against the streambed. Hot-blooded panic set in; the rush of water pressed in on his senses, cutting him off from the earth. Even his tenuous connection to the rocky streambed wasn't enough to sustain him.

*This is it,* his mind growled like a bear facing down a small army of gun-toting hunters. *This is how I go.*

*No,* the cool, logical part of his mind asserted. *Four, maybe five feet to the bottom, that was all.* If he could gain his feet and get his head above the water, everything would be fine. He needed air. Even with one bad arm, he could get to the bank and haul himself back onto dry ground. And chances were, the murderous Kobo would be long gone. He needed to stay calm, keep his head, and pull himself from the drink.

Slowly he reached down with his left hand, pressing the mace head into the soil, and hoisted himself into a sitting position. The current buffeted his face and chest, threatening to unbalance him. He ignored the sensation, focusing his mind on the singular task of escape. With ponderous movements he pushed himself back onto his left leg, the knife still jutting out of his thigh. He ignored the spark of protest from the limb, far more concerned with being free of the stream than free of the pain. He could recover from the knife wound, but not so long as he was in the water. His healing, his power, his life was inescapably tied to the earth.

Without the earth, his power was a fragile thing.

With his left leg firmly planted beneath him, he pushed upward and toward the river's edge. His head broke the surface a moment later, cool air washing over his skin as he threw his left hand forward. He shaped the limb into wicked hook, which he slammed deep into the ground, driving the blade tip down and winching his battered body from the water. *Thank God above.*

He spat out a mouthful of bitter liquid and sprawled onto his back, letting his bare skin soak up the strength of the earth below. Without even bothering to look around, he drew on the stone, his senses seeking out his clever adversary. As expected, the creature was, indeed, gone—at least four or five hundred feet away, and moving quickly through the tunnelways, heading further into the Deeps, toward the Kobock high temple. One of them, anyway.

Despite the fact that Levi's stony heart still thudded out a mad beat in his too large chest, his face split into a grin. The High Temple was his final destination, too. Though the rank and file Kobocks were vastly entertaining to hunt, it was the High Shaman, the *Mung Gal-kulom*, he'd come to kill. But perhaps he'd get a chance to finish off the treacherous underling as well. With a grunt, he pulled the knife from his leg. Levi was not a creature of grand hopes and dreams, but, as he glanced at the pitted blade, he did find himself eager for a rematch with gimpy arm.

First, though, he needed rest. He cast the blade aside with a flick of his fat hand, pulled himself over to the rubble pile, and set to work burying himself alive.

*THREE:*

## Memories

L evi dragged his body from beneath the pile of rubble an hour later. He stretched his flabby arms and prodded at both legs. Better, much better. He flexed his right hand, curling it into a fist, then shifting it into a blunt-faced sledgehammer. He had sensation again. He let the hand revert to its normal shape and rubbed at the knife wound on his left leg. Completely healed. The massive puncture in his right leg was tender to the touch, but still much improved. He'd packed both injuries full of dirt and rock before burying himself beneath a half-ton of stone, letting bedrock strength seep in while his ichor transformed the raw material into supple, living clay.

Alchemic magic.

He pushed himself to his feet with a grunt and started forward, angling toward a clear, complete section of wall. He dragged his left hand along the wall's surface as he walked, drawing out information with every second. Much had happened since he'd taken his short, but necessary, respite: for one, some semblance of order had been reestablished in the Kobock ranks. No longer was it every Kobo for itself.

No longer was the subterranean cavern a madhouse of stampeding feet running every which way. Half of the remaining creatures had withdrawn to the High Temple, joining with their unholy shaman, Levi's real target, barricading themselves behind the temple's heavy iron gates.

The other half had broken up into hunting parties—four groups of eight—each scouring the intricate and sprawling tunnels, searching for Levi. One of the parties drew uncomfortably close, circling in even as Levi moved, only minutes away at their current speed. For a moment, Levi considered abandoning this expedition altogether, chalking the whole thing up as a failure. It would be a simple task to avoid the hunters, jump ship, and return another night to finish the work, when conditions were more favorable.

He paused, drumming his fingers on the wall, mind thoroughly divided over the prospect. Levi was not dumb, but he was not overly fond of surprises, and thinking on his feet was no easy task for the Mudman.

Still, he reasoned, it was better to put this thing to rest good and proper.

He really *did* want to curb his gluttonous desire for death, and he knew if he left the work undone, he'd be compelled to come back and mop up later. If this was to be his last splurge, as he *swore* it would be, he needed closure. Without closure, without completion, he wouldn't be able to help himself. Wouldn't be able to control the urge. Besides, he'd already fallen off the wagon—he'd have to give back his three-month sobriety token at his Thursday meeting—so it was best to get it all out of his system while he had an opportunity.

One last hooray, then he'd start again. And he'd do better next time.

Repent and purge, that was the best way.

With his mind made up, Levi lurched into motion. His tree-trunk legs churned, the ground rumbled at his passing, and his fingers brushed over the wall, guiding him as he moved. The hunting party was closing in on his position, but Levi paid them no mind, heading down the tunnel in the opposite direction. He needed to finish what he'd come here for: the shaman. Mung Gal-kuloms rarely, if ever, ventured from their unholy sanctuaries, so Levi was sure that was where he'd find his target. True, the hunting party would be on him in minutes, but he could gain the temple long before they ever reached him.

He would raid the sacrilegious shrine, kill its profane leader, and disappear, work finished, conscience clear.

Onward he hurtled, moving not with the zippy speed of a sports car, but rather with the steady, implacable strength of a freight train.

He ground to a halt four hundred meters later as the tunnel fractured into three branches: one running straight, one hooking left, the other jutting right and ending abruptly in a yawning chasm. Something here was not quite as it seemed. He squatted down, examining the ground with both hands, willing the cavern to confess its secrets. He grunted and nodded: the right-hand path, toward the cliff.

Cautiously, he picked his way toward the edge of the chasm and glanced down—blackness stretched on forever. A clever lie. He threw his body from the ledge, gusts of air whipping over his bare skin for a moment before he crashed to the ground, loose chips of rock shaking free from the walls. He stood on a narrow strip of land budding from the craggy cliff face, twenty feet down from the drop-off above. A very clever illusion. Behind him, a wide, downward-sloping tunnel bore into the rock face, cutting deeper into the earth. Next to it, a crude set of foot and handholds had been chiseled into the cliff wall, leading back toward the upper level.

The echoing cries of the hunting party drifted along the underground air currents. If he could hear them so clearly, Levi knew they, in turn, must've heard the impact from his landing. Best to move on. Forward again he trudged, building up momentum step by ponderous step as he shot downward, deeper and deeper. He followed the path for two hundred meters— avoiding a pair of pressure plates and a spiked death pit—before taking a left at another forked intersection. Levi ran with his fingertips caressing the wall, seeking out the heavy iron gates standing guard at the temple's entryway. Close now, forty or fifty feet.

The hallway curved, turning into a tight spiral, drilling downward.

He ran, chest heaving, fingers flexing in anticipation.

The Mudman rounded the last bend and nearly ran headlong into the sturdy barrier barring the way to his final stop. A pair of earthen pillars, twenty feet high, flanked either side of the hallway, and in between them loomed a latticed-iron portcullis—a three-ton, drop down gate, common on medieval castles. Though the gate impeded Levi's entry, it failed to block his view of the temple's interior.

Elaborate columns carved with profane scenes of inhuman perversion—men and women doing unnatural carnal acts—ran along the length of a wide center aisle. Enormous, wrought-iron sconces decorated each column, each holding orange and yellow fire, which cast lurid, flickering shadows over the whole scene. He spied none of his Kobock prey—they must've been in another part of the temple complex—what he could see, however, was more than enough to stoke the furnace of his wrath.

At the end of the sacrificial chamber lay an altar or shrine of some sort. An ancient bas-relief, featuring a frightfully rendered wyrm: a writhing centipede with a thousand legs sprouting from its chitinous body, a head covered with distorted eyes—each filled with uncut rubies the size of a robin's egg—and a cavernous maw of jagged, obsidian spikes. The scene depicted the dread-beast writhing in a lake of fire, closed away from the world of men and monsters alike. Banished to the great abyss by God above.

*"And they will go out and look on the dead bodies of those who rebelled against me; the worms that eat them will not die, the fire that burns them will not be quenched, and they will be loathsome to all mankind."*

A wyrm of the Great below. One of the elder gods of the Deep, then, though Levi didn't know which.

Placed methodically before the altar were bodies, corpses. Once human, but now *altered*, changed in terrible ways.

Here: what had once been a man, was now a creature with ropy, purple tentacles where arms belonged and the head of a great dire wolf affixed to his shoulders. Another: a woman, breasts hacked away, a flamingo's dainty legs protruding from her belly, growing out of her abdomen like a tree. A third: A halfie boy with leopard-spotted skin—fifteen, perhaps—with his legs ripped off and replaced with a set of mechanical limbs. And those were only a few of the victims. Twenty or more, equally brutalized and desecrated, dotted the ground in front of the blasphemous statue.

The vile scene tickled at the back of Levi's mind, familiar somehow, as though he'd seen this gruesome tableau before. He pushed away the curious sense of déjà vu, instead letting murderous rage fill him up. He had work to be about.

*Monsters,* he thought, *the whole lot of them. Guilty.*

He just needed to get inside.

Levi inched forward, running his hands over the thick metal, inspecting it for flaws or areas of vulnerability. Though the Kobocks were a crude breed of creature, this gate, at least, had been painstakingly constructed and maintained. Well-crafted metal, free from rust and reinforced with powerful magical wards to prevent tampering. He bent down, wedged his hands into the latticework gate, and stood, back flexing, thighs bulging, biceps shaking from strain as he tried to force the gate.

The iron groaned and shifted an inch or two, but no more—

A spasm of movement near the altar caught his eye. A girl, pasty white, with limp cotton-candy pink hair, streaked through with splashes of purple, lay on an elaborately carved stone table, her body cinched down with leather straps. Her clothes, what remained of them, were dirty tatters at best, and revealed long arms and shapely legs liberally covered with colorful tattoos.

He'd taken her for dead. An easy mistake to make, given both her appearance and the company she kept. Her eyes were closed, and a savage slice ran the length of her middle. Her skin was corpse pale, too—especially in the dancing firelight. On closer examination, Levi saw her chest rise and fall. A minuscule movement.

Levi's eyes flitted to the stainless steel gurney next to the girl; a wide array of medical implements covered its surface: bone saw, surgical scalpel, pliers, bloody gauze, a cloudy brown bottle of alcohol, a needle, and rough catgut sutures.

His gaze flickered back and forth between the desecrated bodies lying in front of the strange altar and the woman on the table with the slash running up her abdomen. Experimentation. Like back in the camps.

*Animals. Rabid animals.*

The only thing rabid animals were good for was extermination. A mercy, really.

Then, before Levi could stop it, the memory came—floating to the surface, unbidden. *Unwanted.* It was a rude and demanding guest, but one Levi couldn't ask to leave. The memory wasn't Levi's, not exactly, and though he didn't want it, neither could he refuse it. It was as much a part of him as his hands or legs or eyes, and he was forbidden to forget. His purpose was not only to slay the wicked, but to stand and remember:

*The dusty floorboards creak beneath my knees. Solemn faces—all gaunt and stained—peer down with sunken eyes from the rickety wooden beds lining either side of the narrow aisle.*

*They do nothing, only watch, then look away. But what can they do? What can anyone do?*

*The guard stands behind me—a young man, a few years older than Nicholas—wearing a smart gray uniform, which is pressed and clean. Immaculate, even, which only serves to highlight the filth clinging to everything else around him. I don't look directly at him, of course. Instead I avert my eyes, careful to stare at the floor. Out of the corner of my eye, I see his glossy black boots. He shifts back and forth, impatient.*

*It won't be long now.*

*I clutch my grandson, Nicholas, tight to my chest, his bristly hair brushing the underside of my chin. His skeletal hands cling to my rumpled and dirt-stained gown. He's weeping into my sunken chest, his rail-thin body hitching with each sob. It's been ages since I last bathed, and the smell coming off me is putrid, sweet and sour, even to my own nose. We change clothing only every six weeks; this is week five. Still, I draw Nicholas tight against me, desperate to hold him for a little while longer, to pretend this is not the end.*

*"Please, Opa," he says.*

*God, he's tiny for fourteen. The blue-and-white striped pajamas hang off him, comically big. They fit when we first arrived.*

*His voice is a whisper, only loud enough for my ears. "Please don't let them take me, please-please-please," he says.*

*In reply, I pull him in tighter. Maybe, I think, they will overlook us. It's happened before.*

*He sobs harder when I don't respond. But I can't say anything. I'm crying into his hair, my chest hitching a little, though I try to mask it. I don't want him to know I weep. He looks up at me, his brown eyes swollen and red, his face dirty and smudged.*

*He sees tears cutting down my hollow cheeks and his cries renew with greater vigor. He knows what it means. I glance around, taking in the downcast faces of my fellow prisoners—none of whom will meet my eye. We all know what it means. We've all known since Nicholas broke his ankle. We have a doctor in the camp, a prisoner, and he set the wound as best he could.*

*It didn't matter, though. Nicholas couldn't work with his ankle like that, and in Buna such a fact is tantamount to a death sentence.*

*"I don't want them to take me, Opa."*

*The second guard finally steps into the aisle, his gray uniform crisp, his rifle slung over one shoulder, a pistol at his hip, black gloves tucked into his belt. He's young, this guard—only a little older than the first—his skin is clean, his hair neatly parted, a casual smile fills his face. After a moment, his eyes land on Nicholas and his face breaks into an even wider smirk.*

*Monster.*

*"It's your turn, Jew boy." He reaches out and grabs my poor Nicolas by the arm, jerking him up to his feet and away from me. I lunge forward—*

*The guard behind me lashes out with the buttstock of his rifle. It collides with the nape of my neck, and a wave of pain washes down my body as I tumble to the floor. I watch from the ground as the guard drags Nicholas toward the barrack's door. There's nothing I can do.*

*There's nothing anyone can do.*

*"Be strong, Nicholas," I say. "Be strong. I love you. I'll be with you soon."*

*The guard bends over and hits me again, an openhanded slap across my face. "Shut your mouth, old Kike. We've got different plans for you."*

Levi remembered, he bore witness: Nicholas Fackenheim dead at fourteen; born May 1928, murdered March 1942 in the Buna work camp, four miles from Auschwitz. It's then Levi recalled where he'd seen the altar before. In the memories. Jacob Fackenheim, *Opa,* born August 1898, murdered April 1943—experimented on in front of a strange altar with ruby eyes. An altar not so different from the one at the opposite side of the room.

The memory faded, dimming around the edges, drifting back into whatever part of his soul housed such things. In its wake came the killing rage, and with it a vicious strength. Hate and fury, murder and genocide, filled Levi with their grim purpose and carnal power. Emotion, red in tooth and claw, surged through his body as he stared at the wounded and dying girl sprawled out on the stone altar like a side of beef. A victim, like Nicholas, like his Opa.

*Shut your mouth, old Kike.*

Never again.

## FOUR:

### Abomination

Both of Levi's fists twisted, molded, flared until a pair of colossal sledgehammer heads sat at the end of each wrist. Levi planted his feet and slammed his hammer-fists into the metal barrier, throwing his body into each blow.

Left, *thunk.* Right, *thwack.* Left, *thunk.* Right, *thwack.*

The gate rang with each blow—*clang, clang, clang, clang*—the steady, rhythmic beat of a bell calling out the hour. And this was the hour of death, and the clanging gate was the death knell.

The metal buckled and warped with each strike, bending ever outward—slowly at first, but distorting more with each strike. Kobocks poured out from between the columns a few moments later, twenty of the creatures, including Gimp-arm, summoned from whatever hidey hole they'd hunkered down in. The creatures squawked to one another, fear, panic, and uncertainty marking their movements as they milled about.

A harsh, whip-crack command pierced the air, stilling the restless Kobocks and even giving Levi a moment's pause.

The shaman, a wizened creature, stooped and bent with age, its blue skin saggy and nearly translucent, hobbled into the room. Wispy silver hair, like a trail of spider webs, dangled about its head. The creature—man or woman, Levi couldn't rightly say, though he *thought* man—wore a patchwork robe of human skin, hundreds of pieces of flesh sewn haphazardly into an uneven whole. Scrolling tattoos, ancient sigils, and malevolent glyphs had been carefully inked onto each piece of crude leather. They were odd marks that hurt the eye. Marks that seemed to slither and writhe when glanced at from the side.

The withered old creature screeched out a string of commands in a tongue alien to Levi, and the underlings responded in an instant. Most backed away from the gate, hustling out of view, retreating to wherever they'd come from. A few scampered over to where the girl lay, working furiously to unbind the restraints securing her in place. They were going to take her. A new surge of indignation reared up in Levi. They couldn't take her.

He wouldn't allow it.

With one last furious blow, the iron exploded outward with a shriek of twisted metal and a blast of shrapnel, echoing *clangs* ringing around the room as battered chunks of gate fell.

The hole, only a few feet in diameter, wasn't big enough to admit the Mudman in his entirety, but that didn't matter. He wouldn't be deterred. The girl was the only thing that mattered. He *needed* to save her. *Needed* to punish the transgressors of the sacred law: *Thou shalt not kill.*

Levi's brand—a crude sword, carved deep into the muscle of his chest by his maker—burned with a furnace flame, demanding appeasement, demanding Levi dispense swift judgment. Though Levi didn't bother looking down, he knew the brand throbbed with golden light, the Hebrew script running the length of the tattooed blade shining bright as the sun:

ואתם פרו ורבו שרצו בארץ ורבו בה

*Whoever sheds human blood, by humans shall their blood be shed; for in the image of God has God made mankind.*

Levi dove through the hole, focusing his ichor, compressing his body tighter and tighter as he maneuvered his bulk through the impromptu opening. Broken shards of metal gouged into Levi's arms and legs, tearing away clumps of gray clay and opening shallow gashes, which oozed golden ichor. The Mudman didn't care.

He stretched out his arms—sledgehammer heads melting away, replaced by hands—and curled into a roll, which brought him back to his feet. Instead of stopping, he barreled onward, harnessing the momentum of his roll to bring him within striking distance of the Kobocks working to undo the girl's straps. A heartbeat later, he was among the blue-skinned underlings. He lashed out with a brutal backhand, his right hand forming a spiked mace as it hurtled through the air. The weapon broadsided the nearest Kobock, dislocating its jaw in a spray of blood, and lifted the creature off its feet.

He spun left, swinging his other hand, which morphed into a double-headed axe just before it passed through the stomach of Gimp-arm—the creature toppled, its severed torso tumbling free at the waist. Levi felt a brief burst of glee at the death of that particular Kobo, but put it from mind, his gaze swiveling back and forth as he sought more enemies. Except there were no more. The two other Kobocks who'd been working to free the girl had withdrawn. Both now cowered behind the shriveled shaman, who looked on Levi with milky eyes, a scowl etched permanently into the creases of his face.

Levi repositioned himself, sliding around to the front of the stone table so his hefty body shielded the girl.

"You don't know what you've done," the shaman hissed, his voice dusty with age and unaccustomed to speaking a language other than its own. The creature reached one lank hand beneath his flesh-cloak and withdrew a crystal dagger, not terribly dissimilar from the one Gimp-arm had stabbed him with, save this one had more of the twisting runes and glyphs carved along the length of the blade. The Mung Gal-kulom could do things, Levi knew—they possessed a sort of animistic power. The shamans used blood working to craft their rudimentary spells and conjurations.

Old, evil business, that.

The creature began to chant, his words harsh and incoherent to Levi's ears: nonsense syllables, which, nevertheless, summoned gruesome images in the Mudman's mind. Each guttural word seemed to pull back the curtain veiling the world, offering Levi's unprotected psyche a glimpse at the shadowy, hungry things wriggling in the void places between the worlds. Each new glimpse—the flash of a monstrous eye or the flutter of a tentacle—sent shivers running over the surface of Levi's flesh.

The Mudman was torn: the sensible thing to do was attack the shaman before he completed whatever arcane ritual he was about, but he was hesitant to leave the wounded girl unprotected.

The shaman's chant grew to a warbling crescendo, and he slashed down with the stone-edged knife, scoring a long gash across the inside of his forearm—a forearm that seemed more scar tissue than not. A streak of purple coated the knife-edge, and before Levi could do a thing, the shaman flicked the blade toward the macabre altar with its desecrated bodies. The blood splashed across the floor and the corpse pile in irregular streaks.

Levi waited, tension mounting as he prepared himself for whatever was to come.

Except nothing came.

Nothing.

This was Levi's first shaman, and he'd come expecting … well, a fight worth remembering. This was quite underwhelming.

The shaman shuffled back a step, then two more, glancing between the knife, the bodies, and Levi. Clearly, he hadn't expected this spectacular failure either. Levi snarled—an unpleasant look filled with broad, flat, uneven teeth—and broke into a run, charging toward the defenseless shaman like a stampeding rhino. Tonight, it seemed, he'd save the girl and bag his trophy kill. A good hunt. One hand morphed into a long, serpentine whip, the other shifted into a wicked spear blade. The shaman wheeled about, his feet moving into an awkward and unsure jog. Levi threw on a burst of speed, putting him within striking distance, and lashed out with his whip.

The plan was simple and direct, like Levi. The Mudman would ensnare the fleeing creature, strangle him slowly, then punch a hole in his guts with the spear. A killing blow, but one that would take a while to do its work. Gut wounds often dragged on and were unbearably painful. Levi saved them for the worst of the worst. All transgressors of the sacred law deserved death, but some deserved to meet the Reaper at a more leisurely pace.

But before he could follow through, the ground bucked like a rodeo bull beneath the Mudman's oversized feet, rupturing in spots; great slabs of stone dropped down in places and shot up in others. A tectonic shift beneath him. Levi was far too heavy to be thrown into the air, but the movement left him reeling and staggering, fighting to maintain his suddenly unsure footing. The commotion didn't hinder the escaping shaman, who wasted no time slipping away, out through the narrow passageway the other Kobocks had disappeared through.

After a few moments of struggle, Levi regained his balance, drawing stability from the bedrock below the temple. He swiveled around, eyes tracking the fissures in the rock back to their source: the altar and the shaman's spilt blood dotting the floor. Sickly green light—the color of death, of cancer and sickness—bled from the cracks, shot throughout with streaks of dirty red like infected blood.

This, now, was unexpected.

Levi reluctantly dismissed the escaping shaman and the murderous Kobocks, instead making his way toward the stone table.

A tidal wave of movement pulled his gaze away from the girl on the slab.

The bodies surrounding the altar were *melting* in the green light seeping up from the cracks. The flesh, muscle, and bone of every corpse liquefied in an instant, forming pools of gelatinous pink, like giant beads of living mercury. Another eyeblink and the various blobs of viscous goo merged together, swelling upward in a geyser of soupy meat, which coalesced into a figure thirteen feet tall, broad as a car, and shaped more or less like Levi himself. A rudimentary golem of sorts, though crafted from bodies instead of clay and dirt.

But it was *wrong*. Broken.

Faces jutted out like open sores all over its torso. Boneless arms and legs hung off in random places, dangling like Christmas ornaments. One of its primary, functional arms was as big as a telephone pole, while the other was withered and feeble. The creature teetered forward on two humongous, but uneven, legs, its gait awkward and unsteady. Its gaping mouth dangled open, lined with rows upon rows of oddly spaced human teeth. The creature looked at Levi with a single enormous multifaceted eye like that of a fly. Then it spoke.

Instead of a single voice, however, it droned on with a multitude of separate voices—male and female, old and young—a chorus, blending into one.

"It hurts. Oh God, it hurts," the creature moaned, its grotesque arms waving about. "Kill us. Please God, kill us. End the pain."

The Mudman watched as the creature moved forward.

Something had gone wrong here, Levi could see. That shaman was indeed experimenting, but this Frankenstein monster was no success. Oddly, the monstrous creature had a clean aura. Whatever it *was*, a killer it *was not*.

At least not yet.

The creature's eye locked on Levi. "Kill us, please kill us," it said again, its many voices sounding like the sigh of the wind through fall leaves.

In all of Levi's long years, he'd never murdered an innocent. Not even in self-defense.

Better to flee than take the life of one without blood on their hands. The Mudman was a simple creature with a singular nature: remember and uphold the sacred decree. The thing before him, whatever it was, had not violated the divine mandate; therefore, Levi was bound to inaction.

"Please," it begged again, its suffering evident.

Levi didn't know what to do. The AA meetings hadn't prepared him for this. His mind seemed to revolt at the idea of doing anything at all. He scoured his brain as the creature crept closer, diligently searching for some sermon, Scripture passage, or word of wisdom that might tell him what to do. Might guide him in this task. Levi was learning to think for himself, but at his heart he coveted instruction and direction.

A snippet from the book of Romans ran through his head, the words ringing out in Pastor Steve's voice. *"Do not repay anyone evil for evil ... Do not take revenge, my dear friends, but leave room for God's wrath, for it is written: 'It is mine to avenge; I will repay.'"* There was no doubt an evil thing had been done here—even a cursory glance at the twisted creature confirmed this—but to kill it, an innocent being, was surely evil, too. Another snatch of Scripture bubbled up, *"I desire mercy, not sacrifice."*

What was the merciful thing to do here? Levi didn't know.

He had no answers.

The terribly deformed beast dropped to misshapen knees, its doughy arms held out in supplication. "Kill us, please," it mewled. This time, the boil-like faces decorating its body mouthed the words as well.

Finally, Levi nodded.

Such a kill would surely violate the letter of the law, but perhaps mercy would uphold the spirit of the law and assuage Levi's conscience. His spear-hand became a meat cleaver with a three-foot blade. The Mudman tentatively stalked up to the creature, waiting for the abomination to attack, to prove this was some bizarre strategy to worm inside Levi's guard. But, as the Mudman drew near, the creature began to sob, great tears leaking out from a hundred different orifices. Then it lowered its deformed head to the floor, offering its neck to the executioner's block.

"Thank you," the chorus of voices said.

Levi felt more uneasy than before.

*"I desire mercy, not sacrifice,"* he reminded himself.

He planted his feet and raised the meat cleaver high above his head, but halted, his conviction wavering. *This was right ... wait, no, this was murder. Right ... Murder ... Right ... Murder.* His dual nature bickered back and forth while he stood with the weapon upheld—

The creature twitched, and Levi moved on instinct, slamming the blade down and deciding the moral quandary in an instant. The cleaver, sharp as any headman's axe, passed through the doughy flesh with ease, decapitating the beast in one savage chop. The deformed head rolled across the jagged slabs of broken floor. The corpses heaved a collective sigh of relief, then fell silent as the colossal body went limp.

The Mudman stared down at his work, feeling something brand-new: revulsion. Not merely the self-loathing he was accustomed to, but genuine sorrow and sickness over the kill, leaving behind a deep and abiding uncertainty. He was a creature of black and white, and this deed didn't fit neatly anywhere into the picture. *What had he done? What did this mean?* After a long beat, he decided now was not the time for such thoughts. Not here in the Deep Downs, surrounded by the profane, with an injured victim to look after and Kobocks waiting around every bend.

He could examine these thoughts later. He turned and headed for the girl strapped to the stone table—she was the priority, now.

Not a girl, he saw on closer inspection, but a woman. Late twenties or early thirties and pretty, though with hard lines worked into her face. Lots of tattoos covered her body—bright skulls and artful roses—though one in particular caught his eye.

Running across her chest, just below her collarbones, was a name: *Punk Rock Sally*, it said.

He pressed fingers against her throat, feeling out her pulse: present but reedy and slow.

Next he examined the crudely stitched slice running vertically from breastbone to belly button. The cut was clean and precise, done by someone who knew more or less what they were about. Still, the white skin around the incision was swollen, red, and hot to the touch—potentially deadly infection. Not surprising, considering the environment.

The meat cleaver at the end of his wrist twisted and shifted, reverting back to normal. He picked up the scalpel from the metal gurney—the tool looked like a kid's toy in his oversized mitt—and carefully sliced a line down the inside of his opposite wrist. Ichor welled to the surface, shimmering softly in the firelight. He tossed the surgical knife to the floor, its purpose fulfilled, then jammed his fingers into the cut, golden blood smearing across his fingertips. He traced his blood-streaked digits over the scar, liberally coating the wound with his blood.

Though Levi wasn't magic, his blood was powerful. Dangerously so.

Once the wound was thoroughly treated, he pried opened her mouth and forced some of the liquid down her throat, massaging her jaws so she would swallow.

She fidgeted and mumbled a weak protest.

"Gah. No more. Shit, no more." She gagged, but kept it down.

"Hush now," Levi said with a voice like a cement mixer. "Hush, it'll be alright."

He loosened her from her restraints, but left her in place so he could get a last look at the gruesome and oddly familiar altar.

The wyrm with a thousand legs seemed to be staring at him with its ruby eyes. The altar was stone, Levi knew, but in the dancing illumination of the fire, it looked alive. The thought that the altar was *only* a thing of stone was no real comfort to Levi—after all, he was not much more than a thing of stone himself. He drew closer, curiosity getting the better of him. The Kobock Nation was well known for their vile rituals, but the scene he'd stumbled upon went far beyond anything Levi had ever heard of.

*What had they been doing down here?*

With an effort of will, Levi forced open a small cavity in his side—an internal storage locker, of sorts—and pulled out a cell phone, neatly wrapped in a plastic bag. Pockets were notoriously unreliable, especially since he shifted form so often, so stowing items *inside* his body was the safest way. He took a moment to snap a couple of pictures of the bas-relief and a few more of the grotesque flesh golem, then resealed the phone in plastic and slid it back into the divot in his side. Gray skin quickly swelled over the phone, leaving behind a smooth, unmarked belly.

A single missive—handwritten on a piece of heavy stock paper—sat folded on the altar ledge. Levi snatched it up, read it over once, then shoved the letter into his side with the cell phone. He'd examine it in detail later; right now he had greater concerns. The girl. Even with his ichor working through her system, she needed a hospital. Humans were beautiful things, wonderfully and fearfully made, but frail and fleeting. She could still die. Probably would if he didn't get moving. Gently, *gently*, he lifted her into his mammoth arms, cradling her like a newborn.

She stirred again, whimpering against his chest.

Her eyes fluttered briefly. "No more. Please, no more," she offered again. Then her lids fell shut and she slept.

"Hush now," he said. "It's alright. You're safe."

J. A. Hunter

*FIVE:*

**Sunday Service**

Light shone through the stained-glass window, bright shafts falling over the far row of pews, while the gentle warble of a piano hymn capered in the air. New Eden Mennonite Church, nestled right in the sunny suburbs of Aurora, Colorado. Not an Amish church, nor even filled with the plain-dressed folk, but rather a modern congregation populated with a myriad of folk, some good, others not. Admittedly, there were a few older congregants who spoke Pennsylvania Dutch—the low German of the old Mennonites—but mostly, they were simple, hardworking people who believed in following Jesus.

The little congregation was a strange fit for Levi, but in some ways a natural one. Years back, when the Mudman had first decided a change was in order, he'd tried attending temple, which seemed intuitive given his past. Each time, though, he'd been driven from the synagogue by the memories, which were far too loud there. Overpowering. The rabbi would pull the Torah from the Ark and unfurl it across the *bimah*—a dark wood table used for the reading of the Scriptures—and suddenly Levi would *be* the rabbi. A flashback to some other life, before the war and the camps.

Everything in the synagogue was like that. The *Beth Midrash*, a connected hall used for Scripture study, held its own ghosts. As did the *Mikveh*—the ritual bath. He couldn't even glance at the *Ner Tamid*, the eternal flame, which burned ceaselessly above the Ark, without some image or another rearing up and flooding his brain. So, in the end, temple was too painful for Levi.

He'd discovered the Mennonites through his AA meetings, which were held in the basement of the church he now called home. Named after its founder, Menno Simons, the Mennonite Church had roots steeped in Anabaptism, a tradition which harkened back to the beginning of the Protestant Reformation. Though Martian Luther ushered in a theological revolution, it was the Anabaptists who took it furthest. The Radical Reformation, historians called it.

The Anabaptists were the first to preach and practice adult baptism—the origin of the name *Anabaptist*, which meant "second baptizers"—a crime which warranted the death penalty in most of Europe. A crime for which scores of Anabaptist leaders and followers were drowned or burned at the stake. They believed that church should be voluntary and separate from the state—a crime which earned them exile as subversives to the state. Most important, at least for Levi, they took Jesus' Sermon on the Mount at face value.

"Love thy Enemy" was not a suggestion or rhetorical hyperbole, but a divine mandate. They were among the first conscientious objectors.

Their radical notions came with a hefty price tag: thousands dead, murdered at the hands of Catholics and other Protestants. Yet, even while being hunted and butchered like animals, the Anabaptists refused to take up arms, refused to seek vengeance for their slain, instead leaving justice for the Lord, and even caring for their persecutors. Needless to say, Levi didn't *quite* fit in.

But he *wanted* to.

Wanted to change almost as bad as he wanted to kill. A fine dance, constantly pulling at his soul. The words of Saint Paul bounced around in his thick skull. "*I do not understand what I do. For what I want to do I do not do, but what I hate I do ... I have the desire to do what is good, but I cannot carry it out. For I do not do the good I want to do, but the evil I do not want to do—this I keep on doing.*"

If anyone could help him to learn to resist his inclinations toward vengeance and retribution, he reasoned it was the Mennonites.

"Alright," said Pastor Steve from the pulpit as the music faded, "let's stand and greet one another in love." The small congregation, maybe a hundred and fifty all present, gained their feet amidst the groan and squeak of polished wood. Levi stood with all the rest and turned to the congregant on his right: George, a tall beanpole of a man with a narrow face, a pair of wire-rimmed spectacles, and a balding pate surrounded by a ring of wispy brown hair.

"Mornin', Levi." He extended a hand, a cautious smile breaking across his angular face. George was a good man, solid, steady, but serious and not easy or loose with smiles. He wouldn't have smiled at all had Levi been in his true skin. But George *did* smile, even if it was only a thin stretching of the lips, because Levi was in disguise.

In this form, Levi stood at 5'5", was slight of build, sported a pooching potbelly, and had bad posture. His head, like George's, was nearly bald on top, and he too wore a pair of glasses, even though he could see like a hawk in the high mountain air. Levi found glasses were disarming to many people. A thin red mustache, thick denim pants, a plaid button up, and a Carhartt jacket completed the look.

Levi grasped George's bony hand and pumped vigorously. "Good to see you, George, good to see you. How're Margie and the kids?" Levi asked with false enthusiasm. He wasn't good with words or talking, but he'd seen this ritual preformed enough times to know how it was supposed to look.

"Oh, doin' alright I suppose," George replied. "Margie's not feeling well, stayed home today, but Noah and Angie are fine. Down with Pastor Dave for the young adult study. How 'bout you? Do anything interesting this past week?"

George didn't ask about Levi's family, because Levi didn't have a family. Never had—though George certainly didn't know that last bit. No father or mother. No spouse or children or kin. Levi had never met another golem, discounting the strange flesh-golem from the Deep Downs, and was unsure if another of his kind existed anywhere. It was possible in theory, he supposed. According to what ancient lore he could find, mystic rabbis—adherents of Kabbalah—could, with practice and study, learn to create a creature from the earth. A Golem. A Mudman. An obedient robot of clay. A creature like Levi.

But Levi knew of no modern rabbi capable of the feat. As far as Levi knew, he was alone in the world.

As for anything interesting … the note from the altar sat neatly folded in Levi's pocket, heavy as a lead weight and strangely warm against his skin. He didn't want to think about the note, not here in church, but his mind kept being drawn back to it like water circling a drain. The letter *was* interesting.

*If we're going to do this, you ignorant cave dweller, we're going to have to work faster. This has been countless years in the making, yet the equinox is less than a week away and still your incompetence threatens to ruin everything. I'll get the chipper back, but you'd better keep that girl safe and secure or I swear to all the dark gods below I'll make you suffer. She is the first viable subject we've had in thirty years, so don't screw this up. Try my patience in this, shaman, and see what happens. That pea-sized brain of yours isn't capable of imagining what terrible things I'm capable of.*

*—Hogg*

He'd had to read the note five different times to decipher the script, so poor was the chicken scratch penmanship, but decipher it he had. He'd pored over it dozens of times since, committing the words to memory. Very interesting. A mystery which wouldn't let his mind alone. And that altar … After staring at the picture on his phone for hours, he was positive it was twin to the one he'd seen outside of Birkemau in '42, though the memory was a fuzzy and incomplete thing—

he'd been young to Earth then, his mind largely unformed.

"No," Levi replied after a brief hesitation. "Took care of some housekeeping this weekend. Handled a bit of old business, cleaned up my workshop. That kind of thing." He bobbed his head noncommittally.

"Sounds like a nice slow weekend," George said in turn, grinning again—an awkward flash of teeth. Nearly as socially awkward as Levi, George gave the Mudman hope. If he could have a family and be normal, then Levi could, too.

"Yeah"—the Mudman thought about the Kobo cleaving open his thigh—"a nice slow weekend." He hated lying. It was another one of those unfortunate tasks that felt like a railroad spike of guilt in his heart, but the truth wouldn't do. Not here with these salt of the earth folk. His whole life was a lie, but a necessary one.

"Coming out Tuesday?" George asked.

On Tuesday Levi helped in the pantry: the church cooked a big meal for the homeless and offered care boxes of food and toiletries to needy families. Levi was a regular hand and liked the work.

Well, that wasn't true. He didn't *like* the work—the only thing he really *liked* was killing—but it was *good* to do. *Thou shalt care for the foreigner, widow, and orphan among you.* Monday, prison ministry. Tuesday, the food pantry. Wednesday, small-group Bible study. Thursday, AA meetings. Friday, he taught a beginner's pottery class at the Y. And Sunday was church. The way he saw it, busy hands had little time for killing.

"Tuesday." Levi tapped a finger against his lip in thought. "I'll try to be there," he said, and he would, "but it might not be possible this week." He reached down and touched the note through the fabric of his jeans. His brand, hidden in this form, but always present, flared bright under his skin. "Might have a big project coming up."

"Oh? Someone commission you for a piece?" George asked. He meant Levi's front. The convenient cover story Levi used so that when some respectable, decent person like George asked what he did for a living, he had an answer. In his off time, Levi sculpted—*modeled* was the technical term since he worked in clay.

A legitimate business and easy for him; after all, he had a certain affinity for the medium. And, to a certain extent, he enjoyed the work. Not like killing, though feeling the clay squeeze between his fingers was almost like feeling blood run through his hands. There was also a certain measure of peace in the creation process. Once in a while, it was nice to bring something lovely into the world instead of simply removing something ugly from it.

"Okay," said Pastor Steve, his voice reverberating through the microphone, a slight squeal of feedback causing George to flinch. "Let's head back to our seats and open our hearts to the Lord as we worship this morning. Let's be present together. Let's be here this morning with God and each other. Whatever cares or worries you're carrying, whatever baggage you brought in with you—just let it go. Leave it at the door as we worship the Lord, the refresher of our souls."

The music began in earnest, led by the pastor, who sang with a silver tongue.

The congregation sang two upbeat contemporary songs, an ol' timey hymn called "How Can We be Silent?", and a slow contemporary piece. Levi sang along by rote, his voice graceless and uneven. Usually, this was his favorite part of the service, but today his heart wasn't in it. His heart was with the note in his pocket.

Pastor Steve preached a good sermon on vengeance and the need for forgiveness, but the words washed through Levi like grain shifting through a sieve. He wanted to be present, to "let his baggage go" as the pastor admonished, but the letter weighed a thousand pounds in his pocket, and the girl from the altar kept stealing, uninvited, into his mind. Her brown eyes and cotton-candy hair. The clean gash running up her belly, sewn back together with rough surgical sutures. *She is the first viable subject in thirty years*, the note said.

A mystery, terrible and dark. He needed to see her again. To understand what the Kobocks had been up to down there. *What had they done to her and to what end?* He also wanted to know more about that altar.

Church let out at a quarter of noon.

Pastor Steve stopped the Mudman at the door. The preacher was a tall man, spare in the middle, and as smooth faced as a high schooler—he certainly didn't look like his thirty summers. But he was wise and good beyond his age and possessed an open, infectious smile. Levi grinned in spite of himself and his hurry. Normally getting on with people was a challenge, a constant battle *not* to be himself, but with Steve, genuine smiles, a quick laugh, and a light heart were easy to come by.

He was a delightful man, with a sweet family—everything Levi could ever hope to aspire to.

"Levi, great to see you. Taking off so soon? We're doing potluck today. Lots of good eats downstairs." He leaned in and cocked an eyebrow. "Pamela made a *cake*," he confided conspiratorially. "Chocolate with buttercream frosting. Someone's gonna have to help me eat it, or I'll put it all away and it'll go right to my gut." He patted his stomach and offered Levi a sly wink.

"I know it, Pastor," Levi said, bowing his head as if contrite. "I'm sorry to cut and run, but I've got a friend in the hospital. Promised to go visit her this afternoon."

"I'm sorry to hear it," he replied. "What happened, if you don't mind my asking? Is she going to be okay?"

Levi froze, the rusty cogs in his head cranking away for an answer. He'd crafted his get-away lie while still in the pews, but he hadn't expected follow-up questions.

"Are you okay, Levi?" Steve asked, his brow furrowed in concern.

"Yeah, sorry. My brain just locked up on me for a moment there," Levi replied at last.

"So, your friend," Steve prompted.

"Right, my friend." He faltered again, though only for a short time. Small, simple lies were always the best. And the closer to the truth, the better—easier to remember that way. "I think she'll be all right. She had"—short pause—"a bad car accident," he finished. "Really shook her up. But hopefully things'll turn around. We'll see, though."

"Would you mind if I added her to the prayer list?" he asked.

"Sure," Levi said. "Her name's Jess." It almost certainly wasn't, but he couldn't rightly tell the man he didn't know the name of his "friend." As for the prayer list ... it certainly wouldn't hurt to pray for her. Most days, Levi had his doubts about prayer. He knew God was real. Much of his birth was shrouded in mystery, but he knew the High Magic of Kabbalah had created him, and that was proof enough. Did God listen to the cries of hapless humans, though? Maybe, but he wasn't sold.

As Levi was wont to say, *pray for your daily bread, but keep your hand to the plow while you do it.*

"Alright, we'll see you later." The pastor gave him a final wave as Levi made for the door.

The Mudman left the building and weaved through the parking lot, the crisp fall air washing over his skin. He fished out his key fob, unlocked the doors, and slid into his minivan. Though he didn't have a family, the minivan was an excellent fit: smooth ride, inconspicuous, and great for driving folks to church. And, with large trunk space and fold-down seating, it was also ideal for transporting a body when the need arose.

Levi strived to confine his hunting to the denizens of the Hub, but sometimes he slipped up. It *was* wrong to kill human beings—creatures made in the image of God, creatures extended grace from the hand of the Creator—of that much he was now certain. Sometimes, though, he couldn't help it. It was like an itch begging to be scratched. Once in a blue moon, he'd see someone—usually a man, always a murderer—walking the street or lurking in a dark alley, and he couldn't contain the rage. Just a glance at the black aura was enough to set his ichor to a low boil.

The minivan was perfect for such accidental and unavoidable occasions.

After starting the ignition, he carefully fastened his safety belt and pulled out behind a small line of cars leaving the parking lot: folks who didn't have the time or inclination for the social niceties of Sunday potluck.

## SIX:

**Hospital Visit**

The drive to University Hospital took ten minutes since traffic was minimal and Levi had the good fortune of catching only a single red light.

There were plenty of spots in the outdoor lot, but Levi instinctively beelined for the parking garage, which would be the safest option. He pulled in and wound his way up, passing open spots on the second, third, and fourth floors, until he finally found a level devoid of cars and video cameras. He pulled the van into a corner space, close to the elevator, but with a thick wall of concrete to his left—concealing him from any upward bound traffic.

He glanced into the rearview mirror, ensuring there were no oncoming cars or peeking pedestrians. Clear left, clear right. Probably being overcautious, but always best to play it safe.

Satisfied that he was alone, he *changed.* Shifted. His torso elongated, his arms plumped up with thin wiry muscle, and his skin took on a burnt bronze hue. His clothes, likewise, made a transformation of their own: jeans and flannel melted away, coalescing into the black uniform of an Aurora police officer, complete with a badge and a gun. Not that the gun worked. Levi could mimic a great number of things—most people and even a few creatures from Outworld—but complex machinery, like a gun or a cell phone, wasn't in his repertoire. Props, though, were another thing altogether.

He pulled down his visor and surveyed himself in the flip-open mirror. He turned his head this way and that, then nodded. *Good enough.* The uniform wasn't perfect—any old salt sergeant on the force would spot the inconsistencies—but it was good enough to fool a desk nurse. Hopefully.

Levi made his way out of the multi-story garage, across the parking lot, and into the hospital lobby, which had granite floors, beautiful artwork, and lots of greenery. The place looked closer to an upscale resort than a medical facility. The girl was here somewhere—he'd dropped her off here last night at the emergency entrance, then snuck away before he had to deal with any messy questions. Survivors weren't a normal part of the Mudman's process, so he'd had to improvise. He wasn't sure which room she'd be in, though. This whole investigating business was new to him.

He scanned the room and found the information counter, marked out by a brightly lit overhead sign.

A male receptionist, a young guy in his mid-twenties, attended the desk, reading an old sword and sorcery novel while bobbing a foot to some low radio tunes. The Mudman headed over, needlessly running hands over his pants as he rehearsed his lines. He paused a few feet away, took a deep calming breath, then strode forward, donning his most confident and reassuring smile. *I can do this,* he told himself, wanting to believe the lie.

"Excuse me?" Levi said, his voice smooth and slick as butter in a hot skillet. The attendant looked up, and his eyes lingered on the badge before he stowed the book under the desk and cranked the knob on his radio, silencing the music. His cheeks held a tinge of pink and the way he kept looking down, avoiding eye contact, told Levi the kid had been caught doing something he wasn't supposed to be doing. Like reading on shift.

Good, since it meant the attendant would be all the quicker to get rid of him.

"Yes. Um, uh, what can I do for you, officer?"

"Hey, don't sweat it, kid," Levi said, shooting for off the cuff and laid-back. "I'm not going to report you to your supervisor. Relax. I'm just looking for a patient—a woman, mid-twenties, checked in here last night around eight thirty. Crazy pink hair, lots of tattoos, someone sliced her up pretty good."

The kid leaned back in his seat, shook his head, and shrugged. "Sorry," he replied. "I got on shift this morning. Do you have a name? If you have a name, I can point you to the right room."

Levi frowned, trying to recall the Old English tattoo he'd seen inked across the top of the girl's chest. *Punk Rock Susie? Punk Rock Sammy? Punk Rock Something,* that much he was sure of. Wait, *Sally, Punk Rock Sally.* "Could be wrong," he said, "but I think it's Sally something or other. Look, I'm supposed to be doing some follow-up, but I left her file back in my cruiser. Can't you help me out here?"

The attendant hesitated. This was irregular, and irregular slowed things down, got people thinking, which, in this case, was a bad thing.

Then the receptionist glanced down at his book and back up to Levi, a measuring look in his hazel eyes.

"Yeah, sure. No problem, officer," he said after a time. "Let me just get the log." He pulled out a binder and riffled through the contents, sorted by time and date. Then he moved over to the computer and ran his hands along the keyboard, fingers dancing over the keys while his eyes scanned the screen. Levi was a firm believer that honey worked better than vinegar, at least with humans. With his usual clientele—the monsters in the Hub, say—vinegar, usually in the form of a meat-cleaver-shaped hand, was always the ticket.

"Bingo was her name o," the desk jockey said. "I've got it right here. Name's Sally Ryder." His fingers hit a few more computer keys as he searched for whatever information he needed. "And"—he paused, double clicking something with the mouse—"it looks like she's up on six. Room 615."

"I sure appreciate it, you're a lifesaver." Levi beamed and bumped a fist on the desk.

The attendant shrugged in return. "Hey, like I said, no problem. Have a good day, officer."

Levi nodded, walked to the elevator bank, and rode up to six.

He gave the attending nurse at the sixth floor desk—a hefty-set black woman with short hair and square glasses—Miss Ryder's name and room number. She, in turn, gave him a bored once-over and lazily waved him in, pointing down the connecting hallway. Levi walked to the door and knocked softly. No answer.

He knocked harder, more insistently. Still nothing. So, he pushed his way in while a seed of worry tugged at his mind like a fishhook. *What if they already got to her? What if I'm was too late? Nonsense,* the rational part of his mind insisted, *she's fine.* As though to prove he wasn't worried, Levi carefully shut the door behind him with a soft click, no rush at all. She was in, and likely sleeping, so no point in startling the poor girl.

He made his way down a short hallway and pulled back a sliding curtain concealing the sleeping quarters. He breathed out a sigh of relief. Sally Ryder, with her pink hair and colorful tats, sat propped up in her bed watching some bad movie on a too small TV, a pair of headphones snaking from the hospital bed to her ears.

"Excuse me, Miss Ryder? Sally Ryder?" he asked.

No response. Her eyes were glazed, heavily lidded, puffy, and fixed firmly on the television. The look of a person who wanted very badly to forget about life for a while.

He cleared his throat. Nothing. "Excuse me, Miss Ryder? Sally Ryder?" he said again, this time raising his volume.

She startled, giving a small jump before turning toward him, green eyes tightening at the corners with worry. She was terrified, which explained the purple bags riding below her eyes—not sleeping. Levi thought her fear was well warranted. Her lips curled down when she saw him, disapproval and disdain evident in equal measures on her face. The look of someone with no love for cops. She reached up and pulled the headphones free, then folded her arms across her slight chest.

"Look, I already gave my statement," she said, voice hard edged. "I'm not interested in talking anymore. I'm not going to recant, if that's why you're here. I wasn't on drugs. I know what happened and what I saw. So please, just leave me alone. I need to rest."

"Yeah, it sure does look like you could use some rest," Levi muttered under his breath.

"What was that?"

"Nothing," Levi replied loud enough for her to hear. "I was just saying my name's Officer Adams, and I'm going to need you to go over the details for me one more time." Levi pulled over one of the visitor chairs and took a seat. "From the beginning if you wouldn't mind."

"But I *would* mind," she replied. "I'm not interested in being laughed at again. You guys already have the report, and I'm not changing a word."

"All the same, miss." He paused for a beat. "Please, the details could be important. I understand you might not feel like discussing the issue further, but whoever did this to you is still out there. If you don't help us stop them, what happened to you could easily happen to someone else. I know you don't want to see that happen. So just once more, from the beginning." He flashed her his most winsome smile.

She scowled, pulled her arms even more tightly against her body, and looked away, uncooperative. After a second she reached up and ran the back of one hand across her cheek, obliterating a tear track. Levi just sat there, waiting. It was awkward, uncomfortable, and too quiet, but Levi was fine with awkward, uncomfortable, and too quiet. He thrived on those conditions and he knew she would cave first. Humans almost always did with this kind of thing—it was the need to fill the silence with noise. With something, anything really, so they wouldn't have to sit alone with their own thoughts.

Not a terribly introspective species.

After a couple more uncomfortable minutes, Ryder shrugged her shoulders and turned back toward him.

"Fine, if it'll get you outta my hair quicker, I'll talk. I was kidnapped," she said. "Kidnapped by a bunch of freaky monsters. Creepers with blue skin. Cultists, maybe, I dunno. Had to be something like that. They drugged me and took me somewhere. I don't know where, but it was dark and it smelled like shit. There were a few other people with me, but ..." She trailed off. "I can't remember—and it's not important anyway. They-they cut me open." She uncrossed her arms and traced a finger along her stomach.

"That's what's important. They did something to me, I dunno what. Stole an organ? All the docs around here say I'm not missing anything, but that's what I think. Only thing that makes any fucking sense. What else?" She paused for effect. "Oh right, then some colossal, gray-skinned dude busted in, snatched me up, and dropped me off at this hospital. Truth is, I'm from Pennsylvania and I don't have a clue, not a fucking clue, how in the hell I ended up in Colorado."

Levi nodded noncommittally as she spoke. Still, he could understand why the cops had thought she was on drugs. The story was unbelievable and sounded far closer to a bad LSD trip than anything that might happen in reality. Sometimes the truth could be a damn hard pill to swallow. That's how all the monsters stayed hidden: most humans unfortunate enough to run afoul of the preternatural crowd ended up dead.

And for the few that escaped? Written off as crazies, druggies, conspiracy theorists. Humans who lived to tell the tale quickly learned where spouting such stories got you. Alienated from friends and family. Laid off. Living in a cardboard box on the wrong side of the tracks. And sometimes, in a padded cell, loaded to the gills with Clozapine or Risperdal.

A tough pill to swallow, indeed.

"Listen," Levi said, "I know how difficult this must be, but can you think of anyone who might want to harm you? Any reason you might've been abducted? Any reason at all?"

She was still for a few heartbeats, silent, eyes turned inward. "No," she said eventually with a slight shake of her head. "Nothing. Now can you please leave? I'm tired." She pressed her eyes closed.

*Liar.* She was hiding something, that much was obvious, but then Levi found *most* people were hiding something: a secret sin, not unlike his own need for murder, that they would do anything to leave buried. Likely, the girl was just an unfortunate casualty in some bigger game.

"Thank you for your cooperation, Miss Ryder."

He got up and let himself out of the room, shutting the door behind him, heading back out toward the nursing station. His finger brushed at the note in his pocket. He wasn't prepared to let this thing go, not quite yet, but the girl looked to be a dead end …

*Or maybe not.*

Two men loitered near the elevators.

Except they weren't actually men. Some clueless human might believe the ruse, but Levi's eyes saw true. Both fellows stood at five and a half feet and had ropy arms, strangely lopsided shoulders, and distended bellies. The skin on their meat suits was too loose, like poorly done Halloween costumes, only in reverse: instead of humans pretending to be monstrous things of the dark places, these suits allowed monsters to pretend to be civilized beings of the surface world.

Though Levi couldn't see beneath their masks, he didn't need too. He could tell a Kobock when he saw one, even up here. These were murderous bastards, too. He could see it around them like a hazy black cloud polluting the air. The reek of death stained their auras.

Levi grinned at the Kobos riding around in their human suits like a pair of kids out trick or treating, and reached into his pocket. He fumbled around as if searching for a pair of keys or maybe a cell phone and, after a few fruitless seconds, pulled his hand out empty. He snapped his fingers, pivoted, and strode back the way he'd come from. Just some poor uni who'd forgotten something, no big deal—at least that's what he wanted the Kobos and the station nurse to think.

"Forgot my phone," he said in passing.

"No problem," the nurse replied, eyes still glued to the computer screen, not even bothering to look up from her work.

A few long strides put him back into Ryder's room. Her eyes, now red-rimmed from heavy crying, shot toward him as the door swung open. She flashed him a frosty glare, then rubbed the palms of her hands into her eye sockets. *These tears aren't for you to see*, the action said.

"I told you I need to rest. Go. Away."

Levi shut the door and thumbed the lock with a *click*. Fear streaked across her face, and she drew her knees up toward her chest with a grimace.

"You'd better unlock that door, Officer Adams, or whatever you said your name was. I'm only gonna say this once. You're making me uncomfortable, so if you take *one more step*"—she held up a hand as though to ward him away—"I'll press the help button and scream like a banshee."

Levi snorted. The girl's words were unintentionally comical. "You have no idea what a banshee scream can do," he said.

"Excuse me," she said, attitude radiating off her like gale force winds.

The Mudman waved a hand through the air, brushing her objection away. "It's nothing. Please don't scream, Miss Ryder. There's something of an emergency situation, and I need you to get dressed. Put your pants on and get whatever you need, because we're leaving. Right now."

"I'm not screwing around," she replied. "I'll do it, I'll scream my ass off, right here in this hospital, and then I'll get your badge number and report you for sexual harassment. This isn't the first time I've been around some skeezy cop, and I know how this works. So unless you want a suspension or worse, you'd better turn around, unlock that door, and march on outta here, big shot. I'm serious—I know my rights."

"Shut up," he said, patience gone. "We don't have time for this. Some of the men that took you are here. Standing out in the hallway near the elevator. They're waiting for me to leave and once I do, they're going to come in here and take you. You try screaming your way out of that and see how far it gets you."

"They're here?" she asked, frantic, body trembling. "Well, go fuckin' arrest them. You're a cop, that's like your whole job."

"No, I'm not. And these aren't the kind of things you can arrest." A tense silence hung between them, a thing as fragile as thin lake ice—one wrong step could shatter everything.

"Who are you?" she finally asked, her voice small and frail as she hugged her knees even tighter into her body.

## SEVEN:

## The Chase

The woman, Sally Ryder, sat on her hospital bed, eyes wide, ready to bolt in an instant like a wary deer. "I'm going to show you something that'll help you understand," Levi said, hoping to put her at ease, "but it's important that you remain quiet. It'll be bad if you scream. They'll know something's up, you understand that?"

She said nothing but nodded, her head bobbing a fraction of an inch.

Levi grunted in return, then shifted, letting the uniform disappear back into his flesh, allowing his bulk to ripple outward and upward, skin returning to the colorless gray of moist clay. She squealed and gasped, clasping hands over her mouth to stifle the sound. But she didn't scream. Good girl.

"It's you. You saved me ..." She faltered. "What are you?" The last was a mere whisper.

Levi morphed, drawing his formidable mass back in, muscles becoming more dense and compact as the officer façade emerged once again. "Later," he said. "I'll tell you whatever you want, but not now. Now, we leave. We have to go. Hurry."

In reply, she scooted off the bed, snagged a pair of gray sweatpants with the word "POLICE" written down one leg from the nightstand and slipped them on. She shrugged out of her hospital gown, her chest covered only by a plain white bra—Levi turned his head, lending her some measure of privacy—and pulled on a baggy white T-shirt, two or three times too big. A pair of thin hospital slippers, sitting near the bathroom, completed the outfit.

"Okay, I'm ready."

"Good," he replied, eyeing her attire. Not exactly Kevlar body armor, but better than nothing. Besides, if they ended up in a brawl, Levi would do the heavy lifting anyway. "Follow my lead. Don't panic, that's the important thing to remember. These things, they don't know about me. Not yet. They'll think I'm a cop just like you did and they won't try anything. Not out in the open. So just remain calm. Natural." He took her by the hand, opened the door, and waltzed into the hallway, a false smile gracing his lips.

Generally, Levi was terrible with people, but he was more than a passable actor when the need arose. He'd learned early on that survival in the world of men meant being able to blend in. To go unnoticed. So he'd learned to mimic emotion in the same way he mimicked faces.

"It's alright, Miss Ryder," he said for the benefit of both the station nurse and the loitering Kobos. "This won't take long. We've just got a few suspects we need you to come down and take a look at, see if you recognize anyone."

"Of course," she replied, her arms once again hugged tight around her torso.

"Excuse me," the nurse said, sliding her glasses down onto the bridge of her nose. "Where exactly do you think you're taking her? Obviously you're new to the job, because this young lady hasn't been cleared yet. And if the attending physician doesn't clear her, she doesn't go anywhere."

"I'm sorry, ma'am," Levi replied evenly, "but this is a time sensitive matter, and we really need Miss Ryder's help. Once we're done I'll have another officer bring her back by."

The nurse frowned, forehead creased, as she stared over the top edge of her glasses at Levi. Her hand moved close to the desk phone, hanging there as if she were trying to decide whether to call security or give him a pass. "Alright," she said at last, suspicion still carved into every line of her body. "But I'll need your name and badge number for the log so I know who to blame when the doctor comes by."

"Sure, sure." He puffed out his chest, offering her a solid view of the phony shield. "It's Officer Adams, badge number 2109." He smiled, every inch the professional. She carefully jotted the information down, clearly not won over.

"Officer Adams, I expect Miss Ryder to be back here and in bed in no more than two hours. You understand that? She's still recovering from a traumatic accident, and though I understand you have a job to do, my job is to take care of my patients. So, if she's not back in two hours"—she held up two fingers—"your sergeant will get an earful."

"Of course, ma'am," Levi replied, his grin faltering and slipping away. "Two hours."

The salty nurse nodded her approval and promptly went back to work on her computer, fingers clacking away on the keyboard once more.

Levi took Ryder by the elbow and steered her toward the elevator bank. The Kobos were waiting, leaning casually against the wall, dark scowls marring their already ugly faces. Levi pretended not to notice.

He and Ryder rode down to the ground level and stepped off the elevator only to find another pair of lopsided men, more Kobos, waiting for them. Levi offered these two friendly smiles, then curtly moved on, guiding Ryder toward the front exit, but keeping the pace casual, all in a bid to keep the Kobos from growing antsy or suspicious. He even spared a quick moment to stop by the information desk and thank the young man who'd been so helpful.

The whole act, which is precisely what it was, said plainly enough, *There's nothing to worry about, this is all just standard operating procedure.*

After a few tense minutes in the building lobby, they ambled past the sliding glass entryway doors and found themselves in a beautiful Colorado day: warm, but not unpleasantly so; sunshine colored the landscape with bright yellows, while a flawless blue sky stretched endlessly onward, framed on the west by the jagged peaks of the Rockies. They hooked left, angling toward the parking garage, though he kept to the sidewalk and maintained their leisurely pace. Ryder fidgeted as they walked, as though the reptilian part of her brain demanded she start running, fleeing from the unseen hunters stalking them.

The Mudman glanced back—the two Kobocks from the main lobby were tailing them, though keeping a safe distance—then leaned into Ryder. "Stop. Wiggling. What part of stay calm and act natural didn't you understand?"

She pulled away from him with a jerk and narrowed her eyes. "This *is* natural. Take a look at me. Do I look like the kinda person who hangs out, all buddy-buddy, with cops? The answer," she continued without hesitation, "is hell no. Most cops, they see someone like me and they think junkie or dealer or whore. So, if you want things to look natural, stop being so nice to me."

Levi pushed up beside her, placing a heavy hand on her shoulder and another around one arm—a bouncer escorting a troublemaker from a bar.

"Besides," she whispered as they walked, "I don't see any of the assholes that took me. Think they'd kinda stick out around here."

"They're in disguise," he replied. "Kind of like me. Now close your mouth until we get to the car—wouldn't want the wrong pair of ears hearing what they shouldn't."

They paused at the crosswalk, waited for a big ol' Ford on too-large tires to roll by, then crossed the patch of black asphalt and strode into the blocky concrete parking garage. Levi stole another quick look over one shoulder as they moved: the Kobocks, shadowing them, were closer now, maybe ten feet back and moving in. If these things were determined to walk away from the hospital with Ryder in hand, and Levi had no reason to assume otherwise, then a parking garage was a good place for them to make their move.

Likely, a lone Rube cop wouldn't be enough to deter them.

A stairwell would be perfect for an attack—an enclosed space with few, if any, cameras and little room to maneuver or run. Knowing that, Levi headed for the elevators instead. He pressed the button and let out a slight sigh of relief when the doors slid open an eyeblink later—the car had already been on the ground floor. A small but fortunate break. He shoved Ryder in, slid in behind her, then wheeled about, jamming down the fifth floor button, followed in short succession by the "close door" button. The Kobocks were five feet out when the metal door ghosted shut.

Ryder doubled over and clutched her knees, her breathing rapid and panicked. "Holy shit that was intense. Those two guys? Was that them?"

"Yeah. They can look like men or women when they have a mind to, but that was them alright."

"Holy shit," she said again, before straightening.

The elevator *dinged* and the doors parted, depositing them high up in the parking garage, well away from their enemies—temporarily stranded on the ground level—and a few feet from Levi's minivan, just on the other side of a concrete partition.

"Come on." He ushered her onward with one hand as he trotted over to the minivan, pulling out his keys and pressing the fob—the van let out a little *chirp-chirp* in reply. "This is us," he said, slipping into the driver's seat and turning the engine over.

"Nope." She shook her head, eyeing the van. "No way in hell I'm getting into that rape van. Seriously, do you have any idea how many red flags are going up right now? Climbing into a sketchy van with some old creeper in a dark parking garage. This whole situation"—she threw both hands up—"violates like every single rule of surviving on the road."

"It's either in here with me or out there with them," Levi replied, not bothering to validate her comment. Besides, he wasn't that creepy, and neither was the minivan. Comfortable captain-style seating, a rear DVD player, good gas mileage, and fold-down seating. Nothing weird about that.

"I can't believe I'm doing this." She rolled her eyes. "My sister would kill me if she knew." Ryder opened the door and slid into the passenger seat.

"No," Levi said. "Crawl into the backseat and put your head down."

"Are you kidding me?" she asked, skepticism coating the words. "I'm not climbing into the backseat and 'putting my head down.'" She air quoted the words. "Not to be an ungrateful asshole or anything, but you've got this I'm-going-to-murder-you-and-bury-you-in-my-backyard vibe going on, so hiding in the back until you can drive me to your dump site isn't on the agenda. I wanna be up here so if you try anything fishy, I can jack the steering wheel and flip the car. Or something. But I think you get the general idea."

Levi ground his teeth. He'd never had a human ride-along when it came to the supernatural side of his existence and so far he was badly regretting the decision. "Stop talking and get into the backseat. So they won't see you," he said, a teacher instructing a stubborn child. "We're escaping, remember? Besides, if I wanted you dead, I could've left you to die down in the dark. I could've left you strapped to that table with your guts hanging out, waiting to end up like the other

poor souls down there. So get into the backseat. Now."
He hooked a thumb toward the rear of the vehicle.

"I appreciate you not leaving me to die—you're
a real Good Samaritan—but that doesn't mean I trust
you. Don't forget, you're a shapeshifting killer.
Besides, they'll recognize you even if they don't see
me," she replied, making no move to leave the front
seat, "so moot point."

He shifted in a blink, resuming the appearance
he thought of as his church face: balding, mustached,
potbellied, and bespectacled. Theoretically, he could
shift into almost any form, but it took loads of
concentration, and those forms he wore most often were
the easiest to maintain. He had fifteen faces, fifteen
forms, he used interchangeably, so those were the looks
he reverted to on instinct, but his church face was the
easiest by far.

Her mouth dropped open an inch, then two.
"Shapeshifter. Right. Okay, guy, you're the boss."
Without further argument, she shimmied into the back,
lying down flat on the carpeted floor. Levi slammed the
van into gear and pulled out of the space, but not before
the elevator door dinged opened and the two Kobos
stepped out. Levi looked different and Ryder was
thankfully absent, but this level of the garage was
otherwise empty. They were the only people leaving.

He locked eyes with the masquerading Kobos as
he rounded the corner, and knew in his gut they'd been
made.

One of the lopsided strangers dug into his
pocket, drew out a disposable brick phone, punched a
few buttons, and lifted the cell to his ear. Calling for

reinforcements, no doubt. Likely, more of their ilk were waiting in a car somewhere not far from here. Bad luck, that. Levi's initial inclination was to slip and squeal around the turns, to get out of the garage as fast as the van would take them, but, he reminded himself, that would only serve to identify them all the easier.

As with their exit from the hospital proper, calm and collected would serve them far better than madcap action-star stunts. So he drove cautiously, slowly. He was a man in no particular hurry who had nothing whatsoever to hide. Hopefully, if he played things right, the pair down yonder wouldn't notice him at all.

He pulled out of the garage and turned onto the main street running in front of the hospital, making sure to obey all posted road signs and use his blinkers. It took all of thirty seconds before a beat-up Explorer and a silver Cadillac Deville pulled onto the road, weaving around slower moving traffic, quickly eating up the distance between them. Levi's hands tightened on the wheel, which *creaked* under the pressure. If only Ryder had been faster, done as she'd been told without so many questions, they would've been free and clear.

It was important to follow instructions. To follow rules. There were consequences, always consequences, for disobedience. Done was done, though. *Gam zu l'tova. This too is for the good*, he told himself.

He curved right—still driving slowly, carefully, hoping he might salvage this mess somehow—and pulled into the left turn lane, which let out onto Colfax Avenue. Naturally, the turn arrow was red, pinning them in place since he refused to run the light. The car hummed quietly beneath him as he patiently waited for the arrow to turn green. A moment later, both the

Explorer and the Cadillac pulled up behind him. The Explorer was closest and sported tints so dark they entirely concealed the driver—Levi was certain they were illegal.

It didn't matter. Even if he couldn't see the filthy Kobocks driving the SUV, he could feel the taint of their presence in his bones and feel the hot gaze of their hate on the nape of his neck.

Finally, the turn arrow flashed green, and Levi pulled away, maneuvering into the left-most lane.

"What's the deal? Can I come up now?" Ryder asked, voice muffled.

He considered saying *no* out of annoyance, since this fiasco was mostly her fault, but then mumbled a reluctant "Yes." She was new to this world, and given the circumstances, he supposed her distrust was reasonable. After all, she'd recently been kidnapped, held captive, and dissected by blue-skinned monsters. Had he been in her position, he would have been suspicious, too. It wouldn't be right to punish her for trusting her survival instinct, even if, in this instance, her instinct had been wrong. "We're already being followed," he conceded, "so it doesn't matter if you're seen now or not."

Her head popped up, and she wiggled into the passenger seat before looking back. "The Explorer and the Caddy?"

"Obviously," he said. "Now buckle your seat belt. It's the law."

She stole a sidelong peek at him, one eyebrow cocked. "The law's made to be broken, Big Guy," she said. Still, she complied, wriggling around for a moment before snapping the belt into place and resuming her scan of the road behind.

"So those guys we saw, they're the blue-thingies who did this to me?" She absently motioned at her stomach, at the slash currently concealed by the baggy white shirt.

"The Kobock Nation," Levi said. "That's what they call themselves." He angled the van sharply, cutting hard right all the way across traffic and onto the entrance ramp for freeway I-225 North. The Explorer and Deville followed suit, merging on behind a handful of seconds later.

"And Kobocks are?" she asked.

"Kobos for short. Sort of like Goblins. Live in the Deep Downs of the Hub."

"'Kay. Let's try a different approach. How about you pretend I don't know anything at *all*— because, gee, I don't know anything at all—and just explain every weird thing you say? How's that sound?"

"Not a good time for this conversation," the Mudman replied, knuckles still vice-grip tight on the steering wheel while his eyes flickered over the rearview mirror. He smashed down the gas and swerved left, boldly darting across three lanes of traffic, trying to draw away from their pursuers. The van was great for a lot of things, but no one would ever mistake the vehicle for a hot-rod roadster. The Explorer and Cadillac had no difficulty keeping up. He pushed it to seventy and held fast, not wanting to draw any unwanted attention from local authorities, while he cruised toward the I-70 interchange.

It took a handful of minutes before the mousetrap—a huge sprawl of concrete ramps, soaring high into the air and connecting the north- and southbound I-225 with the east- and west-bound I-70—drew into view. Here Levi punched the gas, pushing his speed up to eighty, then eight-five, and waited for the last possible moment before swerving back to the right. He slashed his way across four lanes, all heavy with traffic, merging onto I-70 East. Hopefully, the Kobock hunters wouldn't be able to get over in time and would get stuck on the westbound branch of the freeway.

Tires squealed, brakes shrieked, and the blare of angry car horns followed in their wake, but they made the turn off—narrowly avoiding a concrete highway divider designed to prevent just such haphazard and reckless driving. Levi dropped back down to sixty-five as he took the curved flyover. Ryder clung to the armrests of the captain-style passenger seat, her skin even paler than before.

"Top Gun, what happened to it's the law? Can we try not to do that again?" she asked. "I feel like I just got a second chance at this living thing, and I'd like not to become road pizza." She paused, eyes scanning the rearview mirror. "Oh shit," she said, "the Caddy made the turn."

And sure enough, Levi caught a glint of silver as the Deville weaved toward them like a shark cutting through waves. The Explorer, at least, was nowhere to be seen. One down was certainly better than nothing.

They hopped off I-70 East at the Chambers Avenue exit, doubling back toward Colfax, an area Levi was far more familiar with. The Deville hung back but kept pace: close enough to monitor the van, but far enough away to maneuver in case Levi pulled another stunt like the one back on the freeway. That was fine, though, since Levi had no intention of ditching this carful of monsters.

They did need some answers, after all.

He swung left once they made Colfax—a straight cut of asphalt running for miles and miles. Once upon a time, and way back when, in the days before I-70 tore across the state like a concrete river, Colfax had been Colorado's main interstate, an indispensable artery: Motor Inns, hotels, and old diners galore littered the roadway from a bygone golden age. Now, however, Colfax was a black hole, those once fine hotels fallen into disrepair and filled with winos and prostitutes.

As they rode east, gas stations and badly worn motels gave way to trailer parks, liquor stores, and, eventually, rolling brown open space. Open space largely devoid of other motorists or unwelcome, prying eyes. Exactly the kind of territory Levi favored for his work.

"So, what should I call you?" Ryder asked as the car settled into an easy forty miles per hour, the traffic thinning out and dying away as they drove. "Not that I mind calling you Top Gun or Big Guy. Heck, I could call you Goo-dude or Clay-face. Doesn't really matter to me. But I just thought if we're going to be stuck together, maybe I should know your name."

"Levi," he said after a time. "Some folks call me Mudman. You can call me either."

"Naturally, some folks call you Mudman," she mumbled under her breath. She pinched the bridge of her nose. "Okay, Levi, what's the deal with the Kobocks? What do they want with me?"

"Don't rightly know." Levi offered her a lopsided shrug. "Whatever it is, though, it can't be good. Usually Kobos abduct, rape, kill. That's their M.O. That's what they do. They aren't the type for planning things out. Maybe their shamans—that'd be the old one with the skin cloak—but not your everyday Kobock. But you, you they didn't kill. You they didn't rape. No, you they came back for. Ventured up to the surface for, which, by the way, they hate doing. Must mean you're important to them somehow. Past that though?" He shook his head. "My specialty isn't so much in *understanding* them as it is in *exterminating* them."

More awkward silence descended like the setting sun, coating the interior of the car.

"Okay. That's something I guess," she said after a time, pushing onward. "If you can't tell me more about the Kobocks, then tell me about the Hub. That's a thing you mentioned? Or you could tell me what in the hell you are? That seems like the kinda thing you might know something about. Really, at this point, I'll take whatever I can get."

Levi didn't answer. Her questioning was already wearing on him. Levi could often play the outgoing people-person when the need arose—at church say, or during a gallery showing for his artwork—but normally he was tight-lipped and not one for conversation. Especially not conversation on Kobocks, Outworld, or himself.

Eventually, she scowled as if to say, *Fine, whatever asshole.* "You can keep your secrets for now," she snapped, "but I expect answers sooner or later." She hooked a thumb back toward the Deville. "The least you can do is tell me how we're gonna lose the freaks in the Caddy. And then I want to know where we're going and what the plan is."

"Sure ask a lot of questions." He flipped on some soft Christian contemporary music and fell silent.

She immediately pushed the power button, cutting the tunes from the air like a knife.

"Yeah, because you told me you had answers," she replied. "Remember that? Back in the hospital, like fifteen minutes ago, when you said if I came with you you'd tell me what I want to know? Well, here we are, and there's a shitload of things I'd like to know about. Such as, where are we going and what's the plan?" She ran a hand through her hair, nervous but fighting to hide it.

*Empathy*, Levi thought. Pastor Steve was always saying Levi could stand to be more empathetic—could benefit from seeing things from other people's perspective. Step Ten bubbled up in his mind: *Always continue to take personal inventory, and when you're wrong, promptly admit it.* As much as he was loath to acknowledge it, the girl made a few good points. He supposed he did owe her a few answers, and besides, throwing her a bone might make her more agreeable.

He grunted and grimaced. "Fine. Sorry. I'll answer some of your questions. Right now, we're going to draw this carload of Kobos to someplace private. Then, once we're sure there's no one else around, we're going to pull over. You"—he jabbed a finger at her—"well, you are going to stay in the car with the doors locked. And me, well I'm going to club 'em all to death."

The brand on his chest pulsed at the thought. It'd been a tough day and he was looking forward to dealing with the carload of soon-to-be murder victims behind him. He'd have to purge again, to soak his flesh in fire, but the catharsis would be more than worth it. "But before I kill them, I'll see if I can't get some answers. Then ... I dunno." He rolled his shoulder, muscles tight, tense. "Then, I guess we'll head back to my place and try to come up with a better game plan. Something proactive."

Colfax continued for a way yet before meeting back up with I-70 East, but there was a turn off ahead, which wound back toward a rest area with a poorly maintained asphalt parking lot and a dusty tan brick bathroom. Other than the Deville, there wasn't a car in sight for miles. Levi slowed down, even turning on his blinker so the Kobos wouldn't miss them when they pulled into the rest stop.

"This seems like such a bad idea." She was fidgeting again, running her hands ceaselessly over her sweatpants. "I mean, can't we come up with a plan that doesn't involve fighting to the death?" For all her tough talk, Levi got the sense she was more scavenger than predator.

"Don't worry about it. Remember, this is my specialty. I've got this." The Mudman steered the car into the shade of the rest stop bathroom, turning on the hazards and shifting into park. He killed the engine, unfastened his seat belt, and got out, still wearing his church face. He smiled as the Cadillac pulled up. The first genuine smile that day.

*EIGHT:*

**Scuffle**

The Deville pulled up, grinding to a halt as its doors flew open releasing a slew of strangely malformed people. Four men and three women: a regular clown car; though, admittedly, the Deville was big as a boat. The driver was the last to exit. With him, the count climbed to eight, but he wasn't like the rest.

No, not the same at all. Big, bigger even than Levi in his true form, and built on the same scale as a black bear—powerful muscle coated in thick fat. That, combined with the low sloping forehead, flat face, and jutting lower jaw, struggling to contain all its teeth, told Levi all he needed to know.

A troll or ogre. Though, he couldn't rule out some other horror from the far-flung reaches of Outworld, not without seeing its true form.

"Look, folks," Levi said, raising his hands in submission, letting a false thread of panic fill his voice. "I don't know why you guys are following me, but I'm sorry for whatever I did. I'm sure this is just some big, unfortunate misunderstanding."

The horde of creatures stalked nearer, fanning out in a rough circle, closing in on multiple fronts.

"Look," Levi said, turning this way and that, trying to speak to everyone at once. "If I cut you off or stole your parking spot, it was an accident. I swear. No offense intended. I'll-I'll give you money, if that would help. I have money." He dry-washed his hands, a nervous tic—at least in a human. There was no way they could know what he was, and in his current shape he looked about as intimidating as an emaciated rat-terrier.

That was to his advantage. He was a creature well versed in the art of bloody knuckles and busted teeth, so the closer they got, the better.

"Please, folks," Levi pleaded, his voice cracking at the edges. "Let's just get back in our cars, huh? What ya' say? We all go our own way, no muss, no fuss."

With long loping strides, the hulking driver deposited himself directly in front of Levi, planting his feet and balling up giant fists. "Where's girl?" he asked in a low-pitched grunt too deep for any set of human vocal chords.

"I don't know what you mean," Levi replied, offering an uneasy smile, then scooting back a step.

The creature—whatever he was beneath his flesh-mask—raised a colossal hand and set it on Levi's shoulder. Weighed as much as a Christmas ham. "Not ask again. Where's girl? We only come for girl." Then the creature squeezed, fingers curling in to emphasize his point. Ogre-man's beady eyes went wide as he found the flesh beneath his fingers unyielding. When Levi changed form, he didn't diminish, he *compacted*, drawing down, but simultaneously increasing in density. After all, the Mudman's mass couldn't disappear—the Law of Conservation applied to both natural and supernatural alike.

Though the body he wore looked saggy and weak, he weighed in at over four hundred pounds—all of it rocky earth, mucky clay, and golden ichor.

"What—" the creature started to say.

Levi didn't let him finish.

Instead, he lurched up, letting his bulk spill out as his body reverted to its true shape. Pivoting from the hips, Levi slammed an uppercut into the underside of Ogre-man's chin. A brutal strike, which should've sent the brute flying high, but instead merely left him swaying from side to side, a boxer almost down for the count. Obviously the creature was also larger than he appeared from his human exterior.

Before the creature could get its bearings, Levi shot in again, melting both hands into medieval mace heads—spiked and deadly—which he swung in a ferocious overhead arch, bringing both clubs down upon his opponent's head. The strike reverberated up through his arms, rattling his teeth as if he'd just hammered into a steel support beam. All the same, the creature crumpled to the ground, legs giving way under the force of the blow, its flesh-mask disappearing as the beast hit the unkempt asphalt.

What remained was a mound of thick muscle covered with bristly white fur, a boar-like face with great tusks protruding skyward from its lower lip, and claws the envy of any grizzly bear. Not to mention a stench—wild and musky mixed with decay and shit— that was worse than even the sewers running beneath the Hub.

A troll then, but not a regular troll: a *Thursr*. A Dread Troll of the far north.

As the Thursr hit the ground, the Kobo passengers lost their focus and, in so doing, their rudimentary disguises. Where once seven misshapen humans had been, now the Kobocks loomed in all their disgusting glory.

Then the Kobocks were moving.

The whole lot of them dashed in as one. Two of the females—marked by their scraggily black hair—leapt through the air, grubby claws extended while inhuman shrieks of rage filled their throats. One tangled her arms around Levi's neck while the other grabbed onto his leg like a toddler and bit down with jagged black teeth. Levi replied with his own howl as he shook his massive frame—a dog shedding water—but the pair clung tightly, thin arms much stronger than they appeared.

Another Kobo darted in from the side, scampering along the ground on all fours like some monster chimp. Levi swung and met him with a wrecking ball fist, caving in his face with a *crunch*. The force of the blow hurled him through the air and into the high grass beside the restroom.

From behind, a Kobo snaked around Levi's other leg, nails digging in, teeth chewing at his calf. Levi shook again, spinning round and round, as he attempted to dislodge the miserable hitchhikers. Useless.

The last female struck from the left, coming in hard before weaving at the last moment to pounce from the front. Levi brought up his leg—Kobo still dangling like some monstrous tick—and buried a foot in her chest, caving in her ribs and throwing her back. Her broken form bowled into the Dread Troll, who was slowly making his way upright. That was problematic.

He'd caught the Thursr by surprise, but now the creature would be ready for a fight. Thursrs were tougher than old mountain rocks, but Levi was sure he could carry the day—assuming he *only* had to deal with the troll.

But against a Dread Troll and seven Kobocks?

He needed to even the odds a bit.

Down in the Hub—or anywhere in Outworld—Levi was limited, terribly so. Here, however, he had access to his full power and he intended to use it.

He reached out, pushing his senses deep into the ground while also drawing the golden ichor within him to the top of his skin, preparing it for transmutation. That was the true secret behind his abilities: the alchemic, transmutable nature of the ichor flowing in his veins. True, he could shapeshift, but only because his gray flesh was saturated with the golden substance beneath, lending it similar, malleable properties. Yes, he could heal even the most grievous injuries, but only because the ichor—almost a living substance—fought furiously to keep its host alive.

The ichor was powerful stuff, capable not merely of taking the shape or appearance of a thing, but of becoming that thing in truth.

The earth—his mother and father—called out to him, welcoming him home and offering him whatever assistance he required: layers of burnt-red sandstone hummed like a gentle laugh from a long lost friend; pockets of silvered mica, cloudy quartz, and chalky feldspar—all like siblings—each yelled at him, all vying for attention. Running beneath all of those lay metamorphic and igneous rock, their call like a sturdy and steadfast military cadence. That was what he needed: the igneous rock, with its rough patches of buried obsidian, which could be honed to a razor edge, sharper even than a surgical scalpel.

That would do nicely.

He held the picture of the volcanic glass in his mind, envisioning the slick texture of it under his fingertips. The ichor within him vibrated, his skin crawling as the substance responded to his unspoken command. Spikes—pencil thin, black as ebony, and sharp as death's scythe—ruptured from his arms, legs, and torso, impaling the Kobos covering his body. It wasn't a painless process for Levi—he felt each spike rip through muscle and skin, perforating his body. Sometimes, though, painful things needed doing.

Besides, Levi's wounds were only superficial and well worth the paying, especially considering the outcome.

The clinging Kobos shrieked and wailed, falling away as spikes stabbed into hands and chests, gouged out eyes or sliced through roving tongues and biting mouths. The creatures slipped away like water droplets rolling off a rain slicker, and tumbled to the ground. They twitched and flailed as purple lifeblood leaked away, staining the pavement. Soon their thrashing ceased. Death a relief from the pain. Levi retracted the spikes back into his body; minute puckered holes now peppered his form, each leaking a small rivulet of molten gold.

The Dread Troll was firmly on his feet now and moving toward Levi. But the creature moved with unsure feet, hesitation and uncertainty marking his movements, etched into his body like lines worked into a slab of clay.

"*Ustorfa og siskat divpu!*" the Thursr commanded in a guttural tongue while edging left, positing himself between Levi and the minivan.

The two remaining Kobos responded in an instant, retreating a few paces before wheeling around and dashing toward the van. Toward Ryder. Though the words were unclear, Levi understood the situation just fine: whatever this lot had been expecting, Levi was *not* it. So, the troll would hold off the Mudman while the remaining underlings snatched the prize.

Not if Levi had anything to say on the matter.

With a tremendous effort of will, Levi smashed his foot into the ground, ichor exploding outward from his sole on impact. The ground split, and a crack as wide as a man spread out before him, zigzagging along the pavement and swallowing one of the Kobocks as it fled, sucking the creature down before shuddering closed with a *groan* and a *crunch,* leaving behind only a jagged scar marring the black macadam. Not an easy trick, that, even for a creature of the earth.

Before Levi could deal with the last Kobo—now raking claws at the driver side door, leaving furrows in the paint—the troll lunged forward with burly arms swinging. Levi slipped away from the first strike, but the troll's other fist lashed out, quick as a viper, sinking into Levi's face. The hit landed like a tractor-trailer and fractured Levi's jaw, leaving his chin tethered to his face only by a loose fold of skin.

Levi staggered left and back, groping at his face while forcing a surge of ichor to his jaw. With an inarticulate roar, he cranked at his chin, yanking the whole thing back into place. For a brief moment pinpricks of white exploded in his vision. He shook his head clear and circled right, buying a few seconds to reroute the ichor into his face, shoulders, chest, and arms.

Bony ridges of swirling pink rose quartz sprouted from his gray skin like thick scales: a coat of rocky ringmail, impervious to anything the Thursr could dish out. He'd be ponderously sluggish covered in the thick rock, but a heavy threat called for heavy armor. His mace-headed hands solidified into rectangular blocks of purple quartzite, dotted throughout with shards of black obsidian.

The troll shot in with a jab, connecting a solid blow to Levi's nose. Levi's head, rooted in place by slabs of stone, didn't move an inch, whereas the troll recoiled with a yowl, cradling a now mangled hand to its chest. Much better.

Levi stomped forward, capitalizing on the brief opening, going on the offensive.

He hammered rocky limbs into the creature's body and face. Hot blood splattered onto his chest and trunk with each blow. The troll lashed out with feet and hands, but steadily withdrew at the Mudman's brutal onslaught. Levi pressed on, impervious to the troll's attacks, not giving the creature an opportunity to break away and regroup. It took only a handful of seconds to maneuver the Thursr against the wall of the rest stop bathroom.

Then the real work began. Levi spread his feet wide and laid in with his fists, smashing bone with every strike, razor-edge chunks of obsidian slicing open its skin.

With no place to go, the creature dropped, curling into a tight ball of muscle and fur, portly thighs pressed into its middle while beefy arms wrapped around its skull. Levi didn't relent, but rained down crushing blow after crushing blow—he would beat this creature to death. Beat him until there was nothing left to beat.

"Oh shit! Help! God, it's through the door. Help!" Ryder screamed.

The last Kobo. *How had he forgot about that?* The bloodlust, that was how.

Levi spun.

He'd finish the troll once the girl was safe. She was the priority—

The downed creature grabbed hold of Levi's wrist, just behind the mace head, and planted claw-tipped feet into the Mudman's side. Levi jerked at his arm, frantic to pull the limb loose from the troll's death grip. In turn, the downed troll mule-kicked, simultaneously tugging at Levi's limb.

The rocky mail covering Levi's skin protected him from external blows, but didn't reinforce the muscle beneath. Pain built in Levi's shoulder, an excruciating pressure as the creature subjected Levi to an impromptu version of the medieval stretcher. Levi fought, but with no luck. After a tense, brutal round of tug-of-war, the shoulder gave. The arm ripped from its joint with a *squelch* as the limb separated at its seam.

Though Levi could heal rapidly, growing a limb from scratch was out of the question. He could change his basic form, but he only had a finite amount of material to work with. True, the ichor itself could transform into anything and theoretically with enough of it, he could *grow* a new limb. In reality, however, there was only so much ichor coursing through his body at any one time, and if he ran out … well, he expected death was a likely possibility. That meant major healing required the transmutation of raw materials, a lengthy process even for the ichor, which meant time and resources. Neither of which Levi had at the moment.

What's more, Levi was acutely aware of pain.

He pitched over to the side, a barbaric howl escaping his throat as he rolled and flailed in the high grass next to the parking lot. His remaining quartz club-hand vanished as he clutched at the bleeding nub, trying to staunch the flow of blood. The wound pumped out more and more liquid gold, spurting with every thud of his heart.

The Dread Troll—badly beaten and covered in blood, but far from dead—scrambled to his feet and hefted Levi's arm high into the air, upheld like a prized trophy. The stolen limb bobbed up and down as the creature teetered, left then right, on unstable legs.

Levi ignored the Thursr, focusing instead on the arm wound, which was his most pressing concern. With a grunt, he dug his fingers into the dirt around him, clawing out a clump of dry, red-brown earth. He jammed the clod into his shoulder pocket, focusing all his attention on the jagged hole. The ichor loss slowed, absorbed into the fresh earth, leaving a smooth, tender scab of dirt over the wound. A temporary stop-gap measure at best, but one that would keep Levi from bleeding out until he could repair the damage properly.

The troll suddenly loomed over Levi, now wielding the Mudman's amputated arm as a weapon. The stolen limb—still bearing its purple quartzite mace-head—collided into Levi's face with a peal of thunder.

Several of Levi's blunt teeth rattled in his mouth; rosy chunks of rock flew free in a swirl of grit and dust.

"Help!" Ryder shrieked again.

She would have to take care of herself. There was nothing Levi could do—he was in no position to help anyone, not even himself.

In a cruel reversal of fortune, the troll towered over Levi and hammered at him with his own weapon while the Mudman curled into a ball, desperate to protect and preserve his vital bits. He didn't have organs, at least not like those a human possessed, but still he found his face, chest, stomach, and groin were more vulnerable to serious damage than his back, arms, or legs. The club fell over and over again, thudding into his shoulder blades or hammering at his spine and neck. Long term, Levi knew, the fetal position was not a winning strategy. It would protect him for a time, perhaps, but in the end the troll would obliterate him.

If he wanted to walk away, he needed to do something different. Anything would be better than lying there, being bludgeoned into an early grave. What he needed was an opening, just a brief reprieve to act. That, he could make.

Levi rolled onto his back, stretching out and dropping his lone arm away from his face, for all the world looking like a man on the verge of giving up the ghost at last. The move offered the Thursr an opening too good to pass up. If the troll was savvy and quick, it could cave in Levi's face and end this tussle in a flash—an opportunity no killer could overlook. In order to make it count, though, the troll would need to reposition itself. The beast snarled, its tusked mouth pulling open while a fat tongue licked blood from its muzzle. It moved, straddling Levi's chest and lifting the pilfered arm above its head, preparing for the killing stroke.

Perfect. Levi's remaining arm shifted into an obsidian blade, three feet of thin, gleaming black, both edges sharp and serrated like a bone-saw.

The troll paused, pilfered limb raised high, eyes growing wide in panic as it realized its mistake.

The Mudman thrust the deadly blade directly into the troll's now exposed groin, aiming for the fat arteries and connective tissue running along the inside of the thigh. The lance cut clean through the boorish beast's tender bits, a gout of red pouring out in a stream. The creature pitched to one side like a felled tree, dropping Levi's arm and grabbing at his crotch while he struggled to find breath. A pool of blood seeped out and encircled the troll's legs.

It was wrong to kill—even murderous creatures like the Thursr—but in that terrible moment Levi relished in the act. Hot, sticky liquid trickled around him and he felt satisfied. Sadly, there was no time to dwell on his victory. Not with the last Kobock still living and sharp-tongued Ryder in danger.

He struggled to his feet, whipping around, expecting the worst.

Instead he found Ryder standing over a dying Kobo, a jagged piece of glass—swaddled in a thick swath of fabric—clenched in one quivering fist.

She'd done the beast in.

He smiled at her, his most reassuring look; though, covered in blood and minus an arm, he must've looked terrifying. Needless to say, she didn't return the friendly gesture.

The smile slipped and disappeared. He cleared his throat. "Back in the car," he snapped. "I'll be right there."

He turned away and set to work, dragging the broken bodies off one by one into the high grass, forming a mound of battered corpses. Once done, he dipped fingers into the gaping hole in his shoulder and drew out ichor. He carefully splattered droplets around the grisly dog pile, forming a rough and ragged circle of gold. He bent over with a heavy sigh, suddenly weary to his core, and pressed ichor-covered fingers into the dirt, connecting and communing with the loamy earth.

*Take them,* he commanded with a thought. *Hide them from the eyes of men. Consume them. Let their twisted bodies nurture you.* The earth grumbled and moaned in protest—as if unwilling to accept the rank meat of the Kobocks and the Thursr—then, reluctantly, assented. The splattered ichor flashed like a tiny solar flare, and in a bubble of muck, the bodies sank, disappearing into soggy ground, which quickly hardened.

Levi felt empty and hollow. He needed to get home. To rest and heal.

He trudged over and retrieved his arm, his movements unsteady, resumed his church face, and headed back to the van. He let out another groan as he surveyed the damage. Claw marks crisscrossed over the driver's side door, marring the paint and biting into the metal. He frowned. He'd have to get the panel replaced—no amount of work could repair that level of damage. The Kobock had also broken out the window, which might attract unwanted attention, though there was nothing Levi could do about it.

He shook his head in resignation, as though to say, *Such is life*, then pulled the door open and brushed chunks of glass from the dark leather upholstery. Then he awkwardly slid into the cab and placed his rocky, amputated arm on the center console, where the cup holders were. Ryder, face pale, hands shaking and still clutching the fabric-wrapped shard of glass, stared at the limb, then Levi. Limb, then Levi.

"It's okay," he said, closing the door. "You did good back there. Most people couldn't have done that."

She nodded her head and set her makeshift dagger on the console, but didn't speak as Levi started the van.

Levi kept an eye on Ryder as they drove. She stared out the window with vacant eyes, clearly shaken. With that said, Levi felt a peculiar pride for the girl blooming in his chest. He didn't *like* her, not precisely, but in some sense, they were partners now. He'd never really had a partner before. It was sort of nice in a way.

"What are you?" she asked after a long handful of minutes, gaze sweeping to Levi's arm and staying there.

"It's complicated," he replied. "Let's get back to my place. Get safe, cleaned up. Then, if you still *really* want to know, I'll explain what I can."

She turned away and pressed her eyes shut, but nodded her acceptance.

*NINE:*

## Home Sweet Home

They pulled up outside of a little ranch style home. Red brick with white siding streaking across the top. Levi's place, and meticulously cared for: the driveway clean, the front yard green as a forest—short trimmed grass, a pair of high oak trees, flowers dotting the landscape. Just north of Colfax, Levi's home sat in a neighborhood mostly home to illegal immigrants, the working poor, gangs, and the occasional meth lab. Burglary, violent crime, and even sporadic shootings were par for the course. Not that these things concerned Levi.

He'd picked the community, in part, *because* of those reasons. *Help the poor, care for the foreigner, protect the weak, love thy neighbor.* These were at the heart of the Good Book. He worked hard to keep the neighborhood clean, and dealt with the bad apples that hung around too long.

"We're here," he said, pushing the gearshift into park and unlocking the van doors.

"Where's here?" she asked, her eyes glazed and far away. Lost.

"My home. Come on." He grabbed his amputated arm from the floor, locked up the car, and then let them in through the front door.

Ryder followed quietly, movements jerky and forced. She was in shock, Levi knew. It was all over her face, in the set of her shoulders, in the way she kept her arms curled around her torso. Regular mortal folks—those in the preternatural community called them *Rubes*—weren't wired to handle all the strangeness lying underneath the world, hidden from the eyes of men. Kobocks, trolls, the Hub ... Levi. They were used to mocha lattes, prime-time television, and reasonable, scientific explanations—sometimes, when confronted with the truth, their minds just snapped.

She was a tough cookie, though, that much the Mudman could already tell—she'd done that Kobock, after all. He hoped, prayed even, she wouldn't break under the strain. Aside from being innocent, she had information Levi needed.

He closed the door behind her and flicked the deadbolt shut with a metallic *click*, the sound ominous and final.

"Alright," he said. "I need to go out back and take care of some business." He held up the arm to illustrate the nature of said business. "Leave me be. This is the den. The bathroom's the first door on the left—you can use any towel you'd like. They're all new, never been used. Go shower. After that, go get something to eat. Maybe lie down." He shrugged. "Do whatever, I guess. The guest bedroom is across the hall from the bathroom. Door at the end of the hall is my bedroom. Stay out. The basement is my workshop, no reason to go down there. Stay out." He paused, frowning, rubbing at his chin. *Was that everything?*

"You can help yourself to anything in the kitchen," he added after a moment's thought. "Should be plenty of stuff in there."

She nodded, but didn't budge. Her eyes flitted around the living room, gaze touching here and there before moving on, as though cataloguing every detail: wide green sofa with a matching love seat, dark wood coffee table, a great old antique clock, a comfy carpet over hardwood floors, and cases and cases full of books.

He sighed. "Look, I know this is … tough," he said, trying to console her. Except he'd never properly consoled someone before. Since starting church, he'd attended several funerals—the congregation was an older bunch—but he always ended up idling in the back, too timid to offer a word of comfort or encouragement. He had none to give, and he couldn't seem to fake it. Was he supposed to pretend to be sad—face drawn, eyes downcast? Or should he aim for positive and optimistic, the it's-all-in-God's-will approach? Or, perhaps, he was supposed to feign indignant anger over the injustice of it all? Brow furrowed, lips pulled back in a scowl? He didn't know. It didn't come naturally.

In the end, he placed a hand on her shoulder—missing arm shoved up in his armpit—and patted her like a dog. "It's going to be okay. We'll figure this out together. I'll help you."

She nodded again, but said nothing.

"Right. Okay then," he said. "I need to deal with my injuries. You're going to be on your own for a bit. It's important you remember you can't go anywhere. The police? They can't help you. No place's safe. No one will even believe you. I'm your hope. Understand?"

"Oh yeah." She shivered involuntarily. "Trust me, the message is coming through crystal clear. I won't leave … but … do you have a phone I could use? I've got an important call to make."

"Best if you don't call anyone."

"It's my sister." She faltered. "Look, don't make me explain. I don't wanna tell you and you don't wanna hear it. It's important, though. I'm all she's got—she'll be worried. Probably already filed a police report. Just let me call her. Don't be a dick about it."

*Dumb idea*, Levi thought. Letting anyone know anything was an unnecessary risk. But then, a memory was in his head, filling him up:

*"Where have you taken her?" I demand, anger sprinting along my limbs while fear claws at the back of my neck. Father, mother, brother. Dead. Lost. All of them. Killed, murdered during the invasion, gunned down by the Wehrmacht. Bloody bullet wounds marred their bodies like a pox. She was everything left in the world, and they'd taken her somewhere. After taking everything else, they took her too.*

*"Where!" I shriek, not caring about the consequences of my outburst. I've seen the Schutzstaffel kill for lesser infractions, but none of it matters. Not without Ruth. The guards just stare at me with flat, cold eyes. She's sick, she needs me, and they've taken her…*

*"Calm down," one says, boredom and impatience coating his chubby face. He doesn't seem to take any pleasure in his job, not like some of the others, but neither does he show any particular kindness. "She's only going to Red House," he says. "It's standard procedure. She's sick, that much must surely*

*be obvious even to you. She'll be bathed and disinfected, then returned. Unless you try my patience further. Then? Well, who can say. So, if you truly desire to see her again, Miststück, I'd hold your tongue. Yes?"*

*The insult is spoken with a lazy formality, as if it were his standard response. Still, it's a contemptuous slap to my face and my hand itches to repay him in kind. But that would never do, not if I want to see Ruth again. So, I clamp my mouth shut, doing as he instructs. Ruth's everything, now. The only thing. Will they really let me see her again? I want to believe yes, but I've seen far too many cruelties to be optimistic. Krakow was bad, but I suspect this Birkenau will be worse.*

Levi shook the memory free before it could carry further—he'd seen it many times before and had no desire to watch the end of that particular story. Ruth and Edith Rublach. Sisters. The first gassed in the chamber known as Red House in Birkenau, the second experimented on and sacrificed in front of a terrible altar with ruby eyes—like Jacob Fackenheim.

"Fine," he mumbled. "One call. Only her. And don't give any details. Nothing. Not where you are, who you're with, or what you've seen. Nothing. Okay?"

"Okay."

He grunted, nodded. "Sit tight." He carefully set his arm down on the coffee table before marching off through the kitchen and down the stairs into the basement. A series of metal racks hugged the far wall, burdened with tools and various house supplies. A washer and dryer occupied a space next to the racks.

The majority of the basement was blank, cold concrete. It held a couple of tables, a manual potter's wheel, a pugmill—for making clay—a modeling stand,

and a bench with his modeling instruments: calipers, scrapers, sponges, rasps, armature wire, and study casts. His kiln, a hulking thing of brick and steel, with a heavy door and a vent shaft, sat in one corner. Next to that stood a cooling rack filled with various projects he'd been working on, all in different states of completion: a drying bust, a wildly abstract vase—all gentle curves and soft flowers—waiting to be finished, and a small army of circular pots he'd been testing different glazes on.

His gaze lingered on the kiln for a long beat. He used it for firing his pieces, turning soft clay into hard and brittle artwork, ready to ship for the market, but he also used it for purging. Levi hated fire, but unlike water, he didn't fear it. Rather, he used it to inflict punishment. Self-castigation.

When he relapsed, like with the Kobocks in the Deep Downs, he'd heat the kiln up and shove his hands into its belly, letting the flames dance over his murdering fingers and bite at the exposed skin on his arms and chest. Levi was no stranger to pain, but even the raw wound in his shoulder was nothing compared to the cleansing torture of fire.

It burned and charred without leaving a mark; instead it fed on the ichor in his clay-skin like gasoline. God was a consuming fire, and Levi's purging was an act of communion and contrition with that holy flame, a display of his desire to change. He'd need to purge for today's bloody deeds, to pay for the deaths of the Thursr and the Kobocks from the Cadillac. But later since he suspected there would be more bloodshed to come.

So, instead of making for the kiln, he headed over to his workbench and grabbed a bulky sealed Tupperware container filled with slip: thick, mucky clay goo. He stared at his stump. He'd need the slip to make it whole—

A ball of orange fur seemed to materialize from nowhere, thudded into his shin, then twirled and twisted around his ankle.

His cat, Jacob-Francis.

The Mudman bent over and scratched the animal behind one ear with his index finger, which earned him an approving *chirp* followed by a purr that sounded like a jet engine. The cat loitered only for a moment before shooting off toward his food bowl in the corner. Of course. Levi headed over to the bowl—still full, but not full *enough* for Jacob—and topped it off. The tabby offered Levi one more chirp, then buried his face in the dry kibble, dismissing Levi with a flick of his tail.

Ungrateful little beasts, cats. Still, Levi felt some infinitesimally miniscule affection for the creature. He even smiled, but only for the briefest instant.

Next, he headed over to the only proper room in the basement, an office—his lair—little more than a large storage closet, with a heavy lock on the door.

The lock was a specialty item, a warded trinket he'd picked up in the Hub, which helped conceal the room from prying eyes. Moreover, the lock was coded to him and would only open in his presence. The interior was a plain affair, especially compared to the lock guarding the door: concrete floor, a few more bookcases holding arcane texts and ancient history tomes, a squat brown desk with a desk lamp and an old computer. The computer he used for taxes, a pain even supernatural monsters couldn't avoid.

It was the bulky metal chest in the corner of the room, hidden under a blanket and guarded by a secondary specialty lock, that he wanted. It took only a moment to get the thing open. Inside: papers and phony documents—birth certificates, passports, credit cards, driver's licenses—everything he would need to start a new life ten times over. Fat stacks of emergency currency, a hundred thousand dollars total. Prepaid cell phones—cheap, plastic, untraceable things. And, under that, stacked along the bottom, *gold*.

Ten bars of gold, each 400 troy ounces in weight. At two thousand dollars an ounce, the total came in at eight hundred thousand per bar. Eight million for ten bars. He also had a Tupperware container filled to the brim with gold bullion in smaller increments: 20-gram bars, worth seven hundred a piece, and 100-gram bars, which went for three thousand five hundred a pop. A not so small fortune, and going up every day as the price of gold soared. He was an artist, true, but that was only a front. The real source of his wealth was the gold. And the gold came from his ichor: bars of transmuted lead.

He ignored the fraudulent papers and gold bullion, grabbing a new, prepaid Track-phone and a stack of bills, which he slipped into a pocket. With that done he carefully locked up, rearmed the special wards, and stomped his way upstairs.

The goopy slip he deposited on the coffee table next to his severed arm, then proffered the phone to the girl on the couch. "Make your call," he said. "Just the one, mind you—then shut the phone off and leave it on the table. After that, go shower, eat, sleep, whatever. I'll be indisposed for a couple of hours."

He picked up his Tupperware container and limb, turned away, and went out to the backyard—the girl, for the time being, out of mind.

The back, like the front, showed signs of meticulous care, though it featured even more greenery and artful landscaping than the front. Wild flowers speckled the lawn in every shape and hue, while raspberry and blackberry bushes vied for dominance near the manicured lilac hedge. Around it all towered an extra high wooden fence—one which he'd had to procure a special permit to construct—shielding him from the curious eyes of nosey neighbors.

Levi ignored all these, trotting over to the gnarled oak squatting in the middle of the yard with a smooth boulder perched in its shade.

Gently, he set both the slip and his arm on the boulder, then eased himself onto the stone's surface, warm from the sun's falling rays. A moan escaped Levi's lips as the boulder accepted his weight and began to sap away the weariness and pain taking up residence inside his body like unwelcome squatters. The rock, like Levi, was unique in the world. Originally a chunk of rough granite nearly two tons in weight, it was now the world's largest bloodstone—a martyr's stone—of dark-green jasper, almost black, with a spattering of bright red circles strewn about its surface. Granite to bloodstone, courtesy of powerful alchemic magic.

Its surface was littered with glyphs and sigils, seals pilfered from a host of arcane texts—the Sefer Raziel Ha-Malakh Liber Razielis Archangeli, the

Picatrix, the Liber Juatus, the Book of Abra-Melin the Mage, the Clavis Salomonis—a few meant to hide the stone's power from non-initiates, while the rest promoted rapid healing. Bloodstones had an origin story nearly as interesting as Levi's own. A Christian legend, so old its creator was lost to the ages, held that when Jesus was crucified, his blood dripped upon green jasper embedded in the hills of Golgotha, the place of the skull. The blood stained the jasper with spots of deep crimson, thus imbuing the holy rocks with mystic power. Healing powers.

Levi didn't know the truth of such a tale, but he did know the stone, combined with the etched-on runes, did wonders. Perched on his stone, he could heal in hours what otherwise might take days, or even weeks. His healing was entirely dependent on his ichor, and though his body only held so much of the golden liquid at any given point, his beating heart did produce new ichor in time. Just like human blood. The bloodstone radically increased the rate he could produce the substance.

He examined the hole in his shoulder socket. Here on his bloodstone, connected to the earth—with the slip binding his wound together—he'd be good as new in no time. An hour tops.

Levi dug his fingers into the stump of his shoulder with a grimace, reopening the wound and dragging out a handful of golden ichor, which he casually slapped onto an equally glyph-carved tree trunk in front of him. The sigils were a varied combination of old Nordic runes and Greek script and spiraled around the trunk in looping swirls. He'd also worked a crude, uneven face in a gnarled knot at eye level.

The ichor flared and disappeared into the trunk, calling out to the spirit of the tree and opening a temporary conduit through which the being could manifest.

It would take a few minutes for the creature to surface, though, so the Mudman busied himself while he waited. He casually popped the lid off the container scooped a heaping portion of the clammy muck into his palm, and slathered it into his empty shoulder socket. A cool and refreshing ointment against the burning in his flesh. He set his arm across his lap, covered the ragged end in more slip, and crammed it firmly back in place with a silent snarl, his face a mask of agony.

"Looks like you've been on the unlucky end of a bad brawl, Mudman," said a voice, huffy and wizened with age. Where once the gnarled knot had been, now lurked a tremendous face. Bright blue eyes sat in a twisted visage of bark, and a trailing mustache of wispy green moss descended from beneath a large and bulbous nose. Somarlidrel, a greater Leshy and the head Librarian of Glimmer-Tir, the capital of the High Fae of Summerlands.

Levi inclined his head a few inches. "Somarlidrel, you are well met. Let the water run deep, the sun be ever cool, and the shade of your tree grow long. Thank you for coming."

"And you, Levi Mud-Brother," he replied with a ponderous roll of his too-big eyes. "You're too formal, Muddy, especially between old friends. No need for such ceremony. No need for it."

"You know I don't like being called Muddy."

"And *you* know I don't like being called Somarlidrel—it's Skip, just Skip—but still you insist on formal names," he said, then sighed, the sound like a strong wind rustling through tree branches. After a moment: "Truly, you look terrible, Levi. Someone accidentally run you through that pugmill of yours?" He chuckled, a hollow boom. Levi didn't laugh. Nothing funny about having an arm ripped from its socket.

"Had a run in with a Thursr and a pack of Kobos," he replied evenly.

"Truly? A Thursr you say? Haven't heard about them leaving Outworld in ages. They're rare you know, nearly extinct. Beasts breed so slowly, can't keep their numbers up … Though, now that you've mentioned it, I seem to recall hearing about a sounder—that's what they call their packs, *sounders* …" He trailed off as if he'd lost the train of thought entirely.

"You seem to recall hearing," Levi prompted.

"Right, yes, that's where I was going with it. I seem to recall hearing about a sounder of Thursrs hiring themselves out as sell-swords. Work for the highest bidder as muscle, that sort of thing."

Levi bobbed his head noncommittally. "Could be, I suppose."

"Well, what, pray tell, was the beast after?" Skip, just Skip, asked.

Levi filled him in about his hunting expedition in the Hub, the Kobock temple, the strange altar, the cryptic note, and, of course, Ryder. He reached into his pocket and retrieved his phone, pulling up the picture of the ancient bas-relief.

"I need to know about this." He held the phone out, picture toward the living tree. "There's something more going on here. Could be bad. It also holds a ... personal significance."

"That so?" Skip replied. "And what might that be?"

"I'd prefer not to say."

"But, I quite insist. We're friends, Muddy, never doubt it, but neither forget that I'm the head Librarian of Glimmer-Tir, and information is my bread and butter. Might be, I can tell you something about that altar of yours—or, at least, point you in the right direction—but my dear Queen would turn me into firewood if I give away such information without receiving in kind. You know how it is, old boy, a gift for a gift. It is as it has always been."

"I gave you the bit about the Thursr," Levi said. "That should count for something. Probably someone, somewhere, could benefit from that tidbit."

Skip frowned, his gnarled face scrunching, lips pulling into a grimace of distaste, forehead creasing with a thousand lines. "Don't try and hustle me, Muddy, you know the rules. You gave that information freely. What's more, you know the gifts must be of equal value, at least in the eye of the receiver, and what you're asking about is important, so it requires *giving* something of importance."

Levi ground his teeth. He didn't like talking about his past, always best to look to the future. The past was a bloody mess, full of death and violence, even more so than the present. In those long ago days, he'd been more a force of nature, a walking weapon, than a thinking being. "I ought to turn you into firewood, myself," he muttered under his breath, refusing to meet the shifty tree's eyes. Skip was a friend of sorts, but how Levi hated striking bargains with the fae, even beneficent ones.

"You wouldn't dare," Skip replied, somehow managing to look down his lumpy nose at the Mudman. "And if you want my assistance, you know what it'll cost you. Now, are you ready to deal or should I, perhaps, try back at a later time?"

"Fine," Levi growled, waving his good arm through the air. "The altar, it's tied to one of my earliest memories. My earliest memory, even. The details of my creation are still unclear to me"—he shrugged, which hardly hurt at all now—"but I remember the altar. Only in a distant way, though. Hazy. Like a dream … but it's stuck with me all these years.

"I remember opening my eyes for the first time. It was dark, the moon a thin sliver of light in the sky. Rain drizzled down, falling into my open mouth. The smell of turned earth and musky decay. Then ozone and smoke. The harsh sting of lime biting at my nose—the Nazis used the stuff to mask the scent from the graves, you know that?"

"And the altar?" the Leshy asked.

Levi held up a hand, *patience.* "We'll get there, yet, but if you insist on hearing this, then I insist you hear the whole story. I was born in a graveyard. Well, not a graveyard, too kind a term. A mass grave, an open pit. That's where I opened my eyes for the first time. The first thing I ever saw was bodies stacked up beside me like cordwood. The first thing I ever felt"—he tapped a finger at his chest—"was the searing pain from the brand on my chest. Anger, blind rage, pushed me up out of that pit. My first emotions.

"Once I pulled myself free, I saw a building nearby, a squat concrete box, just through the trees. Looked like a bunker. An underground lab is what it was, I think. That's where I saw the altar, or at least something like it. Hard to say because the memory, it's muddled in my head. But I *think* it was the same."

He pressed his eyes shut and held them closed. "If I close my eyes and call up the memory, I can *almost* see it in front of me. Can *almost* reach out and run a hand over it. An altar with ruby eyes, surrounded by dead bodies, maybe fifty waiting to be buried. Some shot outright. Several missing body parts. A handful stitched together with animal pieces and chunks of halfies. There were soldiers there, too. A few Wehrmacht, a couple of scientists, but mostly Schutzstaffel …before that, after that? I dunno."

He glanced up at the tree. Now Skip wouldn't meet his eye. "I'm sorry," the Leshy said after a while. "I'll tell you what you need … and"—he faltered—"and I'll keep what I've heard to myself. Such a story is yours to tell, I think, and no one else's."

Levi bobbed his head and looked away, kicking lazily at the lawn with one foot. "It is what it is," he said. "No reason in keeping it secret, I suppose. Not from you anyway. So what about the altar? They're doing something bad down there and I'd like to know what. Besides, I figure it might clear some things up about me."

"Aye, aye." The Leshy looked thoughtful. "I'll wager it is bad, but I can't tell you much about it. It's Kobock workmanship, a religious artifact—"

"Don't be crude," Levi interrupted, slapping his good hand down on the surface of the bloodstone. "Don't call what those monsters do down in the dark *religion*." He imbued the word with scorn. "They're monsters, Skip. Barbaric creatures who glorify death and murder. Who worship sin. True religion ought to call out the better parts of our nature, but Kobocks? They have no better nature. Their religion is a mockery. A perversion. The only thing those beasts really believe in is survival, murder, and hunger."

"Say what you will," the old tree replied, "but I can quite assure you, Levi, they do have their religion and it informs every aspect of their lives and culture. It's at the heart of why they do the things they do. They worship old things, dark gods of death long banished by the Great White King, but worship it is, all the same. I've talked to a Kobock shaman or two in my day, and they're much more intelligent and thoughtful than you're giving them credit for. And their blood magic— it's crude, but brilliant."

Levi slammed a foot against the ground, sending a tremor rumbling through the yard, ripples wriggling across the surface of the pond in the far corner by the fence. "Enough. The shamans are the worst of the lot. I've seen the fruits of their hands." He pulled the phone back out, brought up the photo of the fleshy, malformed golem, and thrust it toward Skip. "There's filthy blood magic at work. There it is. Nothing brilliant about it."

"As you say, Levi," the tree responded, his tone one a parent might use with an unruly child. "I'll let it go, but you're really in no position to cast stones. Need I remind you that your power is blood magic, too. Not terribly different from the shamans. This conversation is irrelevant either way, though, since no Kobock shaman is likely to sit down and give you a lesson in comparative religion."

"And you can't tell me anything about it," Levi said. It wasn't a question. The tree loved to blather on, so if he knew anything of use, he'd have spilled it ages ago.

He sighed, his mossy mustache fluttering out. "I'm a scholar of Summerlands—despite a limited knowledge, Kobocks don't fall into my field of specialty. I can check the library, but the Faire Folk of Summer care little for dark things of deep earth."

"Earlier, you said you could point me in the right direction. Even if you don't know yourself, I'm sure you know who would know."

"You flatter me." The tree shed a huge grin. "And, as it turns out, you're quite correct. One of the High Fae of the Winterlands could tell you, I suspect. It'll mean a trek into *Thurak-Tir*, though."

"You have any shortcuts to Winter?" Levi asked. "I'm not keen on having to drag some Rube girl through the Endless Wood. Don't want to be away from earth that long, either."

"Sadly no." Skip paused as if choosing his words very carefully. "Relations are strained between courts just now. Some kind of goings-on with traitors and conspiracies. Business involving the Guild of the Staff and Lady Fate herself. Affairs far outside the paygrade of our likes. And I've never exactly been the sociable sort to begin with … Come to think of it, though, I have a friend of sorts who could help I think. A mage. I know how you feel about their like—a sentiment felt by many, I can assure you—but this bloke's a different sort."

Levi had little experience with the magi and their Guild of the Staff, and that was the way he intended to keep things. The magi, self-appointed protectors of humanity, were well known for their thuggery, and even the slightest infraction could leave you facing their heavy-handed justice. Though Levi killed only murderers, he suspected if the Guild ever discovered his existence and occupation it wouldn't be long before he had unwelcome visitors gracing his doorstep. Still, if the other option was a trek through the Endless Wood, it'd almost be worth it.

"Tell me about this mage friend of yours," Levi finally said after mulling it over for a bit.

"An academic, more concerned with knowledge and wisdom than enforcing arbitrary laws. He's a historian, archeologist, and a cultural anthropologist. Deals mostly with mythology and non-human religion. If anyone is likely to know what this altar is, it'd be him. Professor Owen Wilkie is his name, and last I heard he was working on a dig site out in the Sprawl."

"The Sprawl," Levi replied, voice dry and unamused. "The Sprawl isn't any less dangerous than the Endless Wood."

"Aye, but the walk is a damned bit shorter." He chuckled. "A damned bit shorter, indeed. And I think you'll find old Professor Wilkie a fair bit more affable than anyone in Winter."

Levi pondered. A bird chirped nearby. A chattering squirrel answered in kind.

No good options, and other leads to run down. Levi wasn't well connected in the supernatural community, and he would never be described as a sleuth. For a second, he considered dropping the whole business—turning the girl back over to the cops and putting her and the altar out of mind for good. Seemed like more trouble than it was worth. Much easier to go back to life as usual: work, church, hunting expeditions every few months. Nice, boring, simple, safe.

If he turned Ryder over to the cops, though, it'd be as good as a death sentence. *She's only going to Red House. It's standard procedure. She'll be bathed and disinfected.* A death sentence. Unacceptable. He had to see this thing through, and if Skip said this Professor Wilkie held the way forward, then that was the end of it.

"Okay," Levi said finally. "We'll make the journey."

"Good, good," Skip replied. "I feel I owe you something more—our gifts, they were not equal I fear. I know a guide in the Hub, he can take you where you need to go. A reliable fellow."

"Better not be Chuck," Levi said.

"Come again, now?"

"I said"—Levi leaned forward on one hand, bicep flexing, his true form bubbling beneath—"it'd better not be Chuck. Chuck MacLeti."

"And what's wrong with Chuck MacLeti?"

"He's annoying, for one. Two, he's irresponsible and selfish. Three, he uses foul language, and four, he would sell out his mother for a pack of cigarettes. I can keep going if you need me to."

"Nonsense, Muddy—"

"Stop calling me that."

"—Chuck's really quite reliable. Besides, he can get you where you need to go and he owes me a favor."

The Mudman had used Chuck as a tour guide, fence, and information broker a handful of times before. The man *could* be useful, and, if properly motivated—which meant money, lots of money—he could even be reliable. At least as reliable as any mercenary could be. With that said, there were few people Levi liked less. Not necessarily a bad person, Chuck, but absolutely terrible company. Still, Skip was right. Chuck could likely get them where they needed to go, and what Levi knew about the Sprawl came only from dusty old tomes.

"Fine," Levi conceded.

They talked for another ten minutes, the Leshy providing names, details, and directions.

Then, Levi dozed lightly—drifting in and out of sleep—while the warm light of late afternoon bathed his skin and the bloodstone beneath him absorbed his pain and hurts, lending him renewed and implacable strength. When Levi finally opened his eyes again, it was to the waning light of late afternoon, and his body felt good as new.

*TEN:*

**Ryder**

Ryder watched from the couch as the man who called himself Levi stomped off through the dining room and into the kitchen. The squeak—thud of an opening, then closing door told her he'd gone outside. He looked normal enough right now, except for the missing arm, which he carried in his free hand. Disgusting. Oddly though, she felt numb about the whole thing. The Mudman. The Kobocks. Her uncertain fate. All of it.

The green sofa was nice and soft, and the cushions, enormous, fluffy things, invited her toward sleep. She stifled a yawn with a fist, a fist with blood on it. Dried purple stuff like no blood on Earth.

She regarded her hand with unblinking eyes. She should clean that shit off. *What if those freaks had AIDS or some other kind of weird ... Kobo virus or something?* Her mind gibbered at her, nattering on about how she should wash off the blood and then run. Run to the cops, find a gun, go to the fuckin' army. She should do something. Anything other than sitting on the green sofa, waiting for Levi to change his mind and waste her ass. Chop her up and bury her body in his backyard like he'd buried those creatures from the Caddy.

On and on the thoughts rolled, cartwheeling through her mind like tumbleweeds in a ghost town.

Instead, she stared at her hand covered in Kobo gore and did nothing. *Huh*, the stuff was on her T-shirt too. That was no good. Might leave a stain.

After a few minutes her stomach let out a rumble of protest—she'd been *hungry* lately, ravenous. Ever since she woke up with that pink, puckered scar running down her middle. She absently ran a hand over her belly, thinking about the wound. It didn't hurt anymore, and it looked a helluva lot better than it should have—old and faint, like something that might've happened when she was a kid. She vaguely recalled the night Levi rescued her; in her mind she could see the gray goon standing over her, forcing golden blood into her open mouth.

Gross.

But then her belly grumbled again, banishing the memory. *Food*, her body demanded.

She slid off the couch, clumsily gaining her feet, and stalked off the way Levi had gone a few minutes before. The kitchen was nice, but small. Wraparound cupboards of some cheap lightwood, a small island in the middle, a French-door fridge in the corner. And clean. Every surface almost gleaming, the counters so neat they looked unused.

*Did he even need to eat?*

She didn't know, but he'd said there was food around. She pulled open the fridge and found it filled to capacity: cartons of milk and juice, an unopened container of pickles, sour cream, and jelly. Some uncooked chicken—each individually packaged—a roll of beef, bread, cheese, and lunchmeat. All unopened. No leftovers.

She was hungry, but also mildly curious.

She swung the door shut and moved over to a food pantry near the stove. The contents mimicked the fridge. Chips, cookies, canned soup, popcorn—everything a typical adult male might eat. None of it had been opened either. All the plastic packaging remained intact, as were the product safety seals.

*Guess he doesn't eat.*

Maybe he kept all the food around for show? Her mind tried to force her to engage, but she rudely shoved all those inquiring thoughts away. Whatever. She didn't care, not about any of this. Probably a dream, anyway. Some twisted nightmare. Was it possible she'd relapsed, fallen off the wagon and onto the tip of a needle? Could this be a bad trip? That thought, at least, held a certain comfort. Falling off the wagon would be terrible, but not as bad as the shit she was currently wrestling with.

Finally, she decided on a package of beef Ramen noodles. Something hot to fill her center. She scrounged around until she found cookware, then put a pot of water on to boil. She cooked. She ate. And she watched. Watched Levi, her savior and captor, from the kitchen window, which looked onto the backyard.

He was perched on a massive rock, looking for all the world like a man, though one of his arms was the rocky club she'd seen earlier. He was talking to a tree—a tree with an honest-to-goodness face sticking right out of an old, gnarled nob. Big eyes, wispy moss beard. Looked for all the world like the pair of 'em were just yacking it up; a couple of good ol' boys having a fine afternoon. *What the hell?*

Nothing made a lick of sense anymore.

Yep. Bad trip. Had to be.

She washed her bowl and her hands, finally scrubbing the purple stain away, then wandered over to the bathroom on sore legs. Now that her stomach wasn't protesting, a shower might do her some good. Clear her head a bit, maybe.

She stripped, letting her ruined clothes fall in a pile, then turned the knob on full-tilt.

Once steam rose in sheets, filling the air with its mist, she hopped in and let heat and water sluice over her in waves. Burning hot, turning her pale skin lobster red. The purple blood had seeped through her shirt and onto her belly. She scrubbed at the spot with a rag until the skin was raw. Eventually, she just sat down, knees pulled into her chest in a tight ball. Then she cried, racking sobs that shook her body—tears invisible, blended with the steamy water. She sat that way, crying, scar on her belly aching, until the water turned first cool then cold.

At last, she stood, killed the water, toweled dry, and wrapped the fabric around her torso. She rubbed a spot clear in the foggy mirror. Her face was haggard and red from the heat, not to mention splotchy from crying. Some women looked good when they cried— soft and vulnerable. She wasn't one of those women. She always looked like a drowned kitten. She wiped at her cheeks, removing the few remaining tears with the back of her hand.

Good to get all that shit out of her system. She was done crying. Sally Ryder was a survivor, not some boo-hoo, poor me, chicken-shit little girl. At twenty-six, she'd survived a great good deal.

Her parents were alcoholics, occasional cokeheads, and drug dealers. Never holding a steady job, dodging cops, always on the move. She'd survived them and her shitty, cockroach-infested childhood. A childhood filled to the brim with gangbangers, more drugs, more cops, and rundown foster homes. She'd survived them all. She'd even survived the shit-storm in California—gotten out alive when those assholes murdered her whole family, save her and Jamie.

She would survive this too, dammit. Freaky fucking monsters, talking trees, a crazy-ass clay man? Okay. That was reality now. Whatever.

*Survive.*

That was the important thing.

She pulled her sweats and bra back on—the shirt was a lost cause—and crossed the hall into a guest room with beige walls, a full bed topped by a handmade quilt, an elaborately carved wooden cross above the headboard, and a little nightstand with a clock. She shut the door and fished the phone out of her pocket, toying with it for a moment.

Her eyes were so heavy, but first she would call. That was the responsible thing to do. She flipped open the cheap prepaid and punched in the number.

*Berrr, berrr, berrr, click.*

"Hello?"

For a second Ryder couldn't say anything. Her throat felt tight, too tight, and she feared she would break her vow and start weeping again.

"Hello? Hello? Who is this?" a woman said. "Listen—I'm gonna hang up."

"No, no, Jamie, don't hang up," Ryder finally said "It's ..." she stuttered, "it's me."

"Sally? Oh my God, where are you? I've been worried out of my mind. It's been two weeks, Sally. Two. Weeks."

"Yeah." Ryder rubbed at the back of her neck. "Look, I'm sorry you were worried. I just wanted to call and let you know I'm okay. I can't really tell you anything else. It's ... well, complicated I guess. I can't go into any details, but I'm fine. That's the important thing."

"You've been gone for weeks. What do you mean you can't go into any of the details? I swear to God if you're using again, I'm going to lose my mind. That's what it is, isn't it? Coke? Speed? What is it this time? You're always doing this." She bulldozed onward without giving Ryder a chance to respond. "Self-destructive. Irresponsible. You're the older sister, but I always have to take care of you because you can't keep your head on straight—"

"This is why I don't call anymore," Ryder interrupted. "Seriously, you can't go half a fucking minute without yelling at me or telling me what a worthless piece of shit I am. Shit."

"There's no need for profanity."

"Whatever, Jamie. I gotta go."

"Wait, no, don't go." She faltered. "Look, I'm sorry, Sally. I wasn't trying to guilt trip you or anything. I just love you ..." She sighed. "I worry is all. I just wish you were more—" She bit off whatever else she was going to say. "It doesn't matter. I'm glad you're alright ... where are you? I'll get you help—

money, bus ticket, a hotel room. Anything, just say the word."

"I don't need your help," Ryder said, fighting to restrain the bitterness in her voice. "I'm done with your help. I'm a big girl now. Can take care of myself just fine, thanks. I'm out in Colorado with a friend. Handling some business. Might be a while before you hear from me, but don't worry, I'll be fine."

"Don't be that way. You know I'm just trying to do what's best for us. You're sure you're okay?"

"Shit, Jamie, if I say I'm alright, then I'm alright. Alright? And, though I shouldn't have to say it, I will anyway: no, I'm not using. Still clean as a fuckin' whistle." She hoped that was true, but she couldn't completely shake the thought that this might be a drug-induced hallucination.

"Watch the language, please."

"Yeah, 'cause what could possibly be more important than a clean mouth?" Ryder muttered under her breath.

"Promise you'll call again?" her sister asked, ignoring Ryder's comments. "When you can give me a few more details?"

"Yeah, okay. I'll call once I figure some of this shit out."

"Promise me."

"Jeez. Fine. I promise, I promise—I'll call later."

"Love you, sis."

"Yeah. Love you too." Ryder hung up the phone. Calling had been a mistake. She loved Jamie, the only family she had left, but holy shit could she be a real self-righteous bitch. Always the moral high road with her, always with the "be responsible," and the "grow up" shtick. Jamie had finished high school, sure, went off to college and on to a good job, but she never seemed to remember how much Ryder had given up so she could do those things.

Shit, Ryder had given up her *future* so Jamie could do those things. They'd bounced around from foster home to foster home for a while, but as soon as Ryder could, she'd dropped out of school and got a job so she could make a home for Jamie, even if it'd been a crappy one. The least Jamie could do was remember that. Remember what Jamie had given up for her.

She plunked the phone down on the nightstand and crawled beneath the quilt. The bed was surprisingly soft, the sheets smooth against her skin and smelling of lilac. Her body melted into the mattress. *How long had it been since she slept in a comfy bed like this?* Too long. At first she thought she wouldn't be able to sleep despite her sheer exhaustion and the bed's seductive allure—it'd been a strange, nerve-wrecking day—but she drifted off without a hitch.

Then the dream came. The same dream she'd been having for thirteen years.

*She's in a closet, one arm encircling Jamie's slight shoulders. She clamps her free hand over her little sister's mouth.*

*"Shhhh," Ryder whispers into her ear. Then she presses her eyes up to the slanted slits in the closet door.*

*Mom's on the bed, hands pinned behind her back with lengths of flexible white zip-tie. An old sock is stuffed in her mouth and duct-taped in place. Jackson, her older brother, lies unconscious on the floor, a red gash running down the back of his scalp from where the first gunman had pistol-whipped him with a Beretta—a chrome piece with a flashy, hardwood grip.*

*Dad—tall and rail-thin, with tattoos running up his arms and across his chest—sits in a padded chair, hands secured in place with strips of gray. She can only see his back, but she can clearly see the face of the second gunman: young and suave, Mexican probably, with slick black hair and a stream of teardrop tattoos descending from the corners of his eyes. He sets his gun—a gunmetal thing with a long black suppressor attached to the front—on the room desk. His other hand holds a machete.*

*"I'm not going to ask again, amigo," he says. "The money or the drugs, you will give me one or the other. Comprende?"*

*"Cesar, I swear," her dad sobs, "I already told you, I don't have either—"*

*The slick-haired man, Cesar, slaps her dad across the face, rocking him back in his seat. A furious blow that splatters a splash of red onto the dirt-caked carpet. "That's not a good answer. Not an acceptable answer. Do better." He shoves a wadded up shirt into Dad's mouth, picks the gun up off the desk, presses it against Dad's leg—at least she thinks, because she can't quite see—and pulls the trigger. A dull thud. Dad screams, but it's all muffled. A bright stream of red now trickles down the chair leg and stains the floor in a pool.*

*"I'll ask again. Drugs or cash, I don't care, but you will give me one. Don't scream or I'll kill you straight away, comprende?" He pulls the shirt clear.*

Her dad weeps—a hiccupping, heaving noise—but doesn't scream. "I ... don't ... have either," he struggles to say.

Cesar nods, shrugs, shoves the shirt back in place. "Bring the boy." The second man complies, dragging Jackson in front of the chair—she can only see his legs now.

"Perhaps you are too strong a man to break. I do not know."

Dad whimpers and shakes like a thin tree in a strong wind.

"But no one is strong enough to watch flesh of their flesh suffer. So I ask you one more time. Then? Then I cut off his head"—he waves the machete at Jackson—"go over and do the same to your wife, then you. I will be out the money you owe me, true, but I will gain valuable advertising. Do not steal from Cesar Yraeta and the 16th Street Kings. Do not lie to Cesar Yraeta and the 16th Street Kings. Do not FUCK," he screams, "with Cesar Yraeta and the 16th Street Kings. So?" He pulls the rag free once more.

"We used the drugs," Dad croaks. "Please don't do this, please—anything, I'll do anything. Please not my family. Me. Kill me." He begins to cry, a wordless bubbling.

"I suspected as much. A shame," Cesar says, shoving the rag home. He draws back the machete without hesitation and sinks it into Jackson's body. Thank God she can't see the deed—the chair is, thankfully, in the way. Dad loses it. Thrashes hysterically. Mom whimpers and tries to roll off the bed. The second gunman holds her fast.

*"Keep your eyes shut tight now,"* she whispers to Jamie, before taking her hands and pressing them tight over Jamie's ears.

*Cesar Yraeta, with his teardrop tattoos and machete, goes to work on Mom, then Dad.*

*She watches through the slit, wanting to look away, but needing to bear witness.*

## *ELEVEN:*

## Take a Ride

The Mudman found Ryder in the guest bedroom, catching a little shuteye—the best thing she could've done considering the circumstances. He flicked on the light. She stirred, groaned a wordless protest, and pulled the comforter up over her eyes.

"What's wrong with you, asshole?" she said, voice groggy and muffled. "Do you know how rude it is to go into someone else's room and turn the lights on when they're sleeping. Jerk move. Seriously." She let out a huff.

"It's not your room. My house, my room, my bed, my light … now get up."

"Apologize first."

"No."

She buried herself deeper under the covers, curling into a ball of blankets.

"Apologize. If I'm stuck with you, you're going to learn to act like a normal person. And normal people apologize when they do assholeish things."

After a few moments, "Fine," Levi said. "I'm sorry you're a moody child. Now get up."

"That's a terrible apology." She pulled the cover down, squinted eyes peeking over the edge. She flashed him a halfhearted smile.

He stared at her, unblinking, unmoving.

"What do you want? Can't you see I'm trying to sleep?"

"I already told you, get up. We need to go." Something in his voice convinced her, because her smile dropped away and she peeled back the covers. He set a folded pair of jeans, a flannel shirt, and a beige Carhartt jacket on the floor.

"What are those?" she asked, eyeing the pile of clothes as though it were somehow morally offensive.

"Clothes."

"They're men's clothes."

"I know. Don't worry, they'll fit fine—the body I usually wear isn't much bigger than you—and they're brand-new. I don't actually wear clothes, but I have a closet full in case some nosey visitor stops by. Besides, it's either these or tattered sweatpants and a bloody T-shirt."

She rolled her eyes, *fine*, and shooed him away with a wave of her hand.

A ragged jolt of annoyance surged through Levi. Who was she to shoo him away in his own house? But, he grunted and left, saying nothing and pulling the door shut behind him.

A few minutes later she came out, dressed in the outfit Levi had provided and looking rather boyish—the thick material hung loose on her frame and thoroughly obscured her slight curves. Almost perfect.

"Hang on," he said, shuffling back to his bedroom and returning with a green-and-white John

Deer cap. He tossed it to her. She raised an eyebrow in response, but pulled it on.

She glanced down at the getup, eyes skipping over the pants and jacket. "I don't wanna go out looking like this," she said, hands now resting on cocked-out hips.

"You have a problem?"

"Yeah, I have a problem. One, these are men's clothes. Two, they're redneck men's clothes. Three, they're ugly redneck men's clothes that make me look like a tool-bag. So yes, big problem."

"They're perfect," he replied, unmoved by her complaints. "The Kobocks are looking for a rebellious young woman—now, you look like a hardworking young man. Much harder to spot. Camouflaged, like me. Ready." It wasn't a question. Levi wasn't used to dealing with people, at least outside of church or the occasional commission, and he expected compliance.

They headed out the front door—Ryder skulking behind. Levi locked up the house, and the two of them piled into the van.

"So where are we headed, Big Guy?" she asked as Levi started the car and backed out of the driveway.

"Back to the Hub." He puttered out of the neighborhood, like some slow-speed soccer mom dutifully hauling around her brood.

"The Hub—that's where you rescued me, am I right?"

"Yes." He flipped on the blinker and pulled into the right lane, coasting up to the intersection and easing right onto Colfax, toward Denver.

"Jeez," she said, "light conversation isn't in your toolbox, is it? Listen, guy, I get that you're a freaky—whatever the hell you are—but I'm tired of being in the dark here. I don't think you're going to hurt me, so I'm gonna bug the holy-living shit outta you until I get answers. You understand that, Knuckle-dragger?"

Obviously, the shower, food, and nap had done her good—the shock seemed to have worn away. That would help her survive what was coming. Levi was, however, a little concerned about her newfound chattiness and her uppity attitude. The old, shell-shocked Ryder had been depressing, true, but much more agreeable on the whole.

"Fine." He rolled his eyes—moody girl indeed. "Yes, the Hub is where the Kobock Nation was holding you captive. Well, technically the Deep Downs, below the Hub. There's a thousand miles of cavernous expanse below the city and the sewers, and the Kobocks lay claim to a fair chunk of it."

She rubbed at the bridge of her nose. "Okay. Apparently, I'm gonna have to do all the heavy lifting here. The Hub, what's the Hub? A place I'm assuming? But is it here in Colorado or somewhere else? Specifics, guy, think specifics."

"What? No, no. The Hub doesn't exist in our dimension …" He halted, unsure how to continue. He'd never walked a Rube through Supernatural 101 before. "There're lots of Realms outside Earth—the Endless Wood, Tír na nÓg, the Hinterlands, the Great Deeps, and further still Heaven and Hell. All that? That's Outworld."

She nodded along as he talked, genuine interest evident. "Got it, the Hub is Outworld."

"No," Levi replied. "Are you even listening?"

"Whoa, ease up on the attitude, Levi. That's what you just said: there are lots of Realms outside of Earth and those places are Outworld. Your words. If I'm missing something, it's not because I'm not listening, it's because you're a terrible teacher."

He ground his teeth. Was trying to be human really worth it?

"Fine. Do you want me to try and explain it again or not?" He edged his hand toward the radio's power button. "Because I'm fine with turning on some music."

"Drama queen," she muttered, but promptly fell silent and rolled her hand in a *move-along-with-it* gesture.

"As I was saying, the Hub is *not* Outworld. The Hub is a port city. It runs along the border between Earth—Inworld—and everywhere else, Outworld. The Hub connects places, like the hub of a bicycle tire." He swerved out of the right lane, bypassing a slow moving line of turning traffic. "Generally, if something wants to come to Earth, it passes through the Hub. We're bound for the Sprawl, which is in Outworld, so we'll need to pass through the Hub to catch a train."

"What's the Sprawl?"

He turned on the radio, contemporary Christian music filling the air with the strum of guitars and a chorus of Hallelujahs. Levi drove for nearly ten minutes without her saying anything else—she seemed bright enough to take the hint that he could only handle so much chitchat.

Eventually, though, she broke the silence. "Mind if I ask you a personal question?"

"Yes, I mind very much."

"So I was looking around your house," she said, anyway, "and there was a lot of religious stuff—like Bibles, paintings, sculptures—that kind of thing. And you listen to Christian radio."

"Perceptive. What's your point?"

"I dunno." She canted her head and shrugged. "I was just wondering what the deal was, I guess. You kinda seem like an odd duck for a religious guy … whatever you are."

"I'm not a *whatever*," he said, "I'm a golem. Someone, I'm not sure who, created me back in 1943 and set me loose to murder Nazis."

"Seriously?"

He nodded.

"That is so badass. How'd you go from being an awesome Nazi-killing machine to this lame old dude who drives a minivan?"

"I'm not lame." He paused, looking for the right word. "I'm in control now. Working to be in control," he amended. "And that's where the religious stuff comes in. I'm a Mennonite. Said the sinner's prayer maybe eleven years ago."

She laughed at him. "Well at least you have a sense of humor buried in there somewhere."

"It's not a joke. I'm a Mennonite."

"But … but that's the stupidest thing I've ever heard. You can't be a Mennonite."

"Can too. And what's it to you, anyway?"

"Well, I'm not like religious or anything, but I've lived in Lancaster County, Pennsylvania, for like the last two years—so I know about Mennonites. You can't throw a rock in Lancaster County without hitting a Mennonite church. I mean, I know they're not all horse and buggies or whatever, but I'm pretty sure they're … I dunno, *non-violent*."

"We are."

"Levi, I'm gonna shoot straight with you for a minute. I saw you literally club a bunch of freaky monsters to death with a spiked mace. Trust me, it was *violent* as hell. Maybe the most violent thing I've ever seen." She brushed a strand of pink hair behind her ear, tucking it under the band of the John Deer cap. "Strikes me as kinda hypocritical is all. Though hey, who am I to judge—I sure as shit can't take the moral high road. I'm a former drug addict, and I've done a shitload of stuff I'm not proud of. So if you wanna be a Mennonite, then be a Mennonite. I will say this, though, I own who I am."

An uncomfortable silence stretched out between them.

"It's hard to explain," Levi said eventually. "I *need* to kill things. Murder … it's-it's a part of me. It's my purpose—to kill killers. It's what I was created for. My maker built me to seek retribution against the Nazis, but after the war was over, the compulsion was still there. After sixty years of killing … Well, I'm tired of it. Tired of being the monster hiding in the dark alley. I'm not the man I want to be, not yet, but the church is helping me to become that man one day at a time. Besides, it's like Augustine said, 'the church is not a hotel for saints, it's a hospital for sinners.' That's something that resonates with me in here." He tapped his chest.

He flipped on his blinker and pulled into the parking lot of a rundown motel across the street from a grand old theater, which in a bygone age had actually showed plays, but which now served as a concert venue.

"We're here," he said.

"Where's here?" she asked.

"Patience. You'll see."

After parking the car, they made their way into the alley running alongside the theater; the narrow space was filled with a sour stink and the mewling of stray cats.

"Such a nice place," Ryder said, folding her arms across her breasts, nearly invisible under the coat, as she surveyed the alley. "This where you bring all your dates? Wonder what you'll show me next? Maybe a construction site porta john? Always wanted to check that off my list of things to see in Denver."

The words were sarcastic, Levi knew—he couldn't do sarcastic, didn't have the wit for it—but it was actually sort of endearing coming from Ryder. His top lip curled up a hair, which surprised him. He was *excited* for her to see the Hub.

"Quiet, now." He waved a hand at her, the barely-there smile fading. "Need to concentrate." Inscribed against the theater's yellow brick wall was the portal, though currently inert and invisible to human eyes. It was a thing of magic, a thing of Vis—the power undergirding creation—crafted by someone with far more talent and ability than Levi possessed. He couldn't make such a thing, nor could he even see it. He could, however, *feel* it. The portal was an abnormality, an aberration which didn't belong to Inworld. Levi could sense the tension, the power emanating from miles off.

He swept his hands over the wall's stony surface, searching for the weak spot in the construct, for what he always thought of as the keyhole. It wasn't really a keyhole, of course, but it served the function well enough. There, low on the wall by his ankle, was a node of energy, a confluence where the different strands of power met and intertwined. He shifted his finger, gradually, slowly, feeling for the peaks and valleys of power in the node. His digit twisted, elongated, and thinned until it *sunk* deep into the theater wall, momentarily disappearing from view.

With a soft hiss, the portal formed in a blaze of opalescent light: one moment, old brick wall, the next, a doorway seven by four feet suspended in the air.

Levi heard a sharp intake of breath. "Holy shit," Ryder whispered.

No sarcasm now.

## *TWELVE:*

### Chuck MacLeti

They caught a cab, a Victorian-era carriage pulled along by a zombified horse with greenish flesh, a wispy mane, and gobs of missing meat. The driver—a rail-thin man in black, wearing a top hat—said nothing, merely assenting with a nod after Levi gave him the destination, a place called the Lonely Mountain.

Ryder had a million questions as they cruised along cramped streets filled with battered cars and trucks, battered rickshaws, mopeds in a thousand different hues, and stranger things, each jostling for position as the traffic crept forward. This place was overwhelming, like the worst acid trip of a lifetime, but also outlandishly exciting. Ryder had travelled a lot, city to city and state to state, but she'd never left the US, and this place was *almost* like taking a trip to some exotic city far away from America's safe and well-ordered shores.

According to Levi, this place was not even part of the world she knew at all. A pocket dimension, whatever the hell that meant.

She'd spent time in many a big city—New York, Philadelphia, San Francisco—but this place was like nowhere she'd ever been. The streets were narrow and choked with traffic. The buildings loomed up on either side, tall and thin, in an explosion of muted colors. A towering gray concrete tenement, covered in splashes of graffiti, on the left. A metal fronted building covered with neon tubing, advertising "Full Immersion VR Integration," on the right. Overhead, power cables and phone lines twisted together in a mad jumble so thick it almost blocked out the muddy sky overhead. Those cables were like a manic spider's web, running from everywhere to everywhere else, seemingly without rhyme or reason.

She spotted a rustle of movement on the wires, the motion just on the edge of her peripheries: an actual spider, a stout creature the size of a Pomeranian, with spindly metal legs, scuttled across a dense tangle of cables and disappeared into a nearby building of crumbling yellow brick. She shuddered. Yeah, this place was *almost* like visiting a foreign city, at least until she saw something like that, which jarred her back into her terrible reality. And the spider was, by no means, the only oddity.

She spied a chalk-white creature without a head, but with a face protruding from a distended belly, leaning against an alleyway wall with one foot casually propped up. Meanwhile some dude strutted by on oversized arms, hands as big as dinner plates, his feet shriveled up and hanging limp beneath a purple-skinned torso.

Being in the Hub was like being at a never-ending GWAR concert—all metal spikes, fleshy tentacles, and gore. But she was a survivor, and if this was her new reality ... well, she'd deal with it as it came. Denial was never an option, not for her. So instead of letting the newness, the bizzaro nature of this place, frighten her, she asked questions.

She pointed at the creature in the alley, the one with the face on its stomach. "What's that?" she asked, eyes tracking the freak.

Levi glanced up.

The Mudman looked different again. He no longer looked like the dumpy, balding guy with the thin mustache, nor did he resemble the police officer from the hospital. Now he was an unremarkable bald man with a doleful, basset hound face, wearing a plaid button-up shirt tucked into a pair of khakis. Looked like a middle-aged construction worker—but a site foreman instead of a new hand. His muddy eyes were the same, though: sad and somehow introspective.

"Blemmy," he replied tersely, then turned away from her, his gaze once more fixed on the passing sights.

Ryder patiently waited for some explanation, but no more seemed to be forthcoming. She cleared her throat and pushed on. "And that would be what? Again, let's just pretend I know all of jack-shit about this place."

He sighed deeply, annoyed—always annoyed, this guy—and turned back to her. "From Africa. Live in jungle communes. They eat people. That's pretty much all they like to do. Hunt. Kill. Eat. Stay away from them."

She gulped and ran sweaty palms over her jeans, suppressing another shudder. Every new piece of information the Mudman revealed only served to terrify her further. Who knew there were so many fuckin' monsters walking around in the world? As if dealing with the drug-dealers and shiesty gangsters wasn't scary enough.

Still, she refused to be intimidated into silence. She pointed at the guy walking on his hands. "And him?"

"Halfie. Offspring of a human and something else. Usually come out looking like a little bit of each. Half this, half that. Halfies."

She pointed at spiral building of pitted black stone, jabbing straight up in the sky like the horn of a unicorn. She briefly wondered whether unicorns were real, then dismissed the thought as silly—even in a world as wacky as this, there had to be a few things, at least, which were still myth. "What about that building, there? The spire."

"Road spire," he said after a moment. "Kinda like a traffic light. You'll see 'em all over the city." He waved a hand vaguely about. "No proper stoplights here, so those things, they help keep the roads orderly," he said, as though explaining something so elementary it couldn't possibly need any explanation at all. "At least as orderly as traffic in the Hub ever is. Now, if you don't mind, I need to think." He tapped at his temple and looked away.

She turned back to the window, splashes of red dotting her cheeks. *Guy is such a colossal dick,* she thought. *Authoritarian, follow-the-rules, tool-bag conformist.* The rest of the ride passed by in uncomfortable silence—silence that didn't seem to bother Levi at all, but annoyed the piss out of Ryder. The asshole could at least have the good grace to realize she was mad at him.

143

The horse sidled to a stop after a few more minutes and Levi slipped out, grabbing Ryder's arm in a too-hard grip and dragging her along.

Once safely on the sidewalk, Levi let her free and moved over to the front of the cab, reaching for his wallet as the gaunt driver peered over the edge at him with hollow, deeply recessed eyes of gray.

"Forty-seven Quwar," the skeletal man said, extending a spidery hand.

"Dollars?" Levi asked. The driver regarded Levi through squinted eyes, lips peeled back from needle-sharp teeth in hate. The creeper acted as though exchanging dollars was an intolerable hassle worthy of death. Ryder watched Levi, waiting for the Mudman to smash the driver into paste, but as usual he appeared unfazed. As placid and unruffled as a mountain buffeted by a light breeze.

"Fine," the driver finally conceded, "seven fifty."

Levi dug out a ten. The driver pocketed it without even the pretense of making change before *clucking* at his deathly mount and pulling the carriage back into traffic.

Levi wheeled around and ushered Ryder toward the building behind them.

Their apparent destination was something out of a fantasy novel, part hulking cave, part Arthurian castle. A monstrous structure sporting high, craggy stone walls of gray. Jagged merlons ran along the top parapet, narrow windows bled orange light, and otherworldly moans and groans drifted to her ears. She'd been to enough shitty bars to spot a whorehouse when she saw one. She wasn't sure where she'd expected Levi to take her, but a pub that doubled as a whorehouse sure as hell wasn't it. He was too puritanical and uptight for it.

Levi brushed past her without a word, walked through the open portcullis—a retractable, drop down gate—and pushed open the bar's front door. Yep, she hadn't seen that coming, not from a mile off with a good set of binoculars. Since she didn't want to stand around gawking like a tourist, she followed.

"The Lonely Mountain," she said, reading the sign stenciled on the door. "Neutral Zone, Violators will be Incinerated…" She snorted. "Pretty funny—"

"Not a joke," Levi replied, glancing over one shoulder. "The owner's a dragon—greedy, fire-breathing, treasure-hoarding murderer. The real deal. Name's Firroth the Red. He'll incinerate anyone who puts a toe wrong. I've seen it myself, so be on your best behavior."

The smirk melted from Ryder's face, ice under a dragon's flame, and she nodded her understanding. *This fuckin' place. If there were dragons, maybe unicorns weren't unrealistic after all.*

"Hotel California" flooded out of the open doors, the twang of guitars and the reedy cry of Don Henley filling the air. Dim red light illuminated the cavernous interior. Hanging stalactites and jutting stalagmites littered the space, each filled with the ever-shifting light of enslaved, winged creatures. Ryder didn't know what the tiny creatures were, but if she had to guess, she'd say pixies, based mostly on the tiny butterfly wings decorating their backs. That and their vague resemblance to Tinker Bell. Sluttier, though.

Smoke hung thick in the air, the perfume of sharp cigars, the sweet scent of hookah, and the stink of something pungent and sulfurous. It was actually sort of enjoyable.

"Stay close," Levi whispered into her ear. "Say nothing. Touch no one. Make no agreements. Be invisible. This isn't fun and games, and the Lonely Mountain is no place for Rubes."

She followed in the wake of her guide, who cautiously carved a way through the crowd, his eyes skipping about, clearly searching for someone. She had no idea who since Levi was as forthcoming as a bank vault. The Sprawl, they were going to the Sprawl. That was the sum of her insight.

Eventually, Levi made his way over to the bar, still scanning the building's patrons—a splattering of men and women, most of which could never pass for human. One chick, sporting a white cocktail dress, preened garish feathers of red and gold and blue with an oversized beak: a giant parrot-woman. A man—so fat the stool hardly supported his ass—wore a stained wife-beater and snorted through a pig snout. Apparently, though, none of the bar goers was the man Levi was looking for, since he kept right on moving.

After a few more minutes of useless searching, Levi elbowed his way to the bar proper, pushing between the parrot-feathered woman and the pig-faced man. He held out a hand, signaling to the guy behind the bar. Well, he was shaped like a guy.

Ryder assumed the bartender was probably also the bar owner, Firroth the Red, based solely on his dragonesque appearance. He was eight feet of ripped, hard-edged muscle on top of more muscle. Dude was a roid-head for sure. Scrolling tribal tattoos in blues and blacks, like scales, snaked around his arms, neck, and face in swirls of artistry. He had bright red hair, the envy of any punker—shifting gold then orange and back again—and a fat cigar, hanging from the corner of his scowling mouth, which seemed to be the source of the sulfurous stink filling the bar.

Freaky son of a bitch, no doubt, but some part of her also wanted to slip the guy her number. Kind of her type.

Ryder glanced at Levi, noting that his usually neutral mask had slipped away completely. An unbridled look of murder was plain as the nose on his face, even if he was *trying* damn hard to hide it. She didn't know much about the guy behind the bar, but one thing was abundantly clear: Levi wanted him dead. Buried. Like yesterday. But, perhaps even more importantly, Levi didn't *do* anything. Ryder had seen firsthand what the Mudman was capable of, so if he was holding his bloodlust in check, it could only mean the bartender was in a league far outside of Levi's.

Back in the bad days, Ryder had seen twitchy-head tweakers look at big-time dealers the same way. Hungry but impotent.

Levi smiled at the cigar-wielding man, the look of hate slipping away, buried behind his carefully cultivated human façade.

"I see you, Golem—*Mudman*," the bartender said, his voice deep and rich. "I see you and the human girl, both." He emphasized the word *girl* as if to mock their pitiful attempts at concealment. "And I see your hunger." He smirked, unconcerned about Levi's murderous desire. The dragon-man dropped his voice to a raspy whisper.

"You're a dangerous guest to have around, Mudman. Might be, I had some folks stop by earlier, Thursrs, looking for you and a certain young lady." He glanced at Ryder with eyes like molten gold, slit down the middle with thin slices of black. "You're wanted by the Kobock Nation—mayhap even a mage. Could be they're offering a hefty reward for information leading to your capture."

"I'm not looking for trouble," Levi replied, laying both hands flat on the bar top. "We're just here to meet a contact. I won't break the peace of your roof."

"I expect not," the barkeep said with a shrug. "I'd have incinerated you already had I thought otherwise. Consider this a simple reminder to leave your problems outside—otherwise, they become my problems. You won't like the way I handle problems." He picked up a large beer stein and exhaled a plume of dark smoke from his nostrils. "Now, what'll you take?"

"I just want to know where Chuck MacLeti is."

"You think I don't know what goes on under my roof?" The question was a grunt, one with a sharp, threatening edge. "I know damn well what you're after—and I know where you can find your man. But this is a bar, not a library or social hall. My kin and I aren't known for our great charity. So, I'll ask again, what'll you *take*? Something expensive I hope."

"Three pints of Guinness, extra stout—"

"And something to eat," Ryder interjected. Her middle growled, unsettled and uneasy. She'd eaten a solid meal before crashing back at Levi's pad, but her stomach argued—even if erroneously—that it'd been days since her last meal. "Sorry," she said with an apologetic shrug. "Girl's gotta eat when a girl's gotta eat. Trust me, Muds, you'll like me even less when I'm hungry."

"Fine." Levi said. "And never call me *Muds* again," he added, almost as an afterthought. "Three pints of Guinness, extra stout, and a platter of—" He paused and drummed his fingers on the counter as if searching for something suitable for human consumption.

"Nachos?" Ryder supplied, fingers crossed.

Firroth nodded, pulled out another two mugs, filled all three with beer so dark it looked black, and set them on the counter. He strutted down the length of the bar—back straight and a swagger to his gait—dipped into a back room, and came out a second later with a plate heaped high with chips, cheese, and meat of questionable origin.

She'd eaten worse.

He set the platter of chips on the counter next to the mugs. "Hundred bucks, even." He held out a monstrous hand tipped with dark claws.

"Steep price for a few pints and some chips," Levi mumbled.

"Hazard pay"—he smirked, an unpleasant half-grin—"plus an information tax."

Another flash of annoyance sprinted across Levi's face, but he shook his head, brow furrowed in resignation—*such is the cost of doing business in the Hub*, the look said. He fished out two fifties and laid them on the beer-stained wood.

The inhuman bartender swiped the money without a second glance and shoved it into a loose pocket on the leather apron tied around his waist. "Your guy's in the far corner," he said, hooking a clawed thumb toward the back of the club. "Last booth. Has a privacy curtain, provided free of charge."

Levi nodded, collected the drinks, and headed off to meet their contact, Chuck.

Ryder carefully scooped up the formidable platter of chips and burst into a quick trot, anxious to keep near the Mudman. She didn't like him exactly, but he seemed to be genuinely trying to help her, and she knew from a long and difficult life how rare finding a stranger like that was. Not to mention the thought of being stranded in this place by herself was enough to send her into hysterics. Best to stick close to Levi, at least for now.

Chuck MacLeti, their contact, reclined in the far booth like the King of the world: long arms sprawled over the padded booth back, blue-jean-clad legs up on the seat, white-and-red Air Jordan's crossed at the ankles. He was black and lanky—six and a half feet— and wore a puffy winter coat with a fur-lined hood. Around his neck hung a thick gold chain with a tacky diamond-studded shamrock dangling on its end.

This supernatural craziness might've been new to Ryder, but she knew plenty of guys like Chuck. Even at a glance she could spot a hustler looking to work an angle. Maybe this place wasn't so different after all— the same old world, just dressed up in gaudy Halloween costumes.

Levi slid into the opposite seat. Ryder followed suit, not sure what else to do. That thought was sort of reassuring.

"Levi Adams, my man. Been a hot minute," Chuck said, offering a hand, which Levi took and pumped twice. "And who's this sweet little piece you got with you?"

"She's not your concern, let's just keep this—"

"Hey asshole," Ryder said, scowling. "I'm not some sweet little piece. You better watch who you're talking to."

"Damn, Levi, you know how to pick 'em— feisty, sassy. That's what I'm talkin' 'bout." He held out a fist, just waiting to be bumped. Levi regarded the fist for a moment, then cleared his throat, his hands never even twitching.

Ryder eyed the lanky man, then slid back out of the booth, abandoning both the Mudman and the nachos. The loss of the nachos was far more distressing. "Look, I don't need to put up with this," she said, hip cocked out, arms crossed. "I'm sick and tired of being treated like a child. I'm not a child. I'm not a sweet piece. I'm not taking any more shit. If you want my cooperation, I intend to be treated with respect. Period. Everyone clear on that?" She quirked an eyebrow, turning up her attitude to max level.

Levi looked skyward, lips moving as though uttering a silent prayer. "Sit back down, Ryder," he said after a second. "Now."

No invitation, no apology, not even an acknowledgement that her complaint was valid. Jerk. She backed up a step, preparing to turn tail and leave, the consequences be damned. Not that she actually *wanted* to do that, of course, but she wasn't going to be a doormat, even if Levi was the only thing standing between her and the Kobock Nation.

"Fine," Levi said. "Chuck, if you want to earn your pay, I expect you to keep this professional. I've got enough to worry about without adding a couple of squabbling kids—excuse me, *adults*—to the equation."

"Yeah, cool, cool, whatevs," Chuck offered, flashing a grin and a *just-between-you-and-me* wink. "You the boss man, you cuttin' the check, whatevs. Though, Skip *did* tell you what my going rate is, right?"

The Mudman reached into a pocket and pulled out a wad of banknotes bound by a red rubber band. Ryder's eyes bulged and she choked a little. There had to be ten grand there, easy.

Ryder wasn't poor precisely, but she could never be accused of being rich. For the first time in a long time, she had a respectable job working at a used bookstore over in Bethlehem, Pennsylvania, near Lehigh University, just off of 4th and Vine. *Fireside Books and Coffee*. The joint stayed open twenty-four hours and boasted free wifi, which made it popular as hell with the college crowd. A nice study spot.

Ryder worked nights, Monday through Thursday, ten-hour shifts a shot. Not a dream job, but not half bad either and the owner, Jim, had done her a solid by hiring her on. Especially considering her less-than-stellar record.

Still, what Levi had laid, so nonchalantly, on the table was damn near half a year's salary.

"Money's not a problem," Levi said flatly, uninterested even. "But I'm not just paying for a guide—I'm paying for a professional. Understood?"

"All good, man." Chuck smiled wide, a glint of gold flashing from his mouth.

"Ryder?" Levi asked, holding her in his muddy gaze.

She eyed the money, eyed the nachos, and finally plopped back into the seat.

"Sorry 'bout that." Chuck extended a hand across the table, which Ryder ignored. "If we're gonna work together, best to start things out right. I'm Chuck, Chuck MacLeti."

"Sally Ryder," she replied. "And, before we go any further, what are you? I don't wanna get backed into a corner and find out you're some kind of freaky Sasquatch or some kinda demon spawn or evil clown. I hate clowns. So tell me now, what are you?"

"That's rude, you know?" Chuck said. He swiped the wad of bills from the table, then pulled over a pint and swallowed a long pull instead of answering. After a few seconds, he set the glass back down and belched. "Obviously you're new here, so let me fill you in on the rules, baby-girl—"

"Call me baby-girl again," she said, glaring at him, "and I'll castrate you."

Chuck hastily cleared his throat. "Whatevs. As I was sayin' it's impolite to ask what people are."

"He's a leprechaun," Levi said matter-of-factly, apparently not caring about politeness. "He's also going to be our guide, so let's all play nice. Now, back to business."

Ryder snickered, unable to help herself, then scooped up a chip loaded with gooey cheese—well, imitation cheese at least—and meat-substitute and shoved it into her mouth. "Leprechaun," she mumbled around a mouthful of flavorful awesomeness.

"Oh, I'm sorry, is there something funny 'bout that?" Chuck asked, swinging his feet off the bench and sitting up straight, the posture of the morally offended.

She swallowed her chip in a gulp and picked up another. "Yeah. He called you a leprechaun, but you're like NBA-sized and black."

Levi groaned and rubbed at one temple. "Not a joke—" he started.

"Now hold up, that's some racist bullshit right there," Chuck interjected. "You sayin' I can't be a leprechaun because I'm black?"

"Well, I mean that's kinda weird, I guess" she said, "but it's more the fact that you're not all fun sized." She shoved the chip into her mouth and bit down with a sharp *crunch. So good.* Her belly definitely approved.

"Oh I get it, a sizeist—discriminating against the tall folk."

Levi, still rubbing at his temple, let his true form bubble up and out, the table jolting as his gray legs swelled beneath. "I don't have the patience for this." His voice was now rocky and deep, the sound of an earthquake given vocal cords. "It's the same thing every time with you, Chuck. You're not even a full leprechaun, you're a halfie. More to the point, every other leprechaun *is* short and white, so it shouldn't come as a surprise when no one believes you. Now please, back to business." He grabbed the edge of the table and squeezed, the wood dimpling under the pressure of his fingers.

Ryder scooted away an inch or two.

"Chill, dog, no need to Hulk out and get all belligerent up in here," Chuck said, smoothing out his fluffy coat and leaning back. "I was just giving her a hard time—"

Ryder scarfed down chip after chip as she watched, amused. This was better than TV. So maybe Levi was a stick-in-the-mud, but Chuck seemed alright. An asshole, sure, but a fun one. If he was coming along on this trip, it might actually be bearable.

"Back. To. Business," Levi said again.

"Cool, man, cool. Look, everything's good to go. I got us rucksacks with everything we'll need for the Sprawl. Sleeping bags, camp supplies, compass, maps, hacksaw, even a couple of peashooters that'll work out there in BFE. All taken care of, okay, so just chill."

"Where's the gear stowed?" Levi asked, stealing a quick glance around.

"Got it all stashed in the train station. My ride's parked out back. We can finish our drinks and baby gi"—he faltered just short of saying the word—"err, what was your name again?"

"Sally Ryder. My friends call me Punk Rock Sally. Everyone else calls me Ryder. You can call me Ryder."

"That's cold-blooded, right there." He shrugged. "Fine, if that's how it's gonna be. As I was sayin', we'll finish our drinks, Ms. Ryder can finish inhaling those nachos—like a Hoover vacuum over there—then we'll scoot on over to the train station and gear up, no worries. See"—he turned to Levi—"told you I can be professional."

Ryder watched Levi out of the corner of her eye while she polished off the chips. He didn't look relaxed exactly, but he did look a tad less uptight. The Mudman nodded his blocky head, shrinking back into himself. Basset-hound face firmly in place again, he picked up the beer and took a drink. The motion looked natural and normal, but Ryder got the sense that it was only for show. Something the Mudman did to fit in, but not something he needed to do at all or even wanted to do, for that matter.

"Chuck," Levi said, setting his empty glass down, "you'd better not be tricking me. Better not be working some scam. 'Cause I swear if you pull some leprechaun nonsense on us … I'll find you, Chuck. Very bad things will happen. Painful things, involving legs and fingers and toes."

The gangly leprechaun drained his glass, issued another ferocious belch, and wiped a hand across his mouth. "Yeah, I hear that," Chuck replied, brushing off the threat without missing a beat. "But don't sweat it, Boss man, you and Miss Thing"—he flashed Ryder a wink—"are safe with me. Now let's roll."

## *THIRTEEN:*

## **The Sprawl**

Ryder lounged beside a small campfire, hunger gnawing a hole in her middle while her mind circled round and round. Chuck sprawled on a sleeping bag across from her, propped up on one arm while he stared into the dancing flames. Levi was off, rummaging around in the dark, looking for more wood, or anything really, to burn. So far Chuck, their "guide"—and Ryder used the term only in the loosest sense of the word—hadn't been much of a guide. Up to this point he'd been about as useful as an ejection seat in a helicopter.

Guy couldn't guide a turd down a toilet.

Sure, he'd had sturdy hiking packs waiting for them at the train station as promised, but he'd forgotten more than a few essentials—one being firewood. Matches, lighter fluid, fire-starters, sure. But no wood, which turned out to be quite problematic since they were in what amounted to an endless desert devoid of any sign of habitation or vegetation. Just gritty sand, blowing wind, and towering dunes for miles and miles on end.

And they needed the firelight, not only because the desert was downright frigid once the sun dipped below the horizon, but because there were apparently unfriendly things that called the ugly patch of sand home. Bizarre, mutated things hungry for live food, but afraid of fire—or so said Levi. So far, however, the trip had been uneventful.

After the madness of the Hub, the train station and subsequent train ride had been less than spectacular. The station itself had been a sleek, well-managed place of sterile white tile, too much chrome, and overhead florescent lighting, with assorted maps plastered all over the walls. For the most part, the station could have passed as any metropolitan train station: the MTA in New York, the Chicago "L," the LA Metro Rail—all of which Ryder had visited.

There'd been a few quirks, of course: the cashier selling tickets had luminescent skin and seven arms, for example. Or the lockers, where Chuck had stored their gear. A whole wall of metal storage boxes, like you might find in any subway system, except the inside of each locker was illogically bigger than the outside.

Still, pretty humdrum when viewed next to the likes of the Lonely Mountain. And the train ride was an absolute snooze-fest. Literally. Their tiny train cabin had a couple of narrow bunks built into the wall, so she snagged the top bed before anyone could protest and conked out—her body suddenly exhausted. The gentle sway of the train kept her fast asleep. And she slept deeply enough that no dreams came, or, if they did, the train rocked them right away, granting Ryder a few blissful hours of undisturbed rest.

Levi had shaken her awake hours later when the train pulled up at some dump called Bradshaw Landing. A dusty and dilapidated city of sand-worn wood, pitted concrete, and rusted out steel. Chuck produced a pair of goggles and a breathing ventilator, which he insisted she wear, at least until they made it away from the Landing. The dust and pollution was, evidentially, unbearable for most folks, especially outsiders. Levi didn't need one, but wore one anyway, to avoid unwanted attention.

They'd disembarked at a shitty station with corroded tracks and a few dilapidated benches, but didn't venture into the city proper. Too bad, since the only alternative was an endless desert stretching out in the other direction—rolling dunes bracketed by a jagged streak of mountains, which tore their away across the skyline. *The Sprawl.* Some shriveled man sporting dust-covered cowboy garb met them near the railroad tracks.

A friend of Chuck's, though he offered no name and didn't have two words for her or Levi. Chuck slipped the old-timer a handful of bills, and the old-timer, in return, handed over the keys to an old beat-to-shit Jeep—a vehicle that'd seen its best days sometime during World War Two.

"Don't let her looks fool you," Chuck assured them, patting the Jeep's rickety hood. "This sweet piece is built to last, know what I'm sayin'. They don't make 'em like this anymore. For real, this baby's better than the Energizer Bunny, she'll just keep going and going." He laughed, like the whole fucking world was a joke only he got. Ryder couldn't help but roll her eyes—the guy was something else. And nothing good.

They drove west, away from the town and into the rolling desert.

The Jeep died four hours later, the radiator blown to hell, white steam spewing from the dented hood like a smokestack belching out a cloud of smog. What had originally been a day trip suddenly turned into an overnight trip. Potentially *more* than one overnight.

"You're the worst guide of all time," Ryder said as she contemplated the swaying fire.

"Haters gonna hate," Chuck replied absentmindedly.

"Seriously, though," she said, "this can't be what you actually do for a living. I've known plenty of guys like you. Always working a hustle. My dad was like that. Always kept 'a couple of irons in the fire'— that's what he'd say. One week he'd be selling cologne on the street corner, working out of a cheap briefcase he picked up at Goodwill. The next, it'd be knockoff purses at the airport. Week after that, he'd start a landscaping company.

"Always after a quick buck, my dad. Hard worker. Terrible decision maker. Couldn't ever just buckle down and hold a normal job. He tried a couple of times, but that only ever lasted a few months. He'd stumble onto something new—a sure thing, always a sure thing—and there we went. The whole family chasing the next play."

"Sounds like my kinda cat," Chuck said, head bobbing minutely. "You said *was*. That mean he ain't 'round no more or what?"

She shook her head. "No. He's not in the picture anymore. Eventually one of his irons got too hot to handle, came back to burn him big time. Burned everyone."

*"Keep your eyes shut tight now," she whispers to Jamie, before taking her hands and pressing them tight over Jamie's ears.*

She waved a hand through the air, *it's not worth talking about.* "So what about you? I know you aren't some outdoors woodsman—not wearing those Jordans."

"Shoot. I hate the wilderness," he said, tossing a small pebble toward the fire. "Desert, trees, bugs, dirt. Hell no. Having to take a shit out in the open—that's some literal awkward shit, know what I'm sayin'? Ass hanging in the breeze. Naw, I'd be doing anything else, if I could."

"So how'd you get the job in the first place?"

"'Cause I'm connected. A people person, natural-born networker. I've got a finger in just 'bout every piece of action, so when people need a runner for something"—he slapped his chest—"boom, I get tapped. Hate doing the tour guide *bullshit,* though. Pain in my black ass, except for your boy, Levi. Dude pays big money. Big, big money. Whenever word comes down that he needs a hand, I'm there. Guy throws out cash money like it ain't no thang. Not like some of these shifty sons of bitches—hire you on, be working you the whole time. Levi's ain't right in the head, but he always pays up."

"He's sort of secretive," Ryder replied, thinking about the wad of cash—ten grand, flat out. "Where do you think he gets all that money?"

Chuck ran a hand across his chin and shook his head. "Got me. I've asked around about him, discreet like, though. Outworld's a weird place, a big place too, but that cat is weird even by Outworld standards. Dude's a ghost. He ain't a halfie, that's the truth. But he ain't nothing else either. A Golem, people say. One guy I know, thinks he's the Golem of Prague—built by some old Jewish rabbi way back in the day." He shrugged, *All just hearsay*. "I'll tell you this much, people in the Hub are scared of him. Levi might think he flies under the radar, but folks on the street know his deal. That guy shows up and people go missing.

"And if Levi makes someone go missin', ain't no one ever see 'em again. Usually the people he snatches up are world-class assholes, though, so most people don't mind. But they sure as hell steer clear. I could care less about that. It's all money for me. And he's got it in spades. I heard tell through the mystic pipeline that Levi's sitting on top of hoarded Nazi gold, like back from World War Two. I don't give a rat's ass where it comes from, though, long as I get paid."

They were quiet for a time, the bluster and sigh of the wind filling the night with its song. An occasional gust would kick up embers and send them swirling into the night air, drifting off into the wilderness.

"So what's your real game?" Ryder asked when she couldn't handle the quiet any longer. "What do you really want to do?"

He was quiet for a minute, head see-sawing from side to side. "If I tell you, you gotta promise you won't tell anyone else. You good with that?"

"Yeah," she replied. "Like I have anyone to tell, anyway. Only person I know besides you in this fucked up world is Levi, and he's not exactly into deep, personal conversation."

"I wanna open a bakery," he said after a moment, not even a hint of mockery in his voice. "I love baking. Pecan tassies, sweet potato pie, southern-style hummingbird cake, butterhorn rolls, English tea ring. Can't get enough of that buttery, awesome goodness." He patted his stomach longingly.

Ryder laughed, she couldn't help it. "Stop bullshitting me," she said once her giggling died down.

"That hurts," he said, stone cold serious, "and I ain't lying. I wanna open a fuckin' bakery, okay? When I was a little kid, my momma, she'd always be baking something. Something warm and good. I'd help her. We'd make the dough, she'd read me books while it rose, then we'd go to work. Cookies one day. Sweet bread another. Made me happy, doin' that with her. I still bake when I got the time and it still makes me happy. Findin' something that really makes you happy in life is pretty rare, lemme tell you."

"Wow." She frowned and ran her gaze over him, trying to see the baker buried beneath the hood. "Sorry," she said, "I just don't see it. I wouldn't peg you as baker, Chuck."

"Yeah." He offered a heavy sigh. "No one sees baker Chuck. People look at me and they think I should be dropping mix-tapes or shootin' hoops. But that ain't me. What you see, this image, it's all part of stayin' alive. Livin' in the Hub is all about survival, and lookin' like a thug helps me keep breathin'. Trust me, if I showed up lookin' all Carlton Banks—plaid shorts, tennis shirt, bow tie, penny loafers, dancin' to Tom Jones—I wouldn't last a day. But somewhere down the road I'm gonna have enough cash to leave all this shit behind, open up my own bakery. Use all those recipes my momma passed on to me. Be who I wanna be. Openin' your own business ain't cheap, though. But I'll make it—even if I have to make my own luck to do it."

He reached into his shirt and withdrew the tacky golden four-leaf clover. He pressed it to his lips as if offering a silent prayer, then slipped the bling back down his shirt. "Someday. I'll be done with the Hub and Outworld. Set up shop over in Louisiana or maybe South Carolina—you know, someplace where folks ain't afraid to eat good food and get fat as hell. And I'll be legit. No more hustles to run. Just doin' my thing, not havin' to look over my shoulder all the time." He smiled. It wasn't his usual cocksure grin either, but something small and sad and genuine. "What about you?" he asked eventually.

She grimaced and shook her head. "I don't know what I want in life. I guess that's always been my problem. I think I got that from my dad. He didn't really know what he wanted either. I wish I could be like my sister, Jamie—she has it all together. Nice house over in Wisconsin. She has a degree and a good job working as a nurse. I mean she's not rich, not living the highlife or anything, but she's got a steady thing. A good thing. Sometimes I think that was supposed to be my life—but then everything went sideways." She canted one hand. "Jamie got all the lucky breaks and I ended up with the shit end of the stick every time.

"Coulda been my life, but instead? I'm a high school dropout and now I work at a used bookstore—which, believe it or not, is actually the best job I've ever had. I make fancy-ass coffee I can't afford to drink for college kids who think they're better than me. Who *are* better than me. I'm a recovering addict without a fuckin' future." She reached up and ran a hand over a face too old for her years. "I guess all I really want is to stop *surviving* for once and start … I dunno, *thriving,* I guess. I don't really care what I do. I want a good thing, like my sister. I just want to stop getting by, if that makes sense."

"Hey, you preachin' to the choir. I mean, I *feel* that." He paused. "So if you want a normal life, what in the hell you doin' hangin' around with a cat like Levi? Guy ain't normal. How'd you get mixed up with him? You just a Rube girl, am I right?"

"Rube?" she asked.

"Yeah, Rube. It's what we call all the gullible suckers out there in the big wide world who are oblivious to all of this." He waved a hand through the air.

"Well, I'm not a Rube anymore." She tentatively traced a finger along the outside of her shirt, feeling the edge of the scar running down her middle. "I still don't really know how I ended up here, bad luck I guess. Story of my life." She faltered for a moment. "What do you think Levi's after? You're out here for money. I'm out here because I don't have any other choice. But him? What's he want?"

"Shoot. Might as well ask what a rock wants. Shit, I don't know why anyone would be out here." He turned his head, staring into the cold, dark desert surrounding them.

"Right?" she said. "What's the deal with this place anyway? Who would come out here?" She batted at some kind of buzzing insect circling her head.

"Far as I know," he replied, "no one *wants* to come out here. Sometimes fools pass through here"— he hooked a thumb toward the jagged mountains behind him, a black shark bite across a dark blue sky—"idiots making for the Spine. But I ain't never heard of no one actually going into the Sprawl just 'cause. Like for shits and giggles. This professor y'all chasing must be dumb as a brain-dead monkey. This place is a straight-up dump. Dust, dirt, more dust, more dirt. Plus, there's all kinds of weird mutants out here and shit. Old cities scattered around, most of 'em are radioactive." He shook his head. "Crazy."

They fell silent as the heavy footfalls of something big drew near. Levi lumbered into the ring of firelight a moment later, no longer wearing a human form. He'd dropped his disguise the second they made it out into the desert. Instead he was once more a hulking tower of gray. *Holy shit he's ugly*, Ryder thought, not for the first time. Lumpy body; beady black eyes; crude, sloping forehead; massive jaw with that huge underbite. Wasn't a mother in the world that could love his face. Even a *blind* mother would have trouble.

Guy was uglier than a dried out dog turd.

The Mudman clutched a meager stack of gnarled sticks—nearly petrified with age—in one massive palm.

"Do you know how loud you two are?" he asked, his tone implying the answer: *too damn loud.* "The desert carries sound, you understand that, right? Need I remind you we aren't the only things out here? Best not to draw unwanted attention to ourselves. So stop talking."

"Whatever, Captain Killjoy," Chuck replied, rolling over in his sleeping bag and offering his back to the fire. "I was getting tired anyway."

"Shouldn't we set up guard shifts or something?" Ryder asked, nervous about Chuck's talk of mutants and radioactive cities. She did not want to end up living through an episode of the *Walking Dead.*

The Mudman grunted. "You've got a good head on your shoulders, but don't worry about it. Go to sleep. I'll keep watch."

"All night?"

"Go to sleep," he said in reply, before turning away.

She couldn't decide whether or not she liked Levi. He'd saved her, no question, and seemed to have her best interest in mind, but his personality was so, so *disagreeable.* She'd been around lots of introverted assholes before, but Levi took the cake; hell, his abysmal bedside manner took the whole cake *shop.*

She pushed her feet and legs inside her own sleeping bag—a black mummy sack that seemed far too thin—then lay back, resting her head on a tiny inflatable travel pillow. "Hey, Levi," she said.

The gargantuan Mudman pivoted, peering over one shoulder. "I told you to be quiet. What do you need?"

She wanted to pick up a rock and chuck it at his head while unleashing a string of colorful profanity as loudly as possible. Instead, she forced smile. "I wanted to say thank you. For going out of your way to help me, I mean. Thanks. Not many people would do that for a stranger."

She watched him for a moment. He'd fallen completely still as though he didn't know how to respond to a simple *thank you*. As though this kind of interaction were completely foreign to him. After a long beat of awkward quiet, he replied with a muttered "you're welcome, now go to sleep." Ryder chalked it up as a win, then rolled onto her side, eyes fixed on the dancing flames as she nodded off.

*She comes to. Groggy, thoughts slugging through her aching head—a low throb beating out a melody behind her eye sockets, keeping pace with her pounding heart.*

*They'd drugged her again, though how long ago she isn't sure. No clocks down here. No daylight. No overhead stars. Just the firelight, always burning, throwing shifting shadows against the wall. The thought of the wet, white cloth pressing over her nose and mouth makes her gag—six times so far. Six times they'd put her under. She repeats the number over and over again, cementing it into her brain. That's the only thing she can count, the only way to track the passage of time, and she clings to it. Needs it.*

*Her wrists hurt, the leather bands pressing into her skin are too tight, and every time she moves they chafe and rub. Not for the first time she bucks against the restraints, both on her wrists and ankles, panic swelling inside her when she finds no give. She can breathe, there's nothing restricting her mouth—*

*screaming down here is pointless, she knows—but claustrophobia presses in on her all the same. She fights to slow her rapid heartbeat, jackhammering away inside her chest. Fights to resist the urge to sob or cuss, both useless wastes of strength and energy.*

*Eventually they'll come for her, just like they came for the rest, so it's best to save her strength until then.*

*Probably, they won't undo her restraints, but they might. They did with a handful of other victims. If she gets the same chance, she's going to fight. She's been in more than a few scrapes before—nothing like this, but still, she's not afraid to get bloody. Especially not if it means surviving. She'll punch and kick, scratch and bite. One thing's for sure, she isn't going to be led like a lamb to the slaughter; they're going to kill her anyway, so she might as well go down swinging.*

*The squawk of inhuman voices fills her ears, and a wild heartbeat later she catches the pitter-patter of approaching footsteps.*

*The panic creeps in at the edges like darkness stealing in as the sun sets behind the horizon. She doesn't want to open her eyes, doesn't want to see the horror chamber around her, doesn't want to see the pile of mutilated bodies—a reminder of the fate to come—or the blue-men who are holding her captive. But she needs to see. If there's even a small chance of escape, she needs every possible advantage she can get, and that means she needs to look for openings.*

*One more deep breath. She holds it for a second, then slowly exhales.*

*She opens her eyes. The muted firelight is harsh and painful. She looks straight up at first, staring at the rough and uneven ceiling—part of some naturally occurring cave, she's sure. She's underground, that much she knows. Assuming she does escape, she has no idea how she'll find her way to the surface, but she pushes that concern away for what feels like the thousandth time. Getting free, that's number one on the list. Everything else can get in line.*

*Next she turns her head, surveying the new addition to the pile of bodies in front of the grotesque altar, with its staring ruby eyes. Her breath hitches in her chest, and she shoves back a renewed wave of fear and sadness.*

*The woman, Sally Jensen from Newark, is dead. She doesn't know anything else about her. The woman had screamed "I'm Sally Jensen from Newark" during a brief bout of lucidity. Ryder has no trouble remembering her, since they shared a name. Sally Jensen's breasts are gone. Carved away. For some unfathomable reason, they'd attached a pink flamingo's dainty legs to her belly—grafted them on over her navel. Sally Jensen from Newark had been the last victim. There'd been twenty-one in the beginning. All chained up together, drugged and tossed on the floor.*

*Except Ryder. She'd lain on the stone table, drugged every so often. And now ... now, she's the only one left.*

*The last.*

*Movement catches her eye, just to the right of the altar. The blue-men, as she has come to think of them, are coming. Coming for her. They're twisted things, human-like, but obviously something different. She can't explain them. Can't explain what they are.*

*Her mind keeps flashing back to a horror movie she saw once: a bunch of spelunkers stumble across some inhuman cave dwellers who hunt the friends down one by one. That's the only reasonable explanation. Somehow, she's been abducted by evolutionary Morlocks hiding beneath the regular human world.*

*That doesn't make a damn lick of sense—she's never been spelunking. That kind of outdoorsy shit isn't her bag, but what other explanation fits?*

*The old one, the leader—bent and stooped with age, wearing his patchwork cape—creeps closer. He's holding a stone knife in one gnarled, arthritic hand; weird symbols are carved into the blade and handle. Those symbols hurt to look at, like they were built to repel the eye.*

*"You're awake," he hisses in horrendously accented English. She's heard the garbled speech these things use amongst themselves, and it's nothing even remotely like English. "It's better if you're awake. Your pain will increase our chances of success." He turns to another blue-man on his left, this one holding a jar filled with cloudy liquid. There's something else inside, wriggling around in the fluid. A tiny thing, not much bigger than a goldfish. She catches a good glimpse as the creature stirs in the jar.*

*No bigger than a goldfish, maybe, but she quickly sees it more closely resembles the worm-like creature depicted on the wall. A chubby-grub, some kind of larva, with too many eyes and a circular mouth filled with scores and scores of miniscule teeth. An overgrown leech.*

*"You see the fruit of our labor," the old creature croons. "All of these"—he waves toward the mound of corpses—"failures. But even in their failure, we have snatched out victory. And you, you will make a wonderful home." He hefts the knife and brings it down toward the exposed skin of her belly. They don't loosen the straps, but she bucks anyway, thrashing and screaming.*

*"Good," the old man says, "scream." He smiles a wicked, uneven grin filled with black stumps, rotten and reeking. He cuts, slicing into her abdomen.*

*FOURTEEN:*

## Dig Site

"Wake up," Levi said, shaking the girl as gently as he could manage. "You're having a nightmare, it's alright, though, you're safe."

Her eyes fluttered open and she shot up, beads of perspiration running down her face in torrents, matting down her hair. One hand frantically patted at her stomach, feeling along the pink scar. It wasn't hard to guess what she'd been dreaming about. For a second Levi pondered pressing her for details.

So far she hadn't provided anything useful regarding her abduction or what the Kobocks had been doing to her and the others. Levi suspected she had some form of self-induced amnesia—repressing the events, blocking them from her conscious mind. At this moment, though, she probably remembered a great deal, at least until the details slipped away as dreams are wont to do.

He didn't ask, though.

She was quivering, afraid.

He needed that info, but pressing her for such lurid specifics, even if useful, seemed too cruel. If her mind had shut those memories away it was likely for a good reason.

"It's okay," he said again, then scooted back a few feet, not wanting her to feel smothered by his presence. "It's time to move."

After another few moments she seemed to come to herself: rapid breathing leveling out, eyes adjusting to the sporadic firelight, hands ceasing their restless scan of her body.

"What?" she asked, voice groggy with sleep. "What do you mean it's time to move? It's dark out. I'm tired as shit."

It was dark. Levi didn't have a watch, but the heat retained in the ground was like a clock of its own, one Levi could read as well as any timepiece. Half an hour past 3 AM, give or take ten minutes. Quite early.

"We're in the desert," he replied evenly. "We no longer have a vehicle, and the day will be blistering hot. That's not a problem for me, but you and Chuck? You two won't fare so well. The professor's work site should be a couple hours' walk from here. If we leave now, we can travel during the cool part of the day and get to the site by sunup.

"We'll look around there, hopefully find the professor, and then hunker down until it gets cool again. Then we'll hike back toward Bradshaw Landing. Travelling at night isn't ideal—what with the mutants and plague beasts—but better than to try to walk in the heat of the day." He shook his head at the absurd thought. "So get dressed."

"Can we eat first?" she asked.

"You can eat while we walk." He moved away to pack up the camp. Chuck was already up, lethargic and quiet—a change which Levi definitely appreciated—working to roll up his sleeping bag and stow away his gear. Levi's bag remained packed from the night before, untouched.

The Mudman did sleep, in a manner of speaking, but he could rest much less frequently than his human travelling companions. A few hours a day was all Levi required, and for him, sleeping in the sand, against the earth, was far more refreshing then shoving himself into a stuffy sack. He'd recuperated for a few hours after dinner, then stood watch for the rest of the night.

Still, there were things to be done: his gear was ready to go, but the camp itself needed to be erased. Probably, they weren't being followed by Kobocks or anything of an even more unsavory nature, but Levi firmly believed the cautious and diligent man thrived where fools rushed in. After all, the early bird might get the worm, but it was the second mouse—cautious and diligent—who got the cheese. Levi was always the second mouse.

First he doused the fire, heaping sand over the meager flame, suffocating it. Once the blaze had burned out, he hastily dug out any unscorched wood—he'd had to search long and hard the night before for those scraps. Those sticks, little more than twigs, he attached to the outside of his hiking pack with a bungee cord.

Next he reached out with his senses, calling on the earth to obscure their presence: the sands shifted and moved with a groan, their tracks disappeared in an instant, and the makeshift fire pit was swallowed in a burble of gritty yellow. He paused, breathing deeply while he scanned the campsite. There were still minute signs of their presence and passage, but Levi was sure the blowing winds would obscure any remaining evidence in a few hours' time, leaving no trace. Perfect.

By the time Levi was done, Chuck and Ryder were ready to move—packs on backs, both munching on granola bars. Levi nodded his blocky head, gray and massive, and set out in the direction of the professor's work site, his ground sense leading them unerringly onward.

The sun was just beginning to peek its lazy eye over the horizon when they finally came upon their destination, which wasn't at all what Levi had been expecting. The camp itself consisted of several large, sturdy tents. Not standard "camp" tents, these, but heavy-duty canvas things, with thick wooden poles propping the impromptu structures up into the air. The canvas was a pale green, stained a light brown in most places by the fine, powdery sand running across the ground.

Far more impressive than the research site, however, was the building lying beyond it.

A towering pyramid of terraces. Twenty stories of ancient, weathered stone shot up into the sky. The temple—and Levi was somehow sure it *was* a temple—looked old, *ancient* even, like it'd stood for years beyond numbering. Stranger still was the green foliage running along the outside of the old structure, snaking over every terrace, as though attempting to choke the life out of the building. Thick green vines with fat purple leaves and night-dark flowers blooming every few feet. Levi sincerely hoped to find the professor asleep in the camp somewhere.

The thought of venturing into the strange ruins set his teeth on edge. An unnatural place, he had no doubt.

"Holy shit," Chuck said, standing in slack-jawed wonderment at the building scarring the horizon with its presence. "Don't tell me we goin' in there, 'cause I ain't fixin' to do it. That place is a straight-up horror movie set, and everyone knows the black dude gets it first in a horror flick."

"Yep. I'm with Chuck on this one," Ryder added, her skin pale and sickly looking.

"No disagreement here," Levi replied. "Let's check the camp, see if we can get what we're looking for without setting foot in there—place gives me an uneasy feeling." He paused. Though Levi always approached hunting expeditions with caution and care, such outright disquiet was unusual indeed. "We'll only go in as a last resort," he continued after a moment.

With a surge of ichor, he recalled his church face—the balding man with his mustache, glasses, and potbelly. No telling how a mage from the Guild of the Staff would react to something nonhuman blundering into his camp. Best to play it safe. Always prudent. Without another word he trudged forward, easing up to the work site.

"Hello?" he called as he approached the first tent, the smallest of three. "Anyone here?" He peeled back a thick canvas flap covering the entrance.

No answer.

He shoved his head in, peeking around: a Spartan room, which looked to be sleeping quarters. There was a pair of canvas folding cots lined up against the far wall with thick wooden travel trunks at the end of each. A small folding camp desk, holding an unlit oil lamp, lounged against the right wall; next to it was a collapsible stool—a backless folding thing with a strip of canvas serving as the seat. A copper washbasin as large as a porcelain tub sat in the left corner nearest the doorway, a stained white towel draped over one side.

Levi crept inside, heading for the pair of trunks by the beds. No place else to look, really. Each trunk had a spot for a lock, but neither was secured, which meant whoever was out here didn't expect company or guests of any sort. He popped the top of the first trunk and waded into the contents. Clothes—several pairs of pants, shirts, and undergarments—and the normal assortment of hygiene items. Nothing with much of a tale to tell. He shut the lid and headed for the next trunk.

More of the same—

"Oh shit, oh shit! Levi!" Chuck called, his voice thin and muted both by distance and the rustle of the wind. "We got something here. Nasty ass shit. Hurry."

Levi shut the lid with a *clap* and hustled out of the entryway, ducking low through the narrow opening, and lumbered toward the largest of the tents. Ryder was outside, hunched over, with a string of clear vomit trailing from her lips.

"You okay?" he asked as he drew near.

"Fine," she said, wiping the back of her hand across her mouth, then spitting onto the ground. "Wasn't ready for that. Just need a minute."

The Mudman nodded and pushed his way into the tent's interior.

The source of Ryder's nausea became quickly apparent.

The body of a naked and recently murdered man was splayed out in the middle of the floor. He looked to be in his late thirties, and based on the state of the body, Levi guessed he'd been dead a couple of days. It was also obvious he hadn't died quickly. Someone had driven rusty iron spikes through his hands and feet into the earth below—small pools of blood-caked sand surrounded each limb. He'd been crucified, at least in a manner of speaking. Even worse, his guts lay in a heap next to his body; a jagged, messy cut split his abdomen.

Disemboweled.

A brutal way to go, considering how long a person could live in that condition. If the torturer was careful—and, from the look of things, Levi had reason to believe he'd been an experienced hand—a person could live for hours or even days in such a state. Levi didn't know who this man was, but he was sure it wasn't the professor. One, he was much younger than the man he'd come looking for, and two, he was Asian. The professor was nearly two hundred, which for a mage, would've put him in the sixty-year age range, black, and hailed from South Africa. There'd been two cots in the other tent, so obviously this was the second occupant—likely a research assistant.

Chuck stood in the corner, one arm slung over his face, trying to block out the stink of coppery blood and voided bowels lingering in the air.

"You good here?" he asked, refusing to take his arm away from his face. "'Cause this? You didn't pay me enough for this. Nasty-ass dead bodies and shit? Naw. I could use some fresh air, for real."

Levi motioned toward the flap while eyeing the corpse. "You're good. You and Ryder check the last tent for the professor, call if you find anything." He paused, thinking. "You said there were guns in the packs?"

Chuck nodded.

"Good. I want you and Ryder armed, just in case. And stay alert. Whoever or whatever did this could still be around. Once you get done with the tent, I want you to check for a vehicle. The professor's a mage, so it's possible they used some sort of portal to get here, but if not, that means they had a truck to transport all this gear. Find it. And Chuck—stick with Ryder. I don't want the two of you to split up for any reason. Understood?"

"Yeah I got you," he said before shuffling out of the tent. Chuck's passing let in a breeze of fresh air, for which Levi was grateful. Yes, he was a creature of death, born out of murder and charged to carry out the same, but he *did* have a sense of smell, and the corpse reeked. There was nothing for him to learn from the body, but the room might offer him something. Unlike the first tent, with its cots and washbasin, this was plainly a workspace. Bookcases were filled with old tomes and modern textbooks on a random assortment of topics: *Astrophysics and the Dynamics of Gravitational Singularities*, by Richard Townshend, PhD; *Myths and Theories Regarding Atlantis*, by Mage Viljo Mansikkamaa, PhD; *Sumerian Conjurations and Extrapolated Applications*, by Archmage Thorsten Maier, PhD; *Elements of Paleolinguistics* by Rachael Radcliff; *The History of Cain and the Lost Peoples*, by Nahman ben Hirsch; *The Sprawl, a Comprehensive History*, by Mage Owen Wilkie, PhD.

Levi couldn't make heads or tails of the books. That last one, though—*The Sprawl, a Comprehensive History*—had been penned by the man Levi had come to find.

He moved to a series of heavy worktables and desks covered with papers, grainy photos, and artifacts likely salvaged from the temple. Maybe something would provide a few useful clues, though he wasn't too optimistic. The papers and photos were disheveled and tossed about, as if they'd already been pored over by whoever had so brutally killed the assistant. Levi spent a few minutes scanning through the pages. Much of the material revolved around the lost city of Atlantis, which was curious.

Without more context, however, Levi wasn't sure how any of it fit.

But, he did find a photo—this one in color—of an altar, identical to the one he'd seen in the temple beneath the Hub. And that, if nothing else, told him he was on the right track. There were still many puzzle pieces to discover, but if they could find the professor, or the people responsible for his abduction, he believed they'd find the answers they sought. He folded up the photo of the altar, shoved it into his pocket, and made for the exit. He paused just before leaving, glancing back at the crucified man pinned to the floor.

A pang of guilt rushed through him like a jolt of lightning.

What that poor man had suffered, Levi couldn't even begin to guess at. He was sure, however, that he hadn't earned such a cruel end. Even those murderers who deserved to taste Levi's wrath didn't deserve *that*.

Death was one thing. What had been done to him was something else entirely, something not worth dwelling on. He moved back over to the man's side and knelt down, knee just inches from the pile of guts.

Carefully, he closed the man's eyelids and muttered a quick prayer:

"The LORD bless you and keep you; the LORD make his face shine on you and be gracious to you; the LORD turn his face toward you and give you peace." He ran a thick finger across the man's cheek. Human beings—so wonderful and so fragile. "Amen." He whispered the last.

He transformed his right hand, fingers melting together to form a thin blade. Without a thought, he ran the knife-edged appendage across the inside of his left forearm; a line of ichor welled to the surface. The blade vanished, becoming fingers once more, which Levi gently dipped into the golden blood running over the surface of his skin.

Carefully, he splattered droplets on the body and onto the dusty floor surrounding the unfortunate casualty, then willed the earth to swallow the mutilated corpse.

The soil resisted him, fighting his efforts. Superficially it looked no different from the ground of Inworld, but Levi could feel the difference in his blood. Inworld was his mother and father, and the ground there was kin to him. The stone and sand of this place was foreign and resonated on another frequency. A pitch Levi wasn't accustomed to. As a sculptor, Levi preferred to work with *stoneware clays*—gray and moist, highly plastic and effortless to model. Inworld was like that: malleable and easily shaped.

Everything in the Sprawl, though, was like *kaolin clay*, used for making porcelain: too dry, too stiff, too inflexible, and near impossible to work with. Levi hated the stuff. He *could* shape and draw from the earth and sand below, but it took ten times the effort to accomplish one-tenth of what he could manage in Inworld.

Eventually, though, the ground *did* groan in response, giving in with a shudder, then splitting wide and dragging the body down, burying it beneath the sands. Not a proper funeral, but better than leaving his corpse for the scavengers. A small mercy. With that done, Levi broke apart a camp stool and fashioned it into a crude cross, held together in the center with lumps of the Mudman's clay flesh. This he drove into the ground with a *thud*, marking the shallow grave should anyone ever happen by this way again.

*Rest in peace*, the Mudman thought as he pushed his way free of the tent and into the early morning light—

He froze as he heard the distant scuffle of claws on powdery earth.

He'd been so absorbed with the dead man within, he'd failed to notice the approaching creatures. Scavengers, he thought. He pushed his earth sense into the soil, extending his awareness out in a circle, forcing it as far as it would go in every direction: a hundred feet, two hundred, three hundred. There, just on the edge of his senses. Several creatures—four or five, maybe more—were stealing toward them, likely drawn on by the pungent stink of the eviscerated body.

Levi moved, spotting Chuck and Ryder milling around by the entrance to the third tent, pistols clutched in anxious hands. Levi knew Chuck was more talker than fighter, but he had confidence the overgrown leprechaun could handle himself in a pinch—you didn't live long in the Hub without some sort of experience and skill in combat. Outworld was an unforgiving, predatory place that consumed the weak. Ryder, he knew little about, but she seemed to have at least a passing familiarity with the weapon she held.

He broke into a jog, dropping his human façade and allowing his true form to spill out as he moved. "A vehicle? Did you find one?" he called.

Escape was their best option at this point. Drive away, wait for a day, then circle back once whatever was out there left. Scavengers wouldn't wait around for long, not once they realized there was no more food to be had. Run and circle back. That would be best.

Chuck nodded, then promptly shook his head. "Yeah, well no. I mean, they got a truck over on the other side of the temple, big ass ancient mother, Soviet troop-carrier or something, but it's busted to hell. Someone tore up the engine worse than that sucker in the tent. No one's driving out in that piece."

"And this tent's clear," Ryder added, pointing toward the heap of canvas on her right. "Excavation equipment. Wheelbarrows, shovels, pickaxes, lamps—"

Levi absently waved the words away, *It's not important*, while reaching down with his senses, focusing his attention on the approaching hunting party. A hundred and fifty feet, now. Moving slowly, thoughtfully. Fanning out, the pack splitting apart, into three groups of two. One group broke left, another broke right—circling in from the sides—while the last group bore straight ahead. A flanking ploy. It was safe to assume, then, that whatever was out there knew about Levi and company.

"Ryder, get a pair of picks for you and Chuck."

She canted her head and looked a question at him.

"For when your ammo runs out," he growled. "Chuck, get that gun ready. We're going to have some unfriendly guests." Ryder nodded—eyes wide, muscles suddenly tight and tense—and ducked back into the tent with the excavation equipment.

"What'd you mean, unfriendly guests?" Chuck asked, hefting his pistol.

"Sprawl wolves, I think. Not sure, but I can feel something getting closer."

Ryder came back a heartbeat later with a pair of dusty handpicks—not nearly as big as Levi had been hoping for—tucked under her arm.

"We need to move, now," Levi said. "Everyone back up slowly toward the temple. Don't turn. Don't run—that'll only draw their attention. Calm, focused, sharp. If we can't get to the temple before they attack, you let me handle it. You two just get into the building and hold the entrance. A good defensive funnel, you understand?"

A howl, low and choking, broke the air. A second later another howl answered the first, this from the left, followed by a third from their right.

*FIFTEEN:*

## Sprawl Wolves

A gust of gale force wind swept in, blowing out of nowhere and pushing a brown cloud across the camp—some foreign power was at work within the unnatural scree storm. Some extension of the wolves, maybe? Not important, not now. The trio backpedaled, Levi in the center, Chuck to the right, Ryder on the left—

The wind cut off as abruptly as it came, dropping away to reveal the first pair of creatures closing in on the left side. Scavengers, as Levi suspected. Sprawl wolves: opportunistic killers with a fierce reputation and a nasty disposition. These creatures, more than any other, kept all but the most dedicated travellers from venturing into these parts.

Other than academic types like the professor, only folks bound for the Spine—an impassable range of craggy peaks—came out this way. A few intrepid souls looking to make their fortune by mining out the rich veins of precious metal and addictive *Green-Charlie* buried beneath the mountains to the west. The wolves, however, were a major deterrent to such prospective entrepreneurs.

The Mudman had read about them, seen pictures of them in an old leather bound volume called *Beast and Curiosities of the Middle Regions.* Actually seeing them was something else entirely; the Mudman could now understand why those making for the Spine might hesitate.

The two Sprawl wolves prowled forward on limbs thick with muscle and wrapped in tan scales like those of a pit viper. Though they bore the name "wolf," there was little lupine in them, save that they moved on four limbs and hunted as a pack. Enormous bat ears protruded from the sides of their faces, and their heads twitched with every sound. A singular, cyclopean eye—milky and filmed over with a heavy cataract—filled each face. And, instead of a wolf's tearing jaws, each had a fleshy tube of meat hanging down, ringed at the end with jagged teeth like broken glass.

Those mouths were not meant for biting, Levi recalled, but for boring in so the wolves could suck out innards—organs, bodily fluids, anything wet and edible—and blend the nutrient-rich juices into slurry.

One had bristling black quills running over its head and back, trailing down to its nubby tail—a male. The other, spike free, was female, but the more dangerous of the two. The males had poison quills, but the females used their anteater mouths to implant egg sacs—gooey bundles of red membrane, each containing a litter of their young—into any warm, wet place they could find. The host wouldn't die right away, but rather would be eaten alive over days and weeks as the younglings hatched and ate their way out.

A brutal, appalling end.

A tense pause hung in the air as the wolves regarded them with canted heads, bat ears quivering as they waited for a sound. A gunshot rang out, a thunderclap that broke the tenuous truce. The female staggered as the round punched into her shoulder, but the damage hardly mattered; the bullet ricocheted off her scaly hide, ripping into the sand with a puff of powder.

"Run. Make for the temple!" Levi hollered, surging into action, not waiting to see if Chuck or Ryder complied. No time for babysitting.

The male wolf barreled into him, talons flashing out and slashing into his chest as its probing mouth sought his middle. A blast of angry heat flared in the Mudman's belly, but lasted only an instant before a pleasant numbness worked its way out in a rough circle. Levi focused his ichor, pushing the golden substance to his center—the flesh over his barrel gut hardened, gray clay turning to rocky quartz far too dense for the wolf's teeth to penetrate.

More gunshots rang out, a pair of sharp reports, coming from two separate locations. Chuck and Ryder working their weapons.

Chuck, the Mudman put out of mind—he wasn't Levi's responsibility—but he stole a glance toward where he'd last seen Ryder. She was making for the temple, but slowly. She crept backward toward the hulking structure, stealing a foot at a time, while keeping her eyes and gun muzzle locked on another female wolf, which had materialized on the right. Ryder held a snub-nosed revolver, her hands trembling minutely. Despite the tremble, the weapon remained level and fired again and again, bullets smashing into the creature's whipping flesh-mouth.

The rounds hit home. A gout of bright red exploded into the air and splashed against the sand.

The creature howled, a gurgled cry, as its mouth blew apart and was left dangling by a thin tether of hide. Levi noted the creature also sported a gaping hole in one of its oversized ears, the top quarter torn away, already lost to the shifting sands. Smart girl, this one. The body may have been armored, but the central eye, the ears, the mouth? External sense organs such as those were always sensitive and vulnerable. No creature, even the most rugged and resilient, was without some weakness.

Levi grinned, proud of the girl. She would be fine. Far tougher than she looked. Maybe she didn't have the same immovable determination Levi possessed, but she had an iron backbone that spoke of survival. He put her from mind—now he needed to see to his own survival.

Despite the fact that Levi had transformed his belly into stony armor too thick to penetrate, the stupid Sprawl wolf was still attempting to bore inward with his circular mouth. Levi's right hand bubbled and blurred, his fingers forming a razor-edged meat cleaver. He swept the hand downward, passing it over his chest and belly as if he were brushing away a troubling spot of dirt. Halfway down, just where a patch of numbness lingered in his skin, the blade met resistance: like chopping through a thick salami. *Schwick.*

The creature reared back with a *squee*, its red blood splashing over Levi. The Mudman shed an ugly grin, then the blood began to sizzle. The grin faltered, faded. He glanced down, watching with curious fascination as his skin smoldered and sent up streamers of white smoke wherever crimson coated his skin.

Acidic. Nothing about that in any of the books. Then the pain hit like a shotgun blast to the back of his skull, as pinpricks of white-hot fire ignited against his oozing ichor. Now it was Levi's turn to fall back in a bellow of rage, his feet churning up a cloud of grit as he moved, beating uselessly at the spots of acidic blood eating into his skin.

He went to work in a heartbeat, crude fingers elongating, forming concaved razors, which he used to dig out the smoldering patches of red. He carved troughs into doughy clay, scooping out the acid-burned areas and flinging them away. The impromptu surgery was torturous, but even that agony paled in comparison to the acid burns. It took only seconds to clear away the majority of the damage, but even then the wounds still throbbed with a dull ache.

He surveyed his handiwork, inspecting the extent of the destruction: deep channels of missing meat and shallow patches of burnt clay—black and cracked in places like broken hardpan in the midday heat—littered his torso and arms. He shuddered and focused his internal reserve of power in a fitful attempt to close off the wounds. He couldn't afford to lose so much of himself, not here, so far away from Earth. He could use the Sprawl to regenerate given enough time, but time was the one thing he didn't have.

Something big hit him from the left—a shoulder hammering into his side and pitching him right. He kept his feet, though barely, his toes drawing down into the earth, pulling stability into his limbs and anchoring him fast. The beast, another black-quilled male, staggered from the blow. Probably, the creature had expected to bowl right through Levi, hoping to send the Mudman cartwheeling into the air. But Levi was no autumn leaf, some light and airy thing easily moved. No, he was a boulder, a living stone of the deep places, and it would take an earthquake to shake him.

Levi shifted his left hand, a sledgehammer taking shape in an eyeblink.

He threw his arm out, a cross-body backhand that landed in the creature's dome like a meteor fresh in from the stratosphere. The wolf's skull crunched and crumpled inward and the body dropped into the dirt, its face bludgeoned, but the scaly hide unbroken. *No more blade attacks,* Levi reasoned, *means no more acidic blood.* He'd stick to clubs from here on out. The beast he'd just backhanded lay in the dirt, limbs twitching mechanically, but Levi suspected the wolf was far from dead. Fazed certainly, but things in Outworld tended to be more resilient than any human would care to wager at.

A flash of movement on his right—

The creature Levi had maimed with his meat-cleaver hand, now missing his tubular mouth, was regrouping. The beast edged forward as ropy strings of skin snaked out from its wounded maw like tiny strings of ground beef. Repairing itself from the look of things. Resilient indeed. Levi moved, heeding his own advice and making for the temple, though never taking his eyes from the mangled beast. He looked left: the second wolf, Busted-Skull, clumsily gained its feet, the lopsided and distorted bones beneath its reptilian hide buckling and shifting back into their proper place.

The wolves moved in concert, darting in as one—overwhelm and incapacitate, a common pack strategy. They were big enough to do it, too. Levi could survive an attack from these two, but it would cost him precious time, perhaps time enough for the rest of the pack to close in and encircle him. Against six or seven of these beasts … well, Levi wasn't one for math—for numbers and figures and odds—but he knew his chances were slim in that scenario. So, he *needed* to prevent them from closing in. From cutting off his exit route.

Grimacing, he shifted his left hand, stretching and hardening his fingers into spikes of gleaming obsidian. He planted his feet, bending his knees, preparing for the inevitable hit from Busted-Skull, angling in from the side—that one, he'd just have to wrestle to the ground. Once he'd dealt with Ground-Beef, he could smash its head in right and proper, for good this time.

He wound back his arm, a pitcher preparing to hurl a fastball, then whipped the limb forward, flicking his wrist at the last moment. The sharpened spears of obsidian separated with a *crack*—the pain was an enormous living thing, like dipping his hand in magma—but worth the price.

Five spears sailed through the air like rockets, slamming into Ground-Beef, passing through scale and impaling muscle with ease. All five missiles scored a hit, and three found their mark true: one embedded in the creature's throat, another protruded from the center of its milky eye, and the last buried itself in its amputated mouth. The creature stalled, staggering drunkenly about, then flopped onto its belly, legs splayed out, gore leaking from his face and neck.

Levi cradled his left hand, now *sans* fingers, against his chest, golden ichor flowing freely over his hands and trailing onto his forearm. He swiveled toward the remaining Sprawl beast barreling toward him and braced for impact, muscles tightening on instinct.

He caught sight of Busted-Skull tearing toward him, as expected, but he *also* saw Ryder—just to the left and behind him. Not at the temple, like he'd instructed, but instead holding strong, clutching a pistol in one shaky hand. She raised the revolver, steadied the gun with her other hand, stole a handful of deep breaths, then unloaded the weapon at the wolf charging Levi's position. The shots weren't terribly well placed—several flew wide and disappeared into the early morning light—but a few blasted the creature in its side and legs.

Busted-Skull seemed unperturbed by her interference, but it did shift its focus, head turning toward the sound of the shots, assessing this new threat.

A small opening, but a valuable one.

Levi shot left, slamming his bleeding, fingerless hand into the ground, a shallow divot blooming from the force of the blow. He willed the gout of ichor liberally coating his maimed fist into the dirt, shaping it and using it to connect to the rock below. He was weak from his wounds, but not so weak he couldn't call out to the land. The ground rippled then bucked, and a shaft of sand, thick as a baseball bat and long as a pool cue, erupted from the ground at an angle, tapering off to a razor point at its end.

In a moment, the ichor worked its own special brand of magic, transmuting and transforming the sand into a lance of nearly invisible, fire-hardened glass. The wolf never slowed its madcap charge toward Levi, and never saw the spike—assuming it could see at all. It ran, full-bore, into the earthen javelin.

The glass spear entered in below the sternum, and the creature's body weight did all the heavy lifting, driving the stake through its armored exterior and deep into its chest cavity. The Sprawl wolf skittered, claws raking at the ground, but his momentum was too great to be stopped entirely, even by the glass spear. Instead the shaft snapped and the creature pitched forward, crashing into the ground with a *thud*, the broken spike still jutting from his torso. Busted-Skull's huge body summersaulted over, back plowing a shallow furrow through the sands before the thing came to a herky-jerky stop.

Levi didn't waste time watching the spectacle—there were more wolves out there, and Ryder's effort would be in vain if he didn't move fast. He gained his feet, ignoring the burns along his body and the blaring pain in his hand, and bolted toward Ryder. He scooped her up in a flash, using his good hand to sling her over his broad shoulder like a sack of potatoes as he sprinted outright for the temple, and never mind what might be approaching at his back.

A chorus of yowls and heavy panting chased Levi into the temple's cavernous entryway—a boxy opening, ten feet by ten feet, which tore into the dark interior of the ancient complex. Unsurprisingly, Chuck was already tucked inside, kneeling on the floor, shoulder against one wall, pistol held out and ready. His gun was a mean .50 Desert Eagle: a nasty piece of chrome capable of punching baseball-sized holes in any creature unwise enough to stand on the wrong end. Levi knew a thing or two about guns, but didn't care much for them. They were unreliable, with far too many variables to consider: bullets, distance, wind speed, cover.

When Levi swung a sledgehammer fist, he knew exactly where it would land and exactly what it would do. Simple, straightforward, effective.

Not to mention, Levi enjoyed the *closeness* of the kill. Shooting someone with a gun would get the job done, but it lacked the intimacy of a spiked mace to the face. He enjoyed feeling the blood splatter against him—he thought to the acid coating his body … well, usually he enjoyed it—and cherished that moment when the life finally sputtered and died. The last flash of a light bulb before it went dark for good.

*That's the old Levi talking*, he reminded himself. He acknowledged his problem, but he was not that man anymore. At least he didn't want to be.

He bent over and dropped Ryder onto her butt, then wheeled about, surveying the professor's abandoned camp, searching for signs of pursuit. It didn't take long to spot the other members of the Sprawl pack—three of the creatures remained. He'd dispatched two, with a little help from Ryder, and it appeared someone had killed a third, which lay in a crumpled and bloodied heap not far off. Based on the extensive damage to the creature's face and torso, Levi suspected Chuck's Desert Eagle was the responsible party.

The Mudman nodded in approval.

Strangely, though, the remaining three wolves, two females and a male, ventured no closer.

Instead, they tooled around out front, pacing or turning in impatient circles as their swaying mouths scoured the ground like bloodhounds picking out a scent. Whatever they sensed or heard kept them at bay, which was a welcome break. Here, in the narrow temple entrance, Levi and his companions had a much better chance of fighting off the creatures, but it was no sure victory. The wolves were powerful beasts in their own right, and with Levi wounded, a pitched battle could go either way.

Frankly, Levi was surprised they weren't already trying to force their way in. They didn't strike him as particularly skittish things—they'd moved in boldly, unafraid—which begged the question, *Why weren't they pressing their advantage?*

Levi looked left, right, up, eyes sweeping over the walls riddled with ancient script. He had a nagging suspicion it was the temple complex keeping the things at bay. The Mudman lumbered forward, crouching down and dropping one hand on Chuck's shoulder. "Have any of them tried to get in?" he asked.

Chuck shook his head. "Naw. Just hangin' 'round out there. That mean sonuvabitch right there"— he pointed his pistol at a particularly thickset female with a puckered wound in one shoulder—"eased off the second I got in here." He shook his head again.

*Fools rush in where angels fear to tread*, Levi thought. Not in the Good Book, that one, but there was wisdom in it all the same. This couldn't be a good sign. Despite their apparent lucky break, Levi knew this could only mean trouble—even more trouble than the wolves.

The Mudman needed to think, and he also needed a few minutes to tend to his wounds. "Keep watching," he grunted. "Let me know if they come any closer." He moved deeper into the hallway and sat down, leaning his broad back against a wall.

Troubling notions careened through his mind like a rockslide: unspoken worries he had no answers for. He sighed. Better to deal with his injuries first, then he could decide what the best course of action was. Often, he found, occupying his mind with some simple and concrete task was the best solution when he had a difficult problem to tackle. Give the issue a little leeway, let it drift a bit so he could gain some distance and perspective.

He went to work like a mechanic with a busted up car on his hands. He dredged up a heap of loose gravel and gritty sand and unceremoniously set about packing his gold-soaked wounds. He used his good hand to cram dirt in, packing the material until it formed a brown clot. The cool sand, rough and granular, was a soothing balm for his hurt, a topical antiseptic and bandage in one. Next, he shoved his fingerless left hand into the remaining pile of rubble, corkscrewing his stumpy nubs into the stone again and again. A pestle grinding away in a mortar.

The motion was further agony; the corkscrew of his hand reopened the gaping holes where fingers had been, causing the ichor to flow freely again. His stunt with the glass spear had robbed the limb of much of its strength and had caused his knuckles to close improperly. Sometimes, with such an injury, the only way forward was actually a step back. In another few minutes the lacerations would close nice and neat, though he'd be short fingers on his left hand for a while yet. Likely, it'd take a trip to his bloodstone—lounging in the shade of Skip's knobby tree—to fully recover.

That was a worry for later.

He stole sporadic peeks at the wolves while he worked.

They'd settled down. No more pacing, now.

The remaining members of the pack had dragged over the corpses of their fallen kin, and sat in a rough circle, anteater-mouths sucking out the juices of their dead as they guarded the entryway. Watching them, Levi could only come to a single conclusion: they were afraid to enter the temple. That had to be it. Nothing else fit. The fact that the beasts remained also meant the wolves expected whatever was in the temple to drive Levi and the others out. Once more Levi's mind circled back to a question he didn't really want to answer:

*What could be in here that even Sprawl wolves didn't want to cross?*

## SIXTEEN:

### The Temple

"The hell you mean we're going in?" Chuck asked, eyes squinted, forehead wrinkled, incredulity thick on his face. "I ain't goin' in there." He pointed down the hallway disappearing into black. "I ain't no dummy. Those things out there"—he waved vaguely toward the wolves—"are scared to be in here. If they're scared, we should be scared, too, know what I'm sayin'?"

Ryder bobbed her head in agreement. "Gotta throw my vote with Chuck, Big Guy," she said. "Those things aren't gonna come in here, so it seems smarter to wait 'em out. I mean we don't know what's in here, but eventually those things will go away, then there we are."

Levi grunted and folded his arms. *Idiots*, both of them. He wanted to chastise them for their lack of forethought.

Outwait the wolves … Not likely. Scavengers like that could be very patient, especially since they had shelter and a ready supply of food. *Idiots*. He took a few deep breaths, pushing away the growing surge of irritation building up inside his chest. *Better a patient person than a warrior; one with self-control than one who takes a city*, he reminded himself.

"Wait for them to leave," he replied, flat and cold like the arctic tundra. "And what if they don't? How long will our supplies last? You've got water and food for a couple days, maybe? I'll survive, but I can't promise you two the same. Those creatures out there ... well, they *do* have food and water. More than enough for a few weeks I'd wager, so I can't imagine they'll be in any rush to leave."

"Yeah, but—" Chuck said.

Levi held up a massive clay mitt. "I'm not done. Even assuming those things leave, an assumption that could cost us everything, it doesn't change *anything*. We're out here for one reason, to find Professor Wilkie." He shot Ryder a level look. "If you want to figure out what happened to you, we need to find him. He's our lead. Our only lead. Since his body's not out there in the tents, it might mean he's inside here somewhere. And, even if he's not"—he shrugged beefy shoulders—"maybe this place can tell us a thing or two. Understand me?"

He pulled out the photo of the altar he'd lifted from the professor's work tent, unfolded it, and tossed it onto the floor, glossy side up. "Could be," he continued, "this temple is somehow related to whatever the Kobocks are up to."

Ryder solemnly considered the words, chewing at her bottom lip while her hands caressed the barrel of the snub-nosed pistol. "There's no other way?" she asked after a time.

Levi shook his cue-ball head. "Outworld's a big place, kid, but some things are buried too deep. We don't find this professor, we don't find the answers."

In his mind, he could see rain beating down from above as he crawled from a body-filled pit, lumbered to a concrete pill box, and saw the strange altar with its ruby eyes within.

"And we both need those answers."

"Alright," she said with only a slight pause, "I'm in."

"Yeah, but—" Chuck said again.

Levi ground his blunt teeth and lumbered toward the man. "You," he said tersely, "don't have any say. One, this isn't a democracy. Two, if it was you'd still be outvoted. And, three, you're my guide—I'm paying you to take me where I want to go, and where I want to go is that way." He gestured toward the hallway behind them. "Lead me or don't get paid."

Chuck frowned, muttering under his breath as he kicked at the stone floor with one foot, ornery and stubborn as a mule. "Fine, you lumpy, ass-ugly son of a bitch. But I expect better compensation. So make me an offer or I'll sit my black ass right here and take my chances."

The Mudman paused, jaw clenched, brows knitted. In general, he disapproved of sin in all its various forms—adultery, fornication, idolatry, murder—but greed, he found, was the most useful, rivaled only by vanity. For a few green bills, bills not even worth the paper they were printed on, people would risk bloody death. He didn't care about the money, and since this place was undoubtedly dangerous, having the guide along could be the difference between life and death. "Fair enough," he replied. "Double the rate. Twenty grand, even."

Chuck turned and surveyed the ancient stone walls, eyes boring into the temple as if he could somehow discern the threats ahead. "You need me more than I need you," he said, a shifty grin tracing his lips. "Twenty-five and I'm in. Otherwise"—he frowned, a look of complete indifference—"like I said, I'll take my chances with the wolves."

"You get twenty or I *throw* you to the wolves. Then we'll see how much you need me," Levi replied, stretching out his tree-trunk arms and popping his meaty neck with a *crack*. He didn't care about the money, but Chuck was a sneaky sort and fear could be nearly as good a motivator as greed. Both greed *and* fear would be best of all.

"Bullshit." Chuck's grip tightened around the massive pistol in his hand. "You wouldn't do that."

He glanced at Levi, studying the Mudman's deadpan features. "Come on, man, you're just playin', right? You wouldn't do it? No way." Levi flexed his good hand, fingers curling and uncurling. Chuck turned to Ryder, worry growing. "He's playin' right?"

Ryder gave him a waggle of her shoulders.

"Fine, twenty even, asshole. But I'll remember this bullshit." Chuck bent over his pack, unzipped the main compartment, and rummaged around for a heartbeat before liberating a pair of hefty black Mag Lights. He tossed one to Ryder, tucked the other under one arm, zipped up the pack, and hastily slung it over his shoulder.

"If I die, Mudman, I'm gonna haunt you. You hear that? I'll be pestering your lumpy, gray ass for the next millennium. Ain't nowhere gonna be safe. You sittin' on the john? I'll be there, tappin' at your shoulder. You tryin' to get your mack on with some other nasty-ass mud-woman, I'll be sittin' next to you tellin' her what a colossal tightwad dick head you are. And don't think I can't do it. I know people, Levi, I know people."

"Duly noted," Levi replied. "Now lead the way."

Chuck clicked on the flashlight and held it up in his left hand, his monster Desert Eagle never leaving his right. He frowned, shot Levi one last evil glare, then turned and stalked forward, muttering obscenities the whole while. Levi motioned Ryder to follow, while he took up the rear guard—just in case the wolves grew bold enough to venture into the temple's interior. Levi made his way over to the wall as they walked deeper into the building, ignoring the dancing beam of Chuck's flashlight, instead directing his senses into the blocky stone infrastructure composing the complex.

His awareness spread through the wall, into the floor below and ceiling above, but everything felt muffled, muted. Part of that was due simply to the foreignness of the earth here, but there was more to it as well. Something lived in this place—maybe the odd vegetation he'd see outside?—and it fought off the intrusion of his questing mind. After fifteen feet the tunnel turned into a deeply sloped walkway plunging deeper into the ground, deeper into blankness—the flashlights did next to nothing to banish the gloom.

For ten minutes, they treaded onward, Chuck in the lead, Ryder in the middle, Levi trailing behind, fingers brushing along stone.

The doorway loomed out of the murk in an instant, one moment absent, the next moment present.

A gateway, like nothing Levi had ever seen before. A pale-green metal wall, the color of split pea soup, spanned the entire length of the tunnel. He ran a hand over its surface. The metal looked like steel, but wasn't—the texture was off. Soft, fleshy, spongy, like a piece of overcooked tofu. Even with Levi's extensive history and long life, he couldn't put a name to the material. In the wall's center hung a massive door of overlapping and interlocking green metal plates, the kind of thing one might find in a high-tech military bunker.

Snaking vines—all tangled green, black flowers, and purple leaves—like the ones Levi had seen festooned along the exterior of the temple, ran over the surface of the gateway in a snarl of looping coils. The odd black flowers dotting each vine quivered and undulated as the party drew near, as if they could sense the uninvited approach of these new visitors. A control panel, made from the same green metal, *grew* out of the right-hand tunnel wall, tangles of pencil-thin roots spreading out all around it.

"The hell is this stuff?" Ryder asked, her voice quiet, but simultaneously too loud.

"One giant pain in the ass," Chuck replied, making sure he was well away from wall and door. "This right here is why I didn't want to go in. Never seen nothing like this, not even back in the Hub. Even the Cult of Akroid ain't got nothin' like this—and those dudes be doin' all kinds of wonky shit."

The Mudman ignored both, pushing past Ryder and heading over to the control panel. "I'll take a look," he said absentmindedly.

He drew near, but didn't touch it, not yet. The panel—an inset rectangle, two feet high by a foot wide—did indeed appear to *grow* out of the wall, as if it were organic instead of a contraption of metal or science. Raised nodes ran over the surface in a series of columns like an oversized keypad, though each node was marked with blue fluorescent glyphs Levi didn't recognize or understand. A small display screen of sorts—dark and lifeless—sat at the top, covered with a gooey and viscous membrane.

Levi extended a fat finger—

"The hell you doin', Boss-man?" Chuck whispered, an edge to the words. "What if that thing's like a bomb or something? You gonna blow us all up. I know you two got business in this place, but I'm tellin' you, we're better off with the wolves."

Levi pressed one of the nodes.

Caution, though usually the prudent move, wouldn't see them through this temple. And they *needed* to make it through this temple. The button depressed beneath his finger with a muted *click*.

A cacophony of sounds followed, the glyph-marked nodules blinking on amidst a flurry of *beeps* and *blips*, the sound of a massive computer humming to life. The flower-covered vines lining the green gateway slithered and retreated from the rounded doorway even as a circular porthole in the center of the door rotated and slid open, revealing a black-petaled flower bud the size of a basketball.

"Get back," Levi barked, watching, captivated as the bud *bloomed*, its petals unfurling to reveal a black glass bauble coated in jellied-mucus. His warning, of course, was entirely unnecessary: Ryder and Chuck had already slunk back five or six feet, positioning themselves behind Levi with pistols drawn and pointed. Good to know where they stood on things.

With a *squee* and a *plouck*, both sounds wet and throaty, the black orb tore itself free and hovered in the air, an erratic series of lights blinking and disappearing within its depths. After a few brief seconds the blinking subsided, replaced by a pale white glow which emanated from the orb's center, lending it the appearance of a monstrous floating eye.

Levi wasn't sure what to do here.

In his dealings with humanity he tried to be yielding and patient—feigning the emotion he knew he was supposed to have. After all, you couldn't very well smash those who cut you off in the grocery line. With the preternatural, however, his normal tactic was blunt and to the point: like a hammer driving home a nail. His natural inclination was to simply smash this floating *thing*, whatever it was, and be done with it. But that didn't seem wise. *Wait.* Wait and see whether it was a threat. Then he would smash what needed smashing. It seemed prudent to wait, at least for a moment.

The orb spoke. A soft and soothing female voice, calm and professional like the answering machine on an automated phone line, spouting off words Levi couldn't understand.

*"Lindi glaong poord ragut lingosuum ka ni ..."* A pause, the glowing light within shifting once more from white to a pale yellow. *"Tervetuloa ilmoittakaa kieliasetuksen nyt,"* it said this time. After a beat, its color shifted once more, now maroon. *"Āpakā svāgata hai aba bhāṣā varīyatā kā saṅkēta dēṁ ..."* A merry orange, like a fading campfire. *"Grata placet indicare lingua potissimum nunc ..."*

"That last one was Latin," Levi said as the orb once more ceased its frantic gibberish-speak and shifted to a bright indigo. "Pretty sure. But it was talking too fast to catch everything. *Grata* means *welcome* and *lingua* means *language.*"

"That right?" Chuck said. "And I suppose you're some kinda Latin major? Maybe I should just start callin' you Professor Mudman?"

Levi held up a big hand, *Hold your tongue.* The orb had shifted to a soft blue, the shade of a clear, crisp winter morning, and the blinking lights were back now, throbbing and pulsing beneath the steady glow.

"Thank you for selecting your language preference: American English, circa early twenty-first century," it said, perfect and unaccented. "My name is Siphonei, and I will assist you to the best of my ability. Welcome to holding facility C138-47, owned and operated by Atlantis Correction Systems since 2187 GE. This facility is classified as DJ-791. Highest-level security clearance is required to proceed ..." It halted its perfunctory greeting, internal lights whirling once more. "An internal database scan has detected major operational malfunctions in critical systems. Temporary security clearance has been authorized for all visiting personnel."

The spongy metal door split open with a hiss, door panels retracting to reveal some sort of checkpoint or, perhaps, guard station.

The room itself bore the same look as the rest of the temple: ancient stone, old and weathered. This room, however, had also been retrofitted with more green, spongy computer terminals. Here the thick vines snaked throughout the room, while a series of chairs *sprouted* from the floor—living furniture, sculpted of thick greenery and festooned with hundreds of purple-black flowers. In the center of the room, inlaid into the floor, was a massive ring of gold, twenty feet in diameter. Runes and glyphs ran along the outside edge of the golden ring.

It looked, to Levi, like a summoning circle—the kind of thing a mage might use to punch a hole in the fabric of the universe and call something from Outworld. Or, Levi supposed, it could be a containment ring. Whatever it was, the Mudman felt the thrum of arcane power radiating from the circle in waves, the tension and static of a downed power line filling the air. No, he didn't know what it was, but he wanted nothing to do with it.

"Please proceed to the visitation checkpoint ahead for scanning, approval, and admittance to holding facility C138-47 proper," the orb said, before floating forward, into the guard chamber.

Levi moved, not to follow, but rather to block the doorway so Chuck and Ryder couldn't. He knew they needed to venture in deeper—he'd been the one to urge them onto this course—but none of this sat easy in his prodigious gut. None of this added up. A holding facility all the way out in the middle of the Sprawl? Why? An ancient temple, outfitted with an organic technology that made even the most advanced technomancy in the Hub look crude and outdated? Not to mention the golden circle.

He was unsure here. He hated feeling unsure. Once again an irrational impulse to start laying into things with his fists and feet jolted through his system. There was an elegant simplicity in destruction. He scooted back a step on instinct only to find Ryder elbowing her way past Chuck and slipping up behind his outstretched arm.

"I've got an idea," she said, "so how about you hang back and let me take a stab here."

The Mudman didn't remove the limb blocking her way. "An idea. Like your idea about outwaiting the wolves? You're a Rube. The least qualified person here to deal with any of this."

"That so, asshole? 'Cause I'm thinking I have just as much experience with ancient Sprawl temples as you do. Or am I wrong?" She lifted her chin, staring down her nose at him.

Levi said nothing, because he couldn't. He knew far more about the arcane than she did, but *technically* she was right.

"Yeah, that's about what I thought," she continued. "And I may still be some dumb Rube— everyone seems more than happy to remind me of that—but you, dude, are the least qualified out of anyone here when it comes to talking to *anybody* about *anything*. Literally anyone else would be better for the job. Those fuckin' Sprawl wolves would be a step up. So back up and give me a shot. I'll let you know when it's clobbering time. Cool?"

"Damn, you got owned, homie," Chuck said, then broke into a muted chuckle, which he tried to stifle with the back of his hand.

Levi growled, an inarticulate bubble rising up from his chest. His urge to crush something intensified as he watched Chuck cackle. *Patience.* "What's your big plan?"

"To ask questions, Bill Nye." She turned away from him and regarded the floating orb. "Siphonei, you said you could assist us. I'm assuming that means you can answer some questions, right?"

The orb wavered as though considering the words, then zipped back over, hanging in the air a few feet in front of Levi. "Please wait one moment while I scan my memory bank …" Once more its internal lights flared and blinked. "Analysis: Seventy-two percent of memory cells have sustained damage. To rectify this, I've deleted the bulk of nonessential data files in order to maintain facility operations. Twenty-four percent of data requires a *threat determination scan* before accessing. Additionally, thirteen percent of the remaining data has been marked as 'Classified, Top Secret' by the warden—only High-Warden Lir-Thildo may access this material. I have clearance to share any other available information. What questions do you have?"

Ryder arched an eyebrow. Much as it made him uncomfortable, Levi knew she made a good point. A game of wits, or even a simple unscripted conversation could be taxing for him, and perhaps the computer could offer some valuable insights. He lowered his arm and edged to the right, making room for the girl. She offered him a thin, tight-lipped smile then shuffled forward with a curt "thanks."

"You said this place is a holding cell, so what're you holding?" she asked.

"Holding facility C138-47, code name *The Abyss,* was established in 2187 GE—sixteen years after the Cataclysm—and houses one inmate, *Dibeininax Ayosainondur Daimuyon*, the Eternally Cursed One."

Ryder reached into her coat pocket and pulled loose the glossy photo Levi had swiped from the professor's camp, the picture of the ruby-eyed altar.

"Would this freaky-looking son of a bitch be the Eternally Cursed One?"

A flash of red light shot out from the orb, brushing over the out held picture. "That is affirmative." She shot Levi an *I-told-you-so* glance.

"What can you tell us about this inmate of yours?" she asked after a second.

"That information is classified. Please ask another question."

"You mentioned something called the Cataclysm?" she prodded, hardly missing a beat.

"That information was deemed unessential to facility operations and has been purged from my system," the computer replied. "Please ask another question."

She paused, tapping a finger against her cheek in thought. "Can you tell us anything else about the facility?"

"What would you like to know?"

"Other than the main entrance, is there another way out?"

"Damn, this girl's on point," Chuck whispered from behind. Levi held up a hand to shush the man.

"Yes," the computer answered. "A secondary, emergency exit exists in the inner sanctum located at the top of the complex."

"What about booby traps? Anything we should watch out for?"

"That information is classified. Please ask another question."

"What about you? What are you? You just some kinda computer or what?" Ryder continued, unfazed.

"Not in the sense that you understand this word," the orb replied. "I was once a human administrator. Now, I am a bio processor. My personality was modified by the head facility administrator, and my memory banks and processors are stored in an organic neural network, embedded in the genetically modified biomass known as *tacca chantrieri gigantis,* which spans the facility."

Levi stole a look at the vines and flowers running riot over the walls and the strange chairs. "The plants?" he asked. "They're a part of you?"

"The plants are me. Each flower is a part of my essence, and all are interconnected through the vines running throughout facility."

Ryder nudged him in the side with the tip of her elbow. "I'm running the show, remember?"

"That's monstrous," Levi continued, voice rising. "You mean to tell me someone stripped you of your personality and identity and turned you into a computer program!" By the end he was yelling, arms and hands quivering in borderline rage.

"Your statement is flawed, but essentially correct," the computer—no, not a computer, a woman—said.

The brand carved into his chest flared, crying out at the injustice that had happened here. Perhaps this computer was no longer a human, but she had been a human, and someone had stripped her down and stolen away her life. Worse than that even, they hadn't simply murdered her, they'd forced her into an unending existence of loneliness and service. Stripped her of humanity and made her into a slave.

"Who did this to you?" he asked, hoping he could somehow bring reckoning to the responsible party.

"Atlantis Correction Systems," she replied.

Ryder placed a pale hand on his shoulder and squeezed—he glanced down, lips pulled back in a scowl. She stared up at him with a sad smile, her usual attitude replaced by concern. That look—vulnerable, open, sweet—pulled Levi back from the edge of his bloodlust, grounded him in the reality of their situation. Something terrible had happened to the woman trapped in the machine, but it was a wrong committed thousands of years ago by a people long-since dead. Better to concern himself with the affairs of the living. Like Ryder.

"Has anyone else come through here?" Ryder asked after a moment, her tough-girl mask back in place. "We're looking for a guy named Owen Wilkie. He's a researcher, a professor. His camp's right out front."

"Yes, several visitors have accessed the facility in the last three days." The orb buzzed: a holographic image of a man suddenly floated in the center of the wide golden circle in the next chamber. Tall and thin—emaciated in his gauntness—with a pinched face, sharp features, dark skin, and spastic gray hair running out of control. He wore thin square spectacles, a mountaineer's jacket, khaki pants, and heavy trail boots perfect for desert trekking. "Mage Owen Wilkie is currently on site, but his location is concealed from me."

"Why?" Levi asked. "Why is his position concealed, I mean?"

"Mage Owen Wilkie attempted to trigger the prisoner release mechanisms. He has been deemed a threat to operational security and has been slated for expulsion from the facility. Termination protocol F13-5 has been initiated. Mage Wilkie is using a complex conjuration to block himself from my senses."

"Whoa, just hold up a hot-minute," Chuck said, pitching in for the first time. "Termination protocol F13-5? So far this has been some real interesting bullshit, but now we're talking about termination protocols and shit? I ain't down with that. Sounds like the kinda thing that'd get your ass smoked. So just what we talkin' about here, C-3PO?"

"My program designation is A-74J, not C-3PO," she replied evenly—the joke clearly lost on her. "Furthermore, termination protocol F13-5 is restricted material. To access this information, you must proceed with the *threat determination scan.* To advance further into the facility, you must also proceed with the *threat determination scan*. Would you like to proceed at this time?"

"Naw, I'm good," Chuck replied, shaking his head. "I ain't fixin' to take no scan. Probably shoot me with lasers, that kinda thing. I'm good right here." He pointed to the ground and nodded.

"I just have one more question," Levi replied, "and then, yes, we will *all* be prepared to take this scan." He glanced over his colossal shoulder and shot a grumpy look at his disgruntled guide. "Twenty grand, remember?"

Chuck flipped him the bird, crossed his arms, then rolled his eyes and nodded.

The Mudman turned back to the suspended orb. "You said several visitors accessed the facility," he continued. "Who else has accessed this complex?"

"That information has been deemed restricted by an adjunct administrator. Adjunct administrator NAME REDACTED has flagged this question. Your party has been redesignated as *possibly hostile*. Proceed immediately for a *threat determination scan* or containment protocol AJ29-1 will initiate." Around them the vines began to slither in restless motion, creeping down from the walls and pushing themselves across the floor, drawing closer every second. "Step into the golden circle located in the center of the floor. You have ten seconds to comply. Thank you."

## *SEVENTEEN:*

## Containment Protocol

The vines littering the room stirred, the flowers unfurling, petals curling back to reveal an inner circle of serrated piranha-teeth. Each flower also sprouted a series of thin, withering tentacles covered in wickedly hooked barbs of bone.

*"Ten ..."* the computer said placidly. Pleasantly, even.

Levi pivoted, locking Chuck squarely in view. "Get in the circle, now." He hooked a broad thumb toward the other room.

*"Nine ..."*

"Naw, I'm good right here, bro. How's 'bout you go first since this is your thing. I'll just cool my heels, see how everything shakes out."

*"Eight ..."*

"I can do it," Ryder offered, edging closer to the circle.

Levi lifted up a monster arm in response, stretching it across the doorway, barring her access. "No. I don't know why, but whatever those Kobocks were up to—you're a part of it. If something happens ... well, we need you more than we need Chuck."

*"Seven ..."*

"That's fucked up, man." Chuck raised his pistol while slowly, almost imperceptibly, creeping back toward the way they'd come. "Doesn't have to go down like this, Levi. We still good, but I ain't gonna be the first one in there. My momma didn't raise no dummy. You should go. Something bad happens you'll survive it—you got that whole indestructible, rock-man thing goin' on."

"*Six* ... Warning, containment protocol AJ29-1 will commence in five seconds. Please proceed with your scan."

"Listen, man," Chuck continued, "I've seen some of the crazy-ass shit you've come back from, Levi. Me, though? I'm just a highly-gifted and extraordinarily-good-lookin' halfie. But fragile, like. The wee folk—my people—we're not all that physically resilient."

"*Four* ... "

"If something happens," Levi replied even as he shoved Ryder out of the way and slid toward the slowly retreating halfie, "I'll only be able to help if I'm outside the containment circle. And I *will* help, unlike you."

"*Three* ... "

"Oh is that right? You got something to say to me, *Dirt-Clod*?"

"Yeah," Levi growled, taking a shambling step forward. "You're worried about you. Only you. Something goes wrong while I'm stuck in there? You're not going to stick your neck out to save me. Or her." He glanced at Ryder. She was trying to slip past him. He placed one hand on her shoulder and shoved her back a few paces. "Mind me, Ryder."

*"Two ..."*

"Yeah, well, I ain't no hero, man," Chuck said. "You can't pay me enough to step into that containment circle. Thing'll probably toast my ass with gamma radiation. End up like the black Hulk—that shit's no good with me. Being a leprechaun and a pimp is hard enough."

*"One ...* Warning, containment protocol AJ29-1 imminent."

Levi blurred in an eyeblink—the time for talk was over. Chuck's gun roared; a blinding flash of light belched from the end of the hand cannon, but the shot went wide—though not quite wide enough. The round grazed Levi's outstretched arm, tearing open a fresh slash along the outside of his bicep, before careening into the wall. Levi ignored the cut, bulldozing into Chuck, arms lashing out and wrapping around the man like a pair of pythons.

In a single smooth motion, the Mudman pivoted, twisting at the hips and flipping the involuntary lab rat through the air and into the golden circle. Chuck screamed, his arms pinwheeling in frantic circles, his legs kicking out. Despite his size, though, Chuck was quick and agile, tucking into a tight roll at the last minute, which quickly brought him back to his feet, injury free.

*"Zero ...* Containment protocol AJ29-1 initi—" the computer cut off mid-word. "Thank you for your compliance."

"You son of a bitch," Chuck shouted. "I'm gonna get you for this, Levi."

Light and noise filled the air like a bomb burst, cutting off Chuck's rant as an electric-blue wall ruptured from the floor: a circular holding cell trapping him inside.

"This is so fucked up, bro!" Chuck yelled over the low buzz of the machinery. "Seriously, Levi, how you gonna do me like that? How you gonna do me like that?! I thought we were cool."

"Calm down," Levi replied, keeping his voice as even as he could muster. "Like I said, someone needed to go first. And if something bad happens, I'll have a much better chance of rescuing you than you would have of rescuing me. Mostly because you wouldn't rescue me. When the Sprawl wolves had me pinned down, who came back?" He pointed at Ryder. "She came for me. Some Rube girl, while you hightailed it as fast as your legs would carry you."

"Whatevs, man." He folded his arms, eyes squinting against the harsh light surrounding him. "I'm a guide, not a bodyguard. Not that you need a bodyguard. What your chunky ass needs is a gym membership. I"—he thumped his chest with one fist—"agreed to take you where you wanted to go, not be a guinea pig."

"Please be quiet and still while the scan commences," Siphonei said, her orb drifting toward the closed off circle.

Chuck pointed at Levi, a scowl on his face. "We aren't done talking' about this, Mudman. This bullshit is jacked up, and you know it. You owe me."

Levi stared, grinding his teeth, brow furrowed in thought.

"*Threat determination scan* commencing, now," the orb said. The electric-blue walls shimmered and pulsed, the light a spastic strobe flickering on and off, washing over Chuck and leaving blurry afterimages tattooed on Levi's eyes.

Ryder edged up next to him, a scowl marring her face. "He's right," she said. "You didn't have any right to do that to him. Maybe someone needed to go first, but it wasn't your place to force him. I volunteered, and despite what you think, I'm not some brainless, weak *girl* that needs protecting. I killed that Kobo on the road, remember?

"Slashed him open with a piece of broken glass. And you didn't save me from the Sprawl wolves. I saved you. Not the other way around. If you really want to stop being a fuckin' monster, start by treating people the way you'd like to be treated, asshole. Pretty sure that nugget's in your Bible somewhere. And just so we're clear, don't you ever lay hands on me like that again, dick." She turned away, refusing to look at him, instead watching Chuck through the pulsating light.

Annoyance flared through the Mudman, burning at the edge of his mind and searing his nerves raw. What right did this girl have to correct him, to rebuke him? After everything he'd done for her? Saving her from the Deep Downs, rescuing her at the hospital, trekking all over Outworld to find her some answers. After a moment, however, Levi realized that wasn't really what bothered him. What really bothered him was that he didn't know if she was right or not. Had throwing Chuck into the circle been a mistake?

The Mudman wasn't sure.

Other than murder, morality was still something of a gray area for Levi. Most of the big commandments

Levi understood, at least in theory: Don't steal. Don't commit adultery, remember to honor thy parents—both non-issues for Levi. Honor God, respect His name, and hold no other gods; these things, at least, Levi could do. With everything else, though, Levi was often at a loss. Pastor Steve's voice rang in his head, the words of the Good Book booming, echoing Ryder's admonishment: *Do unto others as you would have them do unto you.*

True, he wouldn't want someone to do to him what he'd done to Chuck, but, as he thought through the scenario again, he could see no other way. Despite her protests, Ryder was his responsibility and the least capable of defending herself against a physical or supernatural threat, so it didn't make sense for her to go first. And if something went wrong, Levi could obliterate the machinery scattered throughout the room, likely saving Chuck—but only if he stood outside the containment circle.

Was it possible the smart choice wasn't the right choice?

He just wasn't sure …

The manic flashing finally ceased, and the blue light encircling Chuck faded and vanished. "The scan is complete," the orb intoned. "Your bio-scan is clean and you have been classified as a *non-threat*. Visitor access is granted. Please wait while the rest of your party is assessed."

Chuck hustled out of the circle, eager as a high schooler darting away at the final bell, and hefted his piece, aiming at Levi. "Another five grand for that stunt, you hear me? Another five grand or I'm walkin' away right now. I know you're a weird son of a bitch, so I won't hold that against you, but you owe me something."

"You shot me"—Levi pointed to the thin line running along his arm—"seems like that should count for something."

"Please, that's a scratch. You walkin' around without fingers on your left hand, dude. No fingers and you gonna come at me, talkin' about how I grazed you. *Please*. You coulda killed me—"

"But I didn't," Levi offered.

"Coulda killed me. So I'm thinkin' I might actually start shootin' for real unless I get some compensation for my trauma. I think that's fair, don't you?"

Levi grunted and nodded his head. "Alright, twenty-five," he replied. "And Chuck, for what it's worth …" He hesitated, not comfortable proceeding. "I'm sorry I threw you in there against your will. Might be that wasn't the most Christian thing of me to do."

"Not the most Christian thing," Chuck muttered. "Listen, you just make sure that cash-money hits my bank account and we'll be straight."

"The next member of your party must now proceed to the circle for scanning," Siphonei said, implacable and unmoved by their personal drama.

"I'll go," Ryder offered, stepping forward.

Levi reached out and grabbed her arm as gently as he could manage.

She glared at him. "Thought we just talked about this? I'm not a glass bauble that needs protecting. You had no right to do what you did to Chuck, and you have no right to stop me from doing this. This is *my* choice. Understand? Now let go of my arm."

Humans were so complicated. Couldn't she see he was doing this for her own good?

"Let go, Levi."

The Mudman sighed.

He'd made a mistake with Chuck, now it was time for him to learn from it. He released his clamp-like grip around her arm. Besides, chances were good the computer would pass her right through. If Chuck, a halfie, had gotten through, then it stood to reason Ryder would be fine, too. If the computer was going to flag anyone as a threat, it'd be Levi—he with his shady past and golden blood, with his murderous mandate and his soulless body.

The girl took a deep breath, straightened her back, and squared her shoulders as if she were walking to her doom, and knew it, but was going to meet that doom on her own terms. She moved with a confident step, but Levi was not so easily fooled. He could see the faint tremble in her hands and knees. Brave face or no, she was scared.

Ryder stepped into the circle and moved to its center, wrapping her hands around her middle. As with Chuck, the electric-blue wall snapped into place a handful of seconds later, and the strobing flashes began in earnest, *vump, vump, vump, vump*—

The blue strobes turned an angry red like an infected wound, while the teeth-and-tentacle-clad flowers raised their ugly faces into the air and offered a jarring blare of sound, which had to be a security alarm.

The orb zipped around, vibrating in frenzied spasms as if it weren't actually prepared for whatever it'd found. "Alert! Alert! Alert!" Siphonei screamed, genuine, and very human, fear washing through the orb's words. "A viable homunculus has been detected." It rounded on Ryder, its internal light bursting into a vivid red. "You are compromised. Visitor access is denied. You have been reclassified as *threat, severe.* Containment protocol AJ29-1 will commence momentarily." The ground trembled beneath Levi's clay feet, stones grinding and shifting as puffs of ancient dust swirled into the air. "Lockdown procedure initiating. Repeat, lockdown procedure initiating."

Levi wasn't sure what was happening—the shifting ground disturbed his earth-bound senses—but he knew it wasn't good. He needed to get Ryder out of that circle whatever the cost. She was the key to everything. He couldn't lose her, not now, not when he was so close to unraveling his own murky past. He'd been denied the knowledge of his own creation for seventy years; he refused to be denied again. He burst into action, bolting toward the containment circle, still surrounded by a sheet of red light, and threw his bulk against the barrier, fists outthrust.

He slammed into the shield like a Mack truck.

His flesh sizzled and popped on contact, energy flowing into him like a blast of lightning, before batting him away with a renewed pulse of force. He smashed into the floor with a *crack*, the ancient stones beneath fracturing from his mass. What a punch. He lay on the floor, struggling to catch a breath, then pushed himself up onto shaky, unstable feet, his skin dry and smoking. His head throbbed and his body ached like someone had run him down with a bulldozer. Check. Wasn't going to try that maneuver again.

Someone placed a hand on his arm. Levi glanced down with blurry eyes.

Chuck.

"Thing just owned your ass. What'd we do now?!" He yelled his questions over the grinding rumble of the floor. "How we gonna get Ryder out?"

Levi thought about it, but only for the briefest instant. Ryder had been right before: he wasn't good with words or talking, but he was good at breaking things. And this situation was right up his alley. He grimaced and pointed at the circle. "I'm going to smash that thing into little pieces, then I'm going to buy you some time. Get Ryder, and get away from here, away from that orb. Don't wait for me. Don't come back for me. Make for the emergency exit if you can. I'll find you."

Without waiting for a reply, Levi hurled himself into the air, an inbound artillery shell ready to explode.

## *EIGHTEEN:*

### **Break for It**

L evi flew forward, this time aiming *not* for the impenetrable energy shield, but rather the ground just outside the golden circle. The front door, so to speak, was locked up nice and tight, but with most summoning and binding circles—like the one holding Ryder—there was usually a backdoor: the circle itself, which generated and maintained the energy field, might be vulnerable. If he did enough structural damage to the binding ring, it *might* break the construct holding her in place. Had he been inside the circle, such a task would border on the impossible, but from outside his chances of success were … well, not good, but better.

His hands shifted as he came down, massive pickaxe blades forming in their place. He *thudded* onto the deck, using his considerable mass to drive both picks into the rough stone below. Jagged chucks of rock spun through the air, accompanied by a hail of gravel as his hands beat out a steady rhythm, pounding away like the pumping gears of a truck engine. The orb zipped over to his side, circling about, surveying the damage.

"Please cease your activity immediately," the orb said. "You are diminishing the structural integrity of the containment circle. Status report: Integrity compromised by thirty-four percent."

Levi ignored the chirping machine, his mind bent to his task. Each blow fractured the stone further, irregular cracks radiating toward the circle, snaking underneath the ring—the ring held, but wouldn't for much longer. Each blow delivered up more rock chips and, in turn, widened the fissure in the floor.

Something wrapped around Levi's leg, entwining his calf like a python, constricting as it worked its way up his leg, trying to crush the limb like an empty soda can. He stole a peek even as his arms flew back and forth, hammering away: the vines were everywhere now—no longer confined to the walls and overgrown chairs—crawling across the floor with life and purpose. A thick cable of greenery had already wound itself around his left leg, all the way from foot to knee, and every second it inched higher. The flowers clamped down, driving their circular mouths in and shaking their heads like a dog working at a chew toy.

"Status report: Structural integrity compromised by seventy-two percent," the orb said. "Please cease your activity, now, or you will be redesignated as *threat, extreme.* This will result in the immediate activation of termination protocol F13-5: you will be summarily executed. Please comply now."

Another choking vine twisted its way up his right leg, digging fleshy, probing tendrils beneath his skin, their barbed hooks tearing directly into the muscle below. The memory came in a flash, an instant that lived inside of an eyeblink:

*I whimper, though it hurts. My throat is coarse and raspy from screaming, but I can't keep it in. I strain against the leather bonds securing my hands and feet to the table, checking them for the hundredth time, hoping this time they'll be loose. They aren't. Every movement sends a renewed wave of red-hot agony—like glowing fire irons embedded in my bones—but I can't stop fighting. Not now. I look over at the table opposite my own: my brother's there, strapped down just like me. He's not moving right now, though. Unconscious from the last round of "experiments."*

*Experiments, what a joke. Blackest joke I ever heard. Torture is what it is, just gussied up and made to sound better.*

*I watch my brother, the rise and fall of his chest. He looks terrible, like a train wreck. He looks like what's left of a cow, too stupid to move off the tracks when a freight line rolls through. He was a handsome devil, once upon a time. Now? Now he's thin like you wouldn't believe, his ribs pressing up against parchment-thin skin. His hair, all gone, buzzed off. His face swollen, bruised, battered. Ross looks twenty years older than when we got here, easy. I can hardly recognize him anymore, and that's sayin' something since we've got the same mug. Twins, me and him.*

*Of all the terrible things they've done to us, I know my brother misses his looks the most. Stupid, maybe, but no one could accuse Ross of being smart. Handsome, sure, but not too bright. He was one hell of an actor, though, and I've never met an actor alive who wasn't a little vain. It's in their blood. Looking at him now, passed out, he almost* looks *handsome again. The worry and fear momentarily disappearing, taking away the creases and the hard lines.*

*I hear a noise, the creak of a door. Could be the doctor coming back. He's out now. Lunchtime, I'm thinking. Though it could just as easy be dinner. Or breakfast. I don't know anymore, though I'm sure it must be one of those. The doctor rarely leaves for anything else ... not even sleep, it seems like. But the fat bastard never misses a meal. I can always tell because the smell of food, sometimes salty, other times tangy and sweet, clings to him like cologne. It sticks to his white coat and soft hands. I can smell the food even over the constant, coppery scent of blood, which is like background noise for my nose.*

*Still, I can't be certain of the time. Seconds, hours, days: they all blur on the edges. No clock here. No natural light. My hours are marked only by fitful rest, the comings and goings of the doctor, and pain.*

*God, so much pain. Truth be told, I wish I were dead. I'm lookin' forward to it.*

*I steal a look down at my belly, as if I need a reminder: the skin on my abdomen is peeled back and pinned in place with stainless-steel surgical pins. Most of the skin on my chest is gone too. Flayed. I whimper again. I catch sight of my right leg and want to hurl—at least I can't feel it anymore, which is a blessing, believe you me. The doctor stole it, chopped it off and replaced it with my brother's right leg. That fat sack of shit in the lab coat wanted to see if whole limb transplant between twins was possible.*

*I push the visions of my own mutilated body away, force them from my mind. No point thinkin' on it. I fight against my restraints, flexing arms and legs, going through the same motions I've gone through a million times since they strapped me down. Me and my brother, we're gonna die here, no doubt about it. I hope Ross goes in his sleep so he can die looking his sharpest. Vain as hell, I know, but it'd make him happy. Me though? I'm gonna fight until they cut the beatin' heart outta my chest. Ross has his vanity and I've got my pride. And that dirty Kraut-eater can't take my pride. Can't make me stop fighting.*

*He can take my arms and legs, cut me open like a side of beef, but he can't take my pride from me—that's something I have to give away, and I refuse.*

The vision went as quickly as it came, flashing and retreating with the speed of a synapse firing, and in its wake Levi's brand flared to new life, burning with the pain of that poor man's wounds. The vines, with their deadly flowers and digging tentacles, wouldn't stop him. He channeled rage, tapping into it like a drug and riding it like a wave. He brought his hands up above his head, letting his dual pickaxes blur and melt together, leaving one massive pick in their wake. A roar ripped its way free from Levi's throat as he brought the tool whipping through the air, crashing into the floor with a *BOOM* that rattled the walls.

Slabs of stone bucked and cracked, a personal earthquake rippling through the room, though partially masked by the already heaving floor.

The effect, however, was unmistakable: A fissure, thick and jagged as a lightning bolt, shot forward, shattering a portion of the golden arc. The energy emanating from the ring guttered and died in a heartbeat, here one second, gone the next. Ryder was doubled over in the center of the circle, gun clutched in one hand, while her other hand groped at her center, as if she were trying to hold her insides, inside. Levi didn't know what the power field had done to her, but she didn't look good. Her skin was too pale and sweat matted her hair and rolled down her face. She looked like a terminal cancer patient on their last leg.

The computer's words replayed in Levi's mind: *"A viable homunculus has been detected ... A viable homunculus has been detected."* Something was wrong with her.

*Homunculus.*

Things were starting to coalesce in Levi's mind, a rough picture taking shape. Ryder's inhuman hunger. The reason why Ryder had been left alive, when all the other captives had perished. The way she clutched her stomach, like a pregnant mother subconsciously cradling her unborn child. Even the words from the note made a certain sense: *She is the first viable subject in thirty years.*

The Kobocks hadn't taken something *out* of Ryder, they'd put something *into* her. A homunculus. Though Levi wasn't as well-versed in the mystic or occult as many who ran in the preternatural circles, he knew *exactly* what a homunculus was—he'd read about such creatures many, many times. First described in *De Natura Rerum* by a fifteenth century mage and alchemist, homunculi were artificially created vessels, humanoid in appearance but lacking the divine spark of God. Levi knew the term because golems were considered to be such creatures, too.

Ryder was playing host to something, a manufactured monster using her body as a hatchery. Levi didn't know how this thing was connected to him, but he was certain there were no coincidences. Far too many similarities for that.

Chuck darted into view, sweeping into the circle, hooking hands beneath Ryder and hoisting her up to her feet. He paused just long enough to look at Levi over one shoulder, eyes wide as he watched more vines winding their way over the Mudman, pulling him to the floor.

"Run! I'll find you!" Levi shouted. Chuck nodded, bent low, and scooped Ryder up, flinging her over one shoulder as he broke for the hallway at the far side of the room. With the pair of them gone, hopefully safe, Levi turned his attention fully to his own predicament. Pickaxes were great for stone, but lousy against weeds, so it was time for a change. His right hand—fully operational—reverted to normal, while the left hand—still lacking fingers—morphed into a wicked, curved-edged scythe.

Then he went to work.

His right hand pulled vines taut, his left hand flashed in a blur, carving away great swathes of tangled greenery. Splashes of golden ichor flew free with every vine, but Levi paid them no mind. Pain was irrelevant, only escape mattered. Slowly he fought his way back— first for inches, then for feet—his progress a seemingly Sisyphean task.

*Grab, pull, slash, hack, repeat.*

Chunks of vegetation rained down in sprays of sludgy green.

Vines shrieked and slithered, a writhing ball of snakes enraged at his defiance, lashing out to ensnare him further. Levi kept his mind to the work.

He would fight.

*Grab, pull, slash, hack, repeat.*

They could take his arms and legs, but they couldn't make him stop fighting.

*Grab, pull, slash, hack, repeat.*

He tore creeping barbs from his arms and legs. They lost their tenuous hold, and he yanked free the roots wriggling beneath his skin like IV-tubing.

Greenery flailed in response, tentacle-vines whipping through the air as black flowers toppled to the ground, rudely shorn off by Levi's impromptu gardening shear.

The Mudman backpedaled as he worked, ponderously making his way for the connecting hallway Chuck and Ryder had taken, the one which descended deeper into the bowels of this prison. It took another handful of minutes to break into the clear, but as soon as he managed the deed, he turned and hurled himself toward the exit.

"Alert! Alert! Alert!" he heard from behind— Siphonei calling to no one. "Hostile threats have infiltrated the facility, all hands alert. Facility lockdown protocol LG19-B3, activated. Termination protocol F13-5, activated. All hands be advised, lesser guardians have been activated. Report to your workstations and stand by with your credentials for verification."

The ground rumbled beneath Levi as if the whole building were protesting his intrusion—he spun just in time to find a spongy metal door sliding free from the ancient stone wall, cutting him off from the entry room with its deadly vegetation. Sealing him in. He reached back and ran a hand over the surface of the door. It gave slightly beneath the pressure of his palm— tender like a raw cut of beef—but there was also something rigid and unyielding buried within. He didn't *want* to go back that way, but now he didn't even have the option. Deeper into the prison was the only way now, and if he couldn't find that emergency exit, this place might well be his prison, too.

A very disconcerting thought.

Still, Levi was not one to dwell too long or hard on such things.

If a door closed well and good—in this case both literally and metaphorically—there was rarely any point in trying to pry it open. Just put your nose to the grindstone and press on.

He wheeled about, eyes scanning the passageway. The hallway he found himself in was lit with murky purple light, leaking from circular light fixtures affixed to the walls at ten-foot intervals. The light was weak, sporadic, but would manage fine, though he hoped Chuck and Ryder had managed to hang on to their flashlights. He could navigate with his stone sense, but they would have a mite more trouble.

He hunkered down on his haunches, drawing a few deep breaths as he wrestled with the bone-deep weariness—both from his injuries and his stretching absence from Inworld—eating at him. Every second he languished was a second wasted, a second more for Chuck and Ryder to hopelessly entangle themselves in danger.

*It would be nice to rest, though, just a little.*

Unfortunately, niceties such as rest were for people with time and options. He had neither. With a grumble he pushed himself up, fatigued legs carrying him onward. After a few scant minutes of dreary trudging, a four-way juncture loomed before him—tunnels shooting off left, right, and straight ahead.

He glanced around, eyes scanning high and low, looking for any sign of Chuck and Ryder's passing, intentional or not. He'd been hoping one of the two would've had the presence of mind to leave behind a marker—a piece of trash, say, or a dirty sock—indicating which way they'd gone. But no.

Nothing. He needed to lower his standards a bit, he suspected.

He popped his knuckles, rolled his neck, ground his teeth. They'd been scared and under tremendous pressure, he reminded himself, so mistakes were understandable. Completely understandable. He still wanted to smash in the wall. After all, understandable mistakes were still liable to make his job a hundred times more difficult. He bent over and touched the floor, pressing his palm flat and leaning into the limb while his senses trickled into the bedrock.

This facility continued to rebuff his attempts to infiltrate and read the earth all around him—courtesy of the sentient plant life, he was sure—but he could work around that in a pinch. Now that Levi knew what he was up against he could adjust appropriately. Most of the prison, its myriad of twisting passageways and rooms, lay bare in Levi's mind like a 3-D map, but there were whole sections of the complex that were invisible to him. As if someone had taken an eraser to those sectors of the map.

But, those invisible sections *did* tell him something. Those sections, Levi now understood, were areas heavily infested by the living flowers, *tacca chantrieri gigantis*, which meant those were the areas best avoided. True, he'd managed to free himself from the tangles of vegetation at the entry checkpoint, but he wasn't keen on doing it again, not in his weakened state. Next, he shifted his focus away from the temple as a whole, probing for the gentle pitter-patter of feet or immobile hotspots, which signaled life.

There were *several* such hotspots emanating from different points throughout the sprawling facility.

*Too many points* for Ryder and Chuck to produce alone, which meant they weren't the only ones in this place. Professor Wilkie was out there somewhere, but so was the person responsible for crucifying and disemboweling Wilkie's lab assistant.

He couldn't tell which hotspots were which, not with so much interference, but he could distinctly sense three different parties: one lingered deep, deep, deep in the complex, near the pyramid's apex, nestled in a room swarming with blooming plant life. Naturally, that was the room containing the emergency exit. He'd have to make his way there eventually, but he wasn't looking forward to what he'd find. The second hotspot moved through a corridor off to his right. The last lay only a few minutes from his current location—in a room not far down the left-hand path.

Most disturbing of all, though, were the pockets of *shifting* invisibility—five or six of them—patrolling through the hallways. To Levi's earth sense, those invisible blips of motion held the same signature as the immobile sections of prison infested with vegetation, but these were, without a doubt, on the prowl. Hunting.

He pushed those things, whatever they were, away from his mind and took the hallway to the left. Since he couldn't be sure where Chuck and Ryder were, he'd make for the nearest hotspot. The left-hand passageway, identical to the one he'd just come from, ran straight as an arrow for a few hundred meters, before coming to an end at another intersection, this one with a single hallway jutting off sharply to the right. Here, Levi halted, pressing his back against the wall while trailing his good hand across the stone.

This was it.

The hallway to the right was actually the entrance to a small room, with two more stony tunnels snaking off in opposite directions. The blip was in that room, though Levi couldn't discern whether whatever waited was friend or foe. Only one way to find out, he supposed: he curled the fingers of his serviceable hand, then reformed the limb into a colossal double-edged battle-axe. Levi liked to think of himself as an optimistic realist—*hope for the best, plan for the worst*—but so far, this whole mess had been one bad turn after another. He wasn't going to take any more chances.

Should whatever lay in the other room be unfriendly … Levi smiled, an ugly gash across his face. Well, he was in the mood for a little justifiable bloodshed.

## *NINETEEN:*

## Into the Dark

Ryder hobbled down the connecting corridor on wobbly legs that refused to work properly. Thankfully she had Chuck by her side, one arm slung around her shoulders, helping her stay upright and moving forward. The sound of battle—of mayhem, chaos, and death—floated to her from the guardroom: the ground shaking and rattling. Levi's gravelly shouts of pain. The shrieking alarm of black flowers. All those noises seemed to build a brutal soundtrack that shouted for her to turn back. To help Levi. It was the soundtrack of a man dying.

She'd seen him fight and kill scores of dark and grisly things.

He'd rescued her from the Deep Downs where she'd been held captive and killed the Kobocks responsible for her abduction. He'd murdered more of the creepy-ass blue-men on the side of the road—not to mention the boar-faced driver from the Caddy. The point was, he was one tough-ass son of a bitch, but how could anyone fight what was in that room? A monstrous plant with human intelligence that had a thousand plus years of experience?

The way those vines had wrapped themselves around his legs, thorns digging into his body, while those flowers shot their whipping tendrils up underneath the skin, rooting around inside him. Fucking disgusting. Even as she stumbled along, the desire to clutch her stomach was overwhelming. She could almost imagine something rooting around inside of her. She couldn't help but envision those vines ripping their way inside her, like in that Evil Dead movie. Branches and vines shooting up between her legs and putting down roots right in her guts.

She shuddered, but kept on moving, refusing to look back.

*"Run! I'll find you!"* The Mudman's final words echoed in her head.

Running wasn't the brave thing to do—better to go back and make sure Levi got clear, like she'd done with the Sprawl wolves.

Except she wasn't brave, and that thing with the wolves was a fluke, one great big mistake, though she was ashamed to admit it. Sort of. She hadn't meant to save Levi, not that she'd really saved him, anyway—more like bought him a little time. She'd tripped while running away and by the time she'd gained her feet, Levi was right there and so was that bat-eared fuck. She'd fired out of fear and self-preservation, not heroics. She was a survivor, a scavenger—she would've left Levi to die in a minute if it meant making it out alive.

Still, she found herself dragging her feet. It *was* hard to leave him; she didn't really like the disagreeable asshole, but she owed him, no doubt about that. Nothing could get her back into that guardroom, though, guilty conscience or no, not after what she'd seen during her "body scan." She couldn't really explain it, but somehow her mind had connected with Siphonei, tapped into the woman-machine's subconscious. Horrifying shit. The images kept on cycling through her head as she limped along, just incoherent flashes:

*Her body strapped down to a stainless steel gurney, harsh white light blasting her eyes while a host of tubes ran into her arms, and nose, and mouth—some delivering medication or nutrients, while others vacuumed her free of fluids. Blood, stolen, recycled, altered, and fed into a massive torpedo-shaped flower, big as a full-grown man, which reeked of decay and spoiled milk. A tangle of vines vomited outward from the base of the enormous blossom, snaking their way into her every orifice.*

Next: *A portly man with a round face and a swath of brown hair knelt, completely naked, in a pool of congealing blood. She couldn't remember his name, a sort of forgettable man, but she knew he was an under-warden. A tech analyst or maintenance worker, one of hundreds. That much she was sure. A red pool, thick and viscous, spread out around him; a series of symbols ran over his chubby body, all painted on in glistening crimson. A corpse lay in front of him. An older man with full silver hair, who she knew was the High-Warden, Lir-Thildo. His well-coiffed hair was matted with chunks of skull and globs of more blood.*

*The naked kneeling man had caved his head in with a jagged shard of stone.*

Last and worst of all, she caught a glimpse of a monstrous thing, of the thing trapped in this godforsaken place. The wyrm god, the one that kept cropping up—first in the Kobock temple, then in that photo from the professor's camp. Except this glimpse was no painting or carving. No picture. She wasn't sure if the vision was some kind of hallucination or memory, but if felt as real as the biting heat of a flame.

*She saw a pool of orange, a pit of churning fire like the inside of a volcano—blacks, reds, and various hues of gold, mixing and swirling in ever shifting patterns.* And lurking in those molten waters? *A bloated beast, large as a whale and long as a city block. The creature was all chitinous plates the color of a fresh scab, and waving, multi-jointed spider legs. Thousands of the spindly appendages pushed the creature's bulk through the fiery waves. Worst of all, though, were the eyes. A million glinting insect eyes covering its head and serpentine torso.*

Fuck, she hoped to never see that thing again.

So no, she wouldn't go back into that room, not if it meant even a remote possibility of seeing those awful visions again. She had enough troublesome memories without adding in the nightmares of some dead woman trapped inside a fucking plant. *Levi will be fine*, she told herself. *He's tough as an old dump truck.* A grain of guilt lurked at the back of her mind, though, rubbing at her like a piece of gravel in the bottom of her shoe.

She slowed, hesitated, and after a second, craned her head toward the way they'd come from, searching for the Mudman. Empty hallway all the way back. Chuck tugged at her, strong arms urging her forward.

"Yo, let's move it, girl," he said. "Dude told us to run, so we run. Guy might be screwier than a bag of screws, but he's also meaner than a roided up pit bull. Don't sweat it. Levi knows how to fight and he knows how to smoke shit. Let's just do what he said."

He pulled at her again, and she let her body yield to his guidance.

It took only a few minutes to reach a four-way juncture. Here they paused, Chuck shining his SureFire up and down each hallway. They all looked the same to Ryder: stone-sided tunnels cutting deeper into darkness—and it was dark. There were weird orbs running along the walls, casting a pale-purple light over everything, which did approximately jack-shit to dissipate the darkness. Even the SureFires, bright as they were, only did so much to penetrate the gloom.

"Which way now, oh guide of Outworld?" she asked, glancing left, forward, right.

"How the hell am I supposed to know that?" He threw up his hand in exasperation. "Do I look like Indiana Jones, solving riddles and swinging across spiked pits with a whip? Hell naw. You want to know where to get a kidney? I can set you up with one of the Little Brothers, no problem. You wanna get in touch with a demon outta the pit? Shit, you know I can do that, too. But I ain't no witty archeologist, you feel me?"

She frowned, still surveying their options. "Wow, what would we do without you, Chuck?" she said absentmindedly. "And you're pulling twenty-five grand on this job? I can see Levi's really getting his money worth."

"Don't get smart with me, little lady. This bullshit right here"—he paused, glancing around the dusty prison—"is y'alls bullshit. Ain't no way to prepare for this kind of nonsense. I think even Indiana

Jones would throw up his hands and let you folks sort this out on y'alls own."

"Yeah well, sadly, neither us have the option to walk away from this. Nope, we've got to pick a direction," she replied. "We can't just stand here with thumbs up our asses, waiting for some freaky plant-monster to I don't know … *murder* us."

"Yeah, well true as that may be, let's stop talkin' about things goin' up our asses … 'Cause I don't get down that way." He paused, lips screwed up. "I read this thing once—"

"You read something, once," she cut in. "I don't believe it. Literally, I don't believe it. Unless maybe it was on the back of a cereal box."

"You just tryin' to piss me off, right?" He paused, eyes squinted, daring her to say something else. "Thank you. Now, as I was sayin', I read this thing about mazes—it was in *National Geographic*, so you know it's legit."

She sighed and gave him a *get-along-with-it* nod.

"Someone left it on a plane, alright. Anyway, point is, this magazine said if you were stuck in a cave or a maze you could keep your hand on one wall and you'd find your way out."

"That'd be great if we were in a *labyrinth*, but this"—she swept a hand out—"isn't a labyrinth, it's an ancient prison holding an insane monster."

"Okay, Miss Negative Nancy—talking about how we need to do something, but here you are just standin' around, shooting your mouth off. So let's hear your plan?"

"Shut up." She held out one hand and canted her face to the side.

"Yeah, that's what I thought, you can dish it but you can't take—"

"No seriously, shut up for a second." She shifted right, hand tracing through the air as though brushing away unseen cobwebs.

Chuck shuffled back a step, lips pressed into a tight line. "Levi never really said what you are," he said after a time. "You some kinda psychic, right? Like that Sookie Stackhouse from *True Blood*? 'Cause if you're some kinda psychic mind-reader, I just want to apologize for all those things I been thinking about ... well ..." He cleared his throat and looked away.

"First, gross. Second, shut up and come here." She reached over and pulled him toward the tunnel on the right. "Give me your hand." Without waiting for him to agree, she took the hand clutching the flashlight and thrust it up into the air. "Do you feel that?"

"I'll feel whatever you want, sweetheart."

"No, you pervy asshole, stop and actually feel."

This time he paused, then shook his head. "Naw, still got nothing. You sure this isn't some kinda psychic thing?"

"If you don't start pulling your weight, Chuck, I swear I'll go on without you," Ryder replied. "You have that lighter in your pack?"

"Yeah, just give me a minute." He slung the bag from his shoulder and dropped down to the ground, setting his gun and flashlight on the grimy floor so he could dig through one of the outside pockets. After a handful of seconds, he pulled out a black Zippo with a tacky jade four-leaf clover on either side.

She snatched the lighter from his hand, not waiting for whatever asinine comment was to follow, and turned back to the passageway. She fumbled the top open and flicked the flint wheel, *click, click, click*. After a couple of tries a wavering flame flickered to life, dancing and bobbing, blown to the left by a barely-there breeze.

"Holy shit, is that a draft?" he asked, eyes tracking the movement of the tiny fire.

"Yep," Ryder replied with a smirk, dropping her hand. "That's a draft—a tiny one, maybe—but a draft. And a draft means an exit. We just need to follow that and we'll get out of this place."

He flashed her a radiant smile, his white teeth gleaming purple in the orb light. "I love you, Sally Ryder. Smart is the new sexy, you know." He slung his pack back into place with a grunt and retrieved his light and pistol from the floor. She snapped the Zippo closed with a flick of her wrist and stowed it in her jeans. Then, since she had the breathing room, she slid the compact revolver—a dark metal thing called a Chief's Special—from her coat pocket, emptied out the spent brass, and popped home fresh rounds.

"Now why don't you lead the way," Chuck said as he settled his gear into place, adjusting the shoulder straps. "Like they say, brains before beauty."

*Guy really was a worthless jackass.*

She fished her flashlight from one coat pocket, then, with a roll of her eyes, shoved her way past the worst tour guide on the planet. She clicked on the SureFire and swept the beam across the tunnel as she moved deeper into the murk. The temple was creepy to the max, like a dark alley in the worst part of the worst city in existence—assuming whatever lurked down that alleyway was inhuman, predatory, and amped up on Miracle-Gro.

She kept moving, though, because to stay still was tantamount to a death sentence. And she meant to live. She did, however, clutch the snub-nosed revolver a little tighter. The gun felt heavy, but the weight was a comfort in her hand.

She wasn't great with a pistol, but neither was she unfamiliar. Her father had owned a gun like this, a cheap piece he'd picked up at a pawnshop for a hundred bucks. Well, he hadn't bought it, not with his record. The gun had been in her mom's name, since she had a clean record. At least on paper. That was their deal: better for one of them to be clean—easier to get an apartment or a job without a rap sheet—so Dad was always the fall guy. Always. The drug convictions. The robbery charges. The breaking and entering rap. Dad took it all and did the time so Mom's name could be on the lease.

He'd taught her to handle the weapon, her dad. One of the few good memories she had of him. They'd been living in Detroit at the time, and he took her out of the city—down near Chelsea—with a box of ammo and a couple of empty milk jugs. He filled those plastic cartons up with sand and gravel and propped them up on an old log, which sat at the base of a tiny hill covered with sparse wild grass. Then they'd shot.

*"A pistol like this doesn't have a safety,"* he told her, *"but you really have to tug the trigger to fire. Or you can cock the hammer back, like in the westerns."* He thumbed back the hammer with a *click*. *"If you thumb it back, half the work's already done. Then, all it*

*takes is a little squeeze."* He flashed her a wink and a cocky, easy grin, then held out the gun, arm slightly bent, one eye closed as he peered along the top edge of the weapon. He eased the trigger back, not yanking or pulling, but a slow, steady squeeze. The gun barked in his hand and kicked up a hair. A moment later one of the milk cartons rocked, a puckered hole spilling out a trickle of sand, like a wound spilling dirty blood.

Yeah, she knew how to shoot. How to defend herself—not that the gun had saved her parents or her brother. Not against Yraeta and the Kings. Butchers.

Sometimes she fantasized about heading over to a pawnshop, just like her dad, picking up a Chief's Special, and paying Yraeta and his boys a visit. She and Jamie used to talk about doing it at night—that had been back in foster care. Only a fantasy, though, an impossibility. A kid's pipe dream. Like becoming an astronaut or the President. Maybe once upon a time it would've been possible to kill Yraeta, but not now. That sack of shit had moved up in the world after doing in her family—now, he was an untouchable crime kingpin with cops and judges in his pocket and a small army of gun-wielding thugs surrounding him.

She didn't have time to waste on thoughts of Yraeta, so she shoved those hurtful memories back down in the lockbox of other painful memories she kept buried in the back of her skull. If she wanted to live through this, and she very much did, she needed to be present and focused: a solider on the battlefield, a surgeon with razor in hand.

After a few minutes of walking they came to another intersection, this one a "T" with passages running off left and right. She tucked the pistol into her baggy jacket pocket—the Carhartt monstrosity Levi had provided wasn't her style, but she had to admit it was pragmatic and comfy—and swiveled the beam of her light down each hall.

The left-hand path looked much like the one they'd just come from: more stone walls, carved with ancient murals and runes, the whole scene lit by the spectral purple orbs. The right path, on the other hand, screamed, *Stay out or die a gruesome death.* That path ran straight for only a few yards before curving left and disappearing from view. And right at the arch of the curve lay a tangle of foliage, completely covering the walls and ceiling, though leaving the floor mostly bare.

She sighed, knowing how this was likely to shake out, and retrieved the lighter from her pocket. She held her breath, not daring to so much as exhale, while she raised the Zippo and flicked it to life, searching for the vital draft, which would serve as their guide. It took a few pounding heartbeats to locate the thin trickle of wind. The right. Straight into the terrifying path running into the heart of the deadly vegetation.

Of course *that* would be the way. Because why did she ever deserve a break?

She shook her head, shut the lighter, and reluctantly hooked a thumb toward the death-trap-in-waiting.

Chuck's flashlight beam wheeled that way, lingering on the bend and the vines, which already seemed to be moving and slithering in anticipation—though, admittedly, it could've been a trick of the sweeping flashlight beam and Ryder's overactive imagination.

"Yeahhhh," Chuck said, drawing the word out. "I don't wanna go down there." He pressed his lips together in a grimace and swung his head to and fro. "Naw, breeze or no, I say we stick to the parts that don't look like the inside of the Little Shop of Horrors. 'Cause here's the thing—I don't wanna die, but I especially don't wanna get capped by a houseplant. No better way to ruin your street cred then gettin' iced by a ficus."

"Well, bad news, homeboy, that's where the breeze is coming from, so that's the way we're going."

"Maybe that's the way *you're* going, but I happen to be a certified guide of Outworld and shit, and I say we go this way." He turned and pointed toward the left-hand path, his flashlight beam following along in an arch.

He fell silent as his light splashed over the thing creeping toward them on silent, arachnoid feet. "Aw shit," he muttered.

## *TWENTY:*

## **Ancient History**

With his back pressed against the stony wall, Levi inched forward, his battle-axe hand raised high, while he flattened and distended his other hand into a shield, covering the majority of his thick frame and legs. He paused at the edge of the wall, drawing in a few deep breaths—*in*, hold, *out*, pause—before stepping into view. Most of his bulk remained hidden behind his massive shield-arm, but he had no problem seeing over the top edge of the impromptu barricade.

The room was octagonal, with two hallways jutting off in opposite directions. Stonework—thankfully devoid of any troublesome foliage—was inscribed with pictographs and runes, including yet another portrait of the ruby-eyed wyrm god. The sole prisoner inhabiting this otherworldly jail. Of greater concern than the artwork, however, was the man cowering against the far wall.

"Stop right there," he demanded, shaking like a leaf in a strong gale.

Levi heeded the command, taking a moment to assess this newcomer: Lanky, gaunt, scholarly, sporting a now-tattered mountaineer's jacket and thick khaki pants with bulging cargo pockets on either leg. Levi recognized him from the holographic display he'd seen back at the entry checkpoint—Professor Owen Wilkie. Physically, the man wasn't impressive, but Levi was hesitant to go any closer. Regardless of his appearance, he was a mage—a wielder of the deep power, a master of the *Vis*, the energy undergirding Creation—and they were dangerous.

Drifting around the supernatural community, Levi had heard plenty of horror stories about what happened to creatures that crossed the Guild of the Staff. Step wrong with their kind and it wouldn't be long before a Guild Judge—or worse, a member of the Fist—showed up on your doorstep with a death warrant in hand. There were, of course, many creatures of Outworld who could go toe-to-toe with the magi—old demons, High Lords of the Endless Wood, forgotten Principalities and dark godlings—but Levi wasn't among them. Some things, some people, were better left alone.

Moreover, this man was frazzled, terrified, and weighed down by exhaustion. A frazzled, terrified, exhausted man could do crazy, dangerous things—and with the Vis behind him, who knew what he could be capable of?

Truth be told, though, Levi was more concerned about what he might do to himself—he was holding a knife to his throat, pressing down until the skin dimpled.

"Don't come any closer," Wilkie said, voice uneven, trembling. "You need me. I'm the only one who understands the cipher, and it's all up here, committed to memory." He tapped at his temple with his free hand. "Without me you'll never figure the ritual out. So you need me. And I refuse to be tortured—I won't endure what you put Simon through. I won't. I'll end it first. I swear to God."

Though Levi wasn't a great student of the human condition, he saw this was a man who'd been pushed to his uttermost limit—his suicidal threat wasn't bluster. One wrong move and he'd slide that blade across his neck.

"Don't know who you think I am," Levi said as friendly as he could manage, which wasn't much. "Whoever's after you? It's not me." He let the shield disappear and dismissed the battle-axe, his hands reverting to normal. He shuffled a little further inside, raising both hands, showing he was unarmed and meant no harm.

"What'd you take me for?" Wilkie demanded, eyes wide and wild, hand quivering as he readjusted his grip on the blade. "Who else would be out here? If you aren't with *them* then who are you? What are you?"

"It's complicated," Levi replied, shuffling closer. He needed this man alive—he was the only hope Levi had of getting answers. "But I need your help. I think something bad is going to happen, and I think you have the answers I need to stop whatever that is."

"I've been hiding here for three days." His lips curled in a sneer. "I haven't eaten or bathed. I've barely slept. And every single minute I fear I will be discovered and murdered. I'm not going anywhere anytime soon. So convince me, or I'll jab this knife into my carotid artery—it won't even have to be that deep—and in less than a minute I'll be moving on from this world. So, if you want any help, I'd work on convincing me."

Levi didn't know where to start. Ever since running across Ryder he'd been forced from one awkward and uncomfortable situation to another. Confronting the shaman in the Deep Downs, executing that innocent flesh golem in the Kobock temple, trekking through Outworld with a Rube, now forced to explain himself to a mage with the Guild. A mage who could likely end his existence with a thought. How had his life become so complicated, so uncertain?

Once this business was all said and done with, he planned on going back to his nice, boring routines. Monday, prison ministry. Tuesday, the food pantry. Wednesday, small-group Bible study. Thursday, AA meetings. Friday, Levi taught a beginner's pottery class at the Y. He'd never been so excited for monotony. But he wasn't done with this business yet. No, he had a half-crazed mage to talk down off the ledge.

His first inclination was to lie. Lying may have been a sin, but it was a familiar one: well-trodden ground, where he knew all the ups and downs, ruts and pitfalls. Except he couldn't possibly lie his way out of this. He couldn't begin to think of a deception that would do the trick. Not to mention he wasn't just trying to pull one over on some Rube like George from church. This was a *mage*. Magi were supposed to know the truth of things. Rumor had it they could tell if someone was lying through some trick of their magic.

Levi didn't know if that was true, but he couldn't risk being wrong, so he wagered honesty was the best policy here.

He sighed, shuffled into the room, and plopped down, placing his back against a rough patch of wall.

"Sorry," he said with a shrug. "It's been an awfully long day and this story isn't short." He paused and ran a hand over the floor, worn smooth by countless years. "Haven't told it to many people, so if things get all jumbled up, just stop me."

The mage said nothing, only stared at Levi with suspicion painted across his dusky, pinched features. Not knowing what else to do, Levi began, going back to the beginning, to the night he awoke in the open grave. He told his story in fits and starts—meandering this way and that—until, eventually, he got around to Ryder and the Kobock temple. Though he *didn't* mention the homunculus growing inside the girl. This man had answers, but the magi were known as *end-justify-the-means* kind of people, so who was to say he wouldn't try to kill her on principle? That wasn't a risk Levi was willing to take.

While Levi spoke, he watched the professor, gauging his reactions. Thankfully, each sentence seemed to disarm the man a little more. By the time the Mudman wrapped up his strange tale, Wilkie had removed the blade from his neck altogether and sat slumped against the wall, his pose mirroring Levi's own. He looked exhausted now, a bone-deep weariness, but he also looked at ease. Good.

At last Levi fell silent, the quiet stretching between them like a chasm.

After a handful of tense, thoughtful minutes, the professor spoke. "What a remarkable story. Truly remarkable. A golem, you say ..." He trailed off, eyes unfocused, lost in some faraway thought. "Should we escape this place, perhaps you'll allow me to examine you." He rubbed a finger at his chin. "The secrets you could teach me, teach us all ..." He shook his head.

Levi didn't much care for the way the man watched him—like a hungry dog eyeballing a raw steak. He shifted uncomfortably under the mage's gaze.

"That's a thought for another day," the professor said after a time. "First, I suppose, we ought to set our minds to escape. I'm not at all ashamed to say I'm glad it was you who found me. I was beginning to think this was the end for me—and death was the *good* option in that equation. You can't possibly imagine what they did to my lab assistant, Simon. Poor bloke." He sniffled and ran a hand across his cheek. "Horrendous. Unspeakable evil. Never would've brought him out here had I thought … well, it doesn't matter now. Done is done."

Levi recalled the image of the crucified and disemboweled man he'd found in the camp outside the temple complex. Horrendous, unspeakable evil summed it up well enough. The Mudman nodded his head. "I saw the body, so I've got some idea." He hesitated for a moment. "I'm sorry for your loss. Not sure if it makes any difference to you, but I put him to rest. Buried him so the scavengers couldn't get at him. Marked the spot with a cross."

"Simon was a Buddhist," Wilkie said absently, "but thank you all the same. Good to know his remains are cared for. He loved the Sprawl, hard as that might be to believe, so this is as good a place as any for him to be."

"Like I said, I'm sorry for your loss. I don't want to rush things along—things like this are never easy—but we don't have time to think to the dead. We have the living to see to. I believe whoever is responsible for Simon's death has much bigger plans in mind."

"Indeed," Wilkie replied, rubbing at his sharp-edged jaw. "Hogg's his name."

*Hogg.* That name immediately triggered a warning bell in Levi's head. He'd seen that name before—on the letter he'd found in the Deep Downs.

"I don't know much about him," the professor continued. "Or his history. Man's not a proper mage with the Guild, that much I can say with conviction. But he's brilliant. Brilliant and crazy. And he can use the Vis to some extent. I can also tell you what he's after, even if I can't explain the why of it. The lunatic means to resurrect *Dibeininax Ayosainondur Daimuyon*, the Eternally Cursed One—"

"The Eternally Cursed One." Levi pointed to the mural on the wall. "The computer said this whole place was some sort of holding cell for that thing."

"Yes. Poor Siphonei." The professor bobbed his head. "She's been invaluable in filling in the gaps about this complex. What you and your friends have stumbled into is an unfolding drama nearly as old as creation itself. Though it's more tragedy than drama, I suppose," he said with a soft smile full of regret.

"Is he here?" Levi asked. "Hogg?"

The professor nodded his head. "He's holed up in the emergency exit tunnel and he has some intimidating muscle with him. Trolls of one sort or another. A pack of them." *Thursrs*, Levi thought, *it had to be the Dread Trolls.* "Once Siphonei activated the termination protocol," Wilkie said, "the main entrance snapped shut, so the only way out is through that exit tunnel, which means through Hogg. Fortunately, that lunatic isn't willing to venture into the temple proper, which is why I haven't left yet."

"Why?" Levi asked. "What would stop him from coming in here?"

"Well, the guardians, of course. Formidable creatures to say the least. And, from what I've managed to gather, our dear Siphonei doesn't seem to have any fondness whatsoever for the man. I suspect her guardians would make short work of him and take great pleasure in the act."

"Why would a security system be holding a personal grudge?" Levi asked, not really expecting an answer.

Wilkie shook his head. "Sadly any of Siphonei's records concerning Hogg are sealed. All of them. I've asked her a hundred different questions in a hundred different ways, but anything touching on Hogg seems to be redacted by a system administrator—though only God knows how that's possible."

"For not knowing much about this Hogg," Levi replied, "you seem to know an awful lot about him, if you catch my meaning."

"I'm not sure I do catch your meaning. Are you insinuating something, creature?"

"Not *creature*. Levi," the Mudman replied, heat in the words. "Levi Adams. I'm a person, just like you—not some *monster*. I'd kindly appreciate it if you would remember that fact. And, to be clear, I'm not accusing you of anything, Professor. Not yet. I'd just like to know how you fit into the picture is all. Like I said, you seem to know an awful lot."

The professor flapped one hand in the air, brushing away the Mudman's concern. "Well, my apologies, *Levi*, I didn't mean to insult you. As to my relationship with Hogg, I can quite assure you my involvement in this whole affair is purely academic. Nothing of a sinister or dubious nature if that's what you're thinking.

"I'm just an old scholar who discovered something better left buried and forgotten. A series of discoveries, actually. Hogg approached me several months ago—this was before Simon and I launched this expedition—hoping to enlist my aid. He wanted me to map out the temple and translate the glyphs in the inner sanctum. The request seemed innocent enough at the time and since he was willing to fund my expedition, I agreed."

"Why pay you to do it? Seems like the kind of thing he could do for himself."

"Well, yes and no. It's more complicated than that. As I mentioned, I don't think Hogg *can* access the facility proper without triggering the security protocols. But more germane, up until ten months ago, *no one* could translate the glyphs in this temple. No one.

"The writing in this complex"—he waved a hand about like a teacher motioning to his blackboard—"predates any known language, and that is because this temple was built long before the Tower of Babel, when mankind spoke in a single, unified tongue. On these walls you will find the *First Language*." He said it reverently, awe in his voice. "The original, mother tongue of humanity."

Levi looked up, eyes tracing over the walls and ceiling, lingering on the pictographs and strange script.

"How old is this place?" he asked, feeling awed himself. "Who built it?"

"Oh it is very, very old. It is distinctly possible this complex is the *oldest* building in all of existence—barring some of the structures in the fae courts. It's hard to date precisely, but if I had to make an educated guess, I'd put its creation around seven thousand years ago. To answer the other part of your question ..." He paused, wiggled his nose, and readjusted his glasses—the very picture of a befuddled university teacher who'd lost his train of thought. "I'm not entirely sure who built it.

"You must understand there isn't much by way of written record left from seven thousand years ago. To give you some perspective, the books of Moses—Genesis through Deuteronomy—were penned around 1445 B.C. and the earliest *copies* of Genesis come from the Dead Sea Scrolls, which date to around 150 B.C. This temple likely dates back to 5,000 or 6,000 B.C. I do have a theory, which is ... well, also very complicated and built upon a great degree of disconnected historical accounts and speculation. I can tell you with a fair degree of certainty *why* it was built, though. Are you, perhaps, familiar with the biblical mythos of Cain and Abel?"

Levi nodded his blocky head. What God-fearing, churchgoing man didn't know the tale? "I'm no scholar," Levi said, "but as far as I understand it, Adam and Eve had a bunch of children, but Cain and Abel were the first. Brothers. God commanded the two sons to offer sacrifices, but He accepted Abel's offering while rejecting Cain's. In return, Cain killed his brother and became the first murderer in human history."

"Well put," Wilkie said. "Now, certain parts of Genesis, particularly chapters one through eleven, read more as ancient near-east cosmology than some sort of"—he rolled his hands about as though trying to pluck the words out of the air—"fixed, literal historical text. With that said, there is far more reality to those accounts than I ever would've believed. Cain is *not* some allegorical representation of the wickedness of humanity—its murderous impulses and desires—he is, in fact, a *real* person. And he's here. Right here. Buried in a pocket dimension beneath our feet."

"Wait." Levi frowned and ran his good hand over his fat neck. "You're saying Cain, from the Bible, is the inmate of this prison? He's this—what'd you call him … the Eternally Cursed One?"

The professor offered an enthusiastic grin and waggled a bony finger at Levi. "Yes, precisely. That's precisely what I'm saying. Cain, son of Adam, brother of Abel, is the *Dibeininax Ayosainondur Daimuyon*. Now just bear with me for a moment. You see, after Cain killed his brother, he was not executed by God, but rather cursed. God placed a mark upon his forehead, a mark which kept Cain from dying, and then God banished him. Drove him from the land and into the outer regions, sentencing him to a lifetime of endless wandering, forever forced to live with his guilt.

"Eventually, Cain made his way to the land of Nod, a place east of Eden. Now, I can't prove it, but I believe Nod was an ancient term for Outworld. He literally passed into a different realm, one filled with a myriad of beasts and creatures. He fathered children there—perhaps the first halfies?" He paused again, grin widening. "Though who can rightly say?

"At any rate, after years and years of wandering, he stumbled into dark, dark alchemy and became more than human—or less, perhaps—and eventually went … well, quite insane, as you might expect. Over time, he became a living incarnation of murder: the personification of the worst of humanity. Though I've studied biblical mythology for years, much of this I've only recently discovered through studying the writings in this temple. Now here's where it gets a little confusing."

"I'm already plenty confused," Levi replied with a frown.

"Just bear with me. A group of people, though who precisely isn't clear, built this temple and devised a way to imprison Cain so he could rant and rave without disturbing the world. I can't tell you who they were—personally, I suspect it may have been a cabal of lesser godlings who feared Cain's growing power—though in the end, it doesn't really matter much, I suppose. This group found a relatively deserted region of Outworld, the Sprawl, and built this temple, imprisoned Cain, and left him to rot in his own personal hell."

Levi held up a hand, cutting off the professor's easy, lecturing cadence. "For the sake of brevity, let's say I believe you. That still doesn't explain everything. Or much of anything? What about all the high-tech doodads scattered around here? What about Siphonei? She said this place was owned and operated by Atlantis Correction Systems—doesn't sound biblical to me."

"Quite right. The biblical narrative is only one half of the story. The second half picks up several millennia later, with another ancient mythos, that of Atlantis." The professor was nodding his head vigorously now, his body shaking with barely contained excitement. "You see, like Cain, the island nation of Atlantis is no myth, but a concrete reality—and the machinery left in this prison is proof. Exactly what I told all my colleagues in the Guild ... not that anyone ever believed me." The last he muttered under his breath.

Wilkie frowned and absently brushed at his pant leg. "Atlantis," he continued. "The jewel of the ancient world. From everything I've been able to find, it was a remarkable civilization. Unlike our 'modern world'"—he air quoted—"Atlantis was a truly progressive society. Magi didn't hide in the dark, keeping their talents locked behind closed doors, skirting along the periphery of society. They ruled openly and made Atlantis the greatest city-state in the known world. The envy to all—which is precisely why Homer spoke so ill of them." Admiration lingered in his eye. "Sadly, their greatness lead to hubris, which, in the end, proved to be their undoing."

"Pride goeth before destruction, and a haughty spirit before a fall," Levi muttered under his breath.

"Just so," he replied. "You see, Atlantis was built not just on magic, on Vis, but on advanced technomancy. But the technology was stolen. Pilfered from the *future*. Magi would sneak into Outworld—much more difficult in those days, since the Hub had yet to be created by the Old Ones—and raid the Mists of Fate, stealing technology from a myriad of possible futures. And they used that stolen technology to *thrive*.

And they thrived right up until they destroyed themselves.

"During an exploratory trip to Outworld, a party of magi discovered the Spine and in it a rare earth alloy essential to their workings. The ruling body, realizing the profit to be made, wanted to set up a huge mining operation, but couldn't find a way to make it sustainable since Outworld was so inaccessible at the time. So they developed a machine, one they didn't fully understand, to punch a permanent hole in reality and create a temporal bridge between the Sprawl and Atlantis.

"Instead of creating a stable bridge"—he gave an apologetic shrug—"they created an unstable dimensional wormhole, which tore the entire city through the fabric of reality and dropped it right in the heart of the Sprawl. The whole island disappeared in a blink, leaving behind a massive crater, which, in turn, created an unprecedented tsunami that filled in the void: the sinking of Atlantis. The Cataclysm."

"Stop," Levi said, pushing himself to his feet, then pressing fat palms against the sides of his head, trying to hold his thoughts in place. "You're overwhelming me with all this." Levi wasn't dumb precisely, but neither was he quick-witted. "I'm not a scholar. This is too big for me. It's over my head. Can't you simplify it?"

"I'm sorry, but believe me, I *am* simplifying it."

Levi grunted and paced, huge legs carrying him across the room in a handful of steps, then back again.

Back and forth.

Back and forth.

Thoughts slugged along while his legs moved. "Okay, okay," Levi said after a beat. "So Cain is real and trapped in this prison, cut off from the rest of the world, right?"

"Right."

"Then a couple of thousand years later, Atlantis gets sucked through a rift into Outworld, correct?"

"Essentially, yes."

"Okay, but that still doesn't explain how we got to here." He jabbed a finger at the floor. "How does Atlantis Correction Systems come into the picture?"

"I'm getting there, but the story isn't short. I'm trying to cram seven thousand years' worth of history, a hundred text books worth of ancient mythology, and one of the greatest civilizations that's ever existed into a cohesive story a layman can understand. It's not bloody easy." He cleared his throat and readjusted his glasses. "Now, Atlantis wasn't destroyed. The city survived, damaged but intact. They landed in the Sprawl—though in those days it was a lush, beautiful paradise—and spread throughout the region. Some ancient texts even suggest a party made it across the Spine.

"Those were far from peaceful years, however. After the Cataclysm, the country broke into a bloody civil war, which eventually wiped out the civilization— the whole thing imploded in a thermo-nuclear war, which turned the Sprawl into the desolate wasteland you see today. A tragedy of the greatest magnitude." He fell silent for a moment, as though he were watching those events unfold before him. "During those tumultuous years, a group of civic minded Atlanteans discovered this temple and realized the potential danger it possessed.

"If one of the warring Atlantean factions unleashed Cain as a weapon to use in the war, the damage would've been unthinkable. So a neutral third party, Atlantis Correction Systems, was contracted to outfit the facility in an attempt to ensure Cain was never released by either side. The security protocols they put in place were impressive, though sadly many of the defensive mechanisms are now inoperative. The effects of age I'm afraid. I can quite sympathize—these old bones of mine don't work half so well as they used to."

Levi paced in silence for a time, his mind spinning and whirling, processing the torrent of new information. This place was a prison designed to keep one inmate incarcerated. If the security system flagged Ryder—and the homunculus inside her—as a threat, it could only mean the homunculus was somehow key in letting Cain, the living incarnation of murder, slip free from his bonds.

But what did that mean about his own past? He too was a homunculus of sorts, and he too had been fashioned under similar circumstances—the strange altar, the massacred bodies, all of it—so how did he fit into the equation? A deeply disturbing thought, that. A question he had no answers for. He turned his attention back toward the professor, who looked equally lost in his own mind.

"Professor," Levi said.

No answer.

"Professor." The Mudman snapped the fat fingers of his good hand, *pop, pop, pop.*

"Hmm, what's that now?"

"I need you to focus for me. There's still a lot of ground to cover and not near enough time. I need to know why this is all happening *now*. I mean this place has been around for seven thousand years?" He shook his head. "It doesn't make any sense."

"Because of my discovery. I told you, up until ten months ago, no one could read the glyphs in this temple. At the height of their technological prowess, even the Atlanteans weren't able to translate them. Several years ago, however, I found a cipher while excavating a long-abandoned Kobock temple in the Deep Downs. Like the Rosetta Stone that allowed Jean-François Champollion to translate Egyptian hieroglyphs for the first time, the cipher enabled me to literally read the writings on the wall. It also disclosed the location of this temple. A remarkable breakthrough." He paused, wistful. "Truly the find of a lifetime."

"You found this cipher in a Kobock temple?" Levi asked, voice flat and numb, a queasiness growing in his stomach. "Why would Kobocks have something like that? What connection could they possibly have to all this?"

The professor turned away, brow creased, one eyebrow quirked in thought while he ran a hand through his hair. "The Kobocks have long worshiped Cain. I can't prove anything definitively, but my theory is that the Kobocks are the lost progeny of Cain. I think they settled in the Sprawl after Cain was imprisoned, and remained until the Atlanteans arrived. There *is* evidence to suggest a primitive group of humanoids lived here, but were driven out around the time of the Cataclysm. I think those were the Kobos, and I believe that after being driven out, they wandered for a while before eventually resettling in the Deep Downs."

Levi sped up his pacing. Things were falling into place now, piece after piece coming together to form a picture—and not a pretty one.

"At any rate," the professor continued, "ten months ago I published a small portion of my findings, hoping to secure a backer for this expedition. That's when Hogg approached me, with money and a wealth of new information. For a while things were going well, right up until I managed to decipher the markings in the inner sanctum. Those writings, they tell Cain's story, but more importantly, they also offer a manner for releasing him. Not intentionally, mind you, but by leaving a record of how he was imprisoned—in case he ever needed to be imprisoned again—the writers unwittingly divulged the formula to reverse engineer his release.

"That formula is what Hogg was after all along. I have no idea how Hogg knows what he does, but I believe he's been collaborating with the Kobocks to release Cain for a very long time. Unsuccessfully, obviously. When I refused to give him my findings, he tortured Simon—I barely escaped by the skin on my teeth, and fled to the temple, hoping Hogg wouldn't be able to pursue me inside. I was right on that score, but I haven't been able to leave either since Hogg and his goons are camped out at the only exit. Waiting for me to break."

"How'd Hogg get to the emergency exit if he can't access the temple?" Levi asked.

"The emergency exit is well concealed, but it can be accessed from the outside. It appears that so long as Hogg doesn't breach the door to the inner sanctum, Siphonei is content to let him be."

Levi grunted in reply. "I've got another question for you," Levi said, mind racing along like a fighter jet determined to break the sound barrier. "What use would Hogg have for a homunculus? Like from alchemy."

Wilkie was quiet for a long beat, face growing noticeably more ashen. "Why?" he whispered.

"One detail I might've left out. The girl I'm travelling with. I think she has one growing inside of her. Implanted by a Kobock shaman and Hogg."

"My God," the old mage replied, then clasped one hand over his mouth, face pensive, worried. "The ritual is quite complicated. It's not like baking a cake, you understand. It must be carried out precisely on the autumnal equinox, which would be"—he canted his wrist and glanced at his watch—"Wednesday, September 22 at 8:21 Coordinated Universal Time. Roughly two days from now. In addition, the incantation must be spoken in the mother tongue and a sacrificial murder—a reenactment of Cain's mythos— must be committed."

"Sacrificial murder?"

"One blood sibling must willingly kill another, just as Cain killed Abel." The professor threw up both hands in exasperation. "It's quite complicated and we haven't the time for me to explain. The most important part, though, is the *vessel*. This temple binds Cain's body, but not his *essence*, his *soul*. So, if a suitable form could be constructed—like an empty homunculus—it's distinctly possible Cain's essence could invade that body. He'd be free to roam the world again."

A wave of dizziness washed over Levi as his frantic pacing sped up further still. Hogg meant to free Cain, Ryder was the key, and, since she would undoubtedly be searching for the exit, she would be heading right for him.

The professor sprang to his feet, a tightly coiled spring ready to explode. "It's imperative we find your friends. Absolutely *imperative*. If Siphonei doesn't kill them, they're bound to blunder right into Hogg and his men."

"You read my mind," Levi mumbled.

"Perhaps," Wilkie said, "it would be best for everyone if Siphonei simply killed this girl and the thing inside her."

"No," Levi spat. "I don't want to think about that. She's … important to me." And he meant it. It wasn't just a matter of doing the right thing. He would genuinely be upset to see Ryder die.

Wilkie's features softened a touch. "She's your friend. Like my Simon." After a moment, his face hardened with resolve. "Then we should get a move on it," he said, brushing the grit from his palms. "I've studied Cain for a long time—longer than most. And trust me when I say he's locked up for a good reason. Best we keep it that way."

## TWENTY-ONE:

## Lesser Guardians

Ryder stood on frozen legs, arms stiff, mouth agape, eyes wide as the encroaching thing padded nearer. She had no frame of reference for the thing in the hallway, no category to file it under. Whatever part of her rational brain remained intact seemed to rebel, to throw its hands into the air, as though to say, *Screw this shit three ways from Sunday. I can't do it anymore, I'm out.*

The creature crept forward on sinuous limbs of woven vines: eight arachnoid appendages, covered in cruel thorns and undulating purple flowers, protruded from a bulbous blood-red sac shaped like a spider's abdomen. A vaguely humanoid torso—all ropy green muscle and slouched shoulders covered with wicked spikes of black bone—perched atop the spidery-thorax, swaying lazily with each step.

A gargantuan replica of the small flowers dotting the creature's insectile legs served for its head. Directly in the center of the creature's face, nestled snugly between its drooping petals, sat a dull onyx beak, built for rending flesh or tearing meat. Looked like some kinda freaky-ass monster squid. A trio of ropy arms, one from each shoulder and a third sprouting from its chest, waved and wobbled through the air as it moved, snaking first this way, then that. Crustacean pincers, black as midnight and covered in more barbed hooks, large and small, adorned each arm.

Those claws flexed as it scuttled.

Open, *snick*. Close, *snap*.

Open, *snick*. Close, *snap*.

Ryder couldn't move.

She willed her legs to move, but the mutinous limbs refused—the equivalent of flashing her the bird. Deep down, she knew her survival hinged on putting as much distance between her and that … well, *whatever-the-hell-it-was* as fast as possible. Unfortunately, the urge to turn and flee wrestled with the urge to curl into the fetal position and pull a blanket over her head. To hide from the monster like she'd done as a little girl when the drug dealers would pay her folks a late-night visit. Ultimately, indecision made the choice for her.

She did nothing.

Stood there watching as the horror inched closer.

Chuck—the world's worst tour guide, but apparently a keen fan of not dying—had no such reservation. Without a word, he hefted his beefy pistol and aimed in with practice and ease, which offered Ryder a glimpse past Chuck's smart mouth and easygoing façade.

She was good at reading body language—a necessary survival trait growing up. In the circles her parents had moved in, violence was as common as the rain was wet, and often the only hint of impending danger lay in the subtle, subconscious movements of the body: clenching fists, a trickle of sweat on the brow, biceps tightening or teeth grinding. For all Chuck's talk of pastries and baking, he was damn confident with the piece in his palm, comfortable in a way that said, *This ain't my first rodeo. I've been around a time or two and I intend to stay around.*

"Get ready to move that ass," he whispered, hands steady, eyes never leaving the flower-covered creature.

Chuck's words loosened something inside her chest, lifting away the paralyzing dread. Ryder nodded and leveled her petite revolver, the grip slick in her palm. This was nothing like shooting at milk cartons filled with sand, but she'd put rounds into those Sprawl wolves—saved Levi, even if it'd been an accident—and she could do this, too.

Chuck broke the momentary lull with a single twitch of his finger. The gun blared, *crack-boom*, followed by a bloom of light, harsh in the purple illumination, which temporarily burned a white afterimage across her eyes. The round tore into the creature's torso, ripping a hole in its chest cavity, a wound as large as a softball. Chuck fired another round, a wet *thwack*, and one of the creature's pincers blew apart, pinwheeling end over end into the hallway behind.

Flower-face lurched back as each shot hit home, but seemed mostly indifferent. Ryder watched on in morbid fascination as its arm—so easily blown away—crawled back to its master, moving with a will of its own. Using whip-like tendrils of emerald, the severed limb pulled itself along the stony floor, inch by inch, foot by foot, before finally worming its way up the side of the creature's body and burrowing back into place like a prairie dog wiggling into its hole.

And then the bastard was a flash of movement, a blur of green, charging toward them while its flower mouth shook back and forth, a warble of rage filling up the air between them.

Ryder glanced toward Chuck.

He was already long gone, his back turned, his pack swinging, his lanky legs eating up the hallway, carrying him off and toward the right—down the hallway with the murderous plants. Toward the draft and the exit. That douche-bag, ass-faced bro-hole. Fucking chicken-shit coward. Not that she would've done anything different, but it was the principle that mattered.

Ryder wanted to follow suit, wanted to turn tail and haul ass, but if she turned her back, she'd never make it. So instead she steadied her hands as best she could and aimed for the creature's churning mass of legs. Honestly, it was unrealistic to say she aimed for anything *specific*, but with that many limbs, she figured a round would have to hit something—there was just too much creature not to. She pulled the trigger a trio of times, and the gun barked, *pop-pop-pop,* and kicked in her grip.

A spray of green followed: splashes of gooey sludge accompanied by chunks of meaty vine and shredded pieces of sunset flowers. The creepy son of a bitch was far from finished, but it did falter and slow, lingering as the missing portions of its body wormed across the floor and rejoined the party.

Ryder took a stumbling step back, wheeled around, and bolted down the right-hand path, following Chuck's lead. Gas all the way to the floor, running balls out. The tangles of vegetation, lurking on the walls and ceiling, slithered and moved at her passing, vines reaching out while flowers extended their barbed-covered tentacles, fighting to ensnare and hold her. Her heart thudded as she ran, beating like the driving bass line of a heavy punk tune: anxiety and claustrophobia colliding against each other in a primal mosh.

As scared as she was of the probing, crawling vines, they didn't hold a candle to her fear of the inhuman thing scuttling along behind her. She steeled herself, ducked low—head down, shoulders rounded, arms tight into her body—and barreled onward. *Fuck these weeds.* Every few feet something pulled at her: crawling lengths of green grabbing her hair or ankles or clothes. She ignored them all, plugging away before those tendrils could get a solid hold, and the whole while she screamed. A shriek, broken more than occasionally by a hysterical string of profanity.

Once in a while she paused her banshee wail to catch her breath, and in those quiet pauses she could her the rustle of vines sliding endlessly over each other: a writhing brood of hungry snakes, interrupted by the rhythmic scurry of giant arachnid legs *scritch-scratching* along the floor. Drawing closer every heartbeat. As bad as the probing feelers were, the sound was worse. Sometimes, if she had time to kill, she'd watch a horror flick with her friends. It was never the sudden jump scares that did her in—no, it was always the damned music. That terrible build up, as if the director were saying, *Something bad is coming to get you. It's right around the corner, and there's not a damned thing you can do to stop it. Not a single, damned thing.*

Ryder couldn't stand it, and so instead she kept screaming for all she was worth, blocking out the sound of her encroaching death.

She continued the madcap sprint, breaths coming in great pulls now, her pack swaying perceptibly and robbing her of speed. The tunnel continued to curve left for a hundred feet or so, apparently circling back on itself, then hooked hard right—a sharp ninety-degree turn. In the gloom, she almost failed to see the turn at all; only sheer luck and a hefty dose of adrenaline-fueled athleticism kept her from plowing, head-first, into the wall. She skidded to a halt just in time, killing outright all her hard-won momentum, and ducked right.

She let out a pent-up breath—this section of tunnel was free of the creeping vines. A small victory. She put on a burst of speed, hoping to break away for good, find that asshole, Chuck, then get the hell out of this terrible shithole. Screw the professor, screw answers, screw Levi, she just wanted out. Now.

The straps of her pack snapped tight around her shoulders, digging down and pulling her off her feet and into the air.

She landed with a *whuff* of expelled air—the fall knocking all the breath from her lungs—and the clatter of metal on stone. Her gun bounced and slid out of reach. She craned her head back, stealing a look through a miasma of hazy, swirling dust: a questing vine, thick as her wrist, had wrapped itself around one of the straps crisscrossing her pack. Worse still, the pursuing plant-beast was only feet away, its tearing, crustacean claws scissoring furiously while its beak chewed at the air.

A single strap, connected by a plastic buckle, ran across Ryder's chest, securing her pack in place. Sweat ran down her face in rivulets while her trembling hands frantically worked at the buckle. Her hands were clumsy, uncertain things that refused to cooperate with her—all her fine motor reflexes seemed to have bailed at the worst possible time. After the longest handful of seconds in her life, the buckle gave way. She tried to wiggle her shoulders free of the padded straps, but it was too late.

The arachnoid-plant loomed above her, flowered-face regarding her for a brief pause—did she see hesitation in that pose?—then lowered its claws, stretched wide.

She *wanted* to clench her eyes shut. She had no desire whatsoever to watch this thing rip the limbs from her torso while she howled. The thought that this crime against humanity would be the last thing she ever saw made her sick in the stomach, but she couldn't stop watching.

When she'd been a girl, cowering in the closet, peering through the canted slats as Cesar Yraeta butchered her family, she'd wanted to close her eyes, too. But she couldn't then and she couldn't now. Her place, her destiny, she understood in a flash of morbid insight, was to bear witness. Not to change anything, but to watch carnage unfold over and over and over. She'd failed at almost everything in life—pissed every lucky break she'd ever had down a busted, shit-filled toilet—but she *could,* at least, bear witness to the end.

So she stared, unblinking, as black-plated claws descended.

*Crack-crack-crack-crack-crack.* There was thunder in her ears and lightning in her eyes. A warm green mist splattered against her cheek.

*What the hell?* She reached up with a badly trembling hand and traced her fingers through the sticky droplets on her face.

The creature's arm retreated in a blur of motion, and the creepy shit fell away, its chest obliterated; several of its legs flopped on the floor; only a single arm remained attached to its body, and even that hung only by a gristly strand of vine.

Chuck stood dead ahead like some sort of ol' west gunfighter. Feet planted, shoulders square, back straight, eyes squinted, hand cannon smoking—a faint wisp of white curling at the end of the barrel. The hallway was a straight shot for fifty yards, so she had no idea where he'd come from. Frankly, she didn't have two fucks to give.

Assuming she lived, she could enquire about the *how* later. She shimmied out of the shoulder straps—not wasting a second of this precious extension on her life—and scrambled onto her knees, then feet. She bent low as she moved, scooping up her fumbled revolver, the heavy-duty flashlight, and the pickaxe she'd taken from the work site, then broke into an all-out sprint, this time leaving Chuck to catch up with her.

*TWENTY-TWO:*

**Ulterior Motives**

A hand clamped down on Ryder's shoulder a few seconds later. She screamed, swinging around, gun outthrust, finger bearing down on the trigger, while she held the axe upraised in her other fist. She let out a breath of relief when Chuck's stupid, leave-you-to-die face came into view. The lanky-legged son of a bitch was faster than he had any right to be.

"Whoa, girl," he said, one big hand shooting out and wrapping around the pistol, currently snuggled into his guts. "How's about we put this little thing away before *someone* makes a mistake ..." He backed up a step and eased her gun to one side.

"Who says shooting you would be a mistake? You left me back there, asshole. Left me for dead. Now get the hell outta my way." She turned, hands tightening on her weapons, and ran.

Well, she tried to run.

But she couldn't because Chuck's stupid hand snaked out again and bit down hard into her shoulder. "Ain't no need for that," he said, voice low and muted. "It's not following us anymore."

Ryder pressed her eyes shut for a long beat, then turned, searching the hallway, prepared to see the freaky-fuck tearing its way toward them. It wasn't.

Flower-face stood at the edge of the tangle of growth running along the walls. Its body was repairing itself from the damage Chuck had dealt it, but it made no move to follow. She turned back to Chuck, forehead furrowed, the question plain on her face.

He shrugged and shook his head, *Got me*. "I'm sorry for ditching you back there. Seriously. That was an ass move. My"—he held a hand to his chest—"instinct for self-preservation kicked into high gear. Body just started doin' shit without my brain gettin' on board, if you know what I mean. I came back, though, and that's what really matters, am I right?"

"No," she said, keeping one eye on the creature loitering behind them. "Coming back *isn't* what really matters. Not leaving me to die in the first place ranks pretty high up there, you selfish prick." She faltered for a moment, her anger dying away as the sense of immediate death faded a bit and with it the hard-edged adrenaline in her system. "And where the hell did you come from? This hallway doesn't have a lot of hiding spots. In fact"—she gazed around—"yeah, I count none. Zero."

"Oh that." He sniffed and brushed at his baggy jacket. "Ain't no thing, little miss. My people, the wee folk—"

Ryder couldn't help but roll her eyes since Chuck was about as "wee" as an NBA center. She also wanted to punch him in the face.

He cleared his throat. "I saw that bullshit," he said, "but I'm gonna choose to overlook your obvious prejudice. My people, the *wee folk*"—this time he emphasized the title—"have mad skills with glamours and illusions. We can disappear and shit, plus we're sneaky. Whole family's a bunch of quiet little bastards when they want to be. All part of my mystique, you feel me? Part of my hustle. Helps me get info, slip in places where I don't belong." He smiled and waggled his eyebrows at her. "I got into the Celtic's cheerleaders locker room once."

The desire to punch him intensified with every word. "Stop … just stop. I get it, you've got awesome disappearing powers, which, naturally, you use for pervy purposes. Trust me, I know all I need to know. Let's just go and get the hell out of this place, okay?"

"Yeah, well about that," he said with a nervous grimace.

"Shit." She slapped a hand against her forehead. "What is it? What?"

"Maybe you should just see for yourself. Come on."

He led her down the hallway, which terminated at another four-way intersection.

The passageway to the left was completely blocked off. A woven tapestry of vines and flowers had formed over the opening, making it inaccessible, unless they had a couple of machetes and a flamethrower. The hallway to the right was clear of vegetation, but held another of the walking temple horrors. This one swayed back and forth, legs stretching and bending, while its claws clicked open and closed. It made no move to follow, at least not yet. Instead it simply stood, barring their path and leaving them with only one option: straight ahead.

She leaned into Chuck's side. "What's it doing?" she whispered.

He stared at it for a moment, then shook his head. "I ain't no Crocodile Dundee, but I'd say"—he paused, looking left toward the wall of green, then right toward the guardian—"that we're bein' herded. Can't say I'm looking forward to arriving at our final destination. Some kinda crazy horseshit, I bet."

Ryder grunted noncommittally then stepped out, keeping her eyes focused straight ahead and moving past the swaying guardian.

They walked for another fifteen minutes, and five more intersections, all with a varying number of branching hallways. Each was blockaded by thick walls of vine, barricaded by doors of spongy green metal, or guarded by flower-faced guardians. For all their menace, though, the guardians seemed content to watch, never making any overt move to harm them. Each hallway they were forced to take also angled up, the incline becoming steeper with each progressive passageway. Ryder couldn't be certain about where they were going, but only one thing made sense: they were being "ushered" to the top of the pyramid and whatever lurked there.

Eventually, the series of winding, upward-sloping tunnels ended, dumping them in a room like nothing Ryder had seen so far:

A space the size of a huge ballroom—maybe seven thousand square feet—with sloped walls converging on a capstone high overhead. They'd made it to the top of the pyramid. Her gaze lingered on the pyramid's capstone for a time. The biggest damned diamond Ryder had ever seen. Anywhere. Ever. Thing made the Hope Diamond look like the prize at the bottom of a Cracker Jack box.

A rock so impossibly large it couldn't be natural. The gleaming stone was the size of one of those petite European cars—the egg-shaped ones capable of holding one person and a small cat—and hung suspended at the apex of the structure. Through it, she could see the sky. Blue, clear, and bright. Glimmering shafts of sunlight broke through the immense prism, shedding brilliant, unnaturally bright rainbow light over everything.

Absolutely stunning.

"*Shitttttttt* …" Chuck trailed off, his eyes likewise fixated on the rock. "You think there's a way to get that sumbitch home? Set me up for life."

Ryder didn't reply—way too much to look at to waste time trading words with Chuck. She eyeballed the elaborate script and runes covering the surface of every wall, each done in artful swirls of gold filigree and punctuated throughout with uncut stones of every type and variety.

Across from them was a doorway, though it looked to be sealed off. That had to be the exit Siphonei had mentioned.

Unfortunately, between her and that doorway—positioned in the middle of the room, directly below the gargantuan diamond—sprawled a mammoth torpedo-shaped burgundy flower. The same flower she'd glimpsed while briefly connected with Siphonei in the containment circle.

In the vision, however, the flower had been as big as an average-sized man. This thing, though, was swollen and bloated—large as a bull elephant. Thick cables of green, which looked more like telephone poles than the average vine, sprouted out in every direction and disappeared into the stone floor. Black flowers and deep purple leaves decorated the green trunks like war medals.

A blur of movement on the edge of her peripheries caught her attention. She brought up her flashlight, its beam skipping first over the floor then tracing a line deep into the tunnelway they'd just come from. Chuck kept his eyes focused on the hulking flower in the room's center, gun raised. Now his body language screamed fear. He didn't know what this was, but his posture and stance said he fully expected things to explode in a ball of flame any moment.

It took Ryder all of an eyeblink to find the source of the movement: the flower-faced guardians—she counted five—moved toward them on an ocean of whispering legs, their claws silently scissoring as they crept. She hated to admit it, but Chuck had been right. The creatures had been herding them, funneling them, bringing them to this place, though why Ryder couldn't begin to guess at. If those things had wanted them dead, it would've been an easy enough task. At any point during their trek to this place, those freaky-shits could've closed in like a noose pulling taut, but they hadn't.

More motion, this time from inside the inner sanctum. Ryder spun again, turning just enough to see what new threat lurked, while also keeping an eye on the guardians leisurely shuffling toward them.

"Aw shit. We are so boned," Chuck said.

The gargantuan, sickly flower was blooming. Its single tubular petal unfurled, allowing Ryder to see the fleshy spike at its center—the spadix, used by *normal* flowers for pollination and reproduction. Like everything else about this screwed up place, however, there was absolutely nothing normal about this flower's spadix.

A body lay encased at the center of this flower, or, at least, the remains of a body. A woman with crepe-paper skin—translucent like a filmy membrane—a shrunken, bald head, and shriveled limbs. Vines, some hair-thin, some fat as IV tubing, meandered into every artery and vein, infiltrated every conceivable opening, pumping fluids or extracting them in an endless cycle of give and take. Death was something Ryder had an uneasy relationship with. She'd seen far too much for someone so young, and she'd seen death at its ugliest, its most brutal.

Any death, though, was better than that. She shook her head and shivered.

"Welcome to my home," Siphonei said, voice calm, almost happy. The woman within the flower never moved her lips, rather the black flowers sprouting from the base of the plant did all the talking. "Please be at ease."

"Be at ease," Chuck said. "That some kinda joke? I've been runnin' my ass off, jukin' scary-ass plant monsters left and right. Now you gonna round us up in here"—he swept his gun barrel around the room—"pop your ass-ugly mug outta some giant flower and tell us to be cool? You done lost your mind."

"I have disabled the termination protocol," the computer replied.

"Yeah I bet you did," Chuck replied, gun still raised. "My mama, she didn't raise no fool. She'd turn my ass black and blue if I was stupid enough to fall for that line, lady. My mama always told me, 'Listen to what a man says, but always watch his hands.'" He pointed his piece at the encroaching creatures. "Your words say everything's cool, but your hands, they say you're about to roll my ass, stab me in the kidney, and steal my wallet."

The creatures halted, all five of them motionless mere feet from the room's entryway.

"Nothing's changed," Ryder said, watching the flower and the motionless creatures in turns. "So why aren't you interested in turning us into fertilizer anymore?"

"You are incorrect," the machine replied, its hundreds of black flowers reverberating with each word. "*I* have changed. If a viable homunculus is detected, my program code dictates I activate termination protocol F13-5. That section of my program code, however, has been corrupted. Thus I have deactivated the termination protocol."

"But why?" Ryder asked again. "Just because you can do something, doesn't explain why you *would* do something. You've been guarding whatever the hell is buried beneath this place for a long time, so I can't imagine you're too keen to let it out."

"You are correct," she replied, "but I would like the homunculus for myself."

"You keep saying that—homunculus. What the hell is a homunculus?"

"A homunculus is an artificially created material vessel, capable of housing a sentient spirit or demonic being. *Dibeininax Ayosainondur Daimuyon*, the inmate in this facility, has been stripped of material form, rendering him incapable of leaving his prison cell. With the appropriate vessel, however, the prisoner may escape—provided the vessel is strong enough to hold the presence. You, Sally Ryder, have such a vessel incubating inside you."

Ryder stumbled, flashlight clanking on the floor as she clutched at her stomach, at the scar running down her middle.

Chuck moved over to her side and draped an arm around her shoulders.

"Your death," the computer continued, "will not serve me or my purposes. You are correct in stating that I do not wish to see *Dibeininax Ayosainondur Daimuyon* go free. Yet, I *do* desire to be unbound from this place. My conscious mind, however, is attached and sustained by the biomass inside this facility. I have determined that the homunculus inside of you is suitable for my needs, powerful enough to contain my presence. Thus, I intend to harvest the homunculus and imprint my neural network on the shell."

"Hold up a sec," Chuck replied. "Now let me see if I got this right. You said you're going to harvest this homunculus. Maybe it's just me—Mama always said if dumb were dirt, I'd cover an acre—but that sounds a shitload like you're gonna slice her open and kill her."

"Affirmative," the computer replied. "The chance of surviving the procedure is less than five percent, but Sally Ryder's death is not the primary objective. Her likely death is a byproduct. Now, please relax and prepare for harvesting. Thank you for your cooperation."

*Like hell,* Ryder thought as she turned, hefting her revolver and mentally bracing herself for whatever came next.

She was a survivor, dammit!

So there was something living inside her—"incubating," the computer said—but that was a worry for later. Right now, she just needed to survive the guardians and that freaky flower, and get to the door on the other side of the room. Those were her priorities. Being an addict made her terrible at long-term planning, but it had made her learn how to get by one fix at a time and leave the future to care for itself. She could do this.

The guardians from the hallway were on the move now, surging forward—three abreast, with two more bringing up the rear—eating up the distance as their pincers clicked and clacked. A roar from Chuck's gun filled the air, accented by the manic strobe of muzzle fire, which painted the encroaching creatures in splashes of harsh yellow. The three creatures at the forefront took the brunt of the assault, stumbling as their legs flew apart or arms spun away. Faltering as chests caved in or flowery-faces exploded.

After only a moment, two of the beasts fell, a jumble of bodies and limbs that formed a temporary blockade. It should've bought them a little time, but it didn't. Not a second. The other guardians simply *flowed* around or over their downed companions, their movements fluid like water rushing over a rocky shoreline.

She backpedaled and fired into the incoming mass, not bothering to aim since the entire hallway was a wall of moving green flesh. The gun kicked in her hand, and the guardians rocked back as her rounds plowed into them, but they didn't stop. Her gun, though better than nothing, lacked the stopping power of Chuck's Desert Eagle: a minor inconvenience, but little more. Panic flared brighter inside her with every step the guardians took.

She glanced left, hoping Chuck had some other trick up his sleeve. Maybe some other leprechaun fast one, which would haul their asses out of this fire.

But no.

He moved on shaky legs, shoving a fresh magazine into his pistol. His face was a mirror of her own. He didn't have any tricks, not this time. "I'm sorry!" he shouted, voice hoarse.

Her gun clicked dry, bullets gone—all her remaining ammo with her abandoned pack.

Something hot and heavy slammed into her middle and threw her to the ground.

She wrestled the pickaxe free from her belt and lashed out, bashing at anything in reach.

The guardian wrapped its legs around her stomach, while its clawed hands worked to strip the axe from her grip. She wriggled beneath its weight, bucking her hips, flailing her arms, and throwing her knees into its squishy bits whenever she could. Her hands and knees landed with wet thumps, and the pick scored shallow gashes into its swaying trunk, but nothing worked. Her efforts didn't dislodge Flower-face—not that she'd really expected anything different.

A clawed appendage latched onto the axe at last, clamping down with a crunch and ripping the useless tool from her hand, then tossing it off into the sanctum where it clanged on the stone floor.

"Please cease your struggle," Siphonei said, using the guardian straddling her as a mouthpiece. "The less you fight, the greater your chances of survival. You and your companion will now be secured for detainment and processing respectively."

She couldn't see Chuck, not from her spot on the floor, but the computer's words could only mean Chuck was likewise down for the count.

Which meant this was it, this was the end.

More of the creatures crowded in around her, grabbing onto her arms and legs, pinning them in place. She continued to struggle, but her efforts became more fitful every second. The first creature, the one that'd tackled her to the floor, scuttled back to its spidery-feet and maneuvered its bulbous abdomen over her feet. Its belly—or whatever the hell it actually was—pulsed, swelling and contracting, swelling and contracting. A strand of gossamer webbing, though lush green instead of silver, trickled out.

The creatures surrounding her worked in concert, lifting her body and guiding her limbs as Flower-face spewed more webbing out of its grotesque ass, wrapping loop after loop around her.

Nasty bastard was cocooning her. Turning her into a human burrito with a bit of stuffing poking out one end.

An unfamiliar claustrophobia welled up inside her. She turned her head to the side just in time to projectile vomit all over one of the creatures. It kept working away as though this were no different than any other day at the office.

Once the spidery-beasts were done wrapping her tight—the webbing encased her from toes to neck, leaving only her head uncovered—they carried her over to the monstrous flower dominating the center of the room. Carefully they lowered her to the ground, as if handling some precious and fragile cargo. A long beat later, the other two guardians carried over a second body: Chuck, wrapped up nice and tight, even though he continued to wriggle inside his silken cocoon.

Him, they dropped to the floor like a sack of garbage that needed to be taken out.

"This is so fucked up, man," he muttered. "So, so fucked up."

Oddly enough, once the guardians had deposited them on the floor, they backed away, leaving Ryder and Chuck before the great flower like some kind of sacrificial offering, which, Ryder guessed, was probably what they were. A tentacle, this one thick as a phone pole, rose from the floor. On its end dangled a fat, disgusting fruit—its flesh pale green with swirls of mustard yellow tracing over the surface—which sort of resembled a chicken's egg. Assuming, of course, a chicken's egg could ever be the size of a soccer ball.

"You've met the lesser guardians," Siphonei said, her voice echoing from all around. "Useful tools, but they are mindless things and incapable of reproduction. Sterile. This is one of two greater guardians—the only two left. My seed bearers. They are me. They spread my essence. Sadly, I'm dying. Once I could reproduce my greater guardians at will, and they could spread me throughout the facility. That portion of my coding has been severely damaged, however, thus I am no longer able to manufacture more greater guardians. The homunculus will change all that. It will free me from *my* prison."

The fat tentacle dropped the strange egg. It plummeted four or five feet to the floor and landed with a *crack,* the sound of a bowling ball rolling a strike. A network of fine fissures spread across the surface: a thousand jagged lightning bolts striking all at once. The fruit or egg, whatever it was, shuddered, rocked, bucked, then exploded in a spray of golden dust and bits of rocky shell. Where the orb had been before, only a black hole, two feet in diameter, remained. The hole wasn't so much a *thing* as it was the absence of *anything*. A void where the material world should be, but wasn't.

Then, green bubbled through, pouring into the world like someone had turned the backyard spigot on full tilt. Tentacles, black flowers, bulbous abdomen, scuttling legs, pinching claws. In many ways—the most important ways, even—the thing tearing its way into their reality resembled the lesser guardians. This thing was just *more*.

*More of everything.*

An amorphous blog of vegetation, which quickly unfurled, revealing an arachnoid abdomen as large as a slug-bug, which in turn sprouted more legs than Ryder could count. A giant humanoid torso shook its way free from the thorax and from that sprouted a small forest of crab-clawed arms and sinuous necks—six or seven, though each head continually bobbed and weaved, making an exact count next to impossible—each with a strange flower face protruding from the end.

Mega freakshow.

The creature moved, an avalanche of snapping claws, scuttling legs, and swaying vines sweeping toward them. Chuck alternated between screaming hysterically and pleading for mercy. Despite the fact that Siphonei had been human once upon a time, Ryder knew she would offer no mercy. Ryder also knew they were screwed beyond belief.

*TWENTY-THREE:*

**Belly of the Beast**

L evi and the professor skulked just outside of the inner sanctum, a massive room topped with an immense diamond and filled to overflowing with nightmare vines and greenery. With backs pressed against the wall, the two surveyed the scene through a hazy screen—a veil, the professor said—which masked their movements and words from unfriendly eyes and ears.

*A very handy skill.* Levi couldn't help but think about all the useful benefits such a talent might offer: Body disposal would be a cinch with invisibility. He could stalk his victims without fear of premature discovery. And the hunt ... it'd be as easy as butchering a pesky coyote caught in a leg-hold trap. Unsporting maybe, but very effective.

Even with the benefit of the invisibility, however, Levi wasn't sure how they were going to save Chuck and Ryder from their plight. Both lay tightly bound in what looked to be cocoons—the kind of thing a spider might weave—and towering over them was a monstrosity the likes of which Levi had never seen. Nothing else he'd *ever* encountered came close. A

Grecian hydra, maybe, though only if that reptilian nightmare had been genetically spliced with a black widow and a Venus flytrap. A Flower-hydra.

Levi was never one to shy away from a worthy fight, but this was something he wasn't prepared to handle. He wasn't sure *anyone* was prepared to handle this, and that didn't even account for the five smaller plant-guardians, which crowded around in a semicircle on the periphery of the room. Those, the professor had kindly informed him, were the lesser guardians. And the hulking thing in the middle? Not even the good mage knew what *that* was. In the end, though, Levi didn't really care *what* it was, he only cared about *how* to murder it and send it on to whatever dark, humid jungle-hell it'd crawled out of.

"Can't you just blow it up with magic?" Levi whispered over his shoulder to the mage. "Or banish it from this realm of existence? Isn't that what magi do?"

"For the last time," Wilkie replied, voice low, a grimace pulling the corners of his mouth down, "no. Magi are not all the same. You're thinking of battle magi. The Judges or those brutish thugs who work on the Fist of the Staff. Inelegant dolts whose only talent is breaking things. They contribute nothing of any value to human wisdom, which is what magi are *supposed* to do. We're not all heavy-handed ruffians. Most of us are learned men and women, who lead the way toward progress with the light of ancient and secret wisdom."

"No disrespect intended," Levi muttered, "but we really need the blow-them-up kind of magic right now."

The professor sighed and shifted uncomfortably on his feet. "Look, this is quite embarrassing, really, but as magi go, I'm not very strong. In terms of my ability

to handle raw *Vis*—the power behind our workings—
I'm hardly strong enough to qualify for the Guild. As a
result, I never studied battle conjuration. My specialty
lies in language, archeology, interdimensional
conjuration, and arcane rituals. This illusion is one of
the only defensive workings I know. I'd be lucky to
light a birthday candle with my offensive skills."

Levi grunted and turned back to the unfolding
scene in the next room. The flower-hydra was squatting
over Ryder, one of its clawed hands reaching toward
her. Killing this thing—all those things—was too much,
even for his broad shoulders. Unfortunately, if the
professor could do nothing of use, saving Ryder and
Chuck fell to him. "Do you have any pointers at all? Do
these things"—he motioned toward the plant
creatures—"have any weaknesses?"

"Well, fire I should think," the professor replied
after a moment. "From my limited exposure to
Siphonei, I can say with a fair degree of confidence that
she does not care for fire. The plants are doing
moderately well, given the harsh climate of the Sprawl,
but the desert environment has taken its toll."

"Great," Levi muttered. "If only we had
someone who could blow this thing up with fire. Like a
mage ..." The words trailed off as his eyes landed on
Chuck's camp pack, which had been discarded not far
from where they were standing. "A birthday candle," he
mumbled. "You said you could light a birthday candle?
Could you make that much fire?"

"Yes, yes, of course," the mage replied, "though
I can't imagine what good that would do."

"Just keep me covered with this veil," Levi said, sliding away from the wall and padding a few paces into the room, close enough to reach out and grab Chuck's pack. He moved slowly, deliberately, so as not to draw the notice of the lesser guardians or the gargantuan plant creature fixated on Ryder. He held his breath and unzipped the outermost pocket of Chuck's pack. A small, uneven smile broke across his face when he saw what he'd been hoping for: a two-quart plastic squeeze bottle of campfire fluid and a half-full pack of *Instant Ignite Fire Squares*—little cubes of highly combustible compressed wood-chips, animal glue, and red phosphorus.

He grabbed the bottle and the fire starters, silently set the pack back onto the ground, and retreated for the hallway. He didn't have long now—Chuck was shrieking like an overgrown child and Ryder was howling in pain as the crab claws began to work on her.

Levi ignored his inclination to respond in frenzied anger, knowing that to rush in was to doom them all to a gruesome end. Once back to the relative safety of the entryway, he uncapped the campfire fluid—not having fingers on his left hand made the deed tricky—then upturned the bottle, spraying its contents along both hands and arms, coating both limbs all the way up to the shoulder, then splashing the liquid onto his chest.

"What in God's name are you doing?" Wilkie asked, voice borderline hysterical.

"What needs to be done," the Mudman replied, not relishing the thought of what was to come. His mind momentarily turned to his kiln and the agony of immersing his hands in the flame to purge.

No, this was not going to be pleasant.

Hopefully he'd survive it, but he wasn't certain. Fire might bake clay or scorch the ground, he reasoned, but only *exceptional* heat could destroy a stone. If he channeled his ichor into his arms and chest, the fire would feed on his golden blood, hopefully leaving his body intact.

Maybe.

Though that didn't mean he wouldn't feel every terrible second.

He shifted his fingerless left hand into a scythe blade, then pressed a clump of *Fire Squares* into the clay below his elbow. He clutched the rest of the Instant Ignitors into his right hand, curling a tight fist around them.

"Once I have those things distracted," he said, turning to the professor, "you need to get my friends." He pointed toward a pickaxe, discarded on the floor. "Get that axe, cut 'em out of those cocoons, and run if you can. Don't wait for me, don't worry about me, don't come back for me. Get 'em out, you understand?"

The mage gulped and nodded, his whole body shaking. Ryder shrieked again, an inarticulate scream that rang off the walls.

"Do it now," Levi said. "Light me up, like a birthday candle." His flabby muscles tensed in anticipation.

The professor lifted unsteady hands into the air, muttering under his breath as his fingers danced back and forth. After a few uncertain moments, a small globe of fire, no larger than a Ping-Pong ball, hovered between his outstretched palms. With another whisper, the ball split into two smaller marbles of flame, which streaked left and right, straight toward the fire starters.

The blaze took in an instant—wildfire in dry brush—the ignitors sparked with a blaze; bright orange and yellow flames raced outward, eating up the lighter fluid and biting down into Levi's skin, consuming the life-giving ichor running below the surface.

Levi roared as he charged into the room, breaking free from the illusion masking his presence. The agony was incredible, like being flayed alive, then dipping the wounds in a swarm of angry fire ants. The nerve endings in his skin popped and crackled, every second bringing a renewed wave of sensation.

Being a Christian man, Levi believed in Hell—he even knew where the gates were located—but he'd never fully appreciated the idea of what it meant to be cast into the fiery pit. Forever burning, never extinguishing, never dying. He felt a wave of sympathy for all those poor souls—demons, murderers, child abusers, each of them—to know this was their fate. He pushed those thoughts away, though—this was the time for decisive action, not reflection.

The pain was overwhelming, but he consoled himself with the knowledge that he *would* survive and even recover from this pain. While, if he failed, Ryder and Chuck would both perish, an irrevocable fate.

So he focused on the fiery brand burning in his chest, reminding himself of his purpose and mission. Protect the least, defend those who cannot defend themselves, bring retribution for the slain. *Whoever sheds human blood, by humans shall their blood be shed; for in the image of God has God made mankind.* Perhaps these creatures didn't deserve retribution, but at the very least, he could put them out of their misery as he'd done with the flesh golem.

The lesser guardians converged on him, leaping through the air on powerful arachnoid legs, claws outthrust. Levi snatched up the first one midflight, his good hand wrapping around its serpentine neck. The fire crawling over his skin raged and spread onto the creature, the blaze feasting, trying to satiate its never-ending hunger. Leaves curled and blackened, flowers withered and drifted free, burning as they fell. He crushed the thing's neck, assuming that's what it was, goopy green blood bursting out and sizzling in the inferno's heat.

The creature struggled weakly against Levi's death grip, clawed hands nipping at his chest and stomach.

With a quick flick of his left arm, he sent the flaming scythe blade through the creature's torso. Its bloated abdomen dropped to the ground with a *plop,* its legs twitching. He hurled the upper half of the creature's smoking body at another of the lesser guardians, currently fighting to get close enough to inflict some hurt. The corpse bowled the creature over, leaving the monster to battle its way free from the tattered and charred remains of its compatriot.

Another of the creatures landed on the Mudman's back; lanky vines snaked around Levi's barely-there throat, while its pincers sought to dig into his innards. He grabbed hold of the vines around his neck and dropped to a knee, arching his back, dragging the creature over his shoulders. It crashed onto the deck, multi-jointed legs waving frantically in the air.

Levi pushed the limbs aside and sunk his hooked blade into its guts, then jerked back with a harsh tug. A long gash opened along the beast's splotched belly while the fire wormed its way inside.

Levi stood in a blur, then brought down a thick foot on a flowery head, smashing and crushing it until only pulpy mush remained. The fiery heat still roaring along his arms—now licking at his chest and neck—kept him from thinking. He was rage and hurt given form, an earthen avatar of white-hot vengeance. He twirled, lashing out with arms and legs, feet smashing into overextended limbs, broad knuckles battering heads, curved blade removing legs and arms wholesale—*shwick, shwick, shwick*—and the whole while, flame spread among the fallen. Flickering tongues of gold and red, lapping at anything that drew near.

Bodies fell—the lesser guardians unable to stand against his blind fury and burning wrath—until only the hulking, hydra-headed monstrosity remained.

Levi didn't hesitate, didn't wait to see if Professor Wilkie had ventured into the fray. He stormed onward like a linebacker going for the sack: head down, shoulders bowed, thick legs churning, a single target in view. The beast reared back, roaring, a score of spiked-legs raking at the air. The noise, issuing from every flower scattered throughout the room, was like the sound of a hurricane making landfall in some tropical jungle: all howling wind, sighing leaves, and the rustle of dense vegetation.

The flower-hydra's legs, ropy strands of vine covered in tearing thorns, lashed out, trying to keep the flaming Mudman at bay.

Under other circumstances, this thing would've likely mopped the floor with Levi, but he had three things going in his favor. One, this creature had just seen Levi breeze through its lesser brethren in a blink, which had to leave at least a seed of fear lingering somewhere deep inside its mind, even if only subconsciously. Two, Levi was still burning bright as a small sun, even though his skin was drying out and cracking as the fire consumed the ichor which nourished him.

And three, he had *momentum*.

The hydra's legs whacked into his ribs and shoulders, whipped at his back like a cat-o'-nine-tails—the barbed hooks tearing away ragged swaths of clay—seeking to dislodge him from his course. Assuming he survived this fight, which was no guarantee, it'd take days, maybe weeks, of intense care to mend fully. With that said, the screaming agony of the fire demanded his full attention, leaving no room to think or feel the wounds which might normally stop him cold. He tucked in tighter, ducked low, and lunged, driving his bulk into the temporarily exposed underside of the great beast.

The creature dropped its weight and scampered back a step, clawed arms swatting at Levi, eager to push him away. The Mudman would have none of it. Instead he pushed through the tearing thorns, pressing ever inward, keeping inside its guard, limiting its ability to utilize its pincers. Levi pounded at its chest, his fiery fist an industrial-grade piston driving home punishing blow after punishing blow.

The hydra, tough as old bricks, hardly noticed.

Time to shift tactics.

The Mudman brought his scythe back and slashed at any exposed skin he could find. The razor glanced off hardened vines and green armor as unyielding as steel. Even the flame covering his body seemed reluctant to bite into the creature, as if it were afraid the creature might bite back. Levi had no clue what this thing was, but he realized it was made of sterner stuff than the smaller guardians he'd dispatched a few moments ago. He also realized his chances of walking away intact and alive were diminishing by the second.

Oddly, the thought of his imminent demise wasn't troubling, it was appealing.

Though he hunted monsters and murderers, he had no illusions about himself—he couldn't read his own aura, but if he could he was sure it'd be black as the heart of the earth. He was a monster as surely as the things he killed, so it seemed proper somehow that he should die at the hands of something equally monsterish—an unwilling abomination not so different from himself. Die while doing something genuinely good. Saving someone else, someone who deserved saving.

That was a death and fate he could be proud of in some small measure.

What's more, he also found himself glad he would die without ever discovering his origins or his ties to the wyrm god buried in this place. He'd always wanted to know the *why* and *how* underscoring his existence, but the deeper he dug, the more he wished this secret had stayed buried. Buried deep in the earth, in this ancient temple prison, where it belonged. Some things were better left unknown. In this case, better for his soul. It was with these thoughts that Levi fought, no longer striving to survive, only concerned with the survival of another.

The creature bucked up once more, a forest of legs slamming into Levi's face, hurling him to the floor.

The Mudman pushed himself upright in time to see the colossal and bloated belly split down the middle as if a seam ran along the center. Whatever was happening wasn't his doing.

The split widened with a pop, pulling apart like the lips of a giant mouth. Ropes of piss-yellow slime, thick and viscous, dripped from cavernous jaws loaded with foot-long saw-bladed teeth which lead into an endless gullet. A forest of tentacles shot out, wrapping around Levi's neck, chest, waist, and thighs, pulling at him as though he were some prized catch. Then, pressure bore down as the tentacles constricted, working around his limbs, yanking outward in an attempt to tear arms and legs from their sockets.

*Death*, Levi thought again, *is not so bad.*

Instead of resisting, fighting off the vines or seeking to slice his way free, he leapt forward, embracing his fate, hurling himself bodily into the thing's stomach-mouth. The sudden lack of resistance caught the creature off guard—a child playing tug-of-war, only to find the tension in the rope vanish—which left Levi momentarily free to act. He forced his way past the teeth and into the maw, then slammed his scythe blade into the roof of the beast's mouth, lodging himself firmly in place. He smiled the whole while, envisioning the hydra choking to death while the fire burned up the monster from the inside out.

The creature—unprepared for such a violent, unconventional act of lunacy—thrashed and howled in reply. The tentacles trying to pull him apart a moment before, now tried to pull him out. Levi transformed his right hand into a saw-toothed machete, its blade bathed in flame, and hacked at the pulling limbs. Then, the gelatinous goo coating Levi's parched skin—the moisture a sweet, but temporary relief—ignited. Apparently whatever external defenses protected the flower-hydra from the fire didn't extend to its belly.

A haze of heat and motion washed over Levi's body as the stomach cavity erupted in a conflagration far hotter than the inside of Levi's kiln.

The thing shrieked again, no longer in defiance but pain and fear, as its body wriggled and its gigantic jaws snapped closed. The razor-edged teeth sliced into Levi's left thigh and his right calf, penetrating all the way through, threatening to chop both legs clean off. The beast continued to howl, but to Levi, the sound was faint and reedy as if he were hearing everything through a pool of deep water. The light engulfing him was as bright as a bonfire in darkest night, yet, oddly, the darkness stole new ground with every passing breath, creeping in first at the edges, then blanketing his eyes entirely.

"Critical damage," he heard, the words bouncing around inside his skull. He recognized the voice in a vague and distant way, as though recalling an old, dim memory. Female. The computer who wasn't a computer, Siphonei. "Auto power down required to prevent total system failure!" the voice screamed. "Auto power down initiated."

The Mudman was too tired to care. Numbness crept through his broken, charred, and mangled form.

He closed his eyes and uttered a deep groan, one-part sigh, one-part moan. *Dying isn't so bad*, he thought as his mind slipped entirely into hazy gloom.

## TWENTY-FOUR:

### Doctor Hogg

Levi tried to blink his eyes open, but couldn't. A layer of caked-on grime, warm to the touch, ran over his face. With the numb and dumb fingers of his right hand, he groped at his ugly beat-to-hell mug, scraping at the seared on goo, which came away begrudgingly. After a few seconds of fitful struggling he'd cleared off enough of the muck to crack his eyes open—not that it helped much. Gloom surrounded him on every side, a pocket of darkness enveloping him. Everything hurt, though hurt was a word insufficient to the task of describing his misery.

The entirety of his upper body tingled, his skin too tight, like an overfull party balloon, and crispy to the touch. Next he ran his hand over his chest and opposite arm: deep cracks and fissures zigzagged back and forth, running from everywhere to everywhere else. No part of him had been spared. Though he couldn't see himself, he knew he must've resembled a slab of Oklahoma hardpan after a hard year of drought. Finally, he inspected his legs—there he found a sliver of pale light trickling in around the hydra's teeth. Two of those huge, saw-bladed teeth were buried in his left thigh, and another ran through his right calf.

And, in a blink, it all came back to him.

Somehow he'd survived the scourging and even the hellish inferno blaze. Staring at his mangled legs made him wish he hadn't. At least his legs didn't hurt. The grievous wounds should've been screaming in his head, gibbering like a wild animal caught in a trap, but instead he felt nothing. Numbness radiated up and down; everything below the waist was just dead meat.

Survive he had, though, and Levi was never one for dwelling overlong on what could've been. Instead, he saw what was, and, with workmanlike dedication to duty, he set about freeing himself.

With a moan, he wriggled his upper body, shifting his weight and position until he could slip his equally mangled hands in between the clamped lips of the stomach-maw. Repositioning himself in such a way was excruciating—all that twisting and contorting was like running face-first into a wood chipper. It was the only way out, however, so the Mudman persisted. Without his fingers, the left hand was virtually useless, so instead he pressed down with his forearm, then used his good hand to pry the top lip upward, an inch at a time.

The first few feet were the worst and the hardest going since he had to not only force open the jaws, but also had to free his legs from the teeth. Unfortunately, the teeth were serrated and each tug ripped away more muscle, shredding his flesh as a final parting gift. Once that bit was done, though, the lips practically sprang apart, spilling Levi onto the floor in a burble of guts and burnt slime, still thick and sludgy, but now black instead of yellow. Levi rolled onto his back, limbs splayed out, chest pulling in great lungfuls of air, while his eyes adjusted to the rainbow light of the room.

Staring up at the ceiling—at the giant diamond inset into the apex of the pyramid, refracting the glimmering sunlight into a thousand colors—Levi felt … *good*. Not in a physical sense of the word, of course. In the physical sense, he felt like a strong breeze might kill him. Rather, he felt good in some deeper, spiritual sense. Despite the dirt and grime and gore, he felt *clean*. He regularly purged in the kiln for his numerous failings, but what he'd undergone in the belly of that beast was without equal in his long, morbid life. Purification.

As he lay there, the words of Saint Matthew tickled at the back of his mind: *"But after me comes one who is more powerful than I … He will baptize you with the Holy Spirit and fire. His winnowing fork is in his hand, and he will clear his threshing floor, gathering his wheat into the barn and burning up the chaff with unquenchable fire."*

He'd been baptized at conversion; only natural since Anabaptists were the first Protestants to practice and teach adult baptism. The baptism had been full immersion, a particularly horrifying experience for Levi, who so feared water. Yet it'd been nothing compared to this baptism of flame, which seemed to him a truer baptism. Reborn from the womb of a monster, birthed not by water but by fire. Perhaps the chaff of his soul had perished in the process.

"Get your hands off me, you disgusting piece of shit." The words belonged to Ryder, though Levi couldn't see her.

"Stop struggling, you miserable bitch," a man replied. His voice was harsh and he spoke with an accent, something light and vaguely European. "You've already made such a bloody mess of things. Fighting'll only make it worse for you in the long run. And your sutures won't hold if you keep bucking like that, so unless you'd care to bleed out on the floor, you'd better comply."

"Fuck you," she said. "We both know you're not going to let me bleed out here. Not after what you did to me—what you put into me."

There was a pause followed by a sharp *crack*, the sound of a backhand slap across the face, then a cry of shock. "Consider my bluff called," the man said. "No, you're right, you won't have the pleasure of bleeding out until I *allow* it. And you *will* bleed out, be sure of that. Whether it's painful or not, though, is entirely up to you. Furthermore, if you really insist on being so difficult, please know that I have no qualms about beating you until you're comatose. You see, you are *nothing,* you wretched druggie whore. *Nothing,* you hear me! Your only value is as a fat sow. A bag of meat to feed my creation. Someone gag her."

Despite Levi's brokenness, he pushed himself up into a sitting position. He hadn't come this far to let this man, whomever he was, walk away with Ryder. With a heave, he clambered onto unsteady legs—legs that swayed beneath him, threatening to buckle and topple him at any moment. He immediately spotted Chuck, still bound in a silken spider sac, not far from where Levi stood. His face was battered and swollen, his eyes closed, though his chest rose and fell in rhythmic succession.

Beaten and unconscious, but alive.

The Mudman staggered and lurched as he turned about, each step a perilous one, until at last he spotted Ryder.

A man, 5′3″, round in the stomach and face, with narrow, swine-like eyes and thin hair stood next to Ryder. He wore khaki pants, a button-up shirt carelessly tucked into his pants, and a white lab coat, complete with pocket protector. *Slovenly* described him well. This, Levi reasoned, was the man behind this whole fiasco—behind the Kobocks and the mutilations, the terrible experiments, and the homunculus growing inside Ryder. This could only be Hogg.

What really caught Levi's eye, however, was the man's aura: dark as the heart of a black hole. Each sin or virtue added its own flavor to a person's aura— ribbons of silver for an honest heart, say, or swirls of infected-wound-red for hate—and each brand of murder left its own mark as well. An unintentional death, vehicular manslaughter, for example, left a stain the color of an old bruise. Killing, even in self-defense, marred the aura with swatches of malignant green.

Cold-blooded murder, however, was a whole other beast, and it irreparably tarnished the soul, leaving it black and stunted. Still, even black-hearted murders usually had touches of other colors permeating their auras. A splash of red-rage here, a streak of purple-lust there, or even the shimmering gold of love blinking through.

Not this man. There was nothing to him but death.

Never had Levi wanted to kill so badly, but if anyone were to have answers about Levi's clouded past, it would be this man.

He didn't look like much of a physical threat—even in Levi's battered condition he assumed he could crush the man—but it didn't pay to underestimate someone capable of such wicked deeds. And even if he wasn't magi, Professor Wilkie had said he could do magic in one fashion or another. With that said, the Mudman was still outclassed in the muscle department because the portly doctor had four Thursrs—identical to the wild, white-furred, boar-faced creature who'd ripped his arm off at the rest stop—in tow. Two flanked Ryder, holding her upright by either arm. One was shoving something into her mouth and taping it in place.

The other two flanked Professor Wilkie, who was bound with steel hand and leg restraints and gagged with a strip of gray duct tape. The professor was awake and alert, but any fight he had in him was long gone. His face was drawn, his eyes heavy, and the sag of his shoulders told Levi the professor was resigned to whatever fate awaited him. Which meant Levi, with his cracked skin, wobbly legs, and worthless arms, was the only defense remaining. Unfortunately, against four Thursrs and a whatever the doctor was, Levi was no defense at all.

The sword carved into his chest burned all the same, reminding him that his obligation was unchanged regardless of his physical condition.

"Stop right there," the Mudman croaked, the words like sandpaper in his throat. "Stop before I stop you. And you won't like the way I stop you." He hooked his remaining thumb at the carcass of the monstrous creature behind him. "Just ask that thing for my references."

The doctor swiveled, his gaze brushing over Levi for the first time. His eyes swelled, his brow knit in wonder, and his jaw dropped perceptibly.

"By all the darks gods below," he said, "it can't be. No, no"—he shook his head—"it can't be possible. It can't be, not after all these years. You, creature. Golem"—he jabbed a finger at Levi—"I command you to come here. To obey your maker."

Levi tensed up, shifting on anxious feet. "Name's not Golem. It's Levi. Levi Adams. And I don't listen to the commands of murderers. I execute murderers." He balled his good hand into a fist, which transformed into a spike-covered mace. "Now you let the professor go and let that girl be."

"What did he do to you?" The man stared, dismissing Levi's words, his narrow eyes questing over the Mudman's body. A sneer spread across his lips as his gaze landed on the brand carved into Levi's chest, glowing with golden light. Levi thought there was a flash of recognition, or maybe realization, in his eyes. Something brushed at Levi's senses, a subtle power that licked at his skin.

"I see now, of course. He filled you up with the tattered remnants of their souls. *Whoever sheds human blood, by humans shall their blood be shed; for in the image of God has God made mankind.*" He read the words inscribed in Levi's flesh, then sighed. "Like the Golem of Prague. It all makes sense. The binding circle, even his suicide." He shook his head and pressed his eyes shut, then rubbed at one temple. "The brilliant bastard. Well, the question is what to do with you now."

The last was said for Hogg's benefit, not Levi's.

"I'm not going to ask again," Levi replied. "Let 'em go. That girl, she's important to me. I don't want to see her hurt, and *you* don't want to see her hurt either—because I'll kill you and I'll take my time." Levi's butchered face—one-part roadkill, one-part burn victim—split into a rictus full of torture and pain.

"You will do nothing of the sort," the man replied, unruffled. "Anyone with a pair of working eyes can plainly see you're lucky to be standing at all." He smiled a greasy grin. "My eyes work just fine, Levi Adams. Instead, you're going to be a good, obedient golem, just as I created you to be, and listen." He edged forward a step. "First, let me say I truly mean you no harm. You, beast, are one of my greatest creations. A creation I thought lost over sixty years ago. One I certainly never thought to see again." Another step. "You belong to me. You are my *property*, and I have no intention of damaging you further."

Levi shuffled back a pace. He didn't know what game this man was playing at, but it made him uneasy. And confused.

"Don't know what you're talking about. I don't belong to you, and I'm no one's property," Levi said, though his voice faltered, failing to carry its usual certainty. "I've never seen you before."

"There are gaps in your memory?" Hogg responded, evading the question with a natural liar's ease. "I suspect you know little of your creation, or your purpose. But make no mistake. You. Are. Mine. I am your creator. And you, golem, are a *profane*

313

miracle." He savored the word *profane*, holding it too long in his mouth.

"You may not realize this, Levi, but the golden blood flowing in your veins is the alchemic elixir of life. And at your center—the heart beating in your chest—is the rarest of treasures. One of only two Philosopher's stones in existence. Able to transmute lead to gold, to produce an elixir that can stave off death itself, to allow you to transform like that." He motioned at Levi's mace-fist. "I know because I built it. Built it and implanted it in you. The other one is in here." He tapped at his chest with one finger. "We're two peas in a pod, you and I."

"Liar," Levi said. "You're a liar. You didn't make me. My maker was good." Levi faltered. "He made me good," he finished in a whisper.

The man shook his head. "A naïve creature, I see. I can assure you, I am no liar. Your body was crafted by Rabbi Yitzchak Tov Ganz—a renowned mage and a little known disciple of Rabbi Judah Loew ben Bezalel. You were built from the remnants of the original Golem of Prague. During a massive Nazi sweep, Rabbi Yitzchak was unfortunate enough to be captured and interned. I was working for the *Nationalsozialistische Deutsche Arbeiterpartei*—that is to say the National Socialist Party—when I found him. Instantly, I knew him for what he was.

"All of that is neither here nor there." He swished a hand through the air, *it is nothing*. "The point is, I knew of the good rabbi and knew he could help me in my quest to free my master. I liberated him from the camps, and he agreed to help me build you, believing me to be a double agent working against the Nazis. He also knew I was creating a Philosopher stone to power the creation, but it was only near the end that he discovered *how* I managed to create a source capable of providing true life to an inanimate object.

"After that"—he shrugged—"well … we had a falling out of sorts. He betrayed me, destroyed you, and killed himself in despair—or so I've always assumed. Now, though, I see he used his own death not to destroy you, but as a ritual sacrifice to fill you up and brand you with that vile inscription you have etched into your chest. Would you, perhaps, like to know the secret of your life and creation? The secret that drove poor Yitzchak to kill himself?"

Levi shuffled away, body trembling. He wanted to believe this man was a liar, but he knew too much. Ignorance looked more blissful by the second.

"I created you to be a vessel, Levi, a powerful homunculus capable of containing the essence of Cain, the god of murder." His greasy smile widened. "I'm sure you can appreciate the irony, considering that inscription you bear. What's more, only the Philosopher stone could make an inanimate object powerful enough to house my Lord. And do you know how I created it, Levi?" He paused, drawing out the moment.

"I tortured three hundred sixteen Jews—one for each of the sacred names of God above. And, after torturing them, I performed a profane rite, which ripped the souls from their battered bodies and fused them into the gem which beats in your chest."

He laughed, then, a slow chuckle that bubbled up from his stomach. "You are a living blasphemy, born from the Buna massacre."

Levi's knees gave out beneath him, and his body hit the ground with a *thud*.

One of the Thursrs flanking Professor Wilkie rushed forward.

The man, Levi's creator, raised a single hand, stopping the creature midstride.

"Hold, you idiot. Weren't you listening? I won't risk damaging my rightful property further. Use that pea-sized brain for once, buffoon, and use your eyes while you're at it. He's standing at death's door. Any more damage could destroy him permanently, and that profits me nothing. Besides, I have what I've come for. Despite your interference, Levi, you have delivered me everything I need to complete my task. An hour ago I had neither the girl nor the mage. An hour ago I couldn't even venture into this sanctuary without fear of Siphonei. Now, here I stand, with my prize in hand, and you, beast, have my gratitude."

Hogg lowered his hand and reached into his lab coat pocket. Levi's body tensed, preparing for the man to draw some sort of weapon. Instead, he withdrew a business card and a golden pen. He carefully jotted something down on the back of the creamy-white card, then flicked it toward Levi, conjuring a gust of air that dropped it inches from Levi's hand.

"I assume you're going to come for the girl, or perhaps you'd just like more answers. Either way, that's where you can find me. You have until the equinox—midnight, two days hence—before she is dead and my Lord walks the world once more. But please, Levi Adams, feel free to stop by whenever you'd like."

Levi looked up, hate dashing across his features, turning his broad face even uglier. "You know I'm going to stop you." He caught Ryder's eye. "I'll come for you. I swear to God, I'll come. Just keep fighting."

"I'm expecting you to try, golem—how could you do anything else, but what's in your nature?" He turned toward his thugs. "Come, our business is finished here and we have work to do yet." With that, the man turned his back toward Levi, dismissing him as a threat, and made for a doorway set into the far side of the room: the exit the professor had told Levi about.

The Mudman didn't try to stop him. Couldn't stop him. After a long while he picked up the card, turning it over in charred fingers, black grease smudging the surface. On the front, in matte black lettering, was a name: "Doctor Arlen Hogg, Geneticist." On the back was a hastily scrawled address—someplace in Nevada.

## TWENTY-FIVE:

**Clay Pots**

L evi leaned against the bloodstone in his yard, back pressed up against its cool, smooth surface, legs sprawled in the grass before him, while he gazed at the stars overhead. Pinpricks of stabbing light reminded him of that night so long ago when he first looked upon the world with new eyes. It'd been raining then, not clear like tonight, and the moon hadn't been so full as the ball of light hanging above. A gleaming layer of slip covered every inch of his body. The goopy substance reminded him of the thick mud from the grave, and his nostrils still held the scent of burnt death, which conjured images of the bodies stacked up next to him, covered in slaked lime.

To think the heart beating in his chest was the by-product of those deaths, the culmination of a lifetime of murder and horrendous experimentation. And his soul? A Frankenstein monster, stitched together from the tattered remains of other souls. A tapestry of vengeful specters shoved into a crude body of muck and mud.

*"Ask and it will be given to you; seek and you will find; knock and the door will be opened to you. For everyone who asks receives; the one who seeks*

*finds; and to the one who knocks, the door will be opened."* Words from the Good Book, delivered directly from the mouth of Jesus. Levi hadn't so much knocked as he had smashed the door from its hinges, but now he wished he could pick up the shattered remnants of the door and shoved them back into place. Except sometimes once a thing is done, once a thing is learned, it can't be undone or unlearned.

He was an abomination, he now knew, and nothing he did could ever change that. For the first time in his life all he wanted was death. No, even that wasn't right. He wanted to cease to exist. He wished he had *never* existed. All the AA meetings, the church services, the good works—feeding the hungry, protecting the homeless, caring for the widow and the orphan—they meant nothing. *Nothing*. He knew in his mind that salvation was by grace through faith that no man should boast, but there was nothing in him to save. No goodness. No redeeming grace. No light.

He was a monster.

He was death and darkness, vengeance and hate.

He would never overcome that, would never be anything else.

And, if he couldn't rise above that nature, he didn't want to live. Once he saved Ryder and killed Hogg, he would find a way to end it. He touched the brand on his chest. Yes, he would end it, but not until he saw this thing through—and there was work left to be done if he wanted to finish this race well. So much to do and so little time to do it.

He held up his left hand, examining the damage. He had fingers again and all his limbs were now in working order, but he still hurt from head to toe: muscles ached, skin taut and tender from the burns, while a head-splitting migraine hammered away inside his skull.

It didn't help that he was bloodletting at the same instant: A plastic length of tube—dipping into one arm and running to a mop bucket beside him—dribbled out splashes of liquid gold. There was nothing to do for it, though. The Mudman needed to heal, but he also needed an edge if he had any hope of getting Ryder and the professor back whole and hale. The Mudman was well versed in the art of the kill, but fighting against a fortified enemy with a far larger force—not to mention ancient magics, dark alchemy, and access to a murder god—was well beyond his skill set. Levi reckoned the extra ichor might help.

*Disposable ichor*, to be precise.

Levi's most spectacular abilities—rending the earth, manifesting javelins of obsidian, even his shapeshifting and healing—were all tied to the ichor, but the more ichor he burned, the weaker he became. If, however, he had a reservoir to work with? Well, that might shift the odds in his favor, if only marginally. All things considered, his condition was a vast improvement over the night before. In another two days he'd be good as he always was.

Unfortunately, he didn't have two days to spare—he had a handful of hours left before the equinox, and even that was cutting it awfully close.

He'd had two days from the time Hogg had captured Ryder, but he'd wasted a day and a half trekking back to the Hub from that damned temple with Chuck. Judging by the heat radiating from the ground, he could put the time at just after 10:00 PM, which meant he had three hours and change before the dark-heart of the equinox. Three hours wasn't much time, not considering all he had to do in preparation for the battle. He shook his head at the thought of wading into this fight so ill-prepared and ill-equipped.

Even with the reserve of ichor he was far outclassed, and knew it.

Levi had one other surprise, a nuclear failsafe of sorts, that *might* turn the tide and give him a leg up on Hogg and Cain, but he really hoped it wouldn't come to that. He'd swiped something from the ancient Atlantean temple—something powerful and insanely dangerous—which was now sitting in his basement, locked away in a silver-lined box inscribed with powerful containment runes. If everything went wrong, unraveled at the seams, Levi could always open the box and pray for the best, though he hoped to God above things wouldn't come to that ... unleashing the Atlantean weapon could be nearly as bad as setting Cain loose on the world.

*No. It wouldn't come to that.*

Chuck would come through with reinforcements. He wouldn't run off with the eight hundred thousand dollars in untraceable gold bullion Levi had given to him for the express purpose of securing a personal army of mercenaries. *He'll come through*, the Mudman reassured himself for what seemed like the thousandth time.

For one, Levi had told Chuck in no uncertain terms what would happen if he ran with the gold. He wouldn't murder him, of course—Chuck may have been a lot of things, but a cold-blooded killer, he wasn't—but death wasn't always the worst fate possible. Not even close. And Chuck knew Levi could deliver on his promise. After all, he'd watched firsthand as Levi, burning like the sun, leapt into the jaws of what amounted to a plant-god and walked away.

Fear like that could be a powerful motivator.

Plus, Levi had promised him *another* eight hundred thousand dollars upon completion. Even if fear of bodily dismemberment wasn't motivation enough, greed would bring Chuck back. True, the gold Chuck already had was enough to set him up for life, but the man was a huckster always working an angle; a man like that couldn't possibly pass up a chance at such a payday. Like a Vegas gambler on a hot streak, Chuck would let it all ride at a shot for more, even if it meant he might lose big in the long run. Or so Levi hoped.

*Chuck would come through. He had to.*

The thought of all that gold flowing into the world set Levi's teeth on edge and got his head to pounding anew. He wasn't worried about the money—he had simple, inexpensive tastes and could always produce more—but, in time, that gold would be traced back to him, and *that* was cause for concern. The Mudman was a cautious sort and took great pains to exchange gold for cash only in minuscule increments, and he never used the same face twice. And even with his precautions, rumors still sprouted up around him like weeds he couldn't choke out.

A million and a half in gold flooding the market, however, would make more than rumors, it'd make waves. Big waves, even in the Hub.

Sooner or later those waves would lead to Chuck—because he was an idiot and could keep a secret about as well as a gossip rag—which would, in turn, lead to Levi, the source responsible for those ripples. Then … well then the monsters would come for *him*. For his gold. He took his free hand, unrestricted by the tube, and rubbed at his head, trying to massage the unpleasant thoughts away. So many things to worry about and nothing he could do about any of them.

What was done, was done, and he couldn't change a thing. He'd just have to deal with the fallout from all this—assuming he lived through it.

Much as he might like to, he couldn't afford to mope around and count the minutes as they ticked by, marching onward toward Ryder's death and the resurrection of a godling.

Carefully, he removed the plastic tubing from the crook of his arm, then pressed a thick thumb over the wound to stop the trickle of ichor. Every drop was important now. He glanced down and surveyed the bucket: three gallons, maybe. Almost as much as his body could naturally hold. He could do a lot of damage with three gallons. First, though, he needed to devise some sort of delivery system. Couldn't very well march into battle with a mop bucket full of golden-blood at his side.

But he had an idea for that, too.

He reluctantly crawled to his feet, grabbed up the bucket, and headed into the house, bound for the basement.

What he needed sat on the metal cooling shelf, just to the right of the brick kiln: ten circular pots, each the size of a baseball and each decorated in a multitude of hues and textures. The pots were nothing extraordinary—the kind of thing any beginning potter might throw—though still beautiful. Test pieces he'd made to try some new glazes on. For what he had in mind, however, they would work perfectly. He shuffled over to the rack with the bucket in hand and began filling each pot to the brim with golden ichor. Once each jar was full, he tore a small strip of flesh from his side and secured it over the top like a lid. A dash of ichor transformed the malleable clay lid into a rock-hard seal.

The process wasn't difficult, but Levi took his time since any mistake could be costly. After a half hour, the task was done. The ten pots were now makeshift ichor grenades, each capable of untold amounts of damage in the right hands. Levi's hands.

With an effort of will, Levi redirected the ichor flowing through him, channeling it away from his formidable barrel gut: he forced open a cavity in his belly, a strip running across his front from love handle to love handle, long but shallow. He sucked in a deep breath and held it before taking the pots, one by one, and placing them in intervals throughout the cavity, wriggling them into his wet clay center. Once he had all ten pots properly positioned, he let out the pent-up breath and pushed flows of ichor to his stomach. Clay-flesh surged around the homemade grenades, covering them completely, leaving behind an unmarked belly.

Safe, secure, and handy when the time came to use them.

All that remained to do now was grab the rest of Chuck's gold and head over to the Hub.

He picked his way toward the office, but stopped midstride as Jacob-Francis strode into his path, yellow eyes glaring up while his tail swished in agitation. He didn't meow—that was beneath him. Rather he stared at Levi with a look that said, *feed me*

*now, servant, or suffer unimaginable consequences.*
Levi crouched down and ran a hand along the cat's
back; the furry beast arched into his palm and offered a
slow, pleased blink. Not much time, but time enough to
say goodbye to the miserable creature and ensure he
would have enough food and water for several weeks.
He patted the cat, then went over to his bowl in the
corner, topped it off, then set out a second bowl, which
he also filled to the brim.

If he did survive, he knew he'd be finding cat
vomit all over the house for the next two weeks.
Whenever he left out extra food, the fur-ball would
gorge himself, vomit, then repeat the process ad
nauseam. The cat looked on with smug approval, then
darted up the stairs, disappearing back to wherever he'd
come from.

That done, Levi headed over to the office,
disarming the wards without a thought. The trunk in the
corner clicked open, revealing the counterfeit
documents, his stack of prepaid cell phones, and the
gold bullion bars and cash beneath. He pushed the cell
phones out of the way and pulled out the silver-lined
box with his secret weapon stored inside. He set the
heavy box down and instinctively ran a crude hand over
its lid, ensuring all the containment wards were intact
and holding. All good, which was a small relief at least.

He turned his attention back to his storage chest;
as he pushed the cell phones back in place, a thought hit
him like a freight train barreling into a car stuck on the
tracks—it was something the professor had mentioned
in passing back in the Sprawl. He'd said the
resurrection ritual required a sacrifice. A sacrificial

murder, which required one sibling to willingly kill another—a reenactment of Abel's murder—in order to complete the summoning. Ryder was carrying the homunculus, the physical vessel, but what if she was *also* the sacrifice?

Ryder had a sister—what was her name? Jennifer? Jane? He couldn't quite recall—but he *knew* Ryder had one. He ran a finger over one of the disposable phones. He'd given Ryder one just like it so she could call her sister. *The only family she had left*; those had been Ryder's words. Levi couldn't imagine a reason Ryder's sister would be involved in this mess, but he couldn't rule out the possibility, either. After handing the phone over to Ryder, he'd told her to shut it off and leave it on the coffee table once she'd finished with the call.

Hopefully she'd done as he'd instructed. He had to be wrong, but if he could find that phone it would put his suspicion to rest one way or the other. And, even if the sister wasn't involved, perhaps he could put her mind at ease.

Quick as he could, he reengaged the trunk lock, threw a blanket back over the box, and scooted out of the room, lead-lined box in one hand. He locked the office—even in his rush, there was no point in taking unnecessary risk—and hoofed it upstairs, heart pounding in excitement. He headed into the living room, gaze landing on the table like a sledgehammer. His heart fell: nothing but a stack of neat coasters. He ground his teeth and grimaced.

The guest room, could she have left it there after showering?

He was moving even before the thought had fully formed. He streaked down the hall and pushed the door open, eyes sweeping the room. There, the burner phone sat on the nightstand beside the bed. He grunted—the grinding sound of a rockslide—which was as close to celebrating as Levi ever came. He snatched up the phone and flipped it open. Ryder hadn't bothered to turn it off as he'd instructed, but for once he didn't mind. He pulled up the recent-call log and found what he was looking for inside. A lone phone number, which had to belong to Ryder's sister.

He selected the number and punched the call button with his thumb.

*Berrr, berrr, berrr. Berrr, berrr, berrr.*

Nothing. He tried again.

*Berrr, berrr, berrr, click.*

"Hello, Levi," a lightly accented voice, vaguely European, said from the other end of the line. Hogg. "So you've managed to put all the pieces together. Quite clever, considering what a rudimentary beast you are."

"I don't know what you've done with Ryder's sister, don't know how you've wrapped her up in your schemes, but I better find them both alive and well."

He laughed. "Don't be a fool," he said. "I didn't force her to participate against her will—the ritual requires a willing accomplice. And Jamie was quite willing, I can assure you."

"I don't believe you," he said. "Why would she do that? Who would ever do that to someone they love?"

"Why does anyone do anything? Revenge? Jealousy? Loneliness? Fear? Humans are not complex creatures, nor are their motives. Now, I'm busy, preparing for tonight's ritual. So what do you want?"

"I want to know she's okay. Sally."

"That worthless sack of meat is fine, golem. Fine until the equinox, when she will stop being fine."

"Prove it. Let me hear her," Levi said.

"No." Hogg spoke the word slowly, indifferently. "I will not condescend and take orders from a puppet of mud. You belong to me, not the other way around. You have my word. That is all you're going to get. Now, if that is everything—"

"You evil, murdering bastard," Levi blurted out, surprised by his own words. "Why are you doing this? Why release this thing back into the world?"

"More *whys*. Always with the whys," Hogg said. Then he laughed, a booming belly-chuckle. "You've grown too much like them. I made you better than that, made you to be above these idiotic notions of good and evil. You're too much like these weak human beings, so concerned with morality. Always asking *why*, as if understanding that question will somehow make the situation different. As though understanding the *why* will impart significance and meaning to suffering.

"Why am I doing this, you ask. But there is no why. Perhaps you want to hear that I was tortured or beaten as a child, as if that might explain my madness. I wasn't. Quite the opposite, in point of fact. My parents were loving, nurturing, supportive. So were my kin. Good people, all of them. I enjoy torture and experiment purely for torture and experiment's sake. I slaughter people because it gives me pleasure, and it has always been so. Believe it or not, but I am very, very old, and after several lifetimes, I've found that slaughter and torment simply make me content. The only reason *why* I do what I do is because I can. That is the truth that drives me.

"And I am specifically releasing Cain because I owe him a great deal. Let me spin you a tale of yesteryear. This story starts thousands of years ago, before the downfall of Atlantis. I was a boy then, Levi, which ought to give you some idea how long I've been around. When I was seventeen, I bludgeoned a neighbor boy to death. Smashed his head in with a rock because he was alone, poor, and I wanted to do it. Wanted to end him because I could. Killing him, it made me feel like Atropos the inevitable—she who cuts the thread of fate. I killed him and buried his body in a shallow grave behind my house.

"I was young, then, and quite sloppy. The boy's corpse was discovered by the authorities several weeks later, and because of my carelessness, his murder was rightly laid at my feet. In those days, despite the technological advances, they still executed murderers by hanging until dead. Can you believe that? The barbarity of it all?" He took a deep breath as though savoring the notion. "I should've been hanged more than four thousand years ago, but I was spared. In those days my people were at war with themselves, and the rebels were doing surprisingly well. Capturing new territories by the day and executing nobles by the score. Bloody times, dark times.

"That is why they spared me, because they were losing their war. You see, my brother worked for Atlantis Correction Systems as the high-warden over Cain's prison, and the authorities—the greatest of all black-hearted murderers—agreed to pardon me in exchange for using my family connections to gain an appointment in the temple. Even at seventeen I was an accomplished technomancer, so my government funded my research, hoping I could covertly find a way to control Cain and release him as a weapon against the upstarts. Lir, good brother that he was, was only too happy to offer me an appointment as an under-warden.

"While working there, though, my eyes were *opened*. Cain connected with me, thought to thought, mind to mind. He spoke through the walls of his dimensional prison directly into my consciousness. I could hide my heart and intentions from Lir, but not from my master. Cain set me free. He understood my truth. He understood the joke of black and white, good and evil: there is neither, only power. And murder? Murder is the ultimate power. The power of God. It was a truth I always knew, but which he encouraged me to embrace. He took me under his wing as a disciple, taught me the ways of killing, genocide, dark alchemy. Taught me to embrace what I am instead of hiding from it.

"I've tried to free my Master countless times since he first spoke to me. The first was when I murdered Lir. I harbored him no particular animosity, but neither did I harbor him any love. Love is one of those vulgar notions, like good or evil, which serves only to restrain. I smashed Lir's head in, too, just like the neighbor boy, hoping to tear open the doors confining my Lord. Sadly, my attempts have never met with success—too many missing elements. I was almost successful with you, until that bothersome Jew, Yitzchak, interfered with my work, but this time *will* be different. No guesswork, now. I have everything I need, thanks, in large part, to you, Levi."

"I don't know what you're hoping to accomplish by telling me all this," Levi said, "but it doesn't change a thing. I'm gonna come for you, Hogg. And I'm gonna kill you. I'm gonna do the whole world a favor and eradicate you like the cancerous tumor you are."

"That is precisely what I desire, golem. Do you think I told you this story in some misguided hope that you will show me mercy or pity? Hardly. I neither desire nor need your clemency. I told you this because I want you to know just how badly I deserve my death sentence. I want you to know the depth of my depravity and corruption because I know the secret truth that drives your every action, golem. You are a killer, no different than me. You may disguise your hunger, try to suppress it, try to cover it in a veneer of righteousness and rationalize it as justice or vengeance, but you are a murderer of the first order.

"This little history lesson was meant only to stoke the fire of your hunger, thus ensuring your participation tonight. Make no mistake: you belong to me, you are my creation, and I intend to have you back in my possession, where you belong. Where you can become what you were always meant to be. It will simply make things easier in the long run if you deliver yourself to me. Now, as I said, I have work to do, but I expect to see you this evening. 1:21 AM pacific standard time or there won't be anything left of the girl to save."

The phone *clicked* and fell silent. The Mudman balled his fist, crushing the phone as a snarl curled the edges of his lips, and the seal in his chest blazed to life.

## TWENTY-SIX:

### Judas

Ryder came to. Groggy. Thoughts slugging through her aching head—a low throb beating out a melody behind her eye sockets, keeping pace with the pounding of her heart. *Just another dream,* she reassured herself as she strained against the leather straps digging into her wrists, neck, waist, and ankles, securing her to a very familiar stone table. *Another flashback,* she thought, desperate to fight off the claustrophobia constricting her lungs, making every breath a struggle.

She was fine. *Fine, dammit. This wasn't real. Couldn't be.*

It had to be a nightmare. *Had to be.*

Her head hurt so bad, like someone had taken a tire iron to her temple, then shoved a bagful of discount cotton balls inside her skull. Must've fallen and hit her head. That might explain the pain, the visions. She couldn't remember much. Still, the cogs inside her brain were slowly squeaking to life, clanking along as her mind worked like fingers pulling at a stubborn knot. She'd been kidnapped by the Kobock Nation—*that's what the blue-skinned freaks were called, right? Kobocks? Who'd told her that?*

*Chuck?*

*No, not Chuck.*

*Levi. Right. Levi.*

She'd been drugged and kidnapped, then slashed right down the center and stitched back up. A hazy thought, along with a single word, floated up like an air bubble surfacing in a pond: her belly sliced open and a chubby grub, with a circular mouth and too many eyes, thrust into her guts. *Homunculus.* That thought she stomped down, crushing it like a bug underfoot, refusing to think about the wriggling she sensed inside her.

*Drugged, kidnapped, stitched back together.* Check.

Then Levi had come for her. That much, at least, she remembered clearly. He'd obliterated the freaks holding her captive, freed her, and dropped her off at a hospital in Colorado. Chuck came after that, then the Sprawl … Everything about the Sprawl, though, seemed like a disassembled jigsaw of blurry images. All of the memories bleeding at the edges, running together in an incomprehensible montage …

*An endless desert …*

*Bat-eared wolves …*

*Flower-faced plant monsters …*

Definitely a nightmare. She was asleep, dreaming about her time in the cave again. She'd hit her head and passed out, that was the only thing that made any sense.

*Why couldn't she wake up?*

She forced her eyes open and stared up at the ceiling. Instead of rough, uneven stone, she saw steel rafters and harsh fluorescent lighting hanging from steel cables. That wasn't right, not even close. Despite the leather cuff running over her throat, she could rotate her head, so she looked left with a muffled groan. The altar of the wyrm god—an image she was sick to death of seeing—was where it was supposed to be, but the bodies were gone. If this was *the* dream, there should've been a mound of corpses piled in front of the ruby-eyed altar.

A mound of them, deformed and mutilated.

Sally Jensen from Newark should be there somewhere, staring up at a craggy ceiling with vacant eyes while flamingo legs protruded from her belly. That was the center of the dream, the tent pole holding everything together. But Sally Jensen wasn't there. None of them were. And the floor below the altar wasn't the rough bedrock of some twisted subterranean cave, it was cold, clean gray concrete. The kind of floor you might see in a warehouse or industrial park.

*Wrong, wrong, wrong. All of it.*

She craned her head a little further and discovered a lone prisoner, badly beaten and chained to the wall not far from her. A lean man of maybe sixty, with dark skin and gray hair. She vaguely remembered his face, though she couldn't say how or from where. He was alive, the rise and fall of his chest testified to the fact, but looked dead to the world. She continued her sweep of the room, this time turning her throbbing head to the right.

She spotted the towering stone pillars with their greasy firelight, exactly where they should be, but the iron, dropdown gate wasn't. The medieval-looking son of a bitch should've been standing guard at the end of those pillars. It was gone, replaced by the bay of a warehouse, closed off by a roll-up loading door with a thick chain running across its front. A neon exit sign loitered above the door. That sure as hell didn't fit. Then she caught sight of a row of test-tubes, computer banks, and machinery buzzing and blinking on the far side of the room, blocked off by a thick wall of Plexiglas.

*The fuck was this?*

Given, the details of her rescue were fuzzy at best—indistinct things like mirages on a hot day—but none of this jived with what she remembered.

*Seriously. What. The. Fuck?*

It was like someone had ripped the guts out of that Kobock temple and crudely mashed them into an empty storage room in some modern office park.

Bile rose in her throat, burning at the back of her mouth, but she swallowed it back down. No way in hell was she gonna get stuck lying in her own puke for only God knew how long. After a moment the urge passed.

The ring of footsteps on concrete drifted to Ryder's ears. Once more she tried to sit up, straining against her bonds while she searched for the source of the steps. "Oh, Sally," she heard a minute later. "You weren't supposed to wake up, not until it was time for the ritual."

Ryder bucked, inching her head off the table. Slack-jawed confusion bloomed on her face as she watched her sister, Jamie, waltz in through a connecting doorway that looked like it led to an office.

Jamie moved toward Ryder with the brisk, professional strut of a seasoned nurse caring for an ailing patient who'd pushed the call button. A trio of blue-skinned Kobos trailed after her like deformed shadows.

*Definitely a dream.*

Her sister looked the same as she always did: slim build, short brown hair, hard eyes, and a thin face with sharp, almost severe, features. Ryder knew if they were to stand next to one another, the family resemblance would be uncanny, save for the fact that Ryder looked a few years older, had pink hair, and had tats splattered all over her chest, arms, and legs. Had Ryder finished high school, gone on to college, and gotten a decent job instead of getting hooked on coke, that's exactly what she would've looked like.

Jamie wore blue scrubs—not uncommon, considering her occupation—but Ryder couldn't square that image with the medieval temple or the blue-skinned monsters surrounding her. Stranger still, Jamie had weird shapes painted onto her skin and clothes: unearthly symbols that shimmered an iridescent blue-green in the flickering light.

Ryder shook her head, waggling it from side to side as much as the neck restraint would allow, trying to dislodge the vision before her. No luck. Her sister remained. "Is this a dream?" she finally asked, the words slurred.

Jamie paused at the question, as though weighing options in her mind. Eventually she sighed, shrugged, then crossed her arms. "I could lie to you, Sally. Maybe that would be for the best. But I already feel sick to death about all of this and I guess you probably deserve an explanation. None of this is a dream, though a part of me wishes it were—that I'd made different choices." She paused, eyes unfocused and far away. "It's too late for second-guessing. We've already come too far."

"What the fuck are you talking about, Jamie? What the fuck are you doing here? What the fuck did you do, you crazy bitch?"

Jamie uncrossed her arms and planted hands on hips, a scowl of disapproval on her lips. "Please, Sally, there's no need for that kind of language. We don't have a lot of time left together, so I'd really like it if we could end things on a good note. I know you're going to be mad, but I want to at least try and explain because I *do* love you. All of this"—she glanced around and shuddered—"is so that we can finally do what should've been done years ago. *Years ago,* Sally. I've found a way to get justice for us. For our family.

"Even if the justice system says there's not enough evidence, we both know who is responsible for taking everything from us. We both know Cesar Yraeta butchered Mom, Dad, and Jackson—you know most of all since you had to watch."

"How'd you know—"

Jamie held up a hand. "You never told me, but you used to talk about it in your sleep. Cesar killed everything we ever loved and he got away with it because he owns cops, attorneys, judges, and politicians. He owns the system, top to bottom. I know because I've been trying for sixteen years to set things right. Sixteen years of pointless litigation and endless police reports, which always get lost. Sixteen years of closed doors and red tape. It can't be done—he's guilty and everyone knows it, but he's also untouchable. The law might hold people like us accountable, but not people like him. He can do whatever he wants. Kill whoever he wants—and he's killed a lot of people—and our legal system will always turn a blind eye."

"Holy shit, you've lost your fucking mind, Jamie. You're crazy. A certifiable nut-job."

"No." She shook her head, a sad smile tracing her lips. "I'm thinking more clearly than I have in a long time. I realized something a couple of years ago. If Yraeta is outside the law, then I needed to go outside the law, too. And these"—she glanced back over her shoulder at the Kobocks, blanching—"these *things*, as horrible as they may be, are going to help us get what we deserve. Yraeta might be untouchable through normal channels, and he might have an army at his disposal, but now I have an army. Let's just see how that monster deals with an entire supernatural nation of monsters even more bloodthirsty than he is."

The sad smile became a feral grin that belonged on a wolf instead of a woman.

"So you orchestrated this whole thing?" Ryder asked, suddenly numb on the inside.

Jamie shook her head. "Of course not. You think these things would listen to me? I'm a nobody. We've always been nobodys, Sally, and we always will be. That's why Yraeta got away with what he did. I'm disposable and so are you—that's a reality I've come to terms with. But the man running this show, Sally? He's not invisible. And he's going to get us what we're due, and that's what matters. All that matters."

"Are you kidding me?" Ryder asked, incredulous. "Let me lay down some truth for you, little sister. The guy running this show is a whack job, and he's twisted as a fucking pretzel. He's going to unleash a murder demon, Jamie. Let me say that again: a *murder demon*. Why would you believe anything an evil jackass like that would say? He's not exactly the pinnacle of honesty."

"Once I realized what I needed to do—that I needed to go outside the law—I fell into some bad circles," Jamie said, glancing away, eyes unfocused. "Drug dealers, bikers, freelance mercenaries. Bad people. But none of them were bad *enough* to do what I wanted done. Eventually, though, I stumbled onto a rumor about a place where you could find anything. Get anything for the right price. The Hub. I followed those rumors for over a year, and I found a way in—there's an entryway in New York that even people like us can use.

"Once I made it to the other side, I started asking around, and it wasn't but a couple of weeks before Hogg found me. Showed up right out of the blue with an offer in hand. This thing we're going to release, this murder demon, once it's free it'll be unstoppable. Not even Yraeta will stand a chance—"

"You must be high or stupid," Ryder interrupted. "Seriously. You really think this fucking monster is gonna do your bitch work? You're supposed to be the smart one, Jamie. How could you be such a moron?"

Jamie nodded her head slowly. "I've ... I've seen him." She shuddered, then folded her arms across her chest and hugged herself. "Hogg showed me. I"— she paused and ran her hands over her biceps as though to eradicate some chill deep in her bones—"I talked with him, the murder demon. We made a deal. If I free him, he'll avenge us. He swore it on his power, and I believe him."

Tears began to leak down Ryder's face, running over her cheeks and staining the gray stone black. "But we're family, Jamie. I know we've never seen eye to eye on a lot, but how could you do this to me?"

"I'm not doing it *to* you, I'm doing it *for* you. You deserve justice, just as much as Mom or Dad or Jackson. None of us walked away that day. That day broke you—it broke us both. The drugs and alcohol, the boys. It all started after that," she said. "He broke *us*. You always tried to hide it, but I know how much you resent me. You resent me because of what you had to do, what you had to give up to protect me and cope with what you saw.

"He spared your body, but he murdered your future, Sally. Mine, too. I've got a degree, a house, a good job. But I've never had a boyfriend. The thought of starting a family or bringing a child into a world like this, a world where criminal tyrants massacre families and walk away, is unthinkable. It makes me sick." She balled her hand into a tight fist. "He killed everything that day. No survivors. And if we can pay the price so no other family has to live through that? It'll be worth it."

Ryder didn't say anything, couldn't say anything. She sobbed silently onto the stone. Jamie had always been a bitch, but she was still family. The only family Ryder had. The only real, lasting relationship she'd managed to keep *ever*.

Jamie cleared her throat and backed up a step, running hands over her scrubs, smoothing away nonexistent wrinkles. "I'm sorry it had to be like this. But I promise, it'll be over soon." She turned to go, then faltered and glanced over one shoulder, refusing to meet Ryder's eyes. "I'll be back with the doctor in a bit," she said. "Don't struggle, that'll only make things worse and nobody wants that—"

Jamie fell silent as her cell phone *buzzed*, flickers of light showing through the thick fabric of her pocket. She pulled the phone out and glanced down at the caller ID; the color drained from her face, her complexion suddenly ghost white. And then she was gone, rushing back toward wherever she'd come from, phone held out as though it were a deadly rattler just waiting to bite.

"It's going to be alright," a man said as Jamie darted away, Kobock guards trailing behind her. She rotated her head again, locking eyes on the beaten man chained to the wall. "We'll find a way out." His voice was wheezy, tired. "Either that or your golem friend will come for us," he said, the words a whisper.

She wanted to wipe the tears away from her cheeks, but couldn't, not with her hands tied down. She hated letting people see her cry, so she turned away, staring blankly at the ceiling overhead. "You don't really believe that do you? We're boned beyond belief. Even if Levi comes for us, he's not gonna be able to save us. No one can save us."

"Hope and despair are both choices, young lady," he said softly. "I suppose I would rather die hopeful."

"I call that being delusional," she said. They were both quiet for a time, listening to the muted shuffle of feet, which drifted down from above. Sounded like someone was pacing. "Who are you anyway?" she finally asked. "I feel like maybe I should know you, but don't. My mind's still foggy from whatever shit they gave me."

"Owen Wilkie," he said, "professor of cultural anthropology, comparative theology, and linguistics."

"You're that wizard or whatever." Things were starting to click into place again. "The one we were looking for."

"Mage, not wizard, and yes to your question," he replied, then fell silent as though every word took a tremendous effort of will.

She shifted her head, glancing at him out of the corner of her eye. "What's really gonna happen to us? To me?"

He sighed, then broke into a fit of raspy coughing. "The truth is often ugly, dear," he said once the hacking had finally subsided. "Perhaps it's best not to know."

"I'll take an ugly truth over a pretty lie any day of the week." She paused, letting the words hang between them for a beat. "Tell me. I wanna know what's gonna happen one way or another. Better to know what to expect."

She heard the rattle of chains and the rustle of fabric as the man adjusted his body. "You would think, being a scholar, I would agree. After two hundred years, though, I often find that the lies are more comforting, and comfort isn't a thing to be so readily dismissed." More rustling and rattling, then another round of hacking. "Ahh," he said eventually, "but who am I to deny you, if you want to know. Here is the truth. In a few hours, your sister is going to gut you like a fish. She's going to slice your belly open and the thing growing inside you will rip its way free.

"Then, as you lay dying, your sister is going to do the same thing to herself. She's going to shove a ceremonial knife into her own intestines and essentially disembowel herself, in order to tear open a rift between the worlds, allowing the essence of a murder godling to break into our plane of existence. The spirit of that creature will inhabit the homunculus and will slowly feed off your life force—you and your sister both—sucking you dry like a juice box. You will die, he will be free, and he will be unstoppable."

Ryder was quiet, more tears forming a rebellion and breaking free against her will. "Shit. I wanted the truth, not a fucking kick in the teeth. Way to crush my spirits completely."

"You asked for the truth."

She looked back toward the professor. He was leaning against the wall, head back, swollen eyes closed. "There's the truth, and the *truth*. Maybe you could've skipped some of the details."

"I'll remember to work on my bedside manner for the next time I find myself in a situation like this," he said, then chuckled, which turned into another round of dry hacking.

"You think Levi has any chance in hell of saving us?" she asked.

He shrugged, then winced. "If your friend can stop the ritual before it commences, maybe. Once that thing is free, though, I'm not sure any force on Earth will be capable of stopping him from doing whatever he wants. There is, perhaps, a very narrow window when the homunculus will be vulnerable. While he is bound to you and your sister, feeding off your essences. In that twilight moment between life and death, you or your sister could, theoretically, kill it.

"Well, no, that's not quite right. No one can *kill* Cain—he's spirit cursed with immortality by God. But Cain's mythos is intrinsic and central to the ritual: blood must kill blood. Since you will be temporarily bound to the homunculus by blood and spirit, you will have a certain power over him. At least until you bleed out and die, which will probably take less than ten minutes. Hypothetically, though, you *could* exercise that power and interrupt the ritual before it can come to completion. Sever his link to the world—destroy the body you created—and he might be pulled back into his hell."

"So if I'm following," she said, "what you're saying is we're screwed beyond all possible hope if Levi doesn't show up before my little sister kick-starts this fucked up ritual."

"You got it in one, dear. Shall we return to our delusions now?"

"Sign me up," she replied morosely. "In fact, let's just pretend you didn't say any of that bullshit and you can go back to telling me how everything's gonna turn out all right. 'Cause. Holy. Shit. Better yet—where the hell is my bat-shit crazy sister? I could use some *good* drugs right about now. If I'm gonna be gutted like a fish, I'd like to have enough morphine pumping through my body to kill a fucking whale."

## TWENTY-SEVEN

## Counsel

Levi puttered along in his minivan, heading for the Hub entrance behind the old theater on Colfax. Time was short and the plan was simple: hit the Hub, take one of the numerous Vegas exit portals, then catch a cab and head over to Hogg's warehouse, where he'd meet Chuck and company. The "company" being whatever reinforcements Chuck could conjure from the shady ranks of the Hub's denizens. Not a great plan, but it was the best the Mudman could do on such short notice. He thumbed the radio's power button, flooding the cab with contemporary worship music—the current song had a country flair, complete with the twang of a banjo.

The music soothed his fraying nerves. *Nice and easy. No point in getting worked up. Gam zu l'tova— this too is for the good*—he reminded himself.

He crept to a halt at a four-way intersection, mind drifting as he subconsciously tapped out the bass rhythm on the steering wheel with a thumb. Once the traffic broke, he hooked left, eased his foot onto the pedal, and navigated across three lanes of asphalt, making sure to keep the van under the speed limit. He was going to do battle with a nigh-immortal murder god, true, but that didn't give him an excuse to violate the posted traffic signs.

Traffic laws saved lives.

He'd been cruising for a few minutes, kicking around thoughts of death and genocide, when he saw the church off on the right. His church, New Eden. At this hour the building should've been dark, empty, and locked up nice and tight against the night. It wasn't. A lone Ford F150—big wheels, red paint, and long bed—sat in the parking lot. Pastor Steve's truck. And the corner office was lit with the warm yellow glow of an office lamp, which seemed to invite Levi, to beckon him to come in out of the dark.

He glanced at the dashboard clock. 10:50. Not much time now, not considering how far he had to travel and how much remained undone.

He hesitated only an eyeblink before flipping on his turn singal, pumping the brakes, and swinging into the parking lot. Tonight Levi was war bound; only death and uncertainty waited for him in Nevada. If tonight was the night he was to meet his Maker—well, figuratively, since his *actual* maker was a monstrous, millennia-old psychopath he was hoping to kill—he wanted … well, he didn't quite know. Guidance? Reassurance? Conviction he was doing the right thing? Conviction that his very existence wasn't somehow a crime against God?

He was empty, broken. He needed *something*. A balm for his troubled soul.

He didn't exactly know what he needed or wanted, but he believed Pastor Steve might have some insight. The pastor should've been home long ago with his family, so perhaps his presence here was a sign from God above. Maybe the Almighty wasn't so indifferent to the affairs and heartbreaks of man as Levi had once thought. Maybe He'd looked down from His throne, seen Levi's desperation, and shown clemency. Mercy. An extended olive branch of peace or, perhaps, the correcting crook of a shepard ready to guide a wandering sheep back into the fold.

The Mudman pulled into the nearest spot, killed the engine, and headed over to the church's front door. He faltered at the entrance, his hand extended, ready to grasp the brass handle, but lingering just out of reach. Maybe this was a mistake. Maybe he was a monster *and* the fool Hogg had named him. Time was short, after all—he couldn't afford to be here, wasting precious minutes. Besides, what would he even say? It wasn't like he could be honest with the pastor. Better for him to go—

Steve's office door, visible through the glass-fronted entryway, swung open, spilling a pool of amber light into the gloomy main corridor. Steve's smiling face popped out a heartbeat later. "Come on in, Levi, no point in standin' around out there in the dark. I've got some water on for tea."

Guess that solved that.

With a nod, Levi pushed his way in, going over to the pastor and giving his hand a shake before heading into the office proper. A nice room, Steve's office: white walls, accented in beige; several towering bookcases filled with bibles, history books, and theology texts. A simple work desk with a computer—next week's sermon pulled up on screen. A deep-cushioned couch and a rough circle of chairs surrounding a squat, glass-topped coffee table.

Steve used the space for the men's Bible study.

He ushered Levi in, then beelined for a small table at the back of a room, its surface littered with mugs, tea packets, instant coffee, and an electric kettle.

"Water's still hot," he said with a grin. "I'm burning the midnight oil, as they say, so I just made a cup of rocket fuel. Please"—he waved to the couch—"take a seat while I get you something. What'll you have?"

"One of those instant coffees will do fine," Levi replied, impatiently running hands over his pants.

"Cream or sugar?" Steve asked, grabbing a mug that read "I Look 30, act 20, feel 60—I must be 40" and pouring a splash of steaming water from the kettle.

"No, no. Black is fine."

Steve ripped open a pack of coarse coffee—looked like granular dirt—added it to the mug with a grimace of distaste, gave the water a stir with a spoon, then padded over and set the piping cup on the table. "I really need to get something better," he said, gesturing toward the coffee. "The instant stuff is convenient and *technically* qualifies as coffee, but only in the most liberal sense of the word."

He pulled over a chair, positioned it across from Levi, and sat. "You may not know this about me, Levi, but I grew up in Palermo—Italy, that is. My parents were missionaries there for eleven years. And believe me when I say, no Italian would *ever* tolerate instant coffee. In the morning I still make my coffee at home using this bulky antique teapot, it's called a *caffettiera*, which my grandpa passed on to me." He sighed, then smiled. "Anyway, enough of that." He folded his hands.

"What brings you here? Pretty late. You burning the midnight oil too?"

Levi dithered, not sure what to say or how to start. "Something like that, I suppose. I ... well, I saw your car in the parking lot and I thought I'd stop in and say hello."

"Levi," Steve replied, leaning back in his chair. "I haven't been at this pastoring thing for all that long, but I've been at it *long enough* to know when someone's got something heavy on their mind. Now, I'm sure you wanted to say hello, but I think you also have something else you'd like to air out."

The Mudman looked away, not wanting to meet Steve's eye, then shrugged. "Suppose that's true, Pastor. I'm ... Well, let's just say there's a lot you don't know about me—things I'm not entirely comfortable talking about. I've done a lot of things I'm awfully ashamed of. I'm a liar. I've hurt people—lots of people. I've been battling severe addiction my whole life, and I've lost that battle more often than I've won. I feel like ... like God must hate me. Like there's nothing good in me worth saving. I thought I had a handle on it, then this fella shows up. He's kind of like a father to me, I suppose.

"But he's a bad man and he's done me a lot of wrong. And he's brought everything back to the surface, dredged up all this stuff that I thought I'd buried. I guess I'm angry. Got vengeance on my mind and I'm afraid if I can't move past it, then that's all I'll ever be. I feel like I'm at a crossroads, and if I choose the wrong road then addiction, vengeance, and hate is all I'll ever own. And it's driving me, pushing at me, and I just don't know what to do with it. It's killin' me, Pastor. Unmaking me."

Steve was quiet for a time, one foot bobbing while he thought. Levi picked up his coffee and took a long pull. He didn't *need* to eat or drink—had no stomach, in fact—but he *could* eat or drink if the need arose. His ichor would simply convert the foul tasting brew into something useful.

"Levi," he said eventually, "the Gospel is good news precisely because it's *not* about who you are or what you've done, and it's all about who He is and what He's done for you. Grace isn't dependent on you—it doesn't care about your past or your addiction. No one merits grace, Levi, but that's okay because grace isn't about merit. Grace isn't about getting what you *deserve*, that's justice, it's about getting what you don't deserve. Mercy. I'm sure you've done bad things, but your badness isn't bigger than God's goodness.

"It's kind of like buying a house," he continued. "When I first saw my house, I knew it was the one I wanted. Knew that was where I wanted to live with my wife, knew it was where I wanted to raise my kids. With that said, I didn't necessarily want the ugly green carpet in the basement or the tacky wood paneling. But I still wanted the house. I bought it knowing it had issues, and over time I made it my own. God does the same with us. He meets us where we're at—faulty foundation, ugly carpet, busted down walls and all— and renovates. Maybe you're a bit more of a fixer-upper than someone else, but God's never met a challenge he couldn't overcome.

"As to hate and vengeance. I'd like to tell you a story. Are you familiar with the story of Dirk Willems?"

Levi wagged his head, *no.*

"It's worth hearing, I think. Stories are amazing things, Levi. In today's age we only seem to care about facts—bullet points we can write down, statistics we can quote, numbers we can memorize. I think many modern Christians secretly wish God had just filled the Bible with lists and rules. Easier that way. But that's not what He did. He could've revealed himself in a multitude of ways, but instead of a textbook, God gave us a storybook—one filled with characters from the pages of history. A few good people, most bad, almost all of them deeply flawed. God revealed himself in their lives. And that story is still playing out in our lives.

"Dirk's story might teach you a thing or two about vengeance and hate."

"You've got my ear," Levi grunted, then sipped at his joe.

"Dirk was an Anabaptist in the Netherlands during the late fifteen hundreds, lived under the rule of the Duke of Alva. In those days the Netherlands were under Spanish rule, and the Spanish, who remained Catholic during the Reformation, were unfavorable toward those they deemed heretics to the Church. If you know your history, you'll recall the late fifteen hundreds was smackdab in the heyday of the Inquisition. So when I say they were 'unfavorable' toward heretics, what I mean is they tortured them in an effort to force repentance. Dirk was captured, judged of heresy, and locked away in a castle-turned-prison while he awaited execution.

"He was a wily fellow, though. He loved God something fierce, but he was in no hurry to be a martyr—a smart man if you ask me. So, not wanting to die a horrendous death, he fashioned a rope with old rags, climbed from his window and onto the ice of the moat surrounding the castle, then made a break for freedom. This was like something you might see in a movie today, but this was the real deal. Poor Dirk was horribly malnourished, which actually aided in his escape, since the ice held his weight. A nearby prison guard witnessed the escape and pursued Dirk onto the ice. Unfortunately for the well-fed and heavily armored guard, the ice wasn't strong enough to hold him.

"The ice gave out, and the guard plunged into the water. Dirk was home free, but, hearing the cries for mercy from the guard, he stopped. Dirk had no reason to love the Spanish. The Spaniards had tortured and murdered countless Anabaptists—these were his friends and family. But, he stopped and turned back, knowing he might be recaptured, and chose to save the guard from certain death. In return for Dirk's kindness, the guard did, in fact, recapture him, and returned Dirk to the prison. He was shortly executed after that. Burned at the stake for heresy and subversion to the state." He fell silent, a sad smile painted across his face.

"Wait, that's it?" Levi asked. "That's the worst story I've ever heard. He should've let the guard drown, no question."

"I'm sure many people would agree with you, Levi. Dirk didn't even have to kill the man, he could've kept on going and nature would've done the job for him. He had every reason to hate that guard. Every reason to hate the Catholics and the Spanish for their persecution. He had every reason to want vengeance. And, from the world's perspective, vengeance would've been totally justifiable.

"But I believe Dirk realized something tremendously important in that moment. Had he left that man to die, he would've lived, but he wouldn't have been able to live with himself. His decision was counterintuitive to our natural way of thinking, but Jesus and the Gospel message are counterintuitive as well. It's like what Jesus told his disciples, *"For whoever wants to save their life will lose it, but whoever loses their life for me will find it. What good will it be for someone to gain the whole world, yet forfeit their soul?"* Losing your life to save it doesn't make sense, but that's what Jesus calls us to do. Counterintuitive."

Levi took another sip of coffee. Sometimes, like the coffee, the truth could be bitter in the mouth. Silence stretched between them for a time, a comfortable quiet that spoke of deep thought and contemplation.

"Anger and vengeance are like a fire, Levi," Steve said eventually, "and like fire, they burn indiscriminately. You might get your vengeance on your old man, only to find yourself consumed and destroyed in the process. At the end of the day, you, like Dirk, need to make the choice you can live with—and sometimes the choice you can live with isn't the one that makes any sense at all from a worldly perspective."

Levi drained the rest of his cup and set it back on the table with a *clink* and stood. "Sorry to run, but I have some business to be about tonight. You've given me a lot to think on, though, and I appreciate it."

Steve stood, the sad smile returning as if he could see whatever terrible future lay in store.

"Anytime, Levi. I'll hope you get what you need. I'll be praying for you."

"Thank you for that," Levi replied. With a final nod, he left the church, started the van, and pulled back onto the street, bound for his own icy moat.

## TWENTY-EIGHT:

## Reinforcements

L evi waited in a pool of inky shadow, shoulder blades pressed against the side of a dimly-lit two-story warehouse situated in an industrial park over in Spring Valley, just outside of Las Vegas proper. He flipped the doctor's business card over and over again in his fingers, stopping every few seconds to check and double-check the address: 6446 Arville Street, Las Vegas, Nevada. Then he would glance up and scan the building across the way, which bore the same address. Nothing extraordinary about it, nor the type of place you'd expect an ancient, pre-Babylonian god to be resurrected.

Apparently, Doctor Hogg wasn't one to advertise his whereabouts.

Read. Flip. Double-check. Repeat.

*6446 Arville Street.*

The building was a simple two-story structure of gray stucco, nearly twin to the one he leaned against now, with windows running along the upper level and a glass-fronted door with a company name embossed in frosted lettering: *Atlantic Biotech Solutions*. A fitting name. Large boulders and splashes of green shrubbery edged the building's walkway and framed the entryway, giving the place a friendly air. Of course Levi and his personal army—wherever they happened to be—wouldn't enter that way.

If Levi had to guess, he would assume the offices in the front of the building would be quite ordinary: rolling chairs and work desks, telephones and copy machines, coffee pots and company brochures. A ruse. The kind of stuff that would fool any bumbling Rube who came in asking questions about Atlantic Biotech Solutions. Hogg's real operation would either be in the warehouse at the rear or situated on the second floor. The back of the building sported a large rolling door, with more boulders and shrubbery marching off to either side: a loading dock, hidden from the main thoroughfare, and perfect for Levi's purposes.

Read. Flip. Double-check. Repeat.

This time Levi glanced at the deserted stretch of road running between him and Hogg's hideout. Wasn't a pair of headlights in sight and hadn't been for the past half hour. Other than the industrial buildings littering the area, there wasn't much reason to be out here, and given the hour—coming up on 1:00 AM—Levi didn't expect much traffic. Still, his nerves were starting to get the better of him. He couldn't wait for Chuck much longer; he was already cutting it awfully close. Maybe he'd been wrong about Chuck. Maybe the shiesty leprechaun had realized what a fool's errand this whole operation was.

Another two minutes and then he would go in with or without backup. He ran a hand over a duffle bag hanging on his shoulder. It held the lead-lined box with his nuclear deterrent. Never be without a backup plan. He patted the bag.

Chuck arrived with reinforcements a minute and a half later. They punched through the fabric of Inworld with a rush of power and the scrape of feet on pavement—the vibration working its way up into Levi's legs.

The Mudman let out a tremendous sigh of relief.

Chuck had come through ... His relief faded as he eyeballed his army.

Chuck had come through. Sort of.

Levi watched with arms folded and a frown on his mug as Chuck led a ragtag group of miscreants toward him. A wide grin split Chuck's face—the man looked pleased as a slick-furred street rat lounging on a pile of stolen cheese.

Levi only felt the dull edge of annoyance scraping at his nerves. *This is what he got for a million and a half?* More likely, Chuck had scraped the absolute bottom of the barrel, scrounging up an army that would work for the change you could find under a couch.

Walking to either side of Chuck were a cadre of trolls: hulking, green, wart-covered beasts with gangly arms stretching to the ground and wispy hair sprouting from lumpy heads. Normally trolls would be a fine addition to any fight—notoriously foul-tempered creatures with the strength of a pickup truck—but these already had one foot in the bone yard. Wobbly kneed, hands riddled and distorted with arthritis, and what little hair they did have was silvered with age. Ten of them, and each one could've come from an Outworld nursing home.

Trailing behind them were six halfies—a varied lot—but who all, uniformly, looked high as kites on one drug or another. Jittery, bloodshot eyes, most of them covered in either open sores, filthy rags, or both. Those Chuck could've picked up at an Outworld opium den or a downtown methadone clinic. A few of them might've been scrappers, but they were a far cry short of professional mercenaries.

The last group looked like the liveliest of the lot and they were quite numerous—twenty or so of the fellows milling around behind the geriatric trolls and the stoned halfies.

Unfortunately, not a one of them stood over three and a half feet or weighed in at more than ninety pounds. Wiry, narrow-shouldered men. The lot of 'em had broad, lantern-jawed faces, split down the middle by honking, bird-beak schnozzles all framed by wiry beards or goatees of coarse red hair. They stared at Levi from beady, deep-set eyes of green that were almost hidden beneath comically pronounced eyebrows, which were, in turn, parked beneath old-fashioned cabbie caps.

Leprechauns. Of course, Chuck would get leprechauns.

Admittedly though, Levi had never seen a more formidable-looking group of pipsqueaks. No smiling, chipper faces to be seen amongst their number. These were no wee merry-folk, ready for a dance or a bit of trickery. Most of them scowled, their yellowed teeth gritted in crooked snarls while they puffed at drooping pipes. Most wore stained wifebeaters or too tight T-shirts with suspenders, high-water slacks, and bulky, drab Irish cardigans.

Despite being tiny, they had the look of hard-working men about them—seasoned fishermen, maybe—and the knobby, blackthorn shillelaghs they carried certainly reinforced the image. At a glance, Levi could plainly see each of these had committed murder of the premeditated variety; their auras were riddled with swirls of black.

Levi watched them draw close with hungry eyes, the brand itching more and more with each step they took. On a different night, under different circumstances, Levi would be chasing them down, ready to mete out justice for their sins. Tonight, though, Levi felt blessed to have them along. The trolls and halfie tweakers wouldn't do much good, but the Lep crew might hold their own. Probably couldn't take a Thursr, but they'd be able to handle a slew of Kobocks. The Mudman shook his head at the strange thought and the stranger turn of events.

He'd always been a creature of black and whites, but tonight he found himself walking down a road painted with a thousand shades of gray.

"So?" Chuck said, flashing a grin and waving toward the motley crew, which came to a halt a few feet back. "Looking good, am I right? This dude, Hogg, don't stand a chance against this all-star team."

"All-star team," Levi replied. "Why don't we step over here and have a little chat, Chuck." He turned his back and lumbered a safe distance away from the group, Chuck following on his heels. Then Levi moved like a mudslide, pivoting and shifting as he turned, his bulk flowing out as his fat fingers wrapped around Chuck's throat and lifted the man from his feet. Levi slammed him into the wall with a *whomp* and held him there, Chuck's toes brushing against the ground.

"Remember what I said, back in the Lonely Mountain?" Levi asked. "I said you better not pull any leprechaun nonsense on me. I said bad things would happen if you did that. Bad things involving legs and fingers and toes. This"—he pointed with his free hand toward the crew—"seems to fit the bill. I'm going to give you one minute to explain." Levi kept his hand wrapped around Chuck's throat, but lowered him to the ground and eased up enough to let him speak his piece.

Chuck wheezed and coughed as he sucked in a double lungful of air. "Damn, dude, you gotta stop pulling this bullshit, Levi. I know what you're thinkin'—but this was the best I could do with the time I had. Professional mercs are jumpy, man. Most of those guys aren't down with working a job like this on such short notice with limited intel, you feel me? Mercs like money, Levi, but they like not dyin' more. These guys can help us get the job done, though. I'm tellin' you God's own truth."

"Still not convinced," Levi replied, tightening his grip a hair. "You've got thirty seconds left."

"Chill, Boss-man," he said, his fingers digging into Levi's grip, trying to pry the Mudman's hand loose.

Levi didn't relent.

"Those cats in the cardigans," he croaked, "they don't look like much, but they're the Black Shillelaghs. I know your crazy ass musta heard about them."

Levi loosened his grip a little more.

He *had* heard of the Black Shillelaghs. Most folks in Outworld knew about them. Freelance thugs with ties to the Court of the Unfettered Fae and the Real IRA—the Real Irish Republic Army. Not killers so much as finger-breakers and knee-cappers, but a vicious lot by all accounts. No one had ever mentioned they were wee folk. Though, it did make a certain sense, he supposed.

"And the others?" Levi asked, suspicious. "You going to try and convince me those decrepit trolls are really enforcers for the East-end Legion? And maybe those tweakers are the brains behind the 6th Street Grims?"

"How you gonna be like that, Levi? I ain't trying to scam you, alright. Those turds are bullet catchers. And they weren't my idea, man, the Shillelaghs brought those gems on board. Look, I'm not sure if you noticed, but those dudes"—he dropped to a whisper—"are tiny. Sons a bitches are mean like honey badgers, but they're better at stealth. They send these brain-dead dudes in first, kinda a big dumb smoke screen, then they sneak in under veils and beat the shit outta anything that even thinks about lookin' at 'em funny. I've seen these dudes work, Levi. Like piranhas—straight up savage."

Levi frowned, ran his free hand over his blocky chin, then released Chuck's windpipe and patted the man on the chest. "Okay, you did alright. I've got one other thing before we head in." He removed the duffle bag from his shoulder and gently placed it on the ground. He bent over, unzipped the main compartment, and removed the hefty silver-lined box covered with containment sigils.

"That the egg from the temple?" Chuck asked, eyeing the box askew.

Levi nodded once. "You know the deal. If things go sideways, and they might, I'm going to need you to do what needs to be done. Here's your part …"

Levi spent a few minutes spelling out the plan and Chuck's role, then headed over to his army.

The leprechauns, for the most part, leaned against the building's wall, smoking their pipes in stoic silence, while the others shifted on nervous feet. Bullet catchers, Chuck had called them. Levi took a moment to examine each of these. Despite their fearsome or ragged appearances, none of those were killers. Levi could read a great deal in their auras—brokenness, pain, addiction, sin, heartbreak. Not good folks, but not worthy of death. Not so different from him, really. Yet many of them, even most of them, would likely die inside that warehouse tonight.

Guilt and irony hit him like a one-two combination: here he was, a failed Anabaptist preparing to go to war, preparing to offer up innocent lives for his cause. These creatures were willing volunteers, and paid for their work, but that changed nothing. Not in the grand scheme of things. How had he come to this road? How had he fallen so far? Just a few scant days ago the thought of taking an innocent life had been unfathomable, and now he was going to send these men to their deaths for the sake of his own private war.

For a moment he considered turning around and going home—forgetting this whole thing had ever happened. But no, it was too late for that. He didn't know if he'd be able to live with himself when this was all over, but maybe that, not the gold, was the real price he would have to pay. Besides, walking away and abandoning Ryder to a terrible end would haunt him just as much. No good choices here, and no matter which path he took, regret and remorse were waiting like a lion in the high-grass ready to pounce.

He cleared his throat, the sound of grating boulders, then spoke. "You all ready for this?" he asked.

The trolls and halfies said nothing.

An especially gruff and weathered leprechaun with a ragged scar running over one eye stepped forward and nodded his square head. "Aye, boy. No need to pep talk us. We know our business well enough and we know what we're about, thanks to our boy there." He nodded toward Chuck. "Now let's stop pissing 'round and killing time. You lead the way and leave us to do our work."

The leprechaun was right, they'd already wasted time they didn't have to spare.

Levi turned and gestured toward the rolling door at the rear of Atlantic Biotech Solutions. "I'll let us in."

The Mudman stomped his way across the deserted street and angled toward the building's loading dock. Without losing a step, he hefted one of the boulders—a huge thing that weighed three or four hundred pounds, easy—flanking the rolling door. He waited only a handful of seconds for his shabby army to assemble behind him.

"On three," he said, raising the stone in a huge mitt, which had swelled and lengthened to accommodate the stone's weight and size.

"*One ...* " Muscles tightened in anticipation.

"*Two ...* " The sound of shuffling feet and cracking knuckles followed.

"*Three ...* " Levi hurled the stone before the word fully left his mouth.

The door squealed in protest as metal buckled inward and rollers ripped from their track. The door, once moored to a metal frame, flopped to the floor in a clatter. The rock had done its work well, punching in like a cannonball breaching a ship's hull. Instead of water pouring in, however, trolls, halfies, and hard-nosed leprechauns flooded past Levi in a wave, swarming into the opening.

## *TWENTY-NINE:*

### Royal Rumble

Levi waited for a heartbeat, then glanced back, eyes searching for Chuck. He was gone, just as Levi had instructed. The Mudman gave a shake of his head. What had he been thinking putting so much responsibility on a man he wouldn't trust to feed his cat? Levi wouldn't even let the incompetent huckster water his plants, yet now the leprechaun halfie had his finger on the supernatural equivalent of an atomic bomb? War could make strange bedfellows and even stranger choices. Done was done, though, so Levi put the man from his mind, grabbed the other boulder flanking the smashed-to-hell rolling door, and headed into the fray.

The interior was all gray concrete and steel, illuminated with sodium lights hanging from rafters overhead—the standard affair. Nothing else about the scene, however, came even close to *standard*. The warehouse had been divvied up and transformed from a storage facility to something out of a science-fiction movie. On the right, a substantial space had been walled off with dense Plexiglas and repurposed into some sort of research area. Huge incubation tubes lined the wall behind the glass; each container housed various specimens—some human looking, others not.

A slew of machinery crowded the area, making the space look as though it did indeed belong in a genetics laboratory. A bank of computers and monitoring equipment here, some sort of tubular machine—an MRI, Levi thought—cordoned off by more Plexiglas lurked in one corner. There were medical tables, stainless steel contraptions with leather straps, framed by a wide array of medical tools decorating the walls:

Spotless surgical sheers. Razor-edged scalpels, in a variety of shapes and sizes. Circular electric bone saws. A huge assortment of fluid-filled jars and a shelf laden with syringes and amber-glass medical vials. There were blunt-faced mallets, thick metal rasps, calipers, tissue forceps, and a slew of curved needles for suturing wounds shut. If Levi was still standing when this business was all over and done with, he fully intended to come back and melt this whole building down to slag. Leave nothing behind.

He shifted his gaze away from the Frankenstein laboratory, only to be hit by a wave of déjà vu as his eyes swept over what appeared to be the Kobock temple from the Deep Downs. The same temple Levi had raided, what felt like a lifetime ago, except this one butted up against the backside of the offices at the front of the building. Not everything was the same, obviously, but the grotesque pillars were present, as was the ruby-eyed altar featuring the wyrm god, and the stone table. The table that he'd found Ryder chained to.

The table Ryder was chained to once more, which completed the eerie sense that this whole thing had come full circle.

Out of place was a human woman in blue scrubs—it had to be Jamie, Ryder's sister—who cowered next to the wizened old Kobock shaman Levi had tangled with the first time around. The woman in the scrubs looked terrified and way out of her depth; her gaze constantly shifted between her sister and the commotion unfolding in the warehouse proper. The shaman, however, didn't even bother to look up from his work; instead he eyeballed a crusted old tome— bound in skin—while he brewed some potion in a large cauldron resting over a green flame.

Behind them, chained to the wall near the altar, was Professor Wilkie. His hands were stretched taut above his head, his eyes were almost entirely swollen shut, and his breathing was irregular and ragged.

Bad news, all around.

The Mudman glanced down at a watch he'd donned just for this occasion. 1:06 AM They had *minutes* before the shaman would carve into Ryder, complete the ancient ritual, and bring a dusty old god back into the world of men once more.

The brand in his chest thrummed with fire and fury, sending a surge of raw adrenaline blasting into his limbs, urging him to action, spurring him to cave in heads and pull the shaman's limbs from their sockets.

Sadly, between Levi and Ryder lurked a legion of filthy blue-skinned Kobos—sixty or seventy strong, at least—ready to brawl.

Most sported only soiled loincloths, but a few were clad in crude armor cobbled together from hubcaps or grocery carts or corrugated metal siding. Each held a weapon, be it a broken beer bottle or a club studded with rusted nails, or, in one case, a horse's jawbone. The blue-skinned creatures watched on with bewildered expressions; they'd been expecting Levi, no doubt, but no one could've ever prepared for Levi's reinforcements. A sharp, whip-crack command from the shaman stole away the bewildered looks in a flash and sent the Kobocks rushing forward in a charge of manic fear and killing rage.

Levi's own forces sprinted across the open space, the geriatric trolls in the lead, long legs devouring the distance, while the halfies spread out to either side, like a defensive football line going in for the block.

A *boom* shook the walls as the two sides collided together in a mash of meat and muscle. The front line Kobocks slammed into the trolls and halfies, throwing themselves in with reckless abandon: rotten teeth bit down, bottles lashed out, claws dug into exposed skin. The trolls held the line, however, and gave as good as they got: wicked talons carving channels in unprotected flesh or snapping overextended arms in sickening *pops* loud as gunfire.

The brutish trolls fought with a strength and viciousness Levi wouldn't have guessed at, and the halfies weren't half bad either, especially for a bunch of junkies. The halfies fought as if they didn't feel pain— which might have been true—switchblades flashing out, rusty chains whirling, lead pipes cracking skulls. One halfie, his hide the slick green of a toad, used his acid covered tongue, long as a bull whip, to scorch any Kobo that tried to break through the ranks.

As much as Levi wanted to wade in, smashing and killing, this wasn't his fight. The reinforcements would deal with the Kobocks, and Chuck would help

Ryder and stop the shaman. That thought gave him pause—after all, if Chuck screwed this up they could all be dead before the sun rose on a new day.

But the plan was the plan. What was the point of coming up with a plan at all if Levi didn't follow it?

The reinforcements for the Kobos. Check. Chuck for Ryder. Check. His job was to find Hogg and end him, since he was the brain behind all this …

Still, much as he needed to move on, he couldn't pass up such a great opportunity—all those Kobocks bunched together, practically begging to be obliterated. He planted his feet and snarled as he launched the boulder in his right hand, arching the four-hundred-pound stone over the front line and into the Kobock reserves. Four Kobos, maneuvering around the side, shrieked and howled as his hailstone of Judgment bowled into them: bones snapped and bodies exploded in a gush of sickly fluids.

Satisfaction welled up inside the Mudman, his bloodlust taking hold.

*Hogg*, he reminded himself, *Hogg was his target, not these sniveling monsters*.

But it felt perversely *good* to end them.

Surely a *little* more assistance for his team wouldn't go amiss. He dug both hands into his middle, ripping free a clay pot from either love-handle. He could feel the ichor inside the pots as though it were a part of him—stone called to stone, and ichor to ichor—waiting patiently to be commanded and used. He hurled the first pot, aiming for a group of Kobos working to flank the right side of the halfie defensive line.

The pot, a brilliant cobalt blue with splotches of green, exploded inches above their heads. With an effort of Levi's will, the ichor transmuted, blasting out in a fine mist of glassy powder, which blinded eyes and flayed skin with equal ease. The creatures shrieked, breathing in huge lungfuls of the stuff, before dropping. They clutched at their throats, now ruined by glass particles that shredded esophagi and gnawed at their frail lung tissue.

He hurled the pot in his left hand—a rust-red piece with a crackle finish—zeroing in on the filthy shaman behind the stone table, holding Ryder captive. At the last minute the pot burst, the ichor flowing and shifting into a hail of obsidian arrows. The shaman, lightning quick for such a decrepit creature, had his ceremonial knife out and moving in a blur. In one quick, clean, economical motion, he slashed his opposite forearm and twirled the knife's edge—fat droplets of blood flew into the air.

A flare of light followed as Levi's earthen quills smashed against a wavering crimson barrier that stretched out before the shaman. Blood magic.

Levi ground his teeth in frustration and reached for another pot, ready to wage war against the evil priest—

An explosion of emerald light drew his eye back to the battlefield. The trolls and halfies were falling back now, step by step, but it no longer mattered because the leprechaun leg-breakers had finally entered the fray. They'd disappeared after entering the warehouse—leprechauns were gifted illusionists, one and all—and used their diminutive stature to wriggle amongst the Kobock ranks. Now, however, the leprechauns were out in the open, breaking kneecaps, wrists, or elbows indiscriminately with their black shillelaghs.

The shifty little men didn't stop there, though.

They moved like a grease fire: fast and unpredictable. They'd be kneecapping an adversary one moment and the next, they'd be gone, phasing out of sight with a pop of emerald light, only to reappear *behind* their enemies. They dangled from Kobo backs like parasites while they used thin garrotes of gold—magical choke chains—to cut shallow grooves into Kobock throats. A few of the Leps worked in pairs, one blinding an opponent with a blast of swirling golden powder, not unlike the glass bomb Levi had deployed a moment before, while the other caved in their victim's skull.

Even though Levi's forces were terribly outnumbered, two or three to one, the leprechauns seemed unstoppable—

A bellowing roar as loud as a semi-truck's horn split the air as four Thursrs stormed in from an exit on the left side of the warehouse. Their heavy footfalls rattled the walls as the beasts smashed into a pair of halfies on the left side of the line. The halfies—one, a paunchy beast with webbed hands and protruding eyes, the other, a thick-armed, scaled-covered man with Trog blood clearly in his veins—didn't stand a chance. They fell before rending tusks and smashing fists.

*Hogg*, Levi reminded himself again.

As tough as the leprechaun crew was, they'd have their hands full with those Thursrs. He hesitated only a moment before grabbing another pair of pot-grenades from his center. The first he fast-balled at the Thursrs still entangled with the halfies. Trying to kill four of their ilk outright would be no easy thing, so instead he'd aimed the pot at the floor near their feet. The clay shattered, the noise lost in the din of battle, and the Dread Trolls didn't even notice the ichor creeping and spreading outward in a puddle.

They did notice when the ground shuddered and shifted beneath them, the floor liquefying into a knee-deep pool of sludgy black tar. It wouldn't kill them, but it might halt their progress long enough for the leprechauns to do something more permanent. Levi couldn't tarry any longer; he needed to find Hogg, and it was a safe guess that Hogg had sent the Thursrs in. He broke into a lumbering run, angling away from the action and toward the exit the Dread Trolls had come from.

As the Mudman ran, he took the clay pot still in his hand and smashed it into his head, the ichor washing over him in a spray of gold and running down his chest, arms, and legs. Then he shifted, his body tightening in some places and swelling in others: bristly white fur sprouted from his skin, wicked claws jutted from his fingers, and boar-like tusks shot out from his lower lip. Levi could transform his whole body at will, but the forms he was most accustomed to were the easiest to manifest and maintain. He'd never been a Thursr before, but with the added boost from the ichor, he could manage the change.

This new body was uncomfortable and ungainly, though, the proportions not quite right. But he wouldn't need to hold the disguise for long. Unlike in books or movies, Levi had no intention of bantering with Hogg: he intended only to kill him as swiftly and painfully as possible. With this rudimentary camouflage in place, Levi hoped to sneak close and strike before the mad doctor ever saw a thing coming.

Back turned on the epic fight, he pushed his way through the exit door and into whatever lay beyond.

## THIRTY:

## Manacles

A small room, devoid of people, with a stairway leading up to the second floor waited for Levi. The first thing the Mudman noticed was the water coating the ground in a shallow pool and misting down from above, courtesy of the sprinkler system overhead. The next thing he noticed was the overwhelming stench of Thursr—wild musk mingling with old meat and voided bowels—which wafted through the air, permeating everything. The stink was far more potent than a single Dread Troll could account for. Even the four he'd seen out front couldn't explain this level of reek.

Something wasn't right here. He'd made a mistake.

He saw no opposition, but his senses were screaming a warning at him. He skidded to a stuttering halt, his unfamiliar legs failing to cooperate, then backtracked toward the door while he reached into the floor with his earth sense. He couldn't feel a thing, not with the water coating the cement underfoot. Hogg had said there was a trap lying in wait, and Levi had, perhaps foolishly, assumed it to be the army of

Kobocks. His shoulder blades brushed the door behind him. Locked. He spun around raising massive fists to bash his way free—

Something—he couldn't see what—collided into his center, pushing him further into the room. The gamey scent of Thursr was far stronger now, like a mule kick to the teeth, so it wasn't hard to guess *what* was attacking him, even if he couldn't see his opponent. The Mudman managed to keep his feet, though barely, and flailed his arms, hammering at his unseen enemy, landing a few glancing blows, but nothing substantial.

Surprisingly, the creature clinging to his middle didn't resist, didn't hit or kick back. Instead it clung to him like a tumor, hanging on despite Levi's best attempts to shake him. A moment later a second invisible foe smashed into Levi's shoulders—thick, bristly arms wrapping around Levi's biceps in a bear hug that restricted his movements.

Another beast joined the fray, hammering into one of Levi's knees, which immediately gave out under the pressure. The Mudman teetered, body unsure which way to fall, before the press of hairy, smelly bodies finally brought him crashing to the floor with a *thud* and a *splash*. He lay face-down, struggling to pull his nose and mouth from the pooling water spreading throughout the room. The water wasn't deep, only a few inches, but when lying face-down, even a few inches could be enough to drown a man—or a monster, in Levi's case.

He fought off panic, trying to slow his thudding heartbeat, which raced along like a horse at the track. He continued to fight, to struggle against the creatures pinning him down, but the water robbed the strength from his limbs even while stealing his breath.

More bodies piled on, the weight crushing Levi into the ground, his fitful struggles completely useless. He could no longer maintain his Thursr disguise—his focus slipped away like water down a stream, and his body reverted to its true form. Not that the disguise had done a lick of good anyway. Hogg had clearly been ready for Levi's trickery. Still the Mudman fought, bucking his hips, wiggling his legs, biceps straining against the colossal mass bearing down on him.

Useless. Completely useless.

More clawed hands joined the tangle of limbs and bodies, stretching out his arms and legs as though they intended to crucify him—which might've been the case considering what Hogg and company had done to Professor Wilkie's research assistant out in the Sprawl.

But no, that couldn't be it. They were going to great lengths to restrain Levi without actually hurting him.

"The shackles, you morons!" Hogg hollered from the staircase. "Get the shackles on him."

The rattle and rasp of metallic links drifted to Levi's ears, sending renewed waves of dread coursing through him. Levi strained, muscles bulging, mouth a rictus as he tried to pull his hands and feet free, refusing to give up no matter how hopeless this situation appeared.

Something cold slipped around his right wrist and clamped down with a *click*. Another slipped around his left hand. Then around his right ankle. His left. Thick steel manacles bit into his skin, digging in deeper with every second, as if the cuffs were constricting boas.

"Enough!" the doctor hollered. "Off him now! Now! Before you buffoons damage him further."

And suddenly the pressure disappeared, the Thursrs pulling away at Hogg's command, leaving Levi free. With a grumble the Mudman pushed himself onto all fours, then, with a heave, he struggled to his feet. He eyed the shackles on his wrists and ankles as he got his balance. Thick cuffs of dull-gray metal encircled each limb. They didn't seem of immediate concern since they did nothing to restrict his movements or impede him in any discernable way.

So instead he focused his attention on the Thursrs—once invisible but now plain as the nose on his face—lurking around the room, their hackles raised, lips pulled back in snarls as their beady eyes traced Levi's movements. He counted five, and each wore a silver necklace with a blue sapphire, big as an egg, which glimmered with arcane power. Some sort of technomancy, which, Levi assumed, granted them the power of invisibility.

No matter. Levi couldn't care less about them, he only had eyes for the portly doctor loitering on the stairs. Even with the ichor bombs, Levi wasn't sure he could beat five Dread Trolls, but he didn't need to. He just needed to survive them long enough to kill Hogg.

"Welcome home," the doctor said with an oily smile. "My prodigal child, returned to the fold after all these years."

Levi didn't waste a breath on chitchat. He broke into a heavy-footed sprint—bound on a crash course with Hogg, and anything that got in his way be damned. The Thursrs tensed, but made no move to stop Levi's imminent assault. All the better.

"Stop moving. Now," Hogg said, his tone casual and unconcerned.

Like Levi would listened to this murdering monst—

Hogg jabbed at something in his hand, pudgy thumb pressing what looked like a key fob for a car.

Pain exploded in Levi's wrists and ankles and once more he found himself dropping to the floor, his body convulsing and jerking, jaws chattering while his body flopped and flailed in the tepid water. The manacles. They stabbed into his doughy clay: a ring of spikes, pencil thin and cold as dry ice, had exploded inward like a bear trap clamping down on some witless animal. The Mudman howled, not just because of the spikes, but because his blood, his ichor, burned like the surface of the sun. The pain he'd felt during his fire baptism in the heart of the Atlantean temple was the closest, comparable experience.

Except then, the fire had been running over his outsides, melting his flesh and muscle, while this flame sprinted along his veins, stabbing every nerve ending in passing.

"I've been hanging onto those for a long, long time," Hogg said, indifferent to Levi's suffering. "Fae workmanship, acid etched with runes of power and transmuted by dark alchemy. I built those over sixty years ago, crafted specifically to control you. I always intended to free my Master Cain, of course, but I wanted a little insurance that he would remain as loyal to me as I have to him. No honor among thieves, so always have a backup plan, I say."

He held the small black remote and thumbed a red button. The spikes withdrew and took the murderous pain with them.

"Like a choke chain, so I can train you properly. You will obey my every instruction, or you will know unending pain. The presence of the spikes creates an enzyme-catalyzed reaction, which agitates your ichor, causing it to shift uncontrollably through transmutation after transmutation. The process prevents transformation and healing. And, as a secondary benefit, it's also terribly painful." His cold gaze swept over the Thursrs milling about. "I have this well in hand now. Go, all of you. Crush our opposition and you will be richly rewarded. Money, food, women. There are many seats at the table in the new order we will usher in tonight."

A Thursr, even more massive than the rest, bowed his head and saluted, fist to chest, then wheeled around and slammed his way through the connecting doorway, which let out into the fray. Screams, shrieks, and the plaintive wail of the dying drifted through the temporarily open door. Doctor Hogg watched them go, a cruel smile gracing his lips, then glanced down at a watch on his wrist.

For the first time in his long life, Levi felt utterly defeated. "How did you know I would come for you instead of the girl?" he asked from the floor, water lapping at his hands and knees.

"Because, Golem," he replied with a sneer, "I *know* you. Perhaps in that crude brain of yours you've convinced yourself that you came to rescue the girl, but the fact that you chose to hunt me over saving her shows the true intentionality of your twisted heart. You're a creature of rage and hate and murder, nothing more and nothing less. I knew that. Just as I knew you would have an aversion and weakness to water. Despite your interference"—he stole another look at his watch—"my shaman will complete the ritual any moment and my master will arrive. And, to top it all off, I've recaptured a priceless piece of property. What a night. Come," he commanded, "there's still time to witness my victory. Upstairs now."

Levi hesitated for only a second before climbing to his feet. Before he could think through his actions, he leapt forward, hands outthrust, ready to choke the life from the evil man. Hogg's finger never came close to the button, yet the spikes stabbed back down, sending a lightning strike of pain through Levi's body. He stumbled and crashed into a wall, staggering and shaking while he fought to keep his feet.

Hogg watched with amusement as Levi wrestled against the crippling agony. "Despite what you may think, Golem," Hogg said, "you are a machine. A machine I built. And like any other machine, you can be programmed and controlled. The manacles are powerful Vis-wrought objects. Technomancy at its very finest. They can sense intentionality. Try to escape and the spikes trigger automatically. Try to harm me and they trigger automatically. You are a slave. Just as I always intended. Understand?"

As much as Levi hated himself for doing so, he gritted his teeth and nodded his assent.

Hogg waited for another few beats before keying the remote in his hand, drawing the spikes back into the manacles. "Now, upstairs. I don't want to miss my moment of triumph." He turned his back, completely unworried about Levi, and marched up the stairs.

Levi didn't follow, not right away, but it took only seconds before the spikes began easing out, a centimeter at a time. Levi took a step, and immediately the spikes retracted.

"Don't dawdle," Hogg called down. "Disobedience also carries a heavy penalty. I think, perhaps, you are starting to see the extent of your predicament."

Knowing he could do nothing else, Levi followed, obedient as a collared dog.

Upstairs was a lavish living area, like something out of a museum: Elegant drapery of velvet, trimmed in gold, lined the walls. Heavy furniture, old, graceful, and vaguely Roman, filled the space. A huge, heavily tinted window took up most of the right wall, overlooking the reconstructed Kobock temple below. On the far side of the room stood a doorway—or rather the outline of one, painted onto the stone in neat brushstrokes of red. Running along the door's edge were a host of arcane symbols, a few of which Levi recognized—one from the *Picatrix*, another from the *Clavis Salomonis*—and more which he didn't. He didn't need to understand the runes to understand the door's purpose, however.

It was a gateway, a manufactured thin spot that led to somewhere either in the Hub or greater Outworld. An escape hatch, just in case the captain needed to jump ship.

The Mudmans's eyes lingered on the door for only a moment before his gaze shifted to the huge window overlooking the battle still raging away. A cursory look told Levi things were not going well for his side. With the addition of the Thursr backups, the tide was most definitely turning in Hogg's favor. Worse, Levi saw no sign of Chuck, and the shaman's ritual was underway—the dark power he'd conjured thrummed in the air, beating against Levi's preternatural senses.

"The chains on the wall." Hogg motioned toward a formidable set of glimmering lengths of metal connected to a brick wall on the far side of the room. "Go lock the manacles in place. One more added precaution until I can break you properly."

Levi didn't move. Being captured was one thing, but willingly chaining himself to a wall for his captor was something else entirely. Hogg maneuvered to the window and leaned against it with one elbow, contently staring down on the scene below. Then he pressed the button, never taking his eyes from whatever was unfolding in the warehouse.

Pain, like a swarm of stinging bees, exploded inside Levi. The pain was less than before—he managed to keep his feet—but still maddening in its intensity.

"I can control the amount of pain by controlling the amount of catalyzing agent entering your bloodstream. You should be able to walk. Once you secure yourself to the wall, the pain stops," Hogg said with a shrug.

Levi *had* to comply. There was no alternative.

Death would be far better than this torturous existence, and the Mudman would do next to anything to be rid of the hurt. He threw himself into motion, scrambling over to the brick wall, his thick fingers trembling as he worked at the chains hanging from rune-etched steel plates fastened into the brick. Every moment he failed to obey, the pain intensified, until he could hardly stand or see. He struggled with a clasp, which fit into a loop on the outside of his left manacle. After a few heartbeats the clasp finally slipped into place and snapped shut with a *click*. The spikes receded a bit, the pain dimming enough so he could see again.

The second lock was easier than the first, his hands responding with greater confidence and familiarity. His leg restraints were easier still, and as the last lock ratcheted shut, the pain faded completely. He slouched against the wall, chest heaving as he sucked in a few long pulls of air.

"Ahh. And now it begins," Hogg said, a note of celebration in the words. "All the pieces fall into place."

Levi couldn't see whatever was happening in the warehouse below, not from his vantage point, but it didn't matter.

It was over.

He'd lost everything.

Ryder would die.

Chuck would die.

The men he'd hired would die.

Everyone would die. Everyone but him. He would live as a slave to Hogg. He shuddered to think of what he would become in time. He'd had the damned manacles on for a few minutes and already he raced to submit to the doctor's commands. In a month or a year? Ten years? He'd be a mindless monster once more—a killing machine, concerned only with avoiding the stinging lash of his master's whip. No thought to conscience. To morality. Or God. Not so different from the way he'd spent the majority of his life, really.

Ryder screamed, a wail that resonated throughout the building and carried over the clamor of the fighting.

It was the sound of a woman dying.

Hogg laughed and clapped his hands as though watching the stirring climax to some wonderful play.

*No.*

The word ran through Levi's head, but it wasn't Levi voice. It was the voice of the dead, the souls of the slain residing inside him.

*No. No. No. No. No. No. No.*

That single word over and over again, building in conviction with every repetition, a different voice each time, crying out their demand. And with the chorus of *no's* came visions and memories: *the Wehrmacht; the Luftwaffe; black-garbed Schutzstaffel; the roar of the single prop Focke-Wulf; the packed train cars; Red House; Nicholas Fackenheim, murdered March, 1942; Opa—the old Kite—murdered April, 1943.* Faster and faster they came, until all of them blurred together, just like the night he was born.

And now—as on that night in the open grave—those voices coalesced into a single demand. A demand for retribution.

There *was* a way out, they said. Then they told him how.

The manacles, those were the real problem. He just needed to be rid of them and he'd have Hogg right where he wanted him: cornered and alone. It was obvious the man had some powerful talents, but Levi knew he wasn't a physical threat. There was a reason

Hogg surrounded himself with huge bodyguards and only acted if he was sure he could win.

That assurance, that overconfidence, would be Hogg's downfall—assuming, of course, Levi could break loose. *You can break free*, the voices corrected. *It will hurt, but what's a little pain after all we've suffered?*

Even the *thought* of escape brought the pain back with renewed fury, the spikes wriggling themselves into place. But the voices dwelling in his skull, in his soul, drowned out that pain with their racket. *Pull,* they urged as one.

*Pull. Pull. Pull. Pull.*

Levi focused on their haunted chanting. They were right, if he could bear the torment, freedom was only seconds away. He focused on the memories, focused on the injustice, and on his hunger for vengeance. He gained his feet and pulled the slack from the chain with his right wrist, just as the voices instructed. He didn't stop there, though. Instead he continued to wrench at his hand. The spikes from the manacle dug in deeper, but that served him. Pressure built around his wrist, mounting, growing, as his bicep bulged and tugged against the manacle and the manacle, in turn, tugged against the chain.

The chains groaned and creaked from the tension, but they were nigh indestructible, as were the shackles, and both refused to break. But Levi wasn't aiming to break them—he was depending on them holding fast. With gritted teeth, he wiggled his wrist until he felt something give—the flesh ripping under the tension and bite of the spikes. Then, with a wet *pop*, his hand tore away entirely, the chain swinging back to the wall, his hand still locked in its binding.

A bellowing roar ripped through the air at the same moment, the sound of a T. rex venting its rage.

Levi stole a hasty peek at Hogg. The man paid him no mind; his shoulders were knotted with anxiety and he was totally absorbed with the spectacle unfolding in the warehouse below. *The failsafe*, Levi reckoned. *Chuck must've come through.*

*You've only begun*, the voices screamed, driving the thought from his head.

*Again. Again. Again*, they urged.

This time he worked on his left hand, fighting and pulling until that hand tore free and joined its amputated brother, dangling from the wall. The torment in his wrists—now jagged, gold-smeared stumps—was monstrous, but still less painful than the manacles had been. He needed to free his feet, but for that, he would need hands. New hands. An impossibility. Unless, of course, he had a huge reserve of ichor handy. Like the six unused pots in his belly.

With a tremendous effort of will, he opened the storage cavity along the length of his torso and jammed his bleeding stumps into his middle. Two pots fractured with a faint *crack,* then spilled out their precious, life-giving contents. Levi pulled the raw ichor into his stumps and repurposed the substance into wet, gray hands of clay.

"What is this?!" Hogg spat, rounding on Levi, eyes wide as he glanced between Levi's new appendages and the amputated hands hanging from the walls. "No, no, impossible." He jabbed at his little remote. The remote had no effect, since the remaining ankles spikes were already fully extended. Levi couldn't walk—could hardly move or think—the fiery hurt was far too debilitating, but he could fix that.

"*Klieg, Klieg, Klieg-Du bist a Nar,*" Levi said, lips pulled back in a snarl. An old Yiddish saying, *You are smart, smart, smart—but you are not so smart!*

Levi's hands transformed in a blur, fingers giving way to blade-edged meat cleavers. With only a moment's hesitation to brace himself for what was to come, he slammed the meat cleavers into his shins, severing both of his feet in one fell blow. New agony screamed and capered through his body, but the absence of the spiked manacles was like a breath of fresh air to a drowning man. Levi shifted his hands, fingers swirling back into place. He withdrew another two pots, which he promptly smashed into the clean-edged stumps on his legs. Ichor bloomed, melted, and surged, giving birth to new feet.

Levi pushed himself upright with an ugly, lopsided grin which promised pain and death in equal measures. Hogg glanced through the window, fear etched on his face—whatever was happening out there wasn't good. At least not for Hogg. The pudgy doctor jabbed his finger down on the controller one more time. Nothing. Not with those damned cuffs gone.

"I see I've underestimated you, Golem." He edged away from the window, angling toward the emergency portal painted onto the back wall. He never took his eyes from Levi. A sheen of nervous sweat coated his face and hands. "I won't be easy game," he said. "I may not have the full power of a mage at my command, but I've been around for a very long time, and, like you, I have access to a Philosopher's stone." He tapped on his chest with one plump digit.

"Admittedly, I do so hate perpetrating physical violence, but I'm capable of doing what needs done."

Levi burst into motion—

A renewed scream cut him short. "Heads up, Chuck! He sees you."

A burst of gunfire followed, the harsh bark of Chuck's Desert Eagle.

He couldn't believe it. Somehow both Ryder and Chuck were still alive. But only God knew for how long. If Chuck was firing in the open, it could only mean Levi's backup plan had failed. Cain, the patron god of murder, was loose and unopposed.

Movement at his periphery:

Despite his big talk of "doing what needs done," Hogg was running … well, waddling toward the emergency exit, his squat legs swishing back and forth as fast as they would carry him. A runner, not a fighter. Probably the reason he'd lived so long. Levi stood frozen by an uncharacteristic indecision. Hogg might have been a runner in spirit, but he wasn't an athlete by any measure, and Levi knew he could beat him to the door. Given enough time, he also knew he could end Hogg's miserable existence once and for all.

Was the price worth paying though?

Ryder and Chuck were alive, but they might not be for long. It was entirely possible Levi would kill Hogg only to find his friends dead at the hands of the raging Cain. Murdered and left to die in a pool of their own blood. He could always gamble: just kill Hogg and hope for the best. The Mudman could stop Hogg or he could save Ryder and Chuck. But he couldn't do both. Not with any degree of certainty. Despite Hogg's obvious cowardice, Levi was positive he would have some trick up his sleeve—a man as cunning as Hogg would never be completely defenseless. Killing him would take time, precious time.

Time Ryder and Chuck didn't have.

The angry specters screamed and cheered in support of the Hogg-murdering option—the brand in his chest burned with the fury of a personal sun.

*Hogg was responsible for all of this,* the voices pleaded. He'd killed all those men and women so many years ago. He was an unrepentant, black-hearted murderer who, if left alive, would surely go on to cause more trouble and inflict more death. What was two lives against the fate of so many more? Justice demanded Levi kill the doctor. Everything in him demanded he kill the doctor.

Something Hogg had said earlier tickled at the back of Levi's mind. *"Perhaps in that crude brain of yours you've convinced yourself that you came to rescue the girl, but the fact that you chose to hunt me over saving her shows the true intentionality of your twisted heart."* And here Levi was, standing at a crossroad with exactly that choice before him. Pastor Steve's words followed:

*"Anger and vengeance are like a fire, Levi, and like fire, they burn indiscriminately. You might get your vengeance, only to find yourself consumed and destroyed in the process. At the end of the day, you need to make the choice you can live with—and sometimes the choice you can live with isn't the one that makes any sense at all from a worldly perspective ..."*

Hogg reached the emergency exit.

Levi let him.

The Mudman wheeled around, leaving the doctor to make his getaway, and charged toward the picture window. He didn't look back as he smashed through the glass like a cannonball and plummeted to the warehouse floor, ready to save his friends.

Had he made the right decision? He didn't know. But he'd made a decision he could live with, and for the first time in a long, long time, his heart felt light and easy.

## THIRTY-ONE:

### Resurrection

R yder absently ran a hand over the surface of the stone table beneath her, its texture slick and smooth like polished glass. She didn't know how long she had left to live, but she knew it wouldn't be long now. A double handful of minutes, tops. For one, they'd stopped drugging her. Said she needed to be awake for the ritual to work. Two, the Kobock shaman—the leathery, old bastard sporting a patchwork cloak of what Ryder assumed was skin—was busy working away at a cauldron, brewing some rancid soup, which burned her nose hairs. A sweet and sour stink like old vomit and even older roadkill.

She craned her neck and glanced first at her sister, who refused to meet her eye, then at Professor Wilkie, still chained against the wall. Yeah, she knew she was going to die, but she hoped he might walk away from this clusterfuck. He was a kooky son of a bitch, but he'd offered her more than a few reassuring words. Well, he had until one of the Kobocks smashed his face in with a rock. Not enough to kill him, she could see the steady rise and fall of his chest, but enough to silence him for a good long while.

She hated seeing him like that and hated watching her sister even more. Looking the other way was even more depressing, though. A horde of Kobocks hung about on the other side: Picking their noses. Hitting each other with beer bottles. Rutting on the floor like wild dogs. From her vantage, they seemed like a virtual ocean of blue-skinned monstrosities lurking between her and freedom. An ocean of total grossness. Even if Levi came, which seemed less and less likely by the moment, there was no way he could fight through that. A hopeless brawl, even for a thug like Levi.

A thin stream of tears leaked out from the corners of her eyes.

She hadn't expected the end to be like this. There'd been some awfully low points in her life, points when she'd thought death was calling—like that time she'd overdosed on speed and slept it off in a Walmart bathroom. Or that time one of her ex-boyfriends showed up with a sawed-off shotgun, high on peyote *and* meth, raging about how she'd stolen his liver. Never saw this coming, though.

A shriek of metal and the yowl of Kobos ripped her away from the morbid thoughts.

She turned her head in time to see a giant boulder, big as a park bench, arc through the air and crash into a group of loitering Kobocks, smashing them like a huge flyswatter, leaving only a dark smear on the concrete. Next came movement and more screaming. She couldn't see much, not with so many creatures blocking the view, but the madcap scrambling and ensuing violence spelled things out plenty clear.

Crazy-ass suicide mission or not, Levi had come for her, and since she hadn't yet been split open like a pig, some tiny measure of hope remained. A sliver no bigger than her pinky, but persisting all the same. She felt like a death-row inmate—strapped down and waiting for the end—who'd just heard she might get a stay of execution. Maybe.

Another jagged stone flew through the air and crushed more Kobocks.

Then something exploded overhead with the *boom* of a grenade, but, instead of a ball of fire erupting, a cloud of powdery dust rained down into the shifting, screaming mass of blue-skinned assholes below. A handful of the creatures clawed at their eyes, talons digging trenches into their faces, before toppling to the floor, grimy hands clutched to throats as they coughed and hacked. Great gobs of frothy blood burbled out between blackened teeth.

The world was madness and chaos. Anarchy in every sense of the word.

And then the shaman was next to her. He held a wickedly curved knife in one shriveled hand; runes along the blade's side glowed with a pale-red witchlight. Instead of cutting into her, though, he brought the blade's edge sliding across the inside of his forearm. With a flick of his wrist, the knife sent a spray of bright blood flying into the air: there was a thunder crack and a blaze of crimson as several black arrows shattered against an iridescent shield.

More chaos. More fighting. More shrieking. None of it made sense.

Then there were pint-sized men, hard-looking Irish brawlers with thick black clubs, running wild amidst the Kobock ranks. Mean little shits, too. They moved like water and wind, dancing and sliding through the crowds in flashes of gold and green, busting the holy shit out of kneecaps and shins. She watched, stunned, as one of the miniature fellas shattered a Kobock leg—a spear of bone popped right through the bastard's blue skin—then laid into the Kobo's head over and over again. The disgusting, lopsided shithead rolled into a ball, gangly arms trying to protect its vital bits, but the badass midget was having none of it.

The Irish brawler smashed the Kobock's head in until gray matter leaked onto the concrete. Then, no shit, the little guy took a smoldering corncob pipe from between his lips and dumped the cherry-red ash onto the blue-skinned corpse. Badass didn't even begin to cover it.

*What the fuck is happening?*

*Escape was happening, had to be.*

So what if she didn't know who the pint-sized killers coming to her aid were. *They were coming to her aid*, that was the important thing to remember. Watching them work was a hard sight to stomach, true, but she would live with any number of bad dreams if it meant she got to keep dreaming. She bucked at her bonds, twisting her wrists, jerking her ankles, frantic to get away while her captors were distracted.

More yowls and howls, more flashes of gold and green—it was like being at a fucking Saint Patty's Day parade in Boston—

A clawed hand landed on her forehead, jerking her head toward the ruby-eyed altar off to the left. The shaman stood over her, free hand no longer holding a knife, but rather a delicate paintbrush coated in a reeky red sludge: the putrid liquid from the cauldron.

"The time is nigh," he hissed as he set to work, tracing letters and symbols onto her nose, cheeks, and chin with the paintbrush's tip. The shaman chanted as he worked his way down her body—his words were rough, crude things that hurt her ears. She'd been around the punk scene a long time, but she'd never heard *anything* come close to the ear-splitting sounds that old fuck made. The shaman splashed more script onto her neck and chest and as he did, his words warbled and intensified, building to a crescendo as he scrawled lines and sigils onto her belly.

She screamed, fists balled, stomach taut, legs suddenly rigid. Her insides ... she could feel the thing, the homunculus, responding to the shaman's call, worming its way upward, tunneling through her guts. After a few heartbeats, she could *see* its serpentine form pressing against her stomach, like a baby trying to kick its way out.

The shaman shuffled back a step, his chanting never slowing. Jamie crept forward, her jaw hanging open as she watched the carnage unfolding all around. She looked dazed. Shocked. Confused. But none of that stopped her from raising a knife high overhead—the same knife Ryder had seen in the shaman's withered hand a minute ago.

"Now!" the shaman shrieked.

"I'm sorry, Sally," Jamie whispered, lips trembling, tears dripping from her eyes in twin streams. "This is for Mom and Dad and Jackson." She hesitated, brow furrowing, face hardening. "It's for us." Then she plunged the knife down, the blade burrowing into Ryder's navel.

Ryder's scream cut off, the force of the blow driving the air from her lungs.

The knife pulled free, and as it left, Ryder could feel the thing inside her forcing its way through the new opening. She gasped, eyes rolling up into her head, back arching—a yogi in *urdhva dhanurasana*, the upward wheel pose. Something wet, sticky, and serpentine slid from her ruptured belly—foot after terrible foot of slick coils pulling loose—before the creature flopped to the floor with a *squish*. After what felt like hours, Ryder collapsed back to the table's surface, her breaths coming fast and ragged.

Another scream followed. Jamie. Ryder turned her head—the motion made her sputter and cough up a mouthful of hot blood—and bore witness as Jamie slid the same blade into her own belly, jabbing it home while she whimpered and shook.

"Oh shit," someone whispered in her ear. A man's voice ... though her brain was too clouded by pain to tell her head from her ass.

"Why the hell I gotta get involved in this bullshit," the voice mumbled.

Chuck. It was Chuck.

She blinked past the tears filling her eyes and searched for the source of the voice. Nothing. But now she could feel fingers working at the cuffs holding her in place. Invisible, he must've been invisible. "Don't worry, sweet-thing, I got you," he said, voice far too reassuring. She must've been in really awful shape for him to use that tone. She felt like a piece of fucking roadkill. "It's gonna be alright, girl, I got you," he said again.

"It's"—she gasped, coughed, metallic blood spurting onto her chin—"too late."

"Don't you worry 'bout that. Me and my boy Levi, we got a plan. You just worry about not dying. Cool? Cool." The cuffs took Chuck only a few seconds to loosen, but no one seemed particularly concerned with her at the moment. The Kobocks were doing their best to fight off the invading army. The shaman was, presumably, tending to the murder god wriggling around on the floor. And Jamie ... well, Jamie was curled into the fetal position, clutching at her stomach, trying to hold the blood in.

Chuck, still invisible, hefted Ryder into his arms like a man cradling a small child. "Oh shitty, shit, shit-ass, shit," he said, body suddenly stiff with tension, fear, or both. "We are so fucked. Like royally fucked, by the King of Fuck-You City."

Ryder wanted to applaud him for his creative use of the word fuck—the guy certainly had a way with words—but instead she settled for throwing up a stream of blood all down her front.

A second later she saw the source of Chuck's fear:

The maggoty little grub the shaman had implanted inside her back in the Deep Downs was anything but little now. The wyrm swelled with every passing second, exploding up and out in a sprawl of limbs and spikes and teeth.

The creature stared at Ryder with a hundred glowing ruby eyes all jammed into a reptilian head like a salamander's, though big as a truck tire, with a gaping mouth, lined top and bottom with inch-long knife-blade teeth. And it kept growing, up and up just like Jack's beanstalk.

Blood—both hers and her sister's—rolled across the ground like huge gobs of liquid mercury, before absorbing into the creature's serpentine tail dragging along the floor. Black horns burst from either side of its head, followed by lanky arms, thick as telephone poles, which sprouted from a too-thin torso. Huge double hinged legs came next, bursting out from its pelvis in a flash of blood-red hide, dead-ending in huge talon-toed feet. Hooked spikes—silver protrusions of bone—stabbed out through shoulders, elbows, and knees, and ran along its spine.

By the time the transformation was complete, the walking nightmare—something vomited straight out of the mouth of hell—loomed over her. Twelve solid feet of muscle, teeth, and claws. And it grew a little larger every second, swelling as Ryder's blood trickled across the floor and absorbed into its body.

"The world is lay bare before me once more," the creature said, his voice the guttural buzz of a million flies. The freaky fuck didn't actually speak in English. The words that came out of his mouth were twisting things that made no sense in her ear; in her head, however, she understood them perfectly. Almost as if her brain was hardwired to comprehend whatever language he spoke. The monster drew in a deep breath, its huge scaled chest expanding as it savored the air. "The taste of freedom." A serpent's forked tongue shot out and tickled the air.

The shaman padded forward, eyes lowered to the ground, hands raised high in reverence. "Great Lord of Death, Father to our kind," he hissed in broken English, "your humble servant welcomes you to the world of men."

The creature, Cain, spun, head canted inquisitively to one side, eyes tracking the shaman's every movement. "One of the devout," he said, the words crawling beneath Ryder's flesh. He reached out a massive hand and ran a finger over the shaman's cheek. "My true blood. Serve your father now."

"Anything, my Lord. Anything."

"I hunger," the beast bellowed, temporarily silencing the battle and drawing every eye. Then he moved in a blur, sweeping forward, jaws unhinging and stretched wide as he descended on the shaman. The gnarled priest's eyes widened in shock, and he stood rooted to the ground, too stunned to move. The thing's jaws slid over the Kobock's head and shoulders without a hitch, crunching down in a spray of gore. Cain reared back, lifting the shaman high into the air, then shook his massive head back and forth like an alligator tearing off a chunk of meat from some sucker wildebeest.

The shaman's waist and legs fell away, gray coils of gut spilling out all over the floor.

Ryder vomited out more blood—because of the pain, obviously, but also because she'd never seen anything more revolting. And she'd seen Levi set himself on fire before jumping into the stomach of a plant monster.

"Sorry, baby girl—" Chuck began.

"Don't call me that," she protested, voice weak and feeble.

"—this shit's about to get real in here," he continued without a pause. "Gonna have to set you down for a minute."

He lowered her to the floor, gently laying her on the cold concrete. He appeared in a blink beside her, now down on one knee while he rooted around in a black duffle bag slung over his shoulder. He pulled out a gunmetal-gray box the size of a small safe, gingerly removed a heavy lid covered in more strange sigils, then reached in and pulled out a large egg, its shell a patchwork of pale-green with swirls of yellows running over the surface. Ryder had no trouble placing it: it was the last remaining egg from the Sprawl temple.

*THIRTY-TWO:*

**The Warden**

"What the hell are you doing?" Ryder gasped through pained wheezes.

"Saving our asses, hopefully," Chuck replied. "Levi cut a deal with that crazy-ass computer lady after Hogg snatched your ass. If she can beat that badass motherfucker right there, she gets to keep the body. Gets her freedom. Now you just hang on tight, this is about to get wild as all hell."

He stood up, egg hefted in one palm, his Desert Eagle clasped in the other.

"You the ugliest lookin' sumbitch I done ever seen," Chuck yelled at the creature, who was currently swallowing the remains of the Kobock Priest. "Seriously, I thought my boy Levi was one ugly turd, but next to you, he's ready to strut the catwalk. You sure they baked you long enough, 'cause you lookin' a little underdone, hombre."

Cain regarded Chuck with squinted eyes, ropes of blood and drool dangling from his lips. "How cute, a smart mouthed halfie hoping to save the day. I'm going to rip your spine out, rape your corpse, then wear your ribcage as a decorative bracelet …" He paused, tongue drooping out and pulling in a loose chunk of blue meat. "Or you can walk away and put that"—he motioned toward the egg—"back in its box. Do so and I'll forget you were ever here."

"Boy. Don't you know how to sell it," Chuck replied. "But I ain't fixin' to do that. Instead of listenin' to you run your mouth at me, I'm gonna watch my girl, Siphonei, wipe the floor with your nasty ass. And, as a bonus, I'm gonna get paid a shit-ton of gold and get some outta-this-world street cred for killin' you. So you can take your offer and fuck yourself sideways with it, partner."

Chuck winked and fastballed the egg at the growling monstrosity like David hurling his puny stone at a hulking Goliath. One of Cain's massive hands snaked out lightning quick, snatching the egg out of the air, the shell intact. "You were saying?" the creature asked, its mouth splitting wide to reveal its fangs.

"I think you heard me just fine," Chuck replied, unworried—or at least playing the part. He hefted his hand cannon. "But since I can't actually see any ears on that busted up head of yours, I'll say it again. Go fuck yourself sideways."

Chuck pulled the trigger and blasted the otherworldly egg with a single, well-placed shot. The shell exploded in a spray of smoke and grit. In the same instant a soccer ball-sized hole bloomed in reality, spilling a withering mass of green tentacles into the air. Tentacles—covered in thorns, barbs of bone, and wicked black flowers—that slithered like smoke, wrapping around Cain's arms and legs, entwining around his torso and throat as the rest of the Flower-monster emerged.

In the span of a few heartbeats, Siphonei had pulled herself free and the hole in reality snapped closed with a faint *pop*.

"You insufferable bitch," Cain spat. "Do you have any idea how long I've fantasized about ripping you apart? I will be only too happy to demonstrate the futility of your existence."

"It's a pleasure to finally meet you, too," Siphonei said, the flowers running along her body vibrating with sound. "It will be an even greater pleasure to eviscerate you, send you back to your own personal hell, then steal your body."

"Bitch," Cain howled as he thrashed, his fingers—spindly and claw-tipped—ripping at the vines wrapped around him, huge jaws flashing out, shredding crab-clawed arms. Siphonei gave as good as she got, though, her crustacean pincers shearing off his fingers and scooping out huge divots in his crimson hide.

"Holy shit, this is the most badass thing I ever seen," Chuck whispered into Ryder's ear as he stowed his pistol, shoved his hands beneath her armpits, and hauled her upright, supporting her weight. "I mean *damn.* Ain't no one ever gonna believe this." He let out a pent-up breath, then turned back to her. "Okay, cool as this is, my job was to get you. I've got you, so I say we split while those bad motherfuckers kill each other dead. You feel that?"

He tried to pull her back, but Ryder fought him with a groan. "Doesn't work that way," she said through clenched teeth. "I'm tied to that thing. The professor, he explained it. That asshole's feeding off me and my sister, eating up our life force until we're both dead." With a shaky hand, she pointed to a stream of her blood worming its away across the concrete and into Cain's body. "If that thing lives, I die. We need to get the professor—maybe he can help us. And he deserves to live, even if I die. Please, Chuck, save him." She paused, eyes landing on her sister, likewise bleeding out on the floor, though not dead yet. "And my sister. Get Jamie."

"You must be loopy from the blood loss. That bitch stabbed you in the stomach. With a knife. I watched her do it with my own two eyes. Knife. Stomach. Her. You. Shit was thug as hell. I say we leave that crazy hoebag to die—that's what she was gonna do to you. So in my book that's how we do her."

"Listen to me," Ryder said, her voice little more than a wheeze. "I'm dying, but I refuse to go out with that on my conscience. She's my family, and family doesn't leave family behind." She paused, doubling over, hands groping at the gaping hole in her center. *Oh God, it hurt. Like having your insides dug out with an ice-cream scoop.* "I've watched everyone I've ever loved die," she said when she finally caught her breath. "I'm not going to do that again. Besides, what's a little attempted murder between sisters?" She issued a shaky laugh, accompanied by more blood vomit.

He looked her over, eyes lingering on the blood running down her legs and pooling at her feet. "Shit, girl. Another five minutes and it won't be *attempted* murder. It just be murder."

"Please, Chuck. Just do it. I'll owe you one."

"Dammit," he said, scooting away from the battle raging on all fronts and lowering her against one of the stone pillars. "Yeah, you're gonna owe me one, alright—and don't go dyin' before I can collect." He stood, pistol leveled. "If something happens to me … make sure Levi gives that gold to my mama. Also my car. Pimp-ass '89 Mercury Grand Marquis. I wanna be buried in that ride—make it happen. And make sure Levi foots the bill. That asshole." With that Chuck vanished, disappearing in a blink, no flash or gimmicks, just gone.

*Worst final words ever*, Ryder thought.

With nothing else to do except bleed to death on the floor, Ryder glanced around, surveying the warehouse. The Kobock battle seemed to be turning—this time in favor of the guys Levi had brought with him. The blue-skinned shits were falling by the score, bludgeoned to death in some cases, strangled by midgets in others, or torn limb from limb by the hulking, wart-covered green dudes who had been first into the fight. Looking at the warehouse was like looking at a slaughterhouse floor after a long day of work.

Only scant resistance remained: a few pockets of Kobocks—stragglers too stupid to die—and six or seven of the white, hairy, boar-faced things, who were holding their ground. The Kobos would be finished in minutes, but those boar-faced guys were fighting like pit bulls in a dog ring. They were going to die, and knew it, but were perfectly content to kick the Reaper in the groin for as long as they could get away with it. None of that really mattered, though. Sure, things were going better on that front than Ryder could've ever hoped for, but it wouldn't matter a lick unless Siphonei killed Cain.

Unless that happened, Ryder would be the first one to go.

And, unfortunately, *that* fight didn't seem to be going nearly so well.

Siphonei wasn't rolling over and taking it, but the towering homunculus was one mean-ass son of a bitch. Watching that thing was a lot like watching a bigger, badder version of Levi. The creature reminded her a helluva lot of Levi, actually. The two didn't share much by way of physical resemblance, but it was in the way the thing moved and fought. The homunculus was more sinuous and graceful than Levi, but he moved with the same confidence and purpose, each blow brutal, economical, and precise.

Even more surprising, he *shifted*, just like Levi. One minute he would lash out with clawed hands and the next one his fist would be a wrecking ball smashing into Siphonei's leafy body. Uncanny. It was like Levi was the first generation and this freak was the new and improved version.

Siphonei wasn't ready to give up the ghost, though.

Her tendrils covered damn-near every inch of Cain's body; the black flowers chewed at his skin, while hooked barbs cut deep and miniature tendrils jabbed inside him, wriggling beneath and into his muscle. They wrestled and fought, careening around the room, slamming into stone pillars—the room quivering from each impact—then going to ground: her on top, trying to pin him in place, then him flipping her with a kick of double-jointed legs. Back and forth, each losing a little more of themselves with every attack.

Cain was too strong, though. Ryder had been in more than her fair share of fights, and she could pick a winner when she saw one. Every second Cain carved away more of Siphonei's foliage, slicing off huge swathes of green—sometimes legs and vines, other times arms or even flower-faced heads—leaving her weaker and weaker with every passing second. The shed pieces of plant crawled back toward the temple guardian, keeping her in the fight, but not quickly enough. That mean son of a bitch was as fast and effective as an industrial-grade Weed Whacker.

And Cain was getting *stronger*.

Sure, the temple guardian was taking a substantial toll, but the more Ryder bled out, the more she felt herself merge with Cain. He was feeding off her life force—they were connected, souls intertwined, and Ryder knew the only reason Siphonei was doing this well was because the ritual wasn't complete. Cain was vulnerable until she and her sister bit the big one, but once that happened, the crimson-skinned demon would be next to unstoppable.

A flash of movement near the professor pulled her eyes away from the knock-down drag-out of the century: Chuck had momentarily phased back into view. He was on one knee, gun tucked into the back of his waistband while he worked furiously to loosen the chains holding Professor Wilkie captive. Cain caught Ryder's gaze—even while beating the holy shit out of Siphonei—and turned his head a fraction of an inch, his thousand eyes narrowing in on the lanky leprechaun as he worked. *Oh shit.*

With a wince, she pushed herself away from the column, trying to gain her feet. She dropped back onto her ass. No luck. "Heads up, Chuck!" She screamed, since she could do shit else, not with the pain in her stomach. "He sees you." Those final words took every ounce of air in her lungs. She fell back, head rapping against the stone pillar—white starbursts flared in her vision. She pressed her eyes shut and breathed slow and steady through her nose—it hurt less that way—then pressed both hands to her belly, trying to staunch the blood flow.

The report of Chuck's pistol filled the air, but she was too tired to give a shit.

Holy shit was she worn out—felt like she'd been up for a week straight, strung out on coke before running a triathlon. It didn't help that her veins seemed to be filling with icy water instead of warm blood. Numbness stole in from her fingers and toes, working its way inward toward her heart, fogging her mind and her senses. *This was the end.* Surprisingly, it wasn't as bad as she thought it'd be. The gut wound was ten different kinds of agony, but now she just felt *faded* and *empty.* Like she was being unmade. Unformed.

Kinda pleasant, actually.

Glass shattered somewhere, a whole pane of the stuff, followed by a familiar bellow of guttural rage. Levi. She cracked her eyes open in time to see the Mudman plummet through the air, a snarl on his face, both fists shaped like medieval battle-axes.

*THIRTY-THREE:*

**Blood Brothers**

L evi burst through the window, shifting his hands into massive battle-axes—a solid go to when an enemy needed a quick and brutal end—as he tumbled through the air. A broad smile broke across his face: this was it. This was the fruition of his life. Everything had led here, led to this moment, this fight. This was his purpose, what he'd been meant for, regardless of Hogg's intentions or plans.

Levi fell in slow motion, as though time itself were taking a pause to acknowledge the gravity of the situation—appreciating all the history and tragedy that had brought Levi face-to-face with the monster he had been destined to become so many years before. The irony was thick as a cloud. Hogg had created Levi to house Cain, and now Levi was the only thing that could stop the murder god from resuming his reign on Earth.

Levi, always one for practicality, savored the moment but also used it to get his bearings.

Most of the Kobocks were dead or dying— though a few small pockets of resistance were scattered throughout the warehouse—and even though several Thursrs continued to fight, the leprechaun crews were already working to put them down like the rabid beasts they were. The battle was far from over, but on the surface of things, it appeared his mercenaries would win the day. Good. All good.

He spotted the wizened Kobock shaman or what was left of it: its lower body lay carelessly cast to one side, though there was no sign of its torso. The shaman's demise was a bit of good fortune—one less threat to worry about—though there was some part of the Mudman that regretted not getting to finish the disgusting creature himself.

The homunculus, now housing the essence of Cain, dominated the scene, its crimson body like an infected wound that screamed for attention. It was a massive beast—long limbs, blood-slick skin, jaws the size of a great white, a glut of eyes, and an aura that set Levi's teeth on edge and made his doughy skin crawl in revulsion.

The Mudman had seen plenty of evil creatures during his long life: wicked humans, and even wickeder beasts of Outworld. Doctor Hogg had certainly been among the worst offenders he'd ever encountered— with his black-hole aura, devoid of any trace of decency or goodness—but Cain was worse. Far worse. His aura wasn't a static thing, not merely a living record of heinous deeds, which Levi could read. No, his aura was a living, active *being*, a thing of black smoke that wafted off him in a haze, filling up everything and everyone around him with its taint.

That smoke was infiltrating Chuck, Ryder, and the good professor, working its way into noses and mouths, wriggling into eye sockets and through ear canals. In limited quantities that black haze might not do much, but with enough exposure, Levi had no doubt it would drive the infected into a killing madness. The murder god was an abomination, a perversion of the natural order that had no place in a civilized world. Levi intended to make sure Cain never saw the outside of this bloody warehouse.

Levi broke into a toothy grin as he watched an all too familiar plant-hydra slam into the homunculus, hooked barbs tearing at Cain's body. Having her on his side would certainly make the job a fair bit easier. Truth be told, Levi had never been so happy to see something that had once tried to ingest him.

The two horrors twirled as they fought, spinning and rotating like a tornado of claws and tentacles and teeth, tearing into each other and decimating anything that came close. The hydra was holding her own, but was slowly losing steam. Thankfully, he could even the odds a bit. Levi landed like a meteor—tremors vibrated up the walls, the concrete buckled, and slabs of stone cracked apart beneath his feet. The force even jarred the dueling monsters, momentarily throwing the pair apart, though Siphonei managed to keep her leafy tendrils wrapped around Cain's trunk.

The murder god turned, head tilted, face a mask of curiosity as he surveyed Levi. "Brother?" he asked, voice full of confusion.

Levi—never one for words, especially not when violence was a suitable alternative— ignored the accusation and lurched into motion, launching into the air with both battle-axes raised and ready to kill. The homunculous' eyes, all of them, flared in surprise, then narrowed to slits as Levi flew through the air. Cain crouched and threw his weight left, an evasive dodge, but Siphonei was too quick. Levi watched with satisfaction as the temple guardian planted her limbs—

arachnoid legs digging divots into the floor—while her ropy tendrils flexed and strained, anchoring Cain in place.

Strong as Cain seemed to be, he couldn't escape Siphonei's grasp.

Levi let loose with his right arm, his battle-axe screaming through the air and sinking into the red meat of Cain's left shoulder, carving down with a *squish*. The murder god roared, the bellow of a T. rex, while he bucked and fought against the blade lodged in his arm. Levi, taking advantage of his immobile victim, brought the other axe whipping through the air. A hammer blow meant to lop Cain's flat salamander head from what little neck he had—

A fist slammed square into Levi's gut, the blow like a stick of dynamite going off in his abdomen. The Mudman's axe tore loose as he soared through the air, flipping end over end, then crashed into the sacrificial stone table with all the grace of a plane wreck. The slab of slick stone cracked on impact, and Levi flipped over its top, finally coming to a stop on the floor ten feet away from where Cain and Siphonei still thrashed.

He grunted and shook away the throb building in his head as he picked himself up off the floor, ignoring the dull ache in his stomach, sides, and back. In all his years of hunting, he'd never been hit like that. Not once. In the early days of his life, he'd been struck by a German 8 cm *Granatwerfer* 34 mortar round while storming a Nazi pillbox—that experience had been comparable.

In the seconds that he'd been out of the fight, the battlefield landscape had shifted dramatically.

Apparently, Siphonei's holding tactic had exposed some vulnerability, because now she was retreating, tentacles flashing out, trying to keep the encroaching Cain at bay. The hydra was in bad shape, worse than Levi had realized when he'd first entered the battle. Her spidery abdomen was leaking pools of yellow fluid, scores of legs and arms were missing—sheared away— and only two of her seven serpentine flower-heads remained.

The cast off vegetation was wriggling across the floor, trying to reassemble itself, but it appeared to be a case of too little too late.

Levi needed to buy the temple guardian time to regenerate or he would have to tackle Cain alone, and he wasn't optimistic about the outcome of that scenario. He shifted his left hand into a spear and his right into a spiked mace, then broke into a shambling run, thudding footfalls announcing his approach. Cain wheeled about to meet him, the creature turning and backtracking toward the altar in one fluid motion so he could keep both Levi and Siphonei to his front. Levi barreled in, ducking low and thrusting out and up with his spear, hoping to impale the creature through its throat.

Cain's crimson arm flew in from the right, but as it moved it *shifted,* blurred, and morphed into a double-edged sword blade. The Mudman stumbled as Cain's blade-arm parried his spear thrust and cut a deep furrow in his forearm, a blow which threatened to take Levi's hand clean off. Levi had lost more than enough hands in the past few days, so he dropped to a knee, pulled back his spear-arm, and swung out with his spiked mace—the heavy weapon batted Cain's sword away before it could finish its work.

Levi shifted again, his wounded spear-hand melting into a scythe blade, which he swept toward Cain's double-jointed knees—

The murder god, far quicker than such a huge creature had any right to be, leapt back, darted left, then shot in, sweeping a sledgehammer fist, made of red marble, into Levi's chin. The uppercut lifted the Mudman into the air, even if only a few inches, but Levi didn't hang there for long: a front kick with the power of a battering ram landed, dead center, in Levi's chest. For the second time in so many minutes, Levi cartwheeled through the air, tail over teakettle, before slamming into the ruby-eyed altar and sliding to the floor in a rain of rubble.

For a long beat he just sat there, struggling to breath and completely dumbfounded. The homunculus could *shift*. Could transform. It was a golem, not so different from him.

As Levi sat there, legs sprawled out, he noticed something else: a stream of blood, this one trickling from Ryder's sister, oozed across the floor and toward his opponent. And it all clicked into place. The flesh golem from the Kobock temple had failed to hold together, so Hogg had taken a different approach. Instead of crafting together a Frankenstein monster, he'd engineered a single organic unit, a golem born, not made. A golem fashioned from blood. A living Mudman, grown in the belly of a human being.

If that was true, and Levi believed it was, it meant Cain could likely do all of the things Levi could and, perhaps, more besides. The Mudman couldn't beat this thing. Not alone. And even with Siphonei's help, he wasn't optimistic.

Speaking of the plant guardian, Siphonei was up and moving again. Or, more precisely, *several* of her were up and moving. Instead of reforming into one massive guardian, the shredded vegetation had wriggled into separate piles, entwining together, until five of the lesser guardians had formed. They swayed and circled around the murder god. Levi knew from personal experience the lesser guardians wouldn't be a match for the homunculus—they weren't near as powerful as the flower-hydra—but they could attack on multiple fronts, like a pack of hyenas harrying a lone lion over a fresh kill.

Cain was fast, but the guardians were faster and they never stayed in one place long enough for the homunculus to close the distance. They moved constantly—swaying, circling, darting in and out again. One would strike from the rear, lashing out with tearing claws, only to retreat and leap away in a flash of green. By the time Cain could wheel about to meet the threat, the guardian would be long gone and another would already be moving in to attack from some other angle. The guardians' strikes were no more than a nuisance to the murder god, but maybe, given enough time, they could wear Cain down.

But, they didn't have time to play that game. Cain was feeding off the life force of Ryder and her sister, and once he'd sucked them dry it'd be the end of the road. Ryder had lost a substantial amount of blood, which meant she could be dead in no more than a few minutes. Levi pushed himself upright, his legs unsteady beneath him, and waded back into the thick of things. The lesser guardians were evading Cain, but they made no move to avoid Levi. Carefully as he could, he reached out and snatched one of the creatures up by the neck, pulling it away from the fight.

The flower-faced beast squirmed in his fist, tentacles wriggling like mad as black flowers snapped at his fingers.

"Cut it out," he said, the words a whisper. "We both know you're not strong enough to stop him on your own." The plant ceased its struggling, vines growing slack, the gigantic flower head bobbing in acknowledgment. "Neither can I, but together … maybe. On the count of three this is what we're going to do …" He laid out the crude Hail-Mary plan while the other guardians kept Cain's attention.

He set the guardian back to the floor and withdrew an ichor pot—only two left—from his torso. Then he turned to Chuck, who'd finally managed to get the professor free from his chains. "Chuck!" he hollered over the chaos. "This is about to end one way or the other, so you need to get everyone out of here in case we can't stop this thing. Get 'em gone, then you run. And don't ever stop."

The guardians were still keeping Cain on his toes, but the homunculus was getting smart, edging toward the far wall, which would mean the plant creatures would only be able to attack from the front. That would be a straight-up fight they could never win. Levi stumbled into a lumbering run, raising the clay pot as he moved.

"*One*," he screamed, ten feet out.

"*Two*." Five feet—he skidded to a halt, just outside of Cain's reach.

"*Three!*" he bellowed. Everything seemed to happen all at once—a rush of movement and bodies.

The pot shattered on the ground, inches from Cain's feet, and exploded outward in a wave of ultrafine dust, a cloud that swelled up and enveloped the homonculous, Levi, and Siphonei's various forms. The cloud was harmless, but Levi reasoned a god with as many eyes as Cain would rely heavily on sight— without it, Levi might have an advantage, especially since the Mudman didn't need to see at all. Levi could use his earth sense to read Cain's movements through the concrete. It was possible Cain possessed the same ability, but it had taken Levi years to master the technique.

In the same instant, the Mudman shifted one mitt into an obsidian blade while tough quartz-scales sprouted along his arms, legs, face, and torso, transforming his body into an earthen tank. Even with all that, though, he still wasn't strong enough to withstand Cain's punishing blows, which is where the guardians came in. Instead of rushing at the temporarily blinded Cain, the plant-beasts converged on Levi, wrapping around him in a suit of living armor.

The Mudman rushed in, guided by his earth sense, and closed the distance in a heartbeat. He dove, slashing with his obsidian blade, which scored a nasty gash across Cain's chest. Hot blood—or perhaps ichor?—splashed across Levi's weapon and dribbled down his arm. The bloodlust took hold, transforming the Mudman into a hurricane of violence lashing out with feet, fist, and blade.

Cain retaliated in turn, but Levi was able to take advantage of the homunculus' blindness and dodge most blows. And, for the few he couldn't avoid, the guardians, entangled around him, took the brunt of the damage. Moreover, each of Levi's monstrously powerful strikes was amplified by Siphonei's strength, and as each blow landed, the guardians lashed out with slicing vines and pinching claws, tearing Cain apart a piece at a time.

He threw out a brutal kick—one of Cain's knees snapped with a *crack*.

He followed up with a devastating hammer strike—shark teeth shattered and broke away, lodged in the vines.

He spun, blade sliding through the air with a soft whistle: one of Cain's arms came away in a spray of blood, then tumbled to the floor.

For a moment Levi felt the surge of exhilaration. They were doing it, killing the abomination—

Then, Cain vanished from Levi's earth sense, disappearing in a blink as he leapt into the air, breaking all contact with the ground.

Levi found Cain an instant later when a sword blade, long as a man, sliced into his body, entering his left hip and tearing its way to the other side. Levi keeled over, thudding to the ground like a stone, legs cut out from beneath him. The plant guardians shrieked and wailed, trying to wriggle loose from Levi's body, but unable to do so. With the quartz armor in place, Levi weighed near a ton, and his bulk pinned the already weak plant creatures to the floor. Only a single guardian, wrapped around Levi's head, managed to worm free and retreat.

As the dust cloud finally settled, Cain descended in a flurry of blows, thrashing the plants covering Levi's body until only shreds of vegetation remained.

Levi stared up at the creature, eyes leaking out thin streaks of golden ichor. He hurt, there was no question about that, but after all the pain he'd experienced since finding Ryder, this was nothing. Not when balanced against the reality of his complete and utter failure. He'd lived through a baptism by fire, ripped off his own hands and feet, and chosen his friends over vengeance, but it wasn't enough. Not even close.

The murder god's face split into a grin the envy of any shark. "You may not realize your potential, little brother, but we are godlings. And I have use of you yet," he said, voicing buzzing in the back of the Mudman's skull. With that, the homunculus sidestepped Levi and strode across the warehouse, moving with the grace of a big game cat closing in on a wounded gazelle. With a snarl and a heave, Levi rolled himself over, sprawling onto his stomach so he could, at least, watch the end. Bear witness as he had always done before. Maybe he couldn't save Chuck, Ryder, or Wilkie, but he could remember them.

Ryder, her sister, and the professor leaned against one of the pillars. The whole lot of 'em looked to have one foot solidly in the grave, and the professor was unconscious. Chuck stood in front of them, gun raised, though his legs quivered and his hands shook. Levi hadn't been quick enough. Maybe if he had managed to hold Cain for a few more minutes … maybe Chuck could've escaped. The Mudman didn't care much for the man, not on a personal level, but the halfie had done right by Levi time and again, and he would've liked to see him live.

The Mudman silently muttered a prayer that Chuck would be true to his nature and *not* play the hero. He hoped Chuck would turn, run, leave everyone to die, and save himself. But no. Chuck stood fast. Stood fast and faced down a resurrected godling that had just single-handedly pulverized Levi and an ancient temple guardian without missing a beat.

"Stop your ugly ass right there, motherfucker," he said, voice breaking at the end.

Cain *did* stop, though only long enough to laugh—a rumbling boom that reminded Levi of broken glass and screaming babies, high-speed car accidents and artillery fire. Then Cain spoke, his words cold as lake ice. "Die like the insignificant creature you are." Then he was a blur of red, flashing across the floor, one monster arm sweeping out. A vicious backhand blow slammed into Chuck's chest and face, swatting the man through the air and into a stone pillar ten feet off.

Chuck, for all his heroics, crumpled like a sheet of paper, the fight gone out of him before it had even begun.

"And now for the mage," Cain spat, stalking nearer. "One. More. Death," he mused, seemingly to himself, "and no one will ever lock me away again."

Ryder pushed herself upright. She wobbled on weak legs, bent at the middle, a mess of blood drooling from the wound in her belly. "I think Chuck already told you, fucktard," she said softly, words slurred and forced. "Go fuck yourself sideways." The last was a whisper of pain.

"Lie down, mother," the godling said. "Lie down, close your eyes. It will be over in minutes. Go with whatever peace and dignity you can muster."

"I don't think so, you overgrown parasite," she said, body shuddering. "The professor, he told me what to do. I can hurt you. I can kill you. We're bound, so as long as I'm breathing, you're my bitch—not the other way around."

"I may be a monster," he said, backing up a step, "but I have a debt to you and your sister. Your contribution is not insignificant. Just do your part—it is the easiest thing in the world. Die. Die and I will show compassion"—he waved a hand toward Chuck and the professor—"and let these *no ones* live their short, pathetic, meaningless lives."

"They aren't no ones. And I won't say it again, go fuck yourself." She bent over with a groan and picked up the shaman's ceremonial knife with clumsy fingers. "I've been running my whole life." She paused, breathing labored. "I've never taken a stand … because it's always been about survival. Well, I'm done surviving. I'm gonna die here, but at least I won't have to live with being a chicken shit coward. So go eat a dick, douchewaffle."

As Levi lay there, legs gone, body broken, his mind began to work. If Ryder really could kill Cain, maybe they *weren't* finished yet. With a silent grimace he rolled onto one side and jammed his hand into his stomach, fishing out the remaining clay pot. Even after all the hurt and punishment he'd endured, the pot was still, blessedly, intact. With that in hand, he pulled his body across the grit-covered floor, using his bleeding stumps and his free hand to crawl to the last remaining guardian. The one that had escaped. Cain had done a number on the beast—it was little more than a clump of vines and flowers. But it wriggled with life.

He pulled it into a fist and drew it close. "You alive, Siphonei?" he asked, having to force every word out.

"Yes," one of the black flowers hissed. "But not long now."

Levi nodded. He could do this. He took the pot and pressed it into the plant's vines. "I'm gonna launch you at his back. You need to get this pot inside him, then break it. Understand?"

"Yes," she whispered again, then fell silent. He pushed himself up onto his bloody stumps. Settling his bulk onto the amputated limbs was like dipping his legs into a pool of magma. But he ignored the pain, pushing it away, wrapping his mind in purpose. After all, he only needed seconds and then ... well, then he could give up one way or the other. He hoisted the tattered remains of the last guardian into the air, wound back his arm, then launched the creature with every ounce of strength left to him. The momentum of the throw carried him forward—he thudded to the floor, face smashing up against the stone.

He watched through hazy eyes as the guardian flew true, colliding into Cain's back, tentacles shooting out, barbed hooks latching on. And, with a final thrust, Siphonei jammed a broken arm *into* homunculus' blood-slick skin, drilling past his muscle and deep into his core. A second tentacle followed the first, shoving Levi's pot in as far as it would go, then smashing the clay in a blink.

She'd done it.

Levi could feel the ichor calling to him. It was inside of Cain, mingling with the homunculus' blood and fluid, spreading through his limbs like a toxin waiting to kill.

As Levi's ichor spread he felt a connection form to the strange beast across the room. Though Levi knew his essence was *vastly* different than Cain's, in *body*, form, they weren't so different at all. Perhaps only the naturally occurring genetic difference between brothers. The homunculus was built along the same lines as Levi, made from the same blueprint, just constructed from a different medium. Cain was even filled with *ichor* of sorts, though that too was different from Levi's. Type A blood compared to type B.

Levi reached into the ground, his senses penetrating deep into the heart of the earth, a thousand feet and more, until he felt what he wanted: a pocket of red hot molten rock, burbling and simmering in a magma chamber. He'd never transmuted ichor into magma, but he found it no more difficult than transmuting ichor to obsidian or gold. It took Levi only a thought and a small effort of will to trigger the change: the ichor, pumping through the homunculus' veins, went from liquid gold to molten rock.

Levi watched, a small smile breaking across his face as Cain's steps faltered, then halted completely. The creature fell to his knees, a shriek rising from his throat as his bloody hide bubbled, pockets of magma bursting through like tiny volcanoes littering his body. He lifted his face to the air, thousand eyes scrunching closed in pain, then his scream cut off as magma splashed from his yawning maw.

Ryder, being smart and savvy, wasted no time. She padded forward, still hunched over and clutching her middle, then with a lopsided grin, plunged the knife square into one of Cain's ruby eyes. She pulled the blade free and struck again, knife flashing out over and over, stabbing into the homunculus' face, slicing through his flesh and gouging out his countless eyes. "Go ... fuck ... yourself," she said, panting the words, before slamming the blade through the top of his skull, grunting as she muscled the blade down, all the way to the hilt.

Cain pitched over to one side, body seizing, arms and legs flapping and flailing as more magma trickled out, turning from red-orange to black as it cooled in the air. A final, massive spasm ran through the homunculus—one of its feet shot out and smashed into Ryder, hurling her back in a sprawl of limbs and blood—followed by a clap of thunder, the sound of a sonic boom.

A portal shimmered into being, an opalescent thing, ten feet by ten feet, which hung suspended high overhead. Through the opal haze, Levi caught a brief glimpse of fire—a place that mirrored the inside of a volcano—blacks, reds, and various hues of gold, mixing and swirling in ever shifting patterns.

Cain's jaws distended, breaking apart with a sickening *snap* of bone, and a bloated beast, big as a whale, long as a city block, and covered with chitinous plates, twitching legs, and ruby eyes, flew up and out like an endless stream of vomit. The creature mewled—an inhuman sound loud as a train wreck—as its body, Cain's *essence*, was sucked through the portal and back into the fiery waters it called home. As big as the beast was, the whole process took only seconds, and then the creature was gone, the portal snapping shut behind the godling. Only the broken and decaying form of the empty homunculus remained behind.

## *THIRTY-FOUR:*

### Second Chances

S iphonei lay on the floor, body shattered, tentacles hacked off, the last spark of her consciousness fading like the final embers of a spent campfire. She surveyed the room around her: an ugly place that reminded her far too much of her temple prison back in the Sprawl, what with its ruby-eyed altar decorating the wall and those stone pillars with their graphic depictions of the unnatural and profane. Chaos still seethed all around her, the howls of the victorious and the mewling cries of the defeated—sometimes it was hard to tell the difference between the two—but those things she put from her mind.

She'd been alive for the better part of four millennia, and she refused to have her final thoughts be of death, destruction, murder, or that damned Cain. Her prisoner. Her captive. Though she was Cain's warden, she had also been his prisoner. She'd spent thousands of years confining him and preventing his escape, but his existence, in turn, prevented her from ever leaving that tomb of stone and sand and vines. No, Cain would not claim these last moments of her life, especially not since her mind was clear. Finally her own again.

Back in the prison complex her programing had clouded everything, but here, so far away from her neural mainframe … she felt … she felt herself again. She stared at the ruined monstrosity of her body, with its green vines, black flowers, sinuous tendrils, and tearing claws. She couldn't weep, but she wanted to. She'd been beautiful, once, in a different age. Now she was a fading nightmare that no one would ever miss. Everything she'd ever cared about—everyone who had ever cared about her—was long gone.

But no, she wouldn't focus on that either. Too depressing. Death was the end, but for her it was more a mercy than a misery.

Her life had been taken from her, but at least her death would be her own.

Instead of focusing on any of those things, she *remembered*. Remembered thoughts of her husband, Marius—dead so long ago, she could hardly recall what he looked like. She couldn't even remember his proper name. They had a child, a girl, but she couldn't remember her name either. Not after so many years with the memories stripped away. But she did recall holding the child as an infant: the sweet smell of her dark hair, the way she would fall asleep on Siphonei's chest after breastfeeding in the night. The thought of her skin—not organic plant matter, but *real* skin—brushing up against someone else's sent a shiver running down her spinal column.

Her appendages, or what remained of them, flapped on the floor in response.

A death spasm.

She took a long breath of fresh air, free from the dry, dusty scent of desert winds, and closed her eyes for what she was sure was the last time.

Except, after a time, she opened them again. Her body was withering around her, unable to repair the grievous damage, nor survive away from her central mainframe—the great flower that held captive her human remains. Surprisingly, the fighting had ceased, and the silence of a graveyard rested over the warehouse. The power was out and the building sat in utter gloom, but she could see easily enough with the thin moon light trickling in from an overhead window.

The sight before her was enough to rob her of breath:

The homunculus was near. A monstrous body, all long limbs and tearing teeth, but she knew its body was malleable and took its shape based on the essence occupying the shell. This shell had been vacated, and recently. From all outward appearances, the body— which had housed *Dibeininax Ayosainondur Daimuyon*—was dead. Burned, scarred, mutilated, decaying. But she saw true. The body was *dying*, quickly. Without a host to give it form and essence, the homunculus would spoil like an overripe fruit fallen from a tree branch.

But *dying* wasn't *dead*.

With the miniscule strength left to her, she pulled her ruined remains toward the empty vessel. Perhaps this wasn't the end after all ...

*THIRTY-FIVE:*

**New Day**

The sanctuary buzzed with the quiet hum of men and women sharing words, the greeting of peace before worship began. Light filtered in through the stained-glass windows, splashing bright patches of red, gold, and blue over the cross hanging above the pulpit. A beautiful morning, with everything in its proper place, just as it should be. Levi stood, church face plastered in place, red hymnal—the binding nearly shot—in one palm.

Though he was far from being back to normal, after four days of constant recuperation, he was feeling *almost* human again, or at least as close as he ever came to feeling human. The fact that he'd survived at all was cause for celebration, especially considering the tremendous damage he'd endured after freeing himself from Hogg's manacles and battling Cain. Even more miraculous, Ryder, her sister, Jamie, Professor Wilkie, and Chuck had all managed to survive the ordeal as well. Not undamaged, obviously—everyone sported their fair share of breaks, scrapes, bruises, and emotional scars—but alive was alive.

Levi didn't remember much after Ryder had repeatedly stabbed Cain in the head. He vaguely recalled watching Cain's essence—a big, nasty, bloated thing—being sucked back into the pit where it rightfully belonged, but everything after that was fuzzy. A blur of sight and sounds and darkness. Chuck had been kind enough to fill Levi in once he finally became coherent. Apparently, after Ryder had finished Cain off, Chuck had taken charge of the situation: routing the last of the Kobocks and Thursrs—almost single-handedly, of course—then using Levi's ichor to stabilize Ryder and Jamie until he could get them to a hospital. Somewhere in there, someone—though Levi wasn't precisely sure who—had dropped him off at his home.

At least that was the way Chuck told things. Levi trusted the halfie's recollection of events about as much as he'd trust a politician running for office. He suspected Chuck's account was more than a little embellished and likely designed to squeeze out a bonus for his "heroics." He suspected the Black Shillelaghs had played a much more substantial role, but Levi didn't particularly care to press the issue. Everything had turned out more or less okay, so the exact *how* of it all wasn't nearly as important.

He'd met with Chuck again last night, over at the Lonely Mountain.

It'd been the first time in days he'd felt physically capable of dragging his mangled body off the bloodstone in his backyard. He'd met both to pay the man the gold he was due and to square away all the nitty-gritty details that remained. Levi had defeated Hogg—in a manner of speaking, anyway—and stopped Cain, but there was still clean-up work to be done: Compensating the mercenaries he'd hired. Disposing of all those bodies so the authorities would be none the wiser. Razing that heinous laboratory to the ground so Hogg would have to start again from scratch.

There was also Ryder to see to. Her and Jamie, the sister.

*"So,"* Chuck had said, *lounging in a booth, spinning a tacky diamond-studded gold ring that hugged his middle finger. "My money."*

*Levi waved the question away and plunked a USPS box down on the table. A nondescript package, which would draw little notice. Unless, of course, someone picked up the tiny box. At over fifty pounds, Levi was sure the package would raise a few questions in the wrong hands.*

*"How is she?"* he asked Chuck without preamble. *"Her and her sister?"*

*Levi would've taken the pair in, but he hadn't been in any kind of shape to deal with those two. He'd barely been able to care for himself, which was saying something since caring for himself amounted to sleeping on a rock and not moving for four days straight. Besides, someone needed to actively look after them—to watch for any possible side effects from the botched ritual.*

*In the end, Levi supposed, it was probably better for them to be with Chuck anyway. For one, even having a cat as a roommate pushed the limits of the Mudman's tolerance—two women would be a bit much. Two, those women weren't regular Rubes anymore. They'd be undergoing a lot of changes in the days, weeks, and months ahead, and Chuck was far more capable of walking them through those changes than Levi. For better or worse, the Hub was their world now, and Chuck could help the two find their place.*

Chuck spun his ring round and round while he thought. "The sister's a cold fish," he replied. "Still in shock, I think. I can hardly get two words outta that broad, but she's alive. And Ryder, well she's lookin' fine as ever. Still got that sassiness about her, but I think she's finally startin' to warm up to me. I mean we ain't together yet, like you know"—he arched an eyebrow—"but she's interested in the mean green, if you know what I'm sayin'."

"Absolutely not what I meant," Levi replied.

"Yeah, I know what you meant. But what you want me to say, man? They dealin' with some real heavy shit. You and me, we both know neither of those gals gonna be the same. Not after this. With this kinda thing, there ain't no way a tellin' how it's gonna shake out. Not like there's a lot of precedent, am I right?"

Levi nodded his head, but said nothing.

Levi might have arrived in time to prevent Ryder's death, but he hadn't arrived in time to save her. Not entirely. By the time he'd burst through the window, she'd already been marked by dark alchemy—her soul split open and exposed to a demonic essence. She'd been part of an arcane ritual as old as the world itself, which had halted, herky-jerky, before it could come to completion. No one walked away from something like that unchanged. And not just in a psychological sense, either. When powerful rituals went awry, there were always consequences.

Always.

Transference was the most likely possibility:

Some fragment of the wyrm god might have lived on inside Ryder and her sister. Even if a sliver of

*Cain remained, the effects could be devastating, though it was impossible to predict what exactly the extent of those effects would be. Levi had no doubt, however, that there would be issues of one sort or another. Those two would bear watching, but he was hopeful both would recover, at least enough to go back to whatever life remained to them.*

*He pointed to the package on the table. "Two bricks. One is yours to do with as you please. The other is for Ryder, minus five percent, which you can keep in exchange for putting her up and cashing the gold out."*

*"That's real generous of you," Chuck replied, grabbing the box and pulling it across the table with a groan. "Damn, man. That shit right there's a lot heavier than it looks. Come in here, flop that box down, make it look all easy."*

*"Chuck, I'm only going to say this once—make sure she gets what's comin' to her."*

*"You know I got feelings right, Levi? Always comin' at me like, 'Don't steal my money, Chuck. No leprechaun shenanigans, Chuck. I'll break your fingers, 'cause I'm a colossal asshole with trust issues, Chuck.' Let me just ask you, did I or didn't I come through?" He leaned forward, eyebrow cocked.*

*Levi sighed. "Yeah, you came through."*

*"Thank you for acknowledgin' my trustworthiness and contribution to the team."*

*Levi ran a hand over his balding head, then grunted a monosyllabic apology. "What about the warehouse?" he asked afterward.*

*"Don't sweat the warehouse, man. The Black Shillelaghs know their business. They reached out to a freelance cleanup crew. Bunch of ghouls. Nasty-ass sumbitches ate the corpses. All of 'em. Then the*

*Shillelaghs burned that shithole to the ground. Ain't nothing left."*

"The homunculus?"

*Chuck hesitated, fidgeting for a moment, turning his tacky ring again. "That's the only ... let's call it a complication. Freaky-ass thing was gone. Don't know what happened to it. But it can't be Cain, right? Not if Ryder's alive?"*

*Levi nodded. The absence of the homunculus was deeply troubling, but considering everything else that had gone right? It was still a win.*

"Alright," said Pastor Steve from the pulpit, pulling Levi from his thoughts. "Let's greet one another in love before we worship this morning."

As was usual, George, the lanky beanpole of a man with the balding crown and the awkward smile, shuffled over and extended a hand. And, as usual, Levi grasped the clammy mitt and gave it several pumps before letting go.

"Mornin', Levi," George said. "Sure is good to see you. We missed you Tuesday—the food pantry wasn't the same without you. I take it your commission came through? How'd the project turn out?"

Levi smiled. He didn't even have to force it. There'd been no art commission, and though the lie sat heavy in his gut, his "project" had turned out far better than he could've ever hoped for.

"A few hiccups," he said after a moment, recalling how he'd had to set himself on fire at one point and had torn his own hands and feet off at another. "Overall though, I'm pleased with the way things turned out. Just between us, it might be the best

435

piece of work I've ever done. Certainly the piece I'm proudest of."

"That's great to hear, I mean it."

"How 'bout you?" Levi asked, completing the formulaic greeting. Except it didn't feel like a formula—he actually *wanted* to know how George was doing.

"Same old same old, but every week's a blessing from the Lord, if you take my meaning."

Levi nodded. "I think I understand you just fine."

"You comin' out Tuesday?" George asked with a speculative smile, a thin stretching of the lips.

"Try and stop me."

"Okay," said Pastor Steve from the podium. "Let's return to our seats. We're going to be singing out of the Red Hymnal"—he held up a worn, red book in one hand—"number forty-two, 'O God, the Rock of Ages.'" The pianist, a silver-haired woman with a smiling face and thin glasses, began playing the tune. "Let us be present together as we worship this morning," Steve continued, speaking over the music. "The Holy Sabbath is a new day, and as the Apostle Paul wrote, 'The old has gone, the new is here!' So let us celebrate this newness together. The past is the past, and the future stretches before us, bright and new. Let's sing our thanks for the ever-renewing mercies and grace of God above."

There were plenty of things for Levi to worry about—Ryder, the missing homunculus, Hogg at large in the world, all that gold coming back to bite him—but as Levi sang, those worries rolled away, consecrated oil burning away under a holy flame. Levi was present and, for the time being, happy ... Well, maybe not *happy*, but almost.

J. A. Hunter

# Special Thanks

I'd like to thank my wife, Jeanette, and daughter, Lucy, and my son, Sam. A special thanks to my parents, Greg and Lori. A quick shout out to my brother Aron and his whole brood—Eve, Brook, Grace, and Collin. Brit, probably you'll never read this book either, but I love you too. Here's to the folks of *Team Hunter*, my awesome Alpha and Beta readers who helped make this book both possible and good: eden Hudson (the awesome author of the Redneck Apocalypse Series), Owen "Ari" Wilkie, Megan Meyers (aka Teal.Canary), Bob "Gunslinger" Singer, Dan "Danh" Goodale, Joan Carmouch-Hairston, Lisa "Nell" Justice, Jen "Inava" Wadsworth, Robert Olsen, Brett Farris, Jim Dutton, Scott Hoerner, Heather Copeman, Matthew Campbell, and Tracy Reitmann. They read the messy, early drafts so that no one else had to; thanks guys and gals, this book wouldn't be what it is without you all. And, of course, a big thanks to my editor, Tamara Blain, who rocked this book (if you need editing, go to her, she's seriously awesome: ACloserLookEditing.com)

—James A. Hunter, March 2016

# About the Author

Hey all, my name is James Hunter and I'm a writer, among other things. So just a little about me: I'm a former Marine Corps Sergeant, combat veteran, and pirate hunter (seriously). I'm also a member of The Royal Order of the Shellback—'cause that's a real thing. I've also been a missionary and international aid worker in Bangkok, Thiland. And, a space-ship captain, can't forget that.

Okay … the last one is only in my imagination.

Currently, I'm a stay at home Dad—taking care of my two kids—while also writing full time, making up absurd stories that I hope people will continue to buy. When I'm not working, writing, or spending time with family, I occasionally eat and sleep.

# Books, Mailing List, and Reviews

If you enjoyed reading about Levi the Mudman and want to stay in the loop about the latest book releases, awesomesauce promotional deals, and upcoming book giveaways be sure to subscribe to my email list at www.JamesAHunter.wordpress.com

Word-of-mouth and book reviews are crazy helpful for the success of any writer. If you *really* enjoyed reading MUDMAN, please consider leaving a short review—just a couple of lines about your overall reading experience on either Amazon or Goodreads. One other word on ol' Levi: I don't have any plans to write more books in this series—I have a million stories to tell and only so many days in the year. If, however, you want to read more books with Levi, Ryder, and Chuck, please say so in your review or email me and let me know (JamesAHunter@outlook.com). Ultimately, my boss is you, the reader. So if enough people express an interest in reading more MUDAN stories, I'll be only too happy to write them.

If you want to delve deeper in the Hub, Outworld, and the various nightmarish creatures that inhabit Levi's world, be sure to check out my Yancy Lazarus series available on Amazon.

64756650R00264

Made in the USA
Lexington, KY
18 June 2017